D0849128

STEPHEN LEIGH

THE CROW OF CONNEMARA

DAW BOOKS, INC.

DONALD A. WOLLHEIM, FOUNDER

375 Hudson Street, New York, NY 10014

ELIZABETH R. WOLLHEIM
SHEILA E. GILBERT
PUBLISHERS

www.dawbooks.com

First printing, March 2015
1   2   3   4   5   6   7   8   9

*This book is dedicated to the memory of Walter Leigh, my father,
who introduced me to the Irish side of the family,
and for whom Ireland was always a precious destination.*

*And, as always and ever, to Denise, whose support is what makes all of my
books possible.*

A Note on Dialect

Given that the majority of the people in this novel are Irish, they would speak English with a distinct accent. From my own time in Ireland, I remember that the "depth" of the accent and even the pronunciation of words varied quite a bit depending on the person and their location. There were times I had to "translate" what some of my relatives in Roscommon were saying even though we were all nominally speaking the same language, their accent was so pronounced.

We won't even talk about idioms, which can be very different there.

An author always has choices to make when rendering dialect in fiction. The dialogue and even the exposition could be *entirely* in dialect (à la *Huckleberry Finn,* for example) but to my mind that slows down the reader unnecessarily, requires far too much work on the reader's part, and can lead to confusion. Another author might choose to not use phonetic dialect spelling at all, but leave the sound of the dialect entirely to the reader's imagination.

My personal preference is to take a middle road between the extremes: to try to give the occasional hint of the pronunciation where it doesn't seem to hinder comprehension, with the hope that the reader will begin to "hear" the accent and continue to provide it in their inner hearing for all characters' dialogue. Hopefully, that works for you. If your preference is more toward one or the other pole, please forgive me.

Irish Gaelic provides another issue for those readers who insist on knowing how to pronounce the words. I'm *not* someone who knows Irish Gaelic beyond a few words, though I love the sound of the language. I've rendered the occasional Gaelic word or phrase here in the generally accepted spelling—but be aware that you won't capture the *pronunciation* of any version of Gaelic by using the rules of English any more than you'd get proper pronunciation of French by applying English rules. For instance, in Irish Gaelic "mh" is a single aspirated consonant, and is pronounced as an English "w" or "v" depending on the surrounding vowels—thus, the Celtic festival day Samhain (to a reader of English) looks like it should be pronounced "Sam-hane" when it's actually pronounced more like "Sow-en."

There's the added complication that the same word in Irish Gaelic can be pronounced differently in various regions of the country, in much the same way that we have regional variations in pronunciation in the USA. For instance, how do you pronounce "pecan"? Is it pee-KAHN, puh-KAHN, pick-AHN, pee-CAN or PEE-can? They're all "correct," depending on what part of the country you're in.

There are online guides to pronunciation of the Gaelic consonants, vowels, diphthongs, and so on; check them out if you're so inclined. For this book, I've attempted to give a rough phonetic pronunciation of most of the Irish words in the appendix at the end of the novel, but I apologize in advance if my efforts don't quite match reality.

Contents

Part One: Macha

Part Two: Nemain

Part Three: Badb

"I don't think there's any point in being Irish if you don't know that the world is going to break your heart eventually."

— Daniel Patrick Moynihan

PART ONE

MACHA

◀ 1 ▶

Death and the Sinner

DARCY FITZGERALD LAY DYING in the next room.

His family and friends were gathered in the small front room of Darcy's farmhouse on Ceomhar Head, well outside the town of Ballemór in County Galway. Two and sometimes three of the group took brief turns sitting at Darcy's bedside with the priest and Darcy's sister Margaret Egan, who were holding vigil. The priest—Father Quinlan—had been sent for by Margaret; the truth was that, in living memory, no one could recall Darcy ever trudging into town of a Sunday to attend Mass, but Margaret had insisted that her own pastor come out and sit with her.

"Darcy's been baptized, an' so I'll be having the Last Rites done proper for the repose of his poor soul," she proclaimed. "The good Father will do them, too, or he won't be seeing another pence of mine or m'family's in the offering tray."

Margaret, Father Quinlan, and the occasional friend sat in the stuffy bedroom: listening to Darcy's labored, stuttered breathing and the muffled din of conversation from the other room. They talked quietly to each other over Darcy's form under the blanket once quilted by his twelve-years-dead wife, occasionally glancing at the grizzled, sunken face on the pillow that was, in turn, staring blindly at the candlelit shadows gathering on the ceiling.

In the front room, the evening already had more the aspect of a wake. The dozen folk there had gone through two bottles of Jameson 12-year-old Special Reserve from Darcy's cupboard ("Well, he won't be a'needin' the whiskey now, will he?"), and flasks were regularly being produced from back pockets and passed around. The air was murky with fragrant smoke from cigarettes, pipes, and the smoldering peat fire in the hearth,

3

which didn't seem to be drawing properly. Their voices were loud and boisterous, laughing as they related stories from Darcy's past: purely fiction, embellished, or nakedly raw, they didn't care. Someone had brought along a guitar and another a fiddle, and the stories and conversation intermingled with playing and singing.

Outside, a gale off the North Atlantic howled and shook the shutters and roof beams of the farmhouse. The door to the farmhouse rattled in its frame, causing those closest to glance toward it to check that the latch was still holding.

The door to Darcy's bedroom opened. Margaret stood there with her white hair hanging limply around her face and a rosary clutched in her hand, Father Quinlan a dark presence behind her. The song failed in mid-phrase and the laughter shuddered to a halt. Margaret sniffed and wiped at her eyes. "Poor Darcy's gone," she stated simply. Several of those in the room made the sign of the cross at the news.

At the same moment, the shutters boomed and rattled, and the door visibly quivered with a sound as if wild fists were beating on the planks. "Sweet bleedin' Jaysus!" one of the company shouted in alarm, then glanced guiltily at the priest. "Beggin' your pardon a'course, Father."

The door and shutters continued to rattle as the wind rose with a nearly human, furious shriek. The blue flames of the peat fire shuddered in a sudden downdraft that sent smoke pouring into the room. "What in heaven—" Margaret began as the gathering coughed and waved hands against the invasion, but a new voice interrupted her.

"'Tis *yer* fault, all of yez," the voice said, and as one they looked over to the hearth from where the voice had emanated. A woman stood in front of the fire, and hers was a face that none of them knew. She was bundled in a hooded red cloak, the cloth beaded with rain as if she'd just come in from the weather, though no one could remember her entering the room. Her eyes were a deep, saturated green, and the strands of hair that escaped the cowl were the color of a moonless sky at midnight. Her voice was edged steel wrapped in dark velvet, low and sensual. "There be no door or window open here for the soul to depart through, as is customary. The spirits sent to accompany Darcy are angry."

"Darcy's soul ca'nah be kept from the Lord by doors or windows," Father Quinlan interjected. He scowled. "This blather is simple superstition, woman. Shame on yeh." Both he and Margaret glared at the intruder.

"Darcy Fitzgerald didn't believe in yer foolish God, priest, so shut your gob," the woman said, and half the company drew in their breath at the blasphemy. Several warded themselves again with the sign of the cross.

"Darcy believed in things much older than that, and they've come for him now. Yeh must let him go. Why has no one stopped the clocks here or turned the mirrors?"

Again there came the sound of fists beating at the door, and the shutters were nearly pulled from their hinges. The wind shrieked in the chimney, and the guitar player, sitting on the hearth nearest the woman, looked at the fire, startled. "'Tis the very banshee," he said, then glanced guiltily at the woman.

"Aye," the woman in red answered. She was smiling strangely. "Open the door," she commanded, gesturing to the men nearest to it.

"Nah," Margaret shouted back. "There be no need for that. Darcy's soul is already in heaven, and his body will be placed in consecrated ground."

The cloaked woman laughed as fists continued to hammer at the planks, and she gestured once more. "Open the door," she repeated. Her voice was imperious, commanding, and one of the men sitting next to the door rose to his feet, glancing at his wife who sat alongside him who, in turn, was staring at the woman.

Finally, the wife nodded, faintly, as if she and the woman had exchanged some unheard communication. "What can it hurt?" she half-whispered, though she kept her gaze averted from Margaret and the priest, who remained standing in the doorway of Darcy's bedroom as if defending the corpse. Her husband lifted the latch and turned the knob, pulling at the door.

The door flew from his hands, slamming hard against the limits of its hinges as the mourners shouted in alarm. A hurricane wind as cold as a winter gravestone blew hard into the front room, snatching papers and napkins from the small table and hurling them about, extinguishing all the candles, sending the pictures on the wall swaying and falling, and toppling the empty bottles of Jameson. The few electric lights in the room—Darcy having been slow to have the lines run out to his farmstead—flickered and went momentarily dark. Only the faint, ethereal light of the peat fire remained, strangely untouched. The wind plucked at the coats and pants and skirts of those gathered there as if with invisible fingers, and tugged especially hard at the priest's cassock, enough that they heard him cry out in the darkness. Then the wind abruptly reversed itself, rushing out from the house and slamming the door shut behind itself. Later, some of those in the room would swear they heard a man laughing in the midst of the retreating gale, and that the laughter was that of old Darcy himself.

The electric lights pulsed once and returned. The peat fire crackled contentedly as the gathering blinked and looked around. "That woman . . ." they heard Margaret say. "I swear that she . . ." and they all looked to where the woman had been.

But she had gone as suddenly as she'd come.

This time, it was the priest himself who made the sign of the cross.

✦ 2 ✦

A Dream, Vanishing

THE CHICAGO WEATHER promised to be a shock. Even in early May, the heat threatened to overwhelm the sweater Colin Doyle was wearing. He pushed his glasses back up his nose as he peered myopically at the crowd near the Arrivals gate.

His sister Jen waved at him as he emerged, rushing over to him after a moment's hesitation. Her short hair was disheveled, as if she'd just hurriedly toweled it dry after a shower. She wore her smile in the same way she wore a business suit. When he hugged her, he heard the smile break and a sob escape. "How's Dad?" Colin asked as he embraced Jen.

"No better," she answered, sniffing as she stepped back. "Sorry. I promised myself I wasn't going to cry when I saw you."

"My face sometimes has that effect."

That brought back the smile momentarily. "Silly as always. Good. I've missed that." He saw her glance at the gig bag on his back, his Gibson J-45 safely ensconced within; she said nothing, but her lips tightened a bit, and he wondered if she were going to say something about it. "Let's hit the baggage carousels and get home," she said instead. "You're sure you want to stay with me and not Mom? You know she's expecting you at home, in your old room."

"I'm certain she is. I'm just not sure that's where *I* want to be." Colin gave a shrug. He lifted his glasses and rubbed at his eyes. "Or is that going to be a problem with you and Aaron? You *are* still seeing him, aren't you?"

Jen's quick blush gave him the answer, and suggested more.

The first time he'd heard about Aaron had been last semester . . .

7

Last semester . . .

Colin slid into a booth at the Starbucks on University Way NE with a grande latte. He pulled out his phone, which claimed it was 6:32 in the morning—8:32 back in Chicago. He touched the link for his sister Jennifer. He heard the click of the connection, a long hiss of static, and finally a ring. A second ring. A third.

"Colin? Do you have any idea what time it is here?" Her voice was simultaneously sleepy and irritated.

"8:30, give or take a couple minutes."

"Yeah, in the morning. Saturday morning."

"I wanted to get you before you left the apartment."

"It's a cell phone, dear; you'd get me whether I was in the apartment or not. And on Saturday, 'before I leave the apartment' means, oh, somewhere before one in the afternoon. Maybe later. It's Saturday, damn it."

"You complain a lot. What happened to the 'Don't worry what time it is, little brother, just call me whenever you get a chance' story you gave me when I left?"

He heard her yawn; a male voice muttered something indistinctly in the background. "My brother Colin in Seattle," he heard Jennifer say. "Go back to sleep."

"Oops," he said. "Jen had company last night. Sorry. Anyone I should know?"

Colin thought he heard the sound of bare feet on hardwood; she'd left the bed. "Hah, you're not in the least bit sorry, so don't even try to apologize. And no, you don't know him, and as to whether you *will* ever know him . . . well, that's not decided yet. It probably depends a lot on when you come back here." She yawned again, sounding a bit more awake, and he heard dishes clattering in the background: she'd moved to the kitchen.

"What would Mom and Dad say?"

"I'm not in the habit of discussing my sex life with them. And not with you either, little brother. Speaking of which, how's yours? You know Mom's half-terrified you're going to bring home some young undergrad coed, probably from the Music department, with a grandchild already incubating in her belly." Colin heard something liquid being poured, and Jen taking a cautious sip: coffee. He took a sip of his own before he answered.

"Not much chance of that at the moment, I'm afraid. I'm too damn busy. So who's this paragon?"

"His name's Aaron Goldman."

"Aaron Goldman? He's Jewish?"

"Yes." He could almost see her eyebrows raising with the affirmation, as if in challenge.

"And how has that gone over with the parental units?"

Her sigh scratched at the speaker of the phone. "It's not 1950 anymore, Colin. In case you hadn't noticed, we're in a whole new century, and Irish Catholics marry Jews all the time now. They marry Latinos and African-Americans, too. Guys marry guys, women marry women. Or have you regressed back to another era since you went to the left coast? I thought things were more liberal out there."

"Sure, all that goes on, just not in the Doyle family. Heck, I remember Tommy getting lots of grief back in high school for dating a Methodist. Somehow, I can't see Dad letting his grandchild go to temple wearing a kippah."

Another sigh rattled the speaker. "I'd like to point out that I'm neither married, pregnant, nor considering a conversion. And Mom said she thinks Aaron is very nice, thank you. Now, let's talk about you, since you called . . ."

. . . *They had, though he hadn't told her then what he'd already been thinking.*

"Hello?" he heard Jen saying now. "Earth to Colin." Colin shook away the memory.

"Sorry," he said. "Just not enough sleep. So Aaron's still in the picture?"

"He is, but I do have an extra bed in my office at the apartment, and you can have that if you decide to stay with me instead of Mom."

Colin nodded. "Good. I don't think I slept more than a few hours last night. I'll probably end up crashing pretty soon, and I'd rather do that at your place, if you don't mind."

"Not a problem for me, though it might be for Mom. But we can decide that later. Right now, let's get you to the hospital. Everyone's there."

Colin lifted his chin in agreement and started walking down the corridor to where the signs pointed to the baggage area. "So . . . tell me about Dad," he said as they walked. "He's going to be all right, isn't he?"

He saw her eyebrows raise at that, but he also saw her press her lips together again, as if to hold back the comment she wanted to make. "I'll fill you in once we're in the car . . ."

On the drive to the hospital, Jen told him that there'd been little change since the phone call he'd received the day before, and the changes that had occurred weren't heartening. His father had been found collapsed on the floor of his downtown Loop office by one of the janitorial staff, after his mother became worried about him not answering his phone and called the building owners. No one knew how long he'd been down, unconscious and barely breathing. The doctors were saying it had been a massive coronary event, that their father had been too long without oxygen, that there'd been too much resultant brain damage, and that his body was failing. His kidneys had shut down; the circulation to his extremities was poor.

"They're telling us it's our decision to make. They can keep him on the vent and see if he improves, but . . ." Jen stopped, biting her lip. He saw her eyes filling with tears, and when she blinked, twin streaks rolled down her cheek. She took one hand from the wheel to wipe at them, almost angrily. Colin reached over to place his hand on her shoulder. He could feel her trembling underneath his touch.

"S'okay, Jen. I wish I'd been in town and able to get here sooner."

"You're here now," she told him. "That's all that matters. Mom and Tommy'll be glad to see you."

Colin wasn't quite so certain of that, especially not given the news that at some point he had to relay to them—when the time was right, which it certainly wasn't now, not with his father's condition. *That has to wait. There'll be a moment soon enough.*

He could only hope that was right. He sighed and laid his head back against the seat rest, watching the once-familiar landscape scroll by.

Home. At least it once had been. Somehow, it no longer felt that way.

Colin wasn't so certain that Jen was entirely right as the elevator doors opened on the lounge of the Cardiac ICU unit. His mother and Tommy were sitting in chairs near the nurse's station, conversing with his Aunt Patty and a man he didn't recognize who was wearing a business suit. Tommy was also dressed in a suit; even from this distance, Colin could tell it was expensive. His mother was wearing a black dress and looking as if she were going out for an evening on the town. Diamond earrings sparkled below her carefully arranged and dyed-too-dark hair.

Tommy looked their way as the elevator doors opened and nodded, as if in approval. He leaned down to speak in his mother's ear, and she glanced toward the elevator. There was a frown on her face before she theatrically arranged it in a smile. He would see weariness in the way her face sagged, though, and that told him how much she'd been affected by his father's illness.

"Colin," she said, rising and holding out her hands. "It's so good to see you again, my dear."

Jen nudged him forward before he could move, and he went to his mother, kissing her on a dry cheek as she pursed her lips for an air kiss. "I'm sorry I wasn't here. I came as soon as I heard," he told her. *Great. Starting with an apology right at the start.* She squeezed his arm, and released him.

"At least Tommy and Jen were here for your father and for me," she said. "I was blessed to have that."

He told himself that there was nothing personal in the words; it was only her way. But the sting of them also told Colin that his rationalizing was only a partial success. "Hey, Tommy," he said as his brother came over to join them. Tom Jr. was a decade older than Colin; his hair already touched at the temple with the start of what Colin was certain would soon be a distinguished salt-and-pepper gray. Tommy had always been too old to be a true playmate for Colin; as a teenager, he seemed to consider Colin more a nuisance than anything else. When Tommy had reached college, he seemed to be more like a distant, usually absent uncle than a brother. It was Jen, three years older than Colin, who'd been his true sibling.

Tommy extended a hand—no offer of an embrace there. Colin shook his hand: Tommy had a politician's grip, firm enough to feel solid, but careful. He put his other hand over Colin's as if to make up for the lack of a hug. "Good to see you again, little brother. Just wish it weren't in these circumstances. How's school?"

"School's school," Colin answered. If Tommy noticed the false smile that accompanied that statement, he didn't react.

Behind Tommy, the man in the business suit watched. He looked to be in his forties, with an athletic build that was beginning to sag and paunch, his hair thin on top and gray. Tommy followed Colin's gaze, releasing Colin's hand as if relieved. "Oh, Colin, this is Carl Harris, Dad's campaign manager."

Harris extended his own hand. "So you're the grad student who's also the musician."

"Yep," Colin answered. "The black sheep of the family. They usually keep me carefully hidden." Harris gave that a thoughtful half-smile.

"You're exactly what you should be." Aunt Patty had come up behind Colin. He turned into her full embrace and an enthusiastic kiss on both cheeks. "You and Jen always were more like the O'Callaghan side of the family than the Doyle side. So sorry you had to come back like this, darling." She hugged him again, tightly. Their glasses clashed slightly with the embrace—the O'Callaghans were also uniformly nearsighted. He could smell the musk of her perfume and the shampoo in her hair, which—unlike his mother—she had allowed to go naturally gray, though she kept it unfashionably long. Patty was his mother's older sister, now in her early sixties, the athletic figure she'd always had softening over the years. Aunt Patty had always been his favorite relative. Sometimes he felt that he had confided more in Aunt Patty than in his own parents. She was childless herself. She'd once been married to the stormy and temperamental Andrew Martelli, who had owned a small chain of shops selling Italian ices and yogurt. Aunt Patty had divorced Uncle Andrew two decades ago, for reasons that were talked about in hushed tones but never around Colin or the other children, though it became easy enough to guess why.

After divorcing Uncle Andrew, Patty had never remarried, though Aunt Patty's best friend, Rebecca, had moved into the old Martelli house, which Patty kept after the divorce, not long after. That Rebecca's "best friend" was also her lover was something that was never openly discussed by his parents, though it was an open secret in the family. "Hey, Aunt Patty," Colin said as they hugged. "It's so good to see you. How's Rebecca?"

"She's fine, and thank you for asking, darling. She said to give you a hug when I saw you." She kissed his forehead and hugged him hard. "So there it is," she said, smiling.

Along with Jen, Aunt Patty had supported Colin when he had announced that he wasn't going to go for the PhD in History; that he intended to leave college to pursue playing music full-time. His parents had been appalled; Aunt Patty had been supportive. *"Oh, for Christ's sake," she'd told them. "He's young, and that's the time to do these things. Let him go—he may just surprise you with how well he turns out."*

In the end, Colin had succumbed to the pressure from his parents and from Tommy: *Get the PhD now while you still have the energy. Go now, while that nice offer from Washington University stands. There's no future in music, especially for the traditional music you like to play. You can always do that as an avocation and a sideline, but with a doctorate, you could make a decent living, like Jen . . .* He'd listened to their incessant arguments for continuing his education, though he now regretted his capitulation.

He remembered a favorite saying of his father: *Regretting past decisions is useless. All that matters is making better ones in the future.* He wasn't certain his father would like the one he'd made.

"When can I see Dad?" Colin asked the group.

"I'll take you back to his room," Jen said. "Okay, Mom? Then maybe we can go out and get some dinner and talk."

His mother nodded. "Go on. We'll wait out here—they don't like lots of people in the room. Tommy, come here and tell me what you and Mr. Harris are thinking . . ." She turned away, her mind obviously already elsewhere.

"So has Mom been playing the stoic as usual?" Colin asked as they walked down the hall.

"She's being Mom, so yeah, I guess so. But this has been hard on her. Dad's always been around, and now . . ." She gave a shrug. "Well, you'll see."

Three doors down, she turned into a room. Inside, there was the rhythmic sigh of the ventilator machine. On the bed, laced by tubes from the vent, IV, and catheter, a blood pressure cuff around his arm and an array of graphs on a flatscreen behind him, his father lay on a bed. Colin stopped in the doorway, trying to take it all in. His father's face was pale, the cheeks sunken, his hair disheveled. His hands lay like two dead birds on the sheets. His eyes were closed, a rubber tube ran into his nose, held in place with tape. His mouth was slightly open, and below, the blue bulk of the vent wrapped his neck over the tracheotomy site. The only indication that he was alive was the slow rise and fall of his chest in tandem with the life-support machinery and the relentless, slow beep of the heart monitor.

For a moment, the room seemed to shift in his vision, like an old movie lurching in its sprockets. He saw flecks of light at the edges of his vision. "Oh, my God," he whispered, and Jen took his hand.

"I know," she said. "It was really hard, the first time I saw him this way."

"There's been no change?" Colin blinked, taking a deep breath before moving to the bed. He touched his father's hand; it felt cold, and there was no response when he squeezed his father's fingers.

"No. If anything, there's been further deterioration, according to the docs. The question is, how long do we keep him on the vent, and when do we take him off—or do we? But go on, talk to him. They say that he can still hear you, even if he can't respond."

"Hey, Dad," Colin said. "It's me, Colin, back from school. Sorry that it took this long to get here. I wish you'd wake up, Dad, so we could . . ." His throat closed up then, and he couldn't finish. He felt unbidden tears well up in his eyes, and he blinked them back. He took a long, slow breath, patting his father's hand. "Anyway, you just rest and get yourself better. Everyone's praying for you, Dad." He hesitated, then: "Love ya, Dad."

It was as if he spoke to a cut log or a bronze statue. There was no response, no indication that anything he'd said had been heard or understood. The words hung in the air and vanished. Whatever spark had once inhabited his father's body was gone; he was an empty shell tossed up on a beach. Vacant.

The exhaustion of the long hours of travel and the sleepless night before hung about him suddenly, dark and heavy and silent. Colin stepped back from the bed. Jen's arm went around his waist and she leaned against him, but he could barely stand himself. A nurse came in and slid around them. "Just here to check his vitals," she announced. "You can stay if you like."

"Thanks," Colin said. "But we were just leaving."

Back in the lounge area, they found that his mother had made reservations for the group at *Gene & Georgetti*, an Italian steakhouse on North Franklin Street. Tommy and the mysterious Mr. Harris had already gone ahead, and his mother and aunt were getting ready to leave even as Colin and Jen returned. Colin's eyelids were beginning to feel as if they were made of lead. He sighed at the announcement, thinking of two hours or more in the restaurant with his family, and dreading the inquisition that he knew would come when they'd finished talking about his father, and the revelation that he might have to make then. "I'm a little underdressed for the place, Mom," Colin protested, but she waved her hand.

"They won't care. I've reserved the Bar Room for us, anyway, so no one will see you. We need to discuss the situation with your father, now that you're finally here."

Turning a concern into a criticism. Well, that's normal at least.

"Mary," Aunt Patty interjected. "Look at the boy. He's about ready to fall over. He's not in any shape to talk about anything yet. Let him get a good night's sleep so he can think clearly. We can all talk in the morning."

His mother's lips tightened. "I suppose," she said. "Well, we need to eat anyway, so the rest of us can still go. Colin can take a cab back to the house . . ."

"Mom." This time it was Jen who interrupted. "I need to get back to my place and take care of the cat, and my contacts are killing me, anyway. I'll take Colin home with me; he can have the bed in the back room. Why don't you guys go on to the restaurant; I'm not feeling that hungry right now and we'll fix something at the apartment after Colin gets settled. His stuff's in my car, anyway."

"Thanks, Jen," Colin said hurriedly. "That sounds good to me."

"I thought you'd be taking your old room at the house," his mother protested. "I had Beth come in and clean it."

"I can stay there tomorrow night," Colin told her. "This'll give Jen and me time to catch up a bit."

"Catch up? You call her often enough from school. I've been hearing everything about you secondhand from my daughter . . ." his mother began, then sighed. Colin decided that it was, perhaps, a measure of how worn out she was herself by her husband's crisis that she didn't pursue the accusation—against which, he had to admit, he didn't have a good argument. For the first time, he noticed the heavily-drawn lines in his mother's face and he realized just how much the last few days had cost her, and how much she had to be hurting. *She and Dad have been married over forty years . . .* He knew he had no sense of what that kind of commitment might mean, or how he might feel if someone he'd been with that long might be leaving. The realization humbled him and made him want to apologize again, but he resisted the impulse.

"Fine," his mother said, with a face that indicated that the word tasted sour in her mouth. "Let's all have dinner tomorrow night at the house, and we'll talk then about the decisions we need to make."

"How's your dad, Hon?" Colin heard someone say inside even as Jen unlocked the door to her apartment. He set down his luggage in the hall and took the gig bag from his back, leaning it against the wall. Jen tossed her keys into a bowl on a small table next to the door as she shut it behind the two of them. There was another set of keys already in the bowl, and the implications of that suddenly hit Colin.

"He's about the same," Jen answered the voice as someone stepped out of the kitchen. "Aaron, this is my brother Colin."

Aaron Goldman wore his dark hair close-cropped, his face adorned with a full beard. His eyes were as dark as the hair and deep set. He was wearing a dress shirt and tie; his suit jacket hung over one of the chairs in the front room as if he'd just arrived himself. He had the build of someone who had once been a runner but was now mostly sitting behind a desk. He came forward—expensive shoes, Colin noted—and extended his hand. "Hey, Colin. Jen's told me a lot about you." The handshake was firm and didn't linger too long.

"I'll bet," he said. "Sorry for the interruptions."

Aaron grinned: a pleasant, self-deprecating smile. "No problem. Brothers always rank over boyfriends, as they should." The smile faded into the beard. "Really sorry about your dad. That's a hell of a reason to have to come back home."

"Yeah," Colin answered. "It pretty much sucks all around." He took off his glasses and cleaned them on the hem of his sweater. Without intending to, he yawned, hard and suddenly. "Sorry," he said as he put his glasses back on. "Jet lag, I guess. Plus I think I've had about three hours' sleep in the last thirty hours."

An orange-and-white cat appeared, rubbing against Jen's ankle. She picked it up and scratched its neck. It purred loudly. "This is Finnigan," Jen told Colin, and pointed to the hallway. "Your room's down there on the right. Bathroom's at the end of the hall if you need it. Close the door unless you want Finnigan coming in."

"It's too early to go to bed."

"It's eight o'clock—so don't worry about it. Get some sleep, and hopefully by morning you'll be feeling better. I'll get you up when Aaron leaves tomorrow morning." Jen let Finnigan down and pecked Colin on the cheek, then moved over to give Aaron a kiss as well—that one longer and far more lingering. Aaron's arms went around her, and she leaned against him easily.

They look like they're comfortable and familiar with each other . . . He wondered at that—Jen had had boyfriends enough before, but they had generally been around only a few months before vanishing. Colin had found most of them a bit stodgy and self-absorbed: like Jen, the majority had been academics and university teachers. He'd thought that, now in her late twenties, Jen would never find herself in a long-term relationship; it seemed he might be wrong. "Go on," she said. "We can talk tomorrow and do that catching up."

Colin nodded. The thought of a bed was enticing and made the exhaustion even more oppressive. He yawned again, then picked up his suitcase and the guitar. "Aaron, it's good to finally meet you. I promise I make a better impression when I'm actually awake."

"Hah," Jen laughed. "Aaron, I'm afraid the impression he makes is about the same either way, honestly."

"Love you, too, Sis. I hope my snoring doesn't distract the two of you too much."

Jen laughed. "In that case, it's another reason to close your door. Besides, I'm getting used to snoring." She dug a playful elbow in Aaron's side.

"Guilty," Aaron said. "At least, that's what she tells me." He leaned toward Colin and said in a stage whisper, "She snores, too. She just won't admit it."

Colin laughed. "Yeah, I know. I grew up with her."

"It's good to finally meet you, Colin. I hope we have a chance to chat while you're here."

"I'm sure we will. See you two in the morning, then."

With that, he left them. He went to his room, shut the door, and stripped off his clothes without unpacking anything. The bed beckoned.

He was asleep within minutes.

⤙ 3 ⤚

They Are Gone

*S*HE COULD SEE *the green land spread out before her, tantalizingly close—as if she could step from here into that world. She could hear the lyric melody of some ancient song in the air, as if the strength of the tune itself was holding open the portal. Strands of color danced and shimmered in the sky, and her hand ached to hold them, to use them, but she no longer had the cloch, the jeweled stone that would allow her to do that . . .*

"Most of the Old Ones have gone on, an' we'll never see that land of yours."

Maeve started at the sound of the voice. With the interruption, the vision in the smoke vanished as if it had never been there, and a weariness came over her. She sagged, letting her head drop, her long, dark hair falling around her face like a curtain. The kitchen table at which she sat was scattered with herbs and potions; a brazier with burning peat inside it sat on a brass tripod before her. Keara, the young woman who'd been helping her create the spell, swept a tattered woolen shawl over her shoulder and glared wordlessly at the speaker with pale eyes. Maeve lifted her head, sighing. She glared at Niall herself for having spoiled the work she'd spent the morning preparing.

So close. I could feel the bard; I could nearly talk to him. So close, and now I have to start again.

"Yer wrong, Niall," Maeve told the man, swallowing her anger. Niall's brown eyes were as hard as winter acorns. His nose looked as if it had been broken once or twice in the past, set over tight and thin pale lips cracked with cold and salt. "There's time yet for us to go there."

"So yeh keep saying, year after year, decade after decade. I just wonder whose time it is yer talking about—yers or that of those like me. Like that

18

poor soul yeh took last week, we're too few and dying too fast." Niall tossed a crumpled envelope on the table, ripped open and with an official-looking document sticking up from the torn seal. "They've given us notice. I just talked to a garda at the harbor who came on a boat from the mainland and handed me this. They say this ain't our island and that we have'ta leave. How do we do that, I want t'know, when we got nowhere else to go and yeh say it must be here or nothin'?"

Maeve glanced at the document. "'Tis just empty words the *leamh* are spouting," she told him. Keara laughed at that, as did Niall, though more bitterly: leamh was the right word for those on the mainland—the mundane people, the ordinary ones. "I tell yeh, Niall. I know now what we need, and I *will* get it. Yeh tell yer people that."

"I will, Maeve. But yeh should know that me folk won't wait forever, nor will some of the others who are here. I'll be taking 'em elsewhere if we need to in order to survive. Yeh and those who sleep under the mound see time differently than we do. *We* can't be waiting forever."

"Yeh won't have to. 'Tis certain."

Niall lifted his chin at that, but his eyes challenged Maeve. She held his stare, unblinking, and eventually his gaze dropped. "Yeh better be right," he mumbled to the floor, then turned and left the room. They heard the front door of Maeve's cottage slam. The wind set the flames dancing above the turf fire in the kitchen hearth.

"Sorry," Keara said to Maeve. "Do yeh want me to set it up again?"

Maeve shook her head. "Neh. I'm knackered, I'm afraid." She glanced toward the front door. "Niall," she said, the name summing up everything she felt. Keara gave her a soft smile as she touched Maeve's hand.

"Not to worry, m'Lady. Niall do'nah think before he talks. 'Tis his way. He'll be back tugging his forelock and asking your forgiveness tomorrow."

"Maybe." Maeve rubbed at her eyes, stinging from the peat smoke in the brazier before her. She leaned back in her chair. "G'wan home," she told Keara. "We'll do this again tomorrow and see if the signs are better. And I can reach out to the bard. Aiden must have supper waiting for yeh."

"Should I bring supper to yeh as well?"

Maeve shook her head. "Nah tonight. I'll just make do here. Now, g'wan with yeh."

She watched Keara gather her things, curtsy once to her, then leave the cottage. Maeve waited until her footsteps had faded on the pebbles of the walk. She cupped the brass legs of the brazier, looking at her hands as she pushed it back from her. They were the hands of a younger woman, aye, but there were lines there now that had never been there before, fine creases in the skin. She saw the same thing in the mirrors when she glanced at them.

Yer not so different now. Once yeh were, but no longer. Yer dying slowly, like all of them. Yeh even think like them now sometimes. An' if yeh can't do this now, then they will all die soon enough.

"Nah," she said aloud, her voice no louder than the crackling of the fire in the hearth or the sound of the gulls along the harbor quay. "I won't let that happen."

Her fist pounded the table once with the denial, but it only rattled the crockery there and didn't convince.

4

Visitations

IN THE DREAM, at first, he was in Ireland, and his playing held the audience in thrall. They were silent, listening to every word and every chord, and his voice was like liquid fire coming from his throat. When the song ended, everyone rose in applause, shouting . . .

. . . and the dream, as dreams do, shifted and became dark. He was still on stage, but the magic of his voice was gone, and he was feeling frantic because he was playing a set with several Irish-born musicians. Someone called a new song, and he couldn't remember the chords; when he guessed at the key and strummed a chord, his guitar was terribly and hopelessly out of tune. He frantically turned the tuning pegs, putting the strings seemingly in tune, but the D chord he hit was dissonant. The lead musician—Lucas, his name was—glared at him; and one of the other people on stage with him struck his Gibson from behind, with a sound like a fist knocking on a door. "What the feck?" Lucas snarled. "How can yeh not know this song? Every idjit knows it." Again the knocking came, a little louder than before, and the Gibson shivered in his hands.

"Breakfast in ten minutes," a dark-haired woman said, getting up from her seat in front of the stage. She felt somehow familiar to him, and her full smile made him smile at her in return. Vivid green eyes sparkled in her face, and she pulled a red cloak around herself. "Better wake up."

The dream dissolved and fled, and Colin felt a momentary panic, not sure where he was. The sun was spilling in through blinds, throwing long, out-of-focus slanted stripes across the opposite wall and over the small desk and bed in the room. Colin rubbed his eyes, yawning. His mouth was dry and tasted like someone's trash can. He struggled to bring saliva into his parched throat as he fumbled on the bedside table for his glasses.

He put them on and the room jumped into focus. On the table, a radio with an iPod sitting in the slot atop it proclaimed that it was 9:17 in the morning. Sitting up, Colin saw that someone had unpacked his suitcase. A new pair of jeans, a green long-sleeved polo, underwear, and socks were neatly folded on a chair near the door. The clothes he'd peeled off the night before were gone. He threw aside the covers and sat up, rubbing at his head. He put on the clothes and opened the door. "Hey, sleepyhead," Jen called from the kitchen. "I'm putting stuff on the table now."

"Give me a minute or two," he answered. "I really have to pee."

"Then don't let me stop you. End of the hall, remember?"

A few minutes later, he padded barefoot into the kitchen. Jen was already sitting at the little table near the window. Finnigan stared at him from the counter; Jen also looked him up and down appraisingly. "Not bad," she said. "You look almost human again."

"Right. Where are the rest of my things?"

"In the dresser in the room. The clothes you were wearing yesterday are in the dryer now."

He nodded and sat across from her. "Thanks. You didn't have to do that."

"Yes, I did. Those clothes were beginning to stink. Y'know, you don't have to wear your jeans for a week at a time."

"Yeah," he told Jen. "I should've changed before the flight, but there just wasn't time." He took a sip of the coffee in front of him and a bite of the eggs. "I keep thinking about Dad. That was such a shock when I got your message about him."

"I know. This doesn't seem possible. Just three days ago, I had lunch with him down in the Loop . . ." She pressed her lips together and Colin could see tears gather in the corners of her eyes. She sniffed and scraped her eggs across her plate with her fork. "That first night, after they . . ." She stopped and he saw her throat convulse. ". . . after they found him, I thought I'd wake up the next morning and find that it was just a dream, that Dad was back to his old self."

That brought back Colin's own memories. "I keep thinking about the last time I saw Dad before I left for the university. We argued. As usual."

"Dad knows how you really felt about him. You shouldn't worry about that."

"That's the thing, Jen. I *don't* really know how I felt about him. Sometimes I loved the man; other times I thought he was a gigantic pain in the ass and a totally self-absorbed person, and I'd just as soon be as far away from him and Mom as possible. It's all mixed up. *I'm* all mixed up. Fuck . . ." He took a bite of his eggs, then took a long sip of his coffee. The heat steamed his glasses; he looked at Jen through the fog. His thoughts had drifted into dangerous territory, and he still didn't want to broach the subject, not even with Jen. "Aaron seems a decent guy. He's a lawyer?"

She let him change the subject without comment. "He's actually in Finance," she answered. "But he does have a law degree. And yeah, he's a decent guy." She lifted her own coffee mug, looking at Colin over the rim. He could see a slight blush in her cheeks. "It's too early to say much more."

"Have you used 'those words' yet?"

She laughed quickly and set the mug down. "None of your business."

"Aha. Then you have."

"What about you, Mr. Grad Student, since you're being so nosy about my love life? Have *you* used those words with anyone?"

"No," he answered. "I haven't. I had a couple dates now and then with a few women, but . . ." He shrugged.

Jen didn't look convinced. She took a bite of toast and chewed it, her gaze on Colin, who took refuge in the appearance of his coffee mug. "So what have you been doing with yourself? How's the dissertation coming along? You haven't sent me that draft you promised me."

Colin hid the flush that erupted then behind the coffee mug. "Yeah, I know. Things have been hectic."

"How hectic can they have been? You having trouble with it?"

He shrugged again. "Can we not talk about this now?" he asked.

"And *that* tells me that there's more that you're not saying. I could always read you, little brother. Talk."

"I will. I promise. We'll have time. Just . . . not now."

Jen gave an overdramatic sigh. "Okay," she said. "You don't want to go into details, that's fine. I can wait. But you know Mom's going to notice, too, and she'll worm it all out of you."

Colin shook his head. "Not this time. I promise."

"Right." She put her fork down. "So what do you want to do today? I'm off; with everything going on with Dad, the Chair has some of the other professors in the department covering my classes this week."

"I want to go see Dad again. I'd like to talk to the doctors so I know what's going on before tonight."

Jen nodded. "Sounds like a plan to me. Finish your breakfast, let me get myself ready, and we'll head over there."

Jen stayed in the lobby with their mother, who was also there when they arrived. Colin walked back to his father's room alone.

The doctor on duty that morning—Elizabeth Pearse, the hospital badge clipped to her pocket declared—entered the room just as he pulled up a chair to sit next to his father. He placed one hand over his father's, which felt cold and clammy to him. "Doctor," he said, "has there been any change?"

She shook her graying head. "You're the son who was in Seattle?"

He nodded.

She tapped at the keyboard and monitor next to his bed. "Your family should have already told you how it is."

"Tell me again," he told her. "Without the sugar coating. You know how families are."

She smiled at that, lines deepening around her eyes. "All right, then. Bluntly, all the medical signs indicate that your father has suffered brain death. There's no response to a light shone in his eyes, and when we removed him briefly from the vent, he made no attempt to breathe on his own. None of the other tests have given us any indication that there's any significant activity from the brain stem. Unfortunately, he was brought here to the hospital too late. If he'd been found earlier, or had been able to call for help when the event happened . . ." Dr. Pearse shrugged. It was a more telling statement than anything that she could have said. "In my opinion, and I'm sorry to say this, your father's clinically dead at this point. The only thing sustaining his life are the machines. Your family needs to think of what his wishes would be in this situation. Did he have a Living Will, or had he talked to any of you or your mother about what he might want?"

"I don't know," he told her. "I've . . . been away for some time."

She nodded. "I'm very sorry," she told him. "I wish I had better news for you."

A few minutes later, she logged out of the computer and left the room. Colin turned back to his father. "Dad?" he said. "It's Colin again. I'm here."

There was no answer except the hissing wheeze-and-thump of the ventilator.

It wasn't any better, even knowing what to expect this time. The noise of the machinery keeping his father alive and monitoring him contrasted ironically with the man's silence and obliviousness to the world around him. It was hard to imagine the husk in the bed as the same driven and intense man who had shaped and manipulated Colin's youth, with whom he'd had epic battles and arguments, whom he'd loved, hated, and feared—all at once. And that last time . . .

Colin had entered into the conversation knowing what to expect, but he still hadn't expected the vitriol that spewed at him from the volcano of his father . . .

He'd met his dad in his office in the Loop. Outside the window high in one of the towers, Chicago was spread out around them, gleaming and bejeweled with lights in the evening, with a glimpse of Grant Park and the expanse of Lake Michigan between the buildings around them. Tom Sr. was standing at the window, with a glass of whiskey already in his hand. "There's a bottle of Redbreast on the bar," he said without turning. "Help yourself, son."

He did exactly that, figuring it might fortify his courage. He took a long sip as he stood next to his father. He could see his father's reflection in the glass of the office window, staring outward almost possessively, as well as his own: torn jeans and T-shirt as opposed to his father's gray, three-piece business suit; perfectly trimmed, salt-and-pepper hair against Colin's hand-combed mop of brown. "So what's up?" he asked Colin, still not looking at him. "You said you had something important to discuss."

Colin was sweating even though the office was cool. He pushed his glasses firmly up his nose, took a deep breath as if he were about to dive into cold water, and plunged in. "You know how interested I am in Irish folk and traditional music—right, Dad? Well, I'd like to go to Ireland. I want to get a visa and study music there. I could probably get approval for the visa pretty quickly." He'd glanced up then, but his father wasn't looking at him. Instead, he was still staring out toward the downtown towers. "Especially with your contacts at the Irish consulate," he added.

He'd expected the storm to break then. It didn't. His father took another calm sip of the whiskey without moving. Then, very slowly, he turned. He set the glass down on his desk as he faced Colin. "No," he said. Just the single, simple word.

"I don't need your permission, Dad. I'm an adult, and I've already made my decision. I can do this with or without your help and approval."

"No," his father repeated. He shook his head. "We had an agreement. I expect you to live up to it."

"Dad, you're not listening to me. I know this isn't what we agreed to, but I've made plans and started to set things up over there."

A nod. "So just what have you 'set up'?" he asked. "What plans have you made?"

Colin blinked. "Stop it, Dad. You need to trust me." In truth, about all he'd done was to check the airline prices and determine how long his savings could last at a bare minimum. A visa might give him two years in Ireland, but his savings wouldn't even give him a quarter of that. He would need to make money playing or busking to stay there more than six months, but he figured he could work on that once he was actually there and had surveyed the situation. He'd managed to scrape together a living, if a sometimes precarious one, here in Chicago, playing solo at local coffee shops and pubs and gigging with three or four different bands. He couldn't imagine that making the same kind of living would be harder in Ireland, which at least celebrated its musicians, writers, and artists, and where the cost of living would be decidedly lower.

"Trust you?" An internal mockery laced his father's words. "Your mother and I gave you all the advantages anyone could have, and you've done very little with them. Look at Tommy and Jen, and think about where they were at your age. Tommy had already graduated law school; Jen was getting her PhD and was already teaching. Or just look where they are now: Tommy's a respected partner in this firm, and Jen is on the tenure track at DePaul. Your brother and sister were both *ambitious*, and they went after what they wanted with all the energy and commitment they had. They still do. The decisions they made weren't selfish; they thought of their future and how they could use their skills to enhance the lives of others. They wanted to *do* something, not just indulge themselves."

And what you're talking about doing is selfish, and what you're talking about doing is self-indulgent. Colin could hear his father's subtext perfectly well. He'd heard it through most of his life: in his academic career, even back in grade school. *"The teachers say you spend all your time lost in your daydreams, that you don't pay attention. You need to buckle down and work . . ."*

Colin swept his hands through the air, not caring that his whiskey glass slipped from his finger and went careening away spewing golden liquid. "Stop it, Dad. Just . . ." He swallowed the profanity he wanted to say. " . . . stop it. I really don't need the 'Tommy and Jen' lecture again. You've given it to me a few million times already, and you know what, they *have* done better than me, at least by your standards. But they're not me, and this is what *I* want to do."

"What you want to do is what you *always* do," his father shot back. "You always make the easy choice. And you know what? I'm done with it. You told your mother and me that if we gave you three years, you'd make it in music, and that if you didn't, you'd go to grad school and get your doctorate. You're a good musician, maybe even more, I'll admit that, but it's been three years now and you're just scraping by. Your mother and I still pay your health insurance, your car insurance, and are covering your student loans. Well, it's time to live up to the bargain. So no, you can't go. You made us a promise, and you're damned well going to keep it. We're done supporting you, unless you do that."

Colin snorted derisively. "I don't want your help. I don't need it. Hell, you think you can solve everything by throwing enough money at it."

"So you don't want our money now?" His father gave a bitter, loud laugh. "Whose money was it that paid for at least half of your music equipment? Whose money paid your rent last year when you were four months behind? Whose money bailed you out when you ran into credit card problems your first year out of college? Who let you stay in your old room when you dropped out in your fourth year after changing majors for the third time? Who found you a decent-paying job afterward—a job you quit after three months, as I recall, because it interfered with your precious gigs?" His father nearly laughed. "Right. You can take care of yourself."

There it was, the endless litany of Colin the Failure, to be resurrected again and again until the end of eternity, it seemed.

"Don't worry, Dad. I promise I won't call you or Mom for help. I wouldn't want to give you the satisfaction."

"You know what would satisfy me? You having some drive and responsibility. You keeping your word! You acting like you had an *ounce* of the goddamn sense you were born with!"

The thunder was in his voice now, the volume rising, and Colin knew that this was going to be another shouting match, and that there would be no reconciliation here. They'd both walk away furious, having said things that they'd both regret later.

It was the effect they had on each other. Maybe Jen was right claiming that they were both too much alike—in that way, at least.

And it had ended as he'd expected, a screaming battle that closed with Colin stalking out of the office in full retreat and slamming the door behind him, flushed and with his jaw clenched so tightly that the muscles ached for two days afterward.

And two days later, realizing that he had exactly eleven dollars in his wallet, an over-limit credit card, and a two-figure savings account, he'd relented. He'd kept his promise and enrolled in graduate school—one as far away from Chicago as he could find.

And now . . . now . . . he'd made the decision to renege on that promise once again.

He remembered all that, staring at the wasted figure on the bed and holding his father's cold, unresponsive hand.

Colin wept then, as he hadn't since he returned.

"I don't think we really have had much of a chance, Dad," he said when he felt able to speak again. "There was so much you wanted to do yet, but there's also so much *I* want to do. I'm sorry that I wasn't like Tommy, but the time I've spent as a musician . . ." He patted the hand. "Dad, I can't tell you how much I've learned and how much I've grown, and how good it's been for me."

He laughed then; an incongruous sound that was mixed with a sob.

"Maybe I'm more like Grandpa Rory—I can still remember him telling us all these far-fetched tales about his boyhood in Ireland, how he saw leprechauns and the fair folk. He was never afraid to say what he believed. I have been, and I'm sick of it, Dad. Sick of lying to everyone around me and to myself."

He was staring at the monitor, at the eternal marching of the graphs on the blue screen. He thought he caught movement on the bed from the corner of his eye. When he looked, it seemed for a moment that it was a woman's face that he saw, not his father's: the woman he'd seen in his dream the night before was lying there, her long dark hair spread out on the pillow, her green eyes staring at him. Her lips moved, as if she were trying to speak. "I need you . . ." he thought he heard. For a moment, the whirr and beeping of the machines receded, and he thought he could smell sea air and see a green coastal landscape overlaying that of the hospital room.

Somewhere distant, a crow cawed its shrill note three times.

Colin gaped. He drew his hand back, his spine tight against the back of the chair in which he sat. But he blinked then and the vision vanished, and it was only his father lying there.

The ventilator chuffed; his father's chest rose and fell in concert. He could smell only disinfectants and the faint, sour odor that lingered in the room. The IV bag dripped on its stand, like a sterile hourglass ticking away the last moments of his father's life.

"Shit," he muttered. He was sweating despite the room's chill. Maybe the waking dream was just latent exhaustion from having been up so long the last few days. Maybe he'd never seen or heard anything at all. Now, in the glaring light of the hospital room, it seemed impossible: a momentary and lost dream fragment. Colin leaned forward again to examine the face on the pillow, trying to remember how his father had once looked in motion even though it seemed impossible. The face was pale, the cheeks more sunken than he remembered, just empty flesh hanging from a skull. "I hope you're happy wherever it is you've gone, Dad. I hope you can hear me there. I just wish . . . I just wish your kind of afterlife was something I believed in myself, but I can't. I lost that faith a long time ago, and I especially can't believe it now. Maybe . . . maybe you're where you always expected to be. Maybe that's how it works—you go to whatever afterlife you expect to have, and maybe those of us who believe in nothing end up going nowhere at all."

He chuckled once, dryly and humorlessly. "I guess I won't know until it happens, huh? I remember that when I first told you I'd lost my faith, you said you weren't having 'a goddamn pagan son.' It wasn't the first time I'd disappointed you; I know it certainly wasn't the last. Sorry I couldn't be who you wanted me to be. I wish I could have been less of a disappointment to you, and I'm . . . well, I'm sorry. Sorry for everything."

He rose from the chair. Leaning over, he touched his lips to his father's forehead.

"Bye, Dad," he said.

5

Searching for Young Lambs

*F*OR A MOMENT, *just a moment, she'd seen him as if he were standing over her. He wasn't quite what she'd expected: a young man wearing glasses, his brown hair longish and disheveled, but he looked at her with a sadness she nearly couldn't bear, the emotion so strong in him that the shock of it threw her entirely from the vision . . .*

"M'Lady?" Keara was crouched alongside Maeve's chair, the other woman's hands cradling hers and Keara's face staring up into her own with a look of concern. Maeve took in a breath she hadn't known she was holding. She blinked and realized that she was crying.

" 'Twas him," she said to Keara. "Finally. Almost as I remember him."

"You're certain?"

"Aye. And neh." Maeve took another breath and wiped at her eyes. Even though the kitchen of her small house was warm, she felt cold. Everything around her now was in too sharp a focus, as if she'd been seeing with eyes other than her own: the brazier with its curls of aromatic smoke, the herbal potion that Keara had fixed. Her ears rang with the memory of Keara's long chant, and she could feel the exhaustion from the effort touching every joint in her body.

It had been over half a century now that she'd been searching and calling. At first, she'd been able to touch him, but he fought her every time, ignoring her calls and her signs. Then, for long decades, there'd been nothing at all, and she despaired of ever recovering what she'd lost, knowing that as a mortal, he was gone. She could feel her own slow but inevitable death approaching, and that of those she'd gathered around her. But then she'd felt a sense of that presence again, fainter but growing stronger each time she'd reached out. *Him, but not him. Him, and stronger yet.* "I could nah feel the cloch na thintri with him," she told Keara, "but this one has the gift of song that t'other di'nah. But 'tis the same family, aye. The same line. He'll come to us. I have to nudge the boy, is all, and he'll come."

Keara smiled. "Good. Then nudge him."

Maeve shook her head. "Not yet. Not till I know that he has the cloch. 'Tis near him, I'm certain. I could almost feel it. But we need that as well as the boy himself."

Keara squeezed Maeve's hand. "You should be pleased then, and those must be tears of joy. Niall and the others will be happy to hear this. Fionnbharr, too." Keara stood, releasing Maeve's hand. "I can make a potion 'twill call him from under the mound." Maeve saw her gaze suddenly drop, as Keara evidently realized how that might have sounded. "I di'nah wish to presume, m'Lady. Only if that's what yeh wish, of course."

Maeve gave a low chuckle. "No, yer perfectly correct. Fionnbharr needs to wake, since we'll require him and his people soon enough. And I . . ." She lifted a shoulder. "I'm nah as strong as I once was, either. I'll need yer potion if I'm to call him forth, Keara. I ca'nah do it m'self, not as tired as I am."

She saw the young woman smile at that. "Then I'll get it ready for yeh. 'Twas me mam who knew the recipe and showed it to me, from her máthair before that, an' who knows how many generations back." Keara flashed a grin. "Sorry, m'Lady. I'll prepare it. 'Twill take a day or so; I'll have to do some gathering, and might have to take a trip to Ballemór if I ca'nah find what I need."

"Have Niall take you in, then," Maeve told her. "G'wan, then. No sense waiting."

Keara curtsied to Maeve. "I'll leave me things here, then, an' come back later to clean up. Yeh rest, m'Lady. All this 'tis harder on yeh than anyone."

Maeve waved a hand at Keara, and the woman smiled at her and vanished. A few moments later, she heard the door to her cottage open and close again.

"It will happen, this time," she said to the air. "No matter the cost."

Her voice was grim and dark.

The potion that Keara gave her was so pungent that Maeve was certain the smell alone would wake the dead. Under the stars and the moon, she poured the oily mixture onto the roots of the hawthorn tree that crowned the mound on the seaward side of the island, then stepped back toward the ring of standing stones that surrounded the mound's base.

She waited, the salt wind ruffling her hair and the long dress she wore. Beyond the mound, she could hear waves breaking in the erratic rhythm of the ocean against the rocks at the foot of the cliff. The sound soothed her: an ancient and eternal heartbeat.

She didn't have to wait long.

"I should have known 'twas yeh from the foul stench." The voice was deep and low, like a growl of thunder. Maeve saw a shadowy form appear, stepping from under the darkness beneath the hawthorn branches into the moonlight. He was of average height (though, she had to admit, she would have once thought of him as tall), with a muscular build accentuated by the ringmail he wore, chiming as he stepped forward on the mound's top. His features were hard and marked by jagged scars on his left cheek; his hair was long and fair, caught in a braided golden band. He held a tall spear in one hand.

"Fionnbharr," she said. "It's been a long time yeh've slept."

He yawned dramatically, and his nostrils flared. "I still remember yer face, and not necessarily kindly. It haunted my dreams. What are yeh calling yerself now, m'Lady?"

"Maeve," she answered.

"Maeve." He spoke her name as if tasting its single syllable. "That's appropriate, I suppose. 'Tis a mortal's name, too." His head tilted as he stared at her. "Yeh look more and more like one. I can smell how close death is to yeh. Maybe yeh'll join us under the mound yet."

"Not yet," she told him. "Not ever."

He sniffed. "Why have yeh summoned me, m'Lady?" He sniffed the air again. "Yeh do nah have the cloch, and yeh do nah have yer bard, either. I would know if they were here."

"They'll be here soon enough," she answered firmly. "But the leamh are causing trouble, and I may need yer people to deal with them."

"'Tis why yeh woke some of 'em already, when yeh brought that leamh's soul to the mound a few days past?"

"That one is one of the few left who truly believe in us, and I thought he deserved to come with us—and he can tell us what the leamh world is like now, and what they might do. Yeh should talk to him, Fionnbharr. The world has changed much since yeh last rode." She pulled her cloak more tightly around herself as a cold gust from off the ocean swirled around her. "An' I feel it changing faster with every year," she added, "and I like it less."

"Yet yeh stay in it." His voice mocked her.

"I've made promises. Yeh know that."

"Promises. Aye. Yeh were always so good at keeping yer promises." His sarcasm bit at her, but she said nothing. "Yer half-leamh yerself now," he continued, when she didn't respond. "Yeh've had too many forms and too many names, and now yeh have the smell of 'em. When I knew yeh with another title, yeh would have killed those who stood in yer way without another thought, and yeh would have laughed as yeh did it. This Maeve that stands before me now . . ." He pointed the tip of his spear toward her. "Yer telling me what *I* must do. Can *yeh* do what's needed, or have yeh become too mortal yerself? Can yeh deceive yer bard the way yeh know yeh must?"

"I can," she told him. "And Fionnbharr of the Mound, can yeh do what's needed when I call?"

"If it means we can finally follow the others, then aye, we can."

Maeve nodded. "Good."

"I still smell death on yeh, Maeve-of-many-names. Yeh sure yer not just a mortal?"

She smiled at that. "Death drives us all, mortal or not," she told Fionnbharr. "Some to run from it, some to seek it."

He laughed at that, and with the laughter, he plunged the base of his spear into the mound. There was a flash and the sound of rolling, distant thunder. Maeve blinked, and when she opened her eyes again, Fionnbharr was no longer standing on the mound.

"Stay awake," she said to the night, to the hawthorn. "There will be death and a need for you to ride out soon enough."

◄ 6 ►

There's a Chicken in the Pot

"**W**ELL, THE HOUSE still looks the same," Colin said as they drove up. The tall, three-story dwelling was wedged between two others across from a small park. The house had been heavily renovated and restored by the Doyles when they'd purchased it in the late 1980s, and they'd added a black wrought iron fence with stone pillars along the sidewalk. To Colin, the fencing and general appearance of the house's facade had always felt cold and imposing, an attempt to intimidate any visitor.

That had always seemed to match his father's outward appearance as well.

Aunt Patty greeted Jen and Colin as they entered, hugging each of them warmly. "Where's Aaron?" Aunt Patty asked Jen.

"He knows we're going to discuss Dad's situation, and begged off—said it should be a private family matter. Rebecca didn't come either?"

Patty nodded. "Like Aaron, she thought this should just be a family matter. Your Aaron's a smart boy. I think you might have a good one there."

"So far I think so, too," Jen answered. "Where's Mom?"

"Making sure the table's set. We're still waiting for Tommy and Carl."

"That Harris guy is going to be here?" Colin asked, and Patty pursed her lips as if she was tasting something sour.

"Tommy wanted him here, evidently," Aunt Patty told him. "After all, he is—was—your Dad's campaign manager, and what we decide here will certainly affect that."

Jen nodded. "I'll go in and see if Mom needs help with that table."

"Make sure I'm sitting next to you," Colin said to Jen. "Between you and Aunt Patty would be ideal."

"I will." Jen went off down the corridor. Colin lingered with his aunt.

There was an 8x10 portrait of his father in a frame sitting on one of the tables in the front room. He stared at it, seeing his father as he remembered him, the smile on his face looking somewhat artificial under the stern eyes.

"It's a lousy homecoming, isn't it?" Aunt Patty commented behind him. "I'm sorry, Colin."

"Not your fault." He stared into his father's eyes.

"He loved you. Your mom does, too."

"Yes, and they both showed it so well."

He felt Patty's hand on his shoulder, and he turned to her. Her head was tilted, her gaze now edged. "You're being too harsh on them, Colin. Especially with your mother. She's really hurting right now, more than you can imagine."

He wanted to apologize, to tell Aunt Patty that she was right and he understood what she was saying, but the words were jammed in his throat and something else slipped out. "Love is a lousy word," he answered. "We have way too many definitions for it, and nobody knows what it really means."

"Too many definitions for what?" The door had opened again, and Tommy and Carl Harris stood in the doorway. They were both dressed in suits—Colin had worn jeans and a button-down oxford shirt. Tommy cocked his head in Colin's direction.

"Nothing," Colin told Tommy. "Nice suits. Don't you guys ever take a day off?"

"There are no days off in politics," Tom answered. "At least, that's what Dad always said."

Yes, and look where that's got him . . . Colin smiled, holding back the comment. "Do you wear them to bed, too?" he asked, but Aunt Patty stepped in before Tommy could answer.

"I think dinner's about ready. Why don't we all go in?" She allowed Tom and Harris to precede them, and took Colin's arm as they passed. "You know, you have the most open face in the whole family. I can practically see what you were thinking," she whispered.

"Sorry." Then: "And sorry for what I said before, too. I know you're right. I do, it's just . . ."

She patted his arm. "No need to apologize. Like I said yesterday, I've always told Mary you were more an O'Callaghan than a Doyle."

"And how did Mom react to that?"

Aunt Patty laughed, causing Tom and Harris to glance back at them. She waved them on. "The same way I'd react if you suddenly informed me that you wanted to be just like your father, may God take his soul." She wagged a finger in Colin's direction. "But I'll deny ever having said that if you tell anyone."

Dinner was another memory made solid. Colin could recall dozens of dinners much like this one around the same table, with only the menu and the ages of the diners changing. Even the absence of his father was normal. During his childhood, dinner had always been his mother's affair, his father only making cameo appearances. Tom Sr. would often be working late: preparing a case, at a community meeting, or out of town entirely in Springfield after he'd been elected to the State Senate and the legislature was in session.

It was Mom who prepared dinner, who set the table, who made certain that everyone was seated, that any guests were properly introduced around, that the blessing was intoned before the first bite of food was eaten (and woe betide anyone but a guest trying to filch a roll or take a bite beforehand), and who directed the conversation around the table from her chair nearest the kitchen as if she were a conductor in front of an orchestra, wielding a fork rather than a baton. Colin had often wondered how she managed to get everything on the table and hot at the same time; but she always had. When Colin was still a young child, with the law firm's continued success and both state and national politics taking on more of a role, the Doyles had retained the services of Beth, the housemaid who put in a half-day's work every weekday, but the kitchen was still largely his mother's domain, even if Beth helped set the table before leaving for the day.

"So, Colin," his mother began after grace had been said and the first dishes passed around, "now that you're back, I've had Beth make up your room for you until you go back to the university."

Thanks, Mom, Colin wanted to say. *But I don't want to stay here.* "Mom," Jen broke in before Colin could answer, "Colin and I haven't had much chance to talk yet. I thought he could stay at least a few more days at my place."

"Actually, Mom, that sounds good to me," Colin added quickly. "Jen's place is right on the 'L' so I could get around pretty easily. I don't mind staying there, since it's no bother to her, and she has the extra room."

"Oh." The single, flat interjection contained entire decades of commentary. His mother drew in a long breath through her nose. "I'm just rattling around in a whole empty house with far too many extra rooms, but I suppose that's fine, then. After all, you'll be going back to Seattle soon enough,

I suppose. You've that dissertation and defense to get ready, I'm sure. Another Dr. Doyle in the family; your father would be so proud."

He ignored that. *It's not the time to tell them. Not here.* The others around the table were carefully not watching him, paying too much attention to their plates. Confusion drowned him under a roiling tsunami of doubt.

"You know, I'd love to hear you play music again, Colin," Aunt Patty cut in. "It's been a long time since I last heard you, and you had such a gift for music. Do you still play gigs in Seattle?"

"Not as much as I'd like, but yeah, I still play," Colin told her. He turned to her, thankful for the change of subject, but uneasy with the shift to his music. "There's a strong Celtic music scene there, and I've learned some old songs and variations on them that I'd never heard, and new ways to approach the material that I'd never considered."

"Immersion in another culture can change the way you think." That was Tommy, and when Colin glanced across the table to him, his brother gave him a quick wink, almost as if he knew what Colin was holding back from the conversation. "I don't think you can avoid that. I know that when Dad and I were in Paris for a two-week conference a couple of years back, it completely altered my attitude toward how food is prepared and presented. Speaking of which, this chicken's delicious, Mom. Did you do something different with it?"

As the talk around the table turned to the meal and its preparation, Colin shot a look of gratitude to Tommy, and Jen softly kicked his shin under the table. She leaned over to him. "You see, Tommy inherited Dad's ability to deflect Mom. You and I just let ourselves get dragged into those arguments with her."

"And you'll get into another one if the two of you don't keep your voices down," Aunt Patty commented softly from the other side. "Remember what she's been going through these last few days, and will be going through in the coming ones. This hasn't been easy on anyone, and especially not for her." Then she smiled toward Colin's mother, a bite of chicken on her fork.

"You really need to give me your recipe, Mary," she said, more loudly.

"Leave the dishes," Colin's mother said. "Let's go into the back room—I had Beth set up the coffee urn, there's cake, and I brought up a bottle of your father's whiskey from the office, too. We can . . ." Colin saw her hesitate as moisture visibly filled her eyes. ". . . talk about what we need to discuss more comfortably there."

The back room had been a combination rec room and library when Colin had lived here. It hadn't changed a great deal. The books were still there, hardbacks arranged in colorful rows along the shelves. There was a new flatscreen TV, much larger than the television that had been there when Colin left for Seattle. The game console that had sat next to the television back then seemed to be missing, and the board games were stacked on the top shelf, something for Beth to dust. The two tables that had filled the center of the room were gone, replaced by large, plush leather chairs and a small couch under the window, all arranged in a rough conversation circle around the room. His mother and Aunt Patty took the couch after getting coffee and a plate of the cake. Tommy half-filled a tumbler with whiskey: Connemara Cask Strength, Colin noted. "Colin?" Tom asked, lifting his glass. "Jen?"

Jen shook her head. "Sure," Colin told him.

"Ice?"

"Neat, please."

Tommy handed Colin a glass heavy with amber liquid. He swirled it around, sniffing the fragrance that held just a touch of peat smoke. He sipped. "Thanks," he said. Tommy nodded, then took a chair next to Harris, who was also nursing some of the whiskey. Harris leaned over to talk earnestly in Tommy's ear, with Tommy shaking his head. Jen sat in the chair next to Colin. For several seconds, no one said anything, the air filled with the clatter of forks on plates.

It was Tommy who spoke first.

"Everyone's spoken to the doctors, and now Colin's had his chance as well," he said. Colin thought he saw Harris make a moue of distaste as Tommy spoke. "Sad as it is, we all know what we're looking at, and I'm sure we all have opinions as to what's the best thing to do. But personally, I don't think it's a group decision. Mom, it's yours to make, and I think I can speak for everyone when I say that we'll stand by that decision, whatever it is."

Colin saw tears gathering in his mother's eyes again as she set down the cake, untouched, on the coffee table in front of the couch, and the sight made him feel guilty for not wanting to stay here with her. As difficult as the situation was for him or for Tommy and Jen, it was entirely life-changing for her. For over four decades, she and his father had been making a life together, and even if it wasn't a life that Colin would have wanted, it was the one that they'd chosen together. Their marriage had worked for them and made them happy as a couple from everything he'd seen. And now that life was threatened.

She'll be alone here, and I've just told her I don't want to stay here to help her. I'm really showing lots of empathy for the person who gave me life . . .

"This is all so horrible and so sudden," his mother began, and Patty stroked her arm. "If I thought there was *any* chance that he might recover, any chance at all . . ."

"Then keep him on the vent, Mom," Jen put in. "It's not a question of money, and it's not going to *hurt* Dad to do that. You can take all the time you want or need to make your decision, and maybe in the meantime Dad will come out of it. I know that's what Father Frank told you the Church would want you to do."

"Is that what *you'd* do, Jen?" Colin's mother asked, and Jen shook her head.

"No, Mom," she husked out. "Honestly, I'm afraid it isn't. I know what the Church teaches, but . . . I think Dad's already gone. I'd have them turn off the machines."

He saw his mother give her a faint nod. "I didn't think so," she said. "The doctors are saying that even if he does wake up, he won't be the same person. Tom always said that this was what scared him the most, having his body continuing to live when his mind was gone. He always said he'd rather be dead . . ." Her voice shivered and broke on the last word. Aunt Patty hugged her. Across from Colin, Harris nodded vigorously. "If there was any hope at all, I'd say let's give him a chance to recover, but . . ." his mother half-whispered, but again she was unable to finish the thought and her voice trailed off.

The silence that followed seemed to last minutes. Colin could hear the ice cubes chime against the glass Tommy held. Colin took a sip of his own whiskey and a long breath.

"I feel the same way Jen does," Colin spoke into the quiet of the room. "Dad's already gone. When I was in his room, looking at him . . ." He shook his head. "Mom, I'm sorry, but I think the doctors are right; he's brain dead—and that's more a real death than the physical one. We're just keeping Dad's body here artificially. I'm glad I got the chance to say good-bye to him, but—" He brought his shoulders up in a helpless shrug and sipped at the whiskey again, letting it burn the words in his throat.

"Then you're all in agreement." She looked at each of them in turn. Her eyes were dry now. "What the doctors want to do are the tests to declare him officially brain dead, then to . . . to. . . ." She struggled to say the words, closing her eyes and taking a shivering breath before she could speak again. ". . . harvest his body for organs before they remove him from the ventilator. You're all in agreement with that?"

"Yes," Tommy answered. "Because that's what Dad would want us to do. At the very least, he'd want his death to help others."

Colin nodded in agreement, as did Jen. Aunt Patty continued to stroke her sister's arm.

"I don't know if I could make that decision on my own," Colin's mother said. "I *still* don't know; I'm still not certain. I can't decide tonight and I can't decide right here. I'm sorry."

"Don't be sorry, Mom," Jen told her. "It's okay."

"I know. And I know that the way you all feel isn't wrong at all, no matter what Father Frank might suggest. It's just . . . Let me sleep on it, and I'll talk to Father Frank tomorrow after Mass, and then see the doctors again afterward. I can make the decision then."

With the statement, the atmosphere in the room seemed to lighten perceptibly. Colin noticed the evening sunlight slanting in through the window, catching floating dust specks in its brilliance. He took another long sip of the whiskey.

"I'll let the party officials know tomorrow after you make the decision," Harris said. "After all, Tom here has decided that he'll run in his father's place—no matter what the outcome or the choice you make, Mrs. Doyle, it's obvious that Tom Sr. isn't going to be able to continue his campaign. We're obligated to hold another quick primary election to officially replace him on the ballot, but it'll just be a formality."

The sun seemed to slip behind a cloud again. The room darkened. "Carl," Tommy snapped. "Shut the fuck up."

"What?" Harris said, looking startled. He spread his hands, the ice cubes rattling in his whiskey glass. "You know that no serious candidate would run against you. You have the sympathy vote all locked up."

"Carl . . ." Tommy said again, warningly. He set down his whiskey with a crash on the table beside his chair. Golden liquid sloshed over the rim. "This isn't the time or the place. I don't care what you've been hired to do. We're not going to turn Dad's death into a political circus."

He already has, Colin wanted to say. *And now you can't avoid it.* That also explained why Harris seemed to be attached to Tommy's hip: he was the Heir Apparent. Colin wondered how much that tempered any doubt his older brother might have had regarding whether or not to pull the plug on their father.

The lines of his mother's face had hardened a bit. "Tommy," she said, "why didn't I know this?"

"I didn't know myself until yesterday," he said, "when we met with Dad's campaign staff. You know Dad always said I should move into politics earlier than he did. I was going to tell you after you made the decision—" that with a glare at Harris, "—but I thought you'd be pleased that I was following Dad's path."

Her face relaxed slightly. "I don't know. I have to think some more . . ."

"Well, we're not going to decide right now," Jen commented, rising from her chair, "so I'm going to take care of the dishes. Colin, would you mind helping?"

"No, not at all," he said. He finished his whiskey in one swallow, letting the heat settle into his stomach. He rose and followed Jen to the door.

Both of them said very little on the drive back to her apartment until Jen reached I-90/I-94 East off of North Paulina, heading back to her apartment near DePaul. "Y'know," Colin mused as Jen made the turn, "it's strange how one moment I can feel furious with Mom, and the next I'm thinking that I'm just an asshole who should be much nicer to her."

"That's family," Jen said. She flicked on her turn signal as she merged with the traffic, then nudged it back off. "They're the people we love to hate. She can be a total dragon. But her intentions are always good—she only wants what's best for us, and she'll fight like hell against anything she thinks might be a threat to any of us."

"Even if it's not what *we* want." Colin laid his head on the window, staring at the traffic. His glasses clicked against the curve of the window and pressed uncomfortably against his nose; he shifted position.

"I guess it's hard to stop thinking of your children as kids who don't know enough to make a good decision—even after they've grown up."

"I felt like I should have stayed with her tonight. That bit about cleaning my room and all . . ."

"Aunt Patty's staying with her. She's not going to be alone, and the two of you would probably just have ended up getting into an argument."

"I know, but . . ." He took a long breath. "I'm her son, and she made the offer. It was pretty obvious she expected me to stay."

"Uh-huh." Jen said nothing. He glanced over to her; her eyes were focused on the road though there wasn't—at least by Chicago standards—a great deal of traffic. He could see a muscle clench in her jaw. Colin decided to mention at least one of the herd of elephants in the back seat.

"Dad's already gone," he said. "If he's brain dead, then he's dead. Period."

"I know. It still doesn't make the decision any easier, not when I go into his room and see his chest rising and falling and see his pulse on the monitor. Not when I can lay my head on his chest and still hear his heart beating." The muscle along her jawline relaxed, then bunched again.

"Are you thinking maybe we should give him more time, the way Father Frank suggests?"

"No," she said quickly, then shook her head, glaring at the cars ahead of them. "I don't know, Colin. I just don't know. Not really, I guess. I'll stick by what I said after dinner. But it seems like Tommy, or Harris anyway, doesn't want to waste any time. Tommy's already planning to *be* Dad, at least in the electorate's minds. And somehow I don't think you want to wait, either—the sooner this is done, the sooner you . . ." She stopped. "Well, what *is* it that you're going to do? Somehow I don't think it involves going back to Seattle."

Colin didn't answer; he didn't see any need to do so. They both knew the answer. They listened to the sound of the engine as Jen changed lanes. In the back seat, another of the elephants shifted position.

"You've been reading my mind," Colin ventured.

"I always could, even when you were a kid," Jen answered. He saw her gaze flick over once to him, then back to the road. "What are you not telling me?" she asked him. "Because I think there's a lot." *Another elephant. It's amazing that the car's suspension isn't dragging on the pavement.*

He shrugged although she wasn't looking at him. "I don't know. It's just . . ." He let out a breath, then released the words he'd been holding back since he'd come to Chicago. "I've left school, Jen. As of a week ago. I told my committee that I was taking at least a semester off and wouldn't be starting my dissertation. Every time I play music, Jen, I feel like *that's* what I'm supposed to be doing. Not the research, not the dissertation, not the teaching. Playing music. It's what feels right. And lately, it seems like the audience feels it, too."

"And when exactly were you planning to tell anyone this?"

The elephants stirred in the back seat, guiltily. "I was planning to come back here after I got an Irish visa in hand, and tell Dad . . ." The word made him stop, his voice choking. Visions of his father rose up like apparitions around him. " . . . Dad and Mom, and you and Tommy then. Sometime before the end of the semester, when I'd had time to get everything together. Then all this crap happened, and there wasn't a good time or place to say anything at all."

"So it's the Ireland thing again? What you and Dad were fighting about before you went to grad school?"

He let that sit for a bit, watching the lights of the city slide by. Finally, he let out a nasal breath. "Maybe. Jen, over there, where the music I like best came from, well, it's easy to think that there's something more behind or underneath the tunes. At least that's what some of the musicians I knew who are from there tell me. I've wanted to go over for so long. There are old bones in the earth there, a sense of the presence of all that history and all those old gods. There isn't that sharp separation between the natural and the supernatural there; the boundaries sometimes are all blurred. Over here . . . well, it's different."

"You're just romanticizing the place, Colin. That's all."

"Maybe, but then again, I won't know until I actually get there, will I?" he answered, then stopped as she switched lanes again to exit at East Jackson. Jen wiped at her cheek, almost angrily, and he realized that she was crying. He put a hand on her shoulder. She sniffed and tried to smile at him.

"I'm sorry," she said. "You never quite managed to get along with either Mom or Dad. I've had my issues with Mom, too, but I was always close to Dad. I'm going to miss him so much, and the thought that he's going to die, that we're going to *let* him die . . ." She choked back a sob. "I wasn't ready for this. Any of it."

"We never are," he told her, his own eyes tearing up in sympathy. "We think they're going to be there forever . . ."

Things can be forever. 'Tis possible. The voice that spoke was a woman's, a rich alto with a strong, lilting Irish accent, though it seemed that he heard other voices, both male and female, echoing the words—resonating inside his head. *We need you.* The statement sounded so clearly and so strongly that he gasped.

Jen mistook the sound. Her right hand left the steering wheel and found his. "We'll get through this," she told him. "We'll manage it together, little brother. I'm glad you're here. I really am." Her hand left his as she wiped at her eyes again. "Even if you are still a hopeless romantic."

He knew she tried to say it as a joke, but it sounded more like an accusation.

7

'Tis a Pity to See

AS MAEVE WALKED DOWN Market Street in Ballemór toward the grocery on Bridge Street, she halted, causing Keara, Niall, and Aiden to stop as well. "There," she said, pointing just ahead to the intersection, where the gargoyle-laden spire of St. Joseph's Church strained to reach the gray clouds overhead. A gleaming black hearse was just pulling up to the front of the church, followed by a short line of cars, as a small group of mourners waited on the steps. "That's Darcy Fitzgerald's body in the box," she said. The undertakers had opened the rear of the hearse, and six men shuffled forward to lift the coffin onto their shoulders and carry it into the church.

An older woman in mourning tweed stepped from the sedan just behind the hearse. She watched as the coffin was raised, but then her gaze snagged on Maeve, across the street. Her eyes widened, then narrowed; the stare was long and assessing, as if the woman were trying to remember where she'd seen Maeve before. Maeve favored her with a smile.

The old woman crossed herself, then spat on the ground toward the group. With a nearly audible huff, the woman deliberately turned away. She followed the coffin into the church, as the priest and his servers opened the doors for the funeral Mass.

"Well, that was nice," Niall said. "The old hag. Yeh should'nah been so accommodating to her when yeh went to gather the man's soul, Maeve."

"It's not entirely her fault. The leamh have mostly forgotten the old ways," Maeve said. "There's too few left to teach them anymore."

"Aye," Aiden agreed. His arm was around Keara's waist. "They do'nah even stop the clocks, turn the mirrors, or open a window when one of their own passes, or if they do, it's for the show of it. They send the body to the undertaker immediately rather than have it properly washed and prepared and left at home for the wake. They use their damned vehicles to carry the body instead of carrying it themselves."

"Piss on the feckin' leamh," Niall grunted. "Just like they piss on us."

"Niall . . ." Keara began, but Niall scowled at her, slicing through her reply with a hand through the air.

"Nah," he said. "Yeh need nah say a t'ing. The Old Ones were right to abandon this world an' go through to Talamh an Ghlas when they did. I only wish my ancestor woulda had the sense then to follow 'em." Maeve saw his glance go accusingly toward her.

"We'll follow soon enough," she told them. Niall started to protest, but Aiden nudged him in the side with an elbow, shaking his head.

"Let's get what we need done here and get back to the island," Aiden said.

"Agreed," Maeve answered. "I'll leave the three of yeh to get the supplies we need; I'll go talk to the garda about their little letter. Keara, please make sure everyone else stays out of trouble."

Across the street, the mourners had filed in behind the casket and the doors to the church had closed behind them. Faintly, they could hear an organ's asthmatic wheeze and warbling voices plodding through a song. "G'wan," Maeve said. "I'll meet yeh all back at the boat in an hour or two."

The garda station was on Galway Road. Maeve walked across Bridge Street and onto Low Road, then followed the curve until it met Galway Road—the station was down to the right, another ten-minute walk away: an unimposing, brick-faced edifice with an array of silver cars emblazoned with fluorescent blue and yellow parked in front and a placard proclaiming *An Garda Síochána* in front. A pair of uniformed gardai held the door open for Maeve, then walked out toward the cruisers as Maeve went to the sergeant at the front desk. "I'm here to see Superintendent Dunn."

The sergeant glanced up from the papers in front of him. A finger the size of a sausage tapped the paper as if the sheets were likely to escape if ignored. His florid, heavy gaze traveled from her face, down her body, and back again. He smiled with his mouth, but the folds around his eyes were untouched. "Yeh are now, are yeh? Well, who should I tell him has come calling?"

"Maeve Gallagher, from Inishcorr. I've come about the notice that was delivered to us two days ago."

Thick eyebrows raised slightly. He picked up a phone handset from his desk and pressed a button on it while still looking at Maeve. "Superintendent, I have one of the Oileánach here who wants to see yeh. Maeve Gallagher." Maeve could hear the faint scratch of a reply from the phone, and the sergeant nodded. "I'll send her in, then." He replaced the phone on its cradle and pointed to a hallway to his left. "Down there, missus. Third door on yer left."

Maeve nodded to him and followed where he'd pointed. *Superintendent Cedric Dunn* was painted in black letters on the frosted glass of the third door in plain block letters. She knocked on the glass once, and a voice boomed, "Come in" from the room beyond. Maeve twisted the door handle and pushed the door open.

Cedric Dunn had the build of a former athlete who had seen the inside of a gym only infrequently in the last decade. He rose from his chair as Maeve entered the office. His suit had been tailored for a body twenty pounds lighter; his pants fit tightly under a small shelf of stomach. But the torso was still muscular and retained the general v-shape it had evidently once had. He gestured toward a chair in front of his desk, where a laptop sat surrounded by small hillocks of files and paper, then ran the hand through short, graying hair. He didn't smile, but his blue-gray eyes seemed sympathetic enough as he sat down on his own creaking office chair. Some of the anger she'd brought with her dissipated, seeing him. She'd expected someone harder and harsher, a bureaucrat composed of nothing but laws and regulations, and that didn't seem to match Dunn.

"So, Miss Gallagher," he said, and his voice was a warm baritone. "Are you the person designated to speak for the Oileánach?"

"I can speak for the islanders, aye," she told him. "I led them to Inishcorr."

He nodded. He ignored the laptop sitting on his desk, and instead opened a drawer and took out a notebook. He flipped it open, found a pencil amid the clutter on his desk, and scratched a few notes on the paper. Maeve found that she liked that. "Were you aware that you had no right to establish residence there?"

"The island's been abandoned since the '30s, Superintendent."

"That may be, but the NPWS took title to the island in the 1990s."

Maeve shrugged. "'Tis nah a park, and none were living there when we came. We've been there for over five years now, and we've cleaned up all the tumbledown houses there and made it a better place. No NPWS person ever seemed to take an interest or visit the island a'tall until now." She paused and gave him a tight-lipped frown. "Nah until some a'the superstitious and frightened people in Ballemór decided to complain about us."

Dunn's lips twitched in what might have been an attempt at a smile.

"That may be, but it doesn't change the legalities, I'm afraid. The NPWS says they want you off the island; I'm obligated to carry out that request." He put the pencil down on the notebook and leaned forward on his elbows. "Miss Gallagher, I went out there meself to serve that notice, and I'm not unsympathetic to what yeh've said. I saw the village and yer people, and yeh've taken a wrecked and wretched place and made it habitable again. I can appreciate that. But m'hands, as they say, are tied here."

He spread out his hands, palm up, as if to show her.

"I see no ties, Superintendent, only a piece of meaningless paper." She reached into her pocket and put the notice on his desk, unfolding it in front of him. He didn't look at it, but at her as she rose from her chair. "Inishcorr is our home," she told. "It's where we *need* to be. I came to tell yeh that we will nah be leaving."

He blinked once. "They've given yeh thirty days," he told her. "Look, it's not for me to tell yeh this, but yeh can probably stretch that out some if yeh take this to court. Find yerselves a friendly barrister and see what he can do. He could probably buy you another few months. Maybe longer if he's good at it."

Maeve was already shaking her head. "We're not leaving, Superintendent. 'Tis where we need to be, as I told yeh. We care nah for yer laws and regulations and such. We'll be staying, no matter what papers yeh show us."

"Miss Gallagher, I have my duties and responsibilities. If yeh won't leave, I'll be forced . . ."

She held up a hand to stop him. "Yeh can do whatever yeh need do," she told him. She pointed at the notice on his desk. "That may mean something to yeh, but it means nothing a'tall to us, and that's all I wanted to tell yeh. I'm wishing yeh a good day, Superintendent."

With that, Maeve turned and left the office. She heard Dunn give an exasperated huff behind her, but he didn't call out to stop her.

She could feel the eyes of the sergeant at the desk on her back as she left the station.

8

The Banshee's Cry

IN HIS ROOM THAT NIGHT, as he undressed and put his glasses on the bedside table, Colin slid his Gibson from the gig bag. He sat on the edge of the bed, holding the guitar and slipping the pick out from the front pocket of his jeans. The wear-polished neck felt slick and comfortable in his grip, and he touched the strings lightly: an "E" in a high, open position. The B string was a little flat; he turned the tuning peg, strumming the top three strings with the pick until the tuning fell into place. Faintly, through the closed door, he heard Jen talking to Aaron, then the bathroom door closing. He hit the chord again, quietly, thinking that he'd play for a few minutes until Jen or Aaron came out of the bathroom, then he'd go in and use it himself.

He put the pick back in his pocket, and began fingerpicking quietly: "The Lover's Ghost," one of the oldest of the Irish folk tunes he knew. As he played softly with his eyes closed against the fatigue of the day, his fingers seemed to move across the strings of their accord; he heard the tune shifting, changing slightly, the melody becoming more minor and urgent, as if he were calling up some ancient ghost from which the tune he knew had descended.

"Colin?"

He heard his name called faintly: that strange woman's voice again, with its Irish lilt. He stopped playing and opened his eyes. The room was entirely dark, but the bedside lamp had been on only a few moments ago. He wondered if Jen had come in and turned off the lamp, if he'd been sleeping with his guitar in his hands, but that didn't seem possible. "Jen?" he called out.

A laugh answered him. "Nah," came the answer from the darkness, in a familiar accent. "Yeh should keep playing. 'Tis a lovely tune, that."

There was a faint glow near the foot of the bed, almost like a campfire glimpsed through evening fog. He thought of reaching for his glasses, to try to see more clearly, but he found that he didn't want to move. He could smell briny water and the distinct herbal scent of burning peat. A figure moved in front of the fire, a long skirt swaying, the woman's face hidden in shadow and long, dark hair.

"Yer wondering if I'm real," she told him. "I might be, or yeh might be dreaming and imagining it all. 'Tis difficult to tell. Mayhap a bit o' both." She didn't come nearer, nor could he see her clearly. Her figure hovered against the light, enticing, but he couldn't seem to make his legs swing over the edge of the bed to go to her. He clutched the neck of the guitar, harder.

"I'm waiting for yeh, Colin," she said. "I need what yeh have to give. It hurts, the mistakes I've made. Yeh have no idea how much it hurts." The pain in the woman's voice made him ache, but still he couldn't force himself to move. He lay there, stricken. In a rush of peat-laden wind, she was alongside the bed, her features faint and indistinct in the firelight and smoke and the weakness of his eyes, and she smiled wanly at him as she leaned into him fully. He could feel her breasts, her hips against his body. "Come to me," she whispered in his ear, her tongue dancing along his earlobe. "It's time. Come to me."

The weight of her lifted from him and the firelight in the room faded. He reached for her one-handed, to put his arm around her and bring her body back to his, but there was nothing above him and the room had gone dark again.

He blinked, as if to clear his vision. There was light from the street outside leaking through the blinds: a true light, a solid light, and the bedside lamp was on again. Colin started; there was no one else in the bedroom, and in his hand he was still holding the guitar, clutching it so tightly that his fingers ached as he released it. Faintly, he could hear Jen and Aaron conversing in the other room, and he wondered whether they had heard him talking to the apparition. Seeing her, talking to her—it was all fading in his head, like the wisp of a dream collapsing in the morning.

"Goddamn it," he said quietly. Then, even more softly: "Only crazy people are supposed to hear voices."

He put the guitar back over his lap and sounded the first notes of the song again, but this time he played only the tune that he knew. That older tune, that strange forefather of it, seemed to be gone, the changed melody teasing him from memory but too elusive to catch and hold.

"Damn it," he said, and put the guitar down.

It was Aunt Patty who called Jen's apartment early the next morning.

Colin heard Jen's cell phone ring through the closed door of his bedroom; Jen was in the kitchen. He heard Jen's "Hi, Aunt Patty . . ." then several uh-huhs, and finally "Sure, we'll meet you at the hospital then. Give us an hour." He heard Aaron's voice, though he couldn't quite understand what he was saying. "I have to get Colin up," Jen said, and he heard her footsteps approaching down the hallway, followed by a soft knock on the door. "Colin?"

"Come on in. I'm awake."

The knob turned and Jen's head—in soft focus since his glasses were still on the nightstand—peered around the edge. "Aunt Patty just called."

"I heard. What's up?"

"Mom's made the decision; she's told them to do whatever tests are needed so they can take him off the vent. If . . ." She stopped, clamping her jaw shut. "If we want to say good-bye before they take him, we need to be at the hospital in an hour."

"You okay, Jen?"

Her voice shivered and tears threatened her eyes. "As much as I'm going to be."

"Let me get dressed and I'll be out."

"We've already showered. The bathroom's yours if you want it."

"Thanks," he told her.

"I'm going to fix some toast and coffee. It'll be ready when you get out."

"Sounds good."

All the mundane, everyday words dammed the emotional chaos underneath. The door closed.

Fifteen minutes later, showered and shaved, he went into the kitchen, where Jen and Aaron were sitting at the small table, coffee mugs steaming in front of them. He poured himself coffee and sat across from them. A plate of buttered toast sat untouched on the table. Colin wrapped his hands around the mug, just feeling the pleasant warmth but not drinking; his stomach was in an uproar and he was afraid the coffee would only make it worse. Jen looked at him and shook her head mutely. "God, I'm so scared," she said. Aaron silently put his arm around her.

"I know," Colin told her. "I am, too. Our grandparents . . . Mom and Dad only told me about their deaths afterward; I wasn't there to see them on their deathbeds. This . . . this is different, and yeah, scary. I agree. Part of me doesn't want to be there; the rest of me feels like it's my responsibility. This is too sudden. I never had the chance to reconcile with Dad. I really wish I could have talked with him, or at least had a chance to try to explain to him, one more time, who I am and what I'm doing. Now . . . At least we don't have to watch him die. We don't have to see them take him off the vent. I guess that's good."

From the corner of his eye, Colin saw a darkness fluttering at the window of the kitchen. He glanced that way: a crow, its feathers blue-black and glinting iridescently in the sun, had landed there. The creature seemed to be staring in at them, its satiny black bill nearly tapping at the glass.

"Your mom's made the right decision, though," Aaron said as Colin stared at the crow. "Who knows whose life your dad might save with his kidneys, his liver? Or maybe his corneas might give someone back their sight. You have to remember that—his death will potentially help others."

"Colin?" he heard Jen say, then she gasped as she followed his stare and glanced at the window herself. "Shit! What the fuck?"

The crow opened its beak; they all heard a faint *caw* through the glass, then the bird extended its wings and let itself fall away. The bird's shadow slid over the glass and was suddenly gone. "Okay, that was too weird," Jen said. "What the hell was a damn crow doing on my windowsill?"

Aaron shrugged; Colin sat silent. The crow, the raven, figured often in Celtic mythology—he knew that from his studies of the subject in school. *That wasn't a coincidence,* Colin wanted to say. He remembered the dream— or at least what he assumed was a dream—the night before. *The Irish woman . . . She wanted me to come to her . . .*

Jen's gaze was on him. He wondered whether she knew that the crow was also considered to be a harbinger of the *bean shee*, the "banshee" whose cry foretold a death. Colin took off his glasses and rubbed the bridge of his nose—at least he could no longer see Jen's face except as a blur. That helped; he could pretend that he didn't know what she was thinking.

"I guess we should get going," he said. "Knowing Mom, she'll be there early."

He would mostly remember the smells afterward: the scent of his mother's perfume and Aunt Patty's when he hugged them; the antiseptic tang of the hospital air, the freshly-dry-cleaned scent of Tommy's suit. They gathered around his father's bed in the ICU, standing around him. His mother stood on the right side at the head of the bed, brushing his father's short, gray hair with her fingers; Doctor Pearse—a nurse behind her—stood across the bed from his mother. Colin, Jen, Tommy, and Aunt Patty were arrayed around his father, with Aaron standing behind Jen and Harris sitting on one of the chairs against the wall. Father Frank stood next to Harris in his surplice and stole, his Bible open in his hand. Doctor Pearse addressed her words mostly to Colin's mother.

"A colleague and I performed the tests independently last night, and again this morning, and we both agree. All the criteria for declaring brain death are there." The doctor kept talking, going on about apnea tests, cerebral motor responses, corneal and tracheal reflexes, and more. Colin heard the technical details without really listening, the phrases just empty syllables in his ears. Dr. Pearse's professionally sympathetic gaze swept over each of them. "What all that tells us," she said finally, "is that we have a definitive diagnosis of brain death, which means—legally—he's already passed on. With the DNR release you've signed, Mrs. Doyle, we're ready to go ahead and take your husband's body to the transplant surgical team. I just want to make certain that's still what you want."

Colin saw his mother nod faintly. Her hand pressed her husband's once.

"We have Mr. Doyle on a morphine drip," the doctor continued, "as well as lorazepam for sedation. I want you know that he is feeling absolutely no pain or discomfort. For the viability of his organs, though, we need to keep him on the ventilator until we've harvested all the viable organs."

"You're sure there's no possibility you're wrong?" Colin asked. "I mean, you hear of someone suddenly coming out of a coma after months or years . . ."

Dr. Pearse was shaking her head before he'd finished. "Your father's not in a coma." She wasn't harsh, only factual. Colin wondered how many times she'd said something similar to other families. "I know that you're looking at him and he seems to be alive. You see his chest rising and falling and can see his heartbeat on the monitor. But on an EEG, looking for brain activity—and we did that last night and this morning as well—you'd see no electrical activity at all. That isn't the case for coma patients, and a coma patient would have had responses to the other tests we've done." She took a long breath, and her voice changed, a warmth and sympathy entering her tone and attitude. "I'm truly sorry and I know how hard this is for all of you. But I can tell you that there isn't any clinical evidence of recovery from a patient who has met all the criteria for brain death. None. I promise you that if I had *any* uncertainty, any at all, I would tell you to wait and let nature take its course. But with your father's situation . . . If I were to take him off the ventilator, he would stop breathing, and he'd die within a very few minutes. This way, with the transplant team, some good will come from his death. I hope that can be of comfort to you."

Colin watched his father's chest, which lifted once, then slowly fell. The ventilator hissed in time to the breath. The tableau would be fixed in Colin's mind: all of them leaning forward over the bed; his mother whispering to his father as Tommy put his arm around her. "Tom, you just rest now. I'll miss you, darling. I love you. I love you so much . . ." Her voice broke and she began to cry, an aching, terrible sound that, contagious, rippled around the room. Colin's eyes filled with tears, blurring the scene, and his breath shuddered. He felt someone's hand on his back and didn't know who it was and didn't care. The comfort was all he craved.

"I'll wait outside while you say your good-byes," Dr. Pearse said. "Call me when you're ready for us to take him."

She left the room, closing the door behind her. Father Frank rose from his chair and went to the head of the bed to intone the Last Rites. Colin's mother gave a sharp, birdlike cry of pain as she listened. She bent over the body, kissing her husband softly as Tommy held her. Colin heard Jen crying hard, and he started to go to her, but she had already turned into Aaron's embrace. For a moment, Colin felt adrift, alone in the midst of a terrible pit of black grief, but then Aunt Patty found him; he let her hug him, comforting him as she might have when he was a child. He let himself cry then, fully, pulling away from her several gulping breaths later, wiping at his eyes. He looked at his father lying warm and breathing and empty on the bed; at his mother sitting now in a chair someone had brought her next to the bed, still clutching his father's hand.

"Go on," she said to the room. "All of you should tell him good-bye."

One by one, they made their way to the head of the bed to whisper their last words to him. Colin hung back, watching as Harris came forward to pat his father's hand. "You'd have won, Tom," he said. "Now it'll be Tommy. I'll make sure of that."

Colin went up last. He touched his father's hand, still impossibly warm. His eyes filled with tears again, blurring his vision. The ventilator chuffed; his father's chest rose. "Sorry, Dad," he said, knowing the others were listening to him. "I'm so sorry . . ." His voice choked and he stepped back. "Sorry," he repeated. Aunt Patty put her arm around his waist and he leaned into her as he glanced at his mother, who was crying also. She nodded to him.

For an instant, as if he'd been somehow transported outside of himself, Colin caught a glimpse of himself on some shore, looking out over the cold, gray waves of the Atlantic: gazing eastward and south, toward what he knew was a distant America. *The sea contains the world's tears*, he thought he heard someone say: again, the woman he'd heard before. *The Old Ones say the sea holds all the sorrow there ever was, and all that is to come.* Someone's arms curled around him from behind; he felt her body press against his back. *Come to me. Let me share your grief. Sing your song for us.*

Then she was gone, in a whiff of salt air, and he was back in the hospital room.

"It's time," he heard his mother say. "Tommy, tell the doctor she can come in now."

9

My Sorrow and My Loss

MAEVE LEANED BACK and heaved a long sigh. She could feel Keara watching her from across the table, through the fume of the brazier. The faint images of the bard and his surroundings had vanished from the smoke, though the feel of him lingered along her body. She had enjoyed that sensation; it reminded her of another time.

"M'Lady?" Keara asked.

"'Tis done," Maeve answered, and smiled at the young woman. "Or at least things are put in motion. I couldn't have done this without yeh, Keara. I want yeh to know that."

Keara favored her with a small, almost shy smile. "T'anks, m'Lady. 'Tis m'pleasure." Then her expression settled. "He *will* be arriving, then?"

For a moment, Maeve considered telling her the truth: that she couldn't know that; that all she could do was push and nudge at the bard from a distance; that if he ignored her voice and the signals she sent him, if despite all that he was going to hear soon he decided to ignore her, there was nothing she could do to compel him to come.

That she was bound to this land more than any one of them and couldn't go to him even if she wished to do that.

"Aye," she told Keara, because there was no other answer that any on the island cared to hear, because it was the only message she could send to them or they'd begin to drift away or give up, and any chance for them— and for her—would be lost. "He will come. Soon."

"Good," Keara agreed. "Aiden and the rest will be glad to know that." She began gathering up the herbs and powders into the leather bag she carried, then stopped and swept back her long hair over a shoulder. "Will yeh need me any more today?"

"No," Maeve told her. "Tomorrow, though, I need yer help again with the spell, just so we can put an end to any questions. Come in the morning, and if yeh have some of your scones ready, that would be grand as well. I'll have tea waiting."

Keara grinned. "I will at that, m'Lady. I'll see you then. Sleep well, tonight, and don't forget the stew I brought for yeh. Aiden said it was tasty enough, and yeh need to keep up yer strength." With that, she swept the last of the herbs into her shoulder bag, gave Maeve a brief curtsy, then went out into the night. Maeve could smell the briny wind from the open door and glimpse a starry, clear sky against which Keara was briefly silhouetted, then the odor and the night sky vanished with the closing of the door.

Maeve sat at the table for a long time before finally throwing a few more turves on the hearth. She glanced at the covered bowl of stew on the stones of the fireplace as she sat in the wooden chair facing the flames. She leaned over to lift the cloth napkin and stared at the chunks of lamb, potatoes, and carrots swimming in a thick broth, the savory steam wafting up enough to make her salivate. But she covered the bowl again, watching the flames beginning to lick at the new bricks of peat.

The fire reminded her of another time, another place, another body.

"I love you," he said to her, and the words fell through her like mirror shards, reflecting back to her how much she'd changed. She said the same words back to him—"And I love you"—knowing that in the past the words would have been simply empty vessels, and that she could have put that person to the sword the next day without any regrets at all.

But slow time as well as the slow change of the culture around them had changed her, at least somewhat, though some of the Old Ones seemed entirely untouched. She was no longer the being that she had been, and there was something in her that echoed the leamh, the mortals, around her. There were times when she nearly envied them, because sometimes now her life seemed far too long and far too lonely.

She looked at this leamh, who had just professed his love for her, and she felt that mortal part of her warm to those words. Could she actually feel love for one of them? Could she one day say those words in return and fully mean them, if not for this one, then another in some future time?

"I did love you as much as I could," she whispered now: to the fire, to the night, to the memory. "I did. And maybe . . ."

She remembered the face she'd seen in the smoke, and the momentary feel of his body against hers.

"Maybe . . ." she whispered again, then shook her head. "No, I can't," she scolded herself. Her voice sounded loud against the silence in the cottage. "You know what your duty is, and to do it, you can't let yourself feel that. You can't."

She clenched her fingers in her lap. She inhaled the scent of the peat, and remembered a cave near Rathcroghan, and the man she knew there.

10

At Midnight Hour

THE NEXT FEW DAYS were a whirlwind for Colin: a visitation at the funeral home where he shook hands and exchanged empty condolences with what seemed to be a few thousand relatives, friends of the family, colleagues, and political cronies: a passing collage of faces and names that he forgot as soon as he heard them. Colin wore one of Tommy's suits, borrowed for the occasion, the tie a social noose around his neck. Of that long day, he remembered mostly the overpowering floral scent of the room, and his father's visage in the burnished metal casket, looking more like an eerie sculpture than a once-living man.

The funeral followed the next morning, attended mostly by family with a few friends and relatives. The day didn't match anyone's mood: sunny and too hot. Colin sweated under the suit coat as Father Frank performed the ceremony at the graveside. Colin stared at the now-closed coffin, sitting on straps over the cloth-covered hole. His mother cried during much of the ceremony, with Tommy and Jen on either side of her. Colin sat next to Jen, with Aunt Patty alongside him holding his hand.

There were crows in the trees near the plot. Colin could hear them calling to each other and see them moving in the branches as Father Frank gave his final blessing and sprinkled holy water over the coffin. He scowled past the priest toward the birds. "This concludes the graveside ceremony," the funeral director said. "If everyone would return to their cars, please . . ."

There would be another gathering at the Doyle house, Colin knew—an interminable afternoon with sandwiches and drinks, with everyone paying too much attention to his mother and to Tommy as the Heir Apparent, while Jen and he hovered in the background. There'd be videos and pictures of his father on the flatscreen TV in the back room; his ghost would

haunt the proceedings. Aunt Patty would probably ask him to play something—and some idiot in the group would call out for "Danny Boy"—or,
as most of the Irish musicians Colin knew called it, "that feckin' song."

Colin already anticipated drinking too much.

Everyone was gathering up the bouquets brought to the graveside to
take them back to the cars. He went to help, but Tommy grabbed his arm.
"Hey, little brother, you got a sec?" Tommy led Colin away from the crowd,
into the shade of the tree where he'd seen the crows.

"Are you thinking of heading back to Seattle soon?" Tommy asked him.
"I know you have that dissertation to write . . ."

Colin lifted his hand, stopping Tommy in mid-sentence. "Jen hasn't
said anything to you?"

Tommy looked puzzled, shaking his head. "No. Why?"

Colin took a breath, then launched into what he'd told Jen: leaving
school, how he wanted to return to his musical career, how he planned to
go to Ireland. Talking to Tommy, who looked so much like their father,
was like talking to a younger version of his father, one who, to his credit,
listened patiently rather than angrily.

"Okay," Tommy said when Colin finished. "That's absolutely not what I
expected to hear. You really want to go to Ireland?"

"Yeah. As soon as I can. I need to get a visa first, so I can stay there for
a few years. But as soon as that happens . . ."

Tommy nodded. "I won't try to talk you out of it, Colin. I know you
and Dad . . . well, I know what Dad thought, but I also know that sometimes you have to follow your own heart, no matter what others think. I
want to make you an offer, though. An alternative, if you like."

That sounded more like their father. Colin frowned. "Yeah, what's that?"

"Stay here in Chicago—for the rest of the year, anyway. Help me. Be
part of my campaign staff. I'm going to need all the support I can get."

Colin was shaking his head as soon as he heard "campaign staff."

"What are you talking about? You don't need my help, and that's not the
kind of job that I'm suited for anyway. Besides, Harris says you're a shoo-
in."

Tommy shook his head. "That's what Carl wants everyone to believe,
and it's what he wants to believe himself. But even he's worried about a
candidate who's single and in his mid-30s."

"Okay, so you're not married. So what?"

"Things have changed a lot over the years, and are continuing to change,
but how many politicians do you know who are openly gay?"

Colin blinked, processing what Tommy had just said. "Gay? You
mean. . . ?"

Tommy nodded. "Yeah. That's what I mean. I guess we both had things we weren't saying to each other. Come on, Colin; you mean you never suspected that? Haven't you ever wondered why I was never dating anyone, why I never brought anyone home for Sunday dinners?"

"In high school and college, you did. I distinctly remember a couple girls."

"Yeah. I did back then. First because I was in denial, then because I was using a few friends as beards so no one else, especially Mom and Dad, would suspect. But since then . . . well, if I haven't been open about it, I also haven't exactly been keeping it a secret."

"Wow." Colin didn't know what to say. All the air had gone from his lungs. As Tommy watched him, he took a breath, starting to speak, then shaking his head. "Mom and Dad? Jen? Do they . . ."

Tommy shrugged. "With Mom and Dad, it's always been 'don't ask, don't tell.' They both stopped interrogating me about whether I was seeing anyone four or five years ago—that way they didn't have to be confronted with the truth, and I didn't have to lie. I think we were all happier that way. Jen knows; I think she suspected it even before I did, or before I was willing to admit it. Aunt Patty and Rebecca, too, of course—I told them a while ago. I'd've told you, but you had your own issues with Mom and Dad and were heading off to Seattle, and afterward it didn't seem like something to say in a phone call. And since you've come back . . ." He shrugged. "There really hasn't been a good moment for the two of us to sit down and really talk. I know this isn't one, either, telling you while we're burying Dad, but I was afraid that you might sneak back to the left coast if I waited any longer, and I really wanted . . ." Tommy stopped. "I really *needed* you to know," he finished.

Colin ignored that. "What about Harris?"

Tommy seemed to smile. "Oh, *he* knows better than anyone," he said, and something in his tone and the glance he cast back toward where Harris was leaning against Tommy's car made Colin suddenly suspicious.

"No."

"Yep. 'Fraid so."

"Harris is your . . . partner?"

"How do you think he got himself introduced to Dad?"

"Really? Harris?"

"Carl's a lot nicer when he doesn't have his campaign manager hat on. Honestly."

"I guess I'll have to take your word for that. I haven't been very pleasant with him, though. I'm sorry."

"He's used to it—that's part of the job. He doesn't take it personally. Look,

I haven't come out publicly, but Carl says that the subject *will* come up once we're in the general election, so I need to do it soon before someone springs it as a surprise in the middle of the election. And honestly, I don't intend to lie if someone asks me the question directly . . ." His shoulder lifted again. "It's anyone's guess how things will go when the news gets out. When that happens, I'll need people around me I can trust, people I care about. That's why I'm asking. So . . . have I weirded you out sufficiently?"

Colin managed a wry grin. "You've managed to shock me a bit, yeah. It'll take me a while to wrap my head around this, but in the end, it doesn't change anything. You're still Tommy, you're still my brother, and I don't have a problem with anyone's sexual orientation. Don't worry."

"Thanks. You don't know how much that means, little brother." The two of them hugged, Tommy taking a long, slow inhalation that told Colin how unsure his brother had actually been. When they broke apart, Tommy looked back at the gravesite, where the workers were already preparing to fill in the grave. "I wish I'd told Dad the truth, even though I'm sure he'd already figured it out."

Colin was also staring toward the casket. "Yeah. There's a lot I wish I had talked to him about, too. I hadn't left things in a very good place with him, and now . . ." The emotions threatened to overwhelm Colin again, and he let the rest trail away unsaid, not able to trust his voice.

"Yeah, I know." Tommy's voice was rough and husky, and his hand touched Colin's shoulder and fell away again. "I know. I also know that he loved you and he was hoping to patch things up between the two of you when you came back next."

"Why are you going to run for office, Tommy? Yeah, it's Dad's legacy and all that, but this is going to put a huge spotlight on your life, with all that entails, and there are people who are going to be upset and angry and furious with you. You could let someone else step in and save yourself all the grief. You could just keep your position at Dad's firm and not have to deal with any potential nastiness."

"I know. But . . . this just *feels* right, like something I'm supposed to do. You understand that, don't you? It's like you with your music. Jen's the same way; teaching is exactly what she wants to do and what she enjoys doing. Dad . . . he wasn't any different, really. We Doyles have this sense of destiny, or a calling, of something that we're *supposed* to do, and we're most unhappy when we're not allowed to pursue it. That's when we get into trouble. Know what I mean?"

For a moment, the scene around them shivered, and Colin thought he could smell the sea and burning peat. Then it was gone. "Yeah. I know the feeling."

"So . . . you'll stay? Or go to Seattle and take care of whatever you need to take care of there, then come back here. I really could use you. I'd be able to pay you a consultant's salary—a good one—and if I'm elected, well, I could use someone I know I can trust on my staff, if that interests you."

Above them, in the branches, a crow stirred, cawed, and flew away.

"I don't know. I'll think about it," he told Tommy. "That's all I can say right now." He clapped his brother on the back. "Thanks for trusting me, Tommy. That means a lot . . . even if I have to apologize to Har . . . I mean, Carl."

Tommy laughed. "Well, c'mon and get it over with, then."

The reception at the house was worse than Colin had imagined it would be.

The house had been filled with bouquets from the funeral home, their sickly sweetness competing with the smell of coffee and the various hors d'oeuvres Beth had prepared. The struggle between the clashing odors threaded through the haze of a dozen conversations and dutiful, apocryphal remembrances of Colin's father. Colin wandered the house, smiling and shaking hands, and enduring the pats on the back and the hugs from people he barely knew, the mindless niceties and clichéd condolences. He fled to his old room on the second floor after an hour or so, sitting on the bed his mother had prepared for him and staring at the walls—freshly-painted, with all his old posters and paintings carefully removed. It was a stranger's room. The only thing of his in it was a large plastic model of the *Millennium Falcon* he'd put together when he was twelve or thirteen, carefully dusted and sitting on an otherwise unadorned dresser top.

He sat there in the dimness, listening to the chatter from downstairs echoing up the staircase. His guitar was there, leaning against a wall—his mother had insisted that he bring it along. He unzipped the gig bag and held it, closing his eyes and strumming a few aimless chords.

"A wee bit overwhelming, is it?" It nearly sounded like the dream-woman's voice, in her lilting Irish accent, but then he realized with a start that the voice had come from the doorway of his room. He opened his eyes to see Aunt Patty standing there. In one hand, she was holding a small, leather-bound book, like the moleskin notebooks he'd seen in stationery stores and bookstores, except that this one appeared to be old and battered; her other hand was closed around something, though all he saw was the long loop of a silver chain hanging from between her fingers.

"Yeah," he told her, putting the guitar aside. "A wee bit. I thought I'd escape up here for a few minutes."

"Your room looks nice."

"It looks like Mom's vision of what she wanted my room to look like back when I was a teenager. Which it never, of course, actually looked like."

She gave him an understanding nod, then came into the room and sat on the bed alongside him. "I brought a couple things for you," she said. "First, hold out your hand . . ."

Colin did so, and Aunt Patty turned her closed one over his, opening her fingers. Something fairly heavy dropped into his palm; in his hand was a green, crystalline stone about the size of his top thumb joint. The stone hadn't been cut into facets, but was polished and transparent enough that one could see into its crannied depths. It was set in filigreed silver, with the fine chain put through a loop at the top. The gem seemed to hold aquamarine ribbons of color within it, and the stone was warm in his hand—most likely from Patty's hand, he thought. "What's this?" he asked.

"Your grandfather—Daiddeó Rory—brought that stone from Ireland when he came. He always had a habit, whenever he went somewhere new and memorable, or if something unusual happened, to pick up a rock and bring it back with him. He always said it helped him remember where he was and what he was thinking then." Aunt Patty laughed. "I picked up the same habit. Whenever I'm traveling somewhere, I'll find a rock—any old rock, actually, though I do try to find an interesting one—and bring it back with me."

"That explains all the rocks I remember on your bookshelves. So Daiddeó Rory brought this one to the States when he came here?"

Aunt Patty nodded, then sat on the bed alongside him. Her fingers caressed the stone in Colin's hand. "Strange," she said. "I only found that pendant a few days ago, but I've never had it out of my hand or off my neck since then. It was like I was supposed to have it."

"Then keep it," Colin said. He held it out to her. "I don't need it."

Aunt Patty shook her head. Reaching out, she closed her fingers around the pendant. "This is going to sound strange, but as soon as I walked in here and saw you, I *knew* you were supposed to have it. Not me."

"And how did you know that?"

Aunt Patty shrugged. She didn't answer directly. "I also brought this for you," she said, handing him the notebook. He took it from her, turning it over in his hands. The cover was well worn, the leather nearly worn away and frayed at the edges, and the paper had the yellow of age and the griminess of much handling. Colin opened it and glanced at the first page where, in faded sepia ink and an ornate handwritten cursive, he saw a title and subtitle. *The Light of Other Days: The Story of My Wanderings.* "That's your Daiddeó Rory's journal," Aunt Patty told. "He started it back when he was growing up in Ireland; it ends a year after he came to the States, when he met your Maimeó Bridgett. I only found it a few days ago, shoved in back of some other books on the bookshelves. Strange, all the years it had been sitting there. I must have missed it a dozen times in the past. The chain of the pendant was wrapped around the book." Aunt Patty had inherited the O'Callaghan house after Colin's grandparents died, and she and Rebecca lived there. The house was still much the same as Colin remembered it from his childhood, with large rooms and many bookcases stuffed with books. He could well imagine that a notebook like the one he now held could have been lost among the other volumes.

"I thought I'd pass it on to you to read," Aunt Patty continued. "You're the most like Daiddeó Rory of all of us. I think you'll find it interesting. All of it's interesting, but I think I'd start reading it around the September 4th of 1947 entry first, if I were you. It explains, or at least I think it does, that emerald or whatever it is I just gave you. I think you're supposed to have both of these—when I read the journal, I kept hearing your voice in my head. Somehow I think Daiddeó Rory intended you to be the one to read this."

"Thanks, Aunt Patty," he told her. He put the stone in the pocket of his suit coat and patted the cover of the notebook. "I'll take a look at it."

Another nod. Aunt Patty put her hand on his, on top of the journal. "I saw you and Tommy talking. I assume he's told you about . . ." Her voice trailed off.

"Yep. He did."

Her fingers pressed his. "And did he ask you to stay, to work on his campaign?"

"That, too."

"He meant that. He could use the help, and he could use the support. Did you give him an answer?"

"Said I'd think about it."

"Ah." The exhalation held sentences. There was almost a satisfaction in it.

"I was serious about that," he said, almost defensively. "I'm considering it. Maybe it's time I did something for the family."

"There's family you're born with, and there's family that you choose and make yourself."

"What are you saying, Aunt Patty?"

She squeezed his fingers again. "I'm saying that it's good you're thinking about things, that's all."

"Jen been talking?" he asked.

"No. I can tell just by looking at you. You're a lot like my dad—he was one of those restless souls, too. And he kept secrets just like you." She glanced at the guitar on the bed. "That's what you always wanted to do, more than anything else."

"So what do you think I should do now?"

She shrugged. "I think it's up to you, honey," she said. "One thing I can remember your Daiddeó Rory telling me when I was about your age is to never let anyone else make decisions for you, because you'd never be happy with them. I take it you've discovered that for yourself."

Colin chuckled at that. "Yeah, I kinda have. And Grandpa always had a saying for every occasion."

"That he did. He'd tell you to always listen to your heart: 'That may not make you rich, but it'll make you happy,' he used to say. I always thought it a silly saying, except for the times I didn't follow the advice. And I think, with you, that your heart will speak loudly enough that you'll be able to hear it plainly."

Colin looked at the stained leather cover of the journal on his lap. "Following your heart . . . I always wondered why Daiddeó Rory never went back to Ireland to visit, since he always talked so much about it."

"He always told me he'd found enough Ireland here to keep him content, and that there was too much of the rest of the world to explore," Patty told him. "But then I found the journal, and now I wonder myself."

Colin cocked his head toward his aunt, waiting, but she only smiled at him as she released his hand and stood. "Read the journal when you get a chance and you'll see what I mean. In the meantime, I'm going downstairs to brave the crowd and see how your mom, Jen, and Tommy are holding up. You coming?"

"I'll be down in a minute."

"Take your time. But not too long. Your mother was looking around for you. She wanted you to sing something, I think." She smiled. " 'Danny Boy,' probably."

He sighed. "I'll be down." Aunt Patty nodded again and left him. He heard her padding down the stairs toward the roar of the wake. He picked up the guitar by the neck and swung it around in front of him again. He put his fingers in position, but played nothing. After a few moments, he gave up. He picked up his grandfather's notebook, jammed it into the pocket of his suit coat with the green jewel, put the Gibson back in the gig bag, and followed Aunt Patty downstairs.

"You sounded good, Colin," Aaron said as he drove back to Jen's after the reception. He glanced into the rearview mirror toward Colin, in the back seat of the car with his guitar. "Jen told me you had a decent voice, but I had no idea just how good it was. You had everyone's attention, and for good reason."

"Actually," Jen interjected as Aaron made the turn onto I-90, "I think you've improved a lot since I last heard you. Everyone shut up when you started to sing, even in the other rooms. That's quite a gift."

"I'm loud," Colin answered. "Lots of playing in noisy clubs, and you learn how to sing over conversations."

Jen gave a snort of amusement, but shook her head. "It was more than that, little brother. Like Aaron just said, you're good."

"Even if one of the songs was 'Danny Boy,'" Aaron added, grinning back toward Colin in the mirror. "I suspect that for you that's like playing 'Hava Nagila' at Jewish functions—it's expected, even required, but the musicians hate it."

Colin nodded. "Pretty much. The words were written by an Englishman, anyway, even if the tune's Irish. But Dad liked it." He would have said more, but with the words, the feeling of loss rose up again and choked him. He leaned back against the seat, and his hand brushed against the journal in his suit jacket's pocket. He reached his hand in, closing his fingers around the pendant as Aaron slid into the late traffic.

It was just after midnight. Colin had expected his mother to ask him to stay with her at the house and he'd already decided that he had no option but to stay: leaving his mother alone in the house for the first time wasn't something he wanted on his conscience. Aunt Patty—perhaps sensing that conflict—had spoken up as people were starting to leave, saying she was tired and a little hung over, and was going to stay there in Colin's old room, and that Colin should go home with Jen again. Colin had shot her a grateful look; she had smiled back at him.

Now he sat back and listened to Jen and Aaron talk softly to each other. He enjoyed watching them, looking like an old established couple that already had their own shorthand. Aaron's hand was on Jen's neck; he saw her lean her head down to her shoulder to capture his fingers. "Thanks for being with me tonight," he heard Jen say. "I really needed you there."

"Where else would I be?" Aaron answered.

"I'm going to miss him so much . . ." Her voice trailed off in a sob she quickly cut off, and Aaron pulled her to him, his arm around her shoulder.

They were mostly silent after that, each caught up in their own thoughts and grief.

It wasn't until they were back at Jen's, that Colin had a chance to open the notebook again. He flipped through the pages until he found the September 4th entry, and started to read what his grandfather had written.

He got very little sleep that night.

11

The Light of Other Days

*E*XCERPTS FROM *the Journal of Rory O'Callaghan*

September 4, 1947:

I met the strangest, yet most interesting woman today.

I've decided to stay a few days in Roscommon before moving on. Today I was out roaming, just wandering the paths around the tumbledown ruins of the medieval Roscommon Castle just outside the township. I thought I was alone, for I saw no one else about as I approached the ruins. Today was a gorgeous one, with a sky the color of a deep lake overhead, and clouds like fine lace floating through it. I'll admit I was staring upward past the ruins to the clouds, imagining that they were ships and aerial ramparts, and I nearly bumped into a fine bit of stuff who was sitting on a hillock near the lake, overlooking the south turret of the old castle. She laughed at my gawking and my awkwardness, and I, shamefaced, spread my hands in apology.

She was no one I knew from the town, though I certainly haven't been so long in Roscommon to have seen enough of the townsfolk to really be certain. I did notice immediately that she had the most lovely eyes: grass-green pupils flecked with darker emerald, set under strands of long midnight hair. I judged her age to be close to mine, and the smile she gave me could make the very sun jealous.

I'll admit that I found myself wanting to know her better, as if her presence somehow filled an emptiness I didn't even know I had inside me. Sure, I'd had girlfriends aplenty before I'd started wandering, but none of them had struck me like this—as if I were supposed to have met her, as if

I'd somehow already known her, though writing these words now, that already sounds like overblown, poetic blathering. But it's true, nonetheless. It's nothing I would have said to her, but I can say it here, where no one else but me will ever read it.

"'Tis a lovely day," she said to me, still laughing, "one where watching the clouds is certainly better than watching the feet, but more dangerous, 'twould seem." That started our conversation. She gestured to the ground next to her and I sat, and we must have conversed for an hour or more. I learned that her name was Máire, and that she was here with several of her family, who'd come to County Roscommon from the east up near Tara, she told me, and with each minute I felt that odd connection growing inside me.

I could hardly bear it when she said that she must leave.

I offered to walk Máire back into town, but she said her people weren't staying there. I offered to escort her to wherever it was she was staying, but she refused me, though with laughter and more smiles. "If yeh happen to come here tomorrow at noon," she told me, "then yeh might find me again, if yeh want." And with that invitation, she left me, walking away through the grass to the north, away from the town. I watched her go until she passed through a hedge and was gone from sight.

For the rest of the day, I've been able to think of little but that promised tomorrow. For now, my intention to leave Roscommon and continue on my walk to the west is forgotten. I think I'll see what else the lass might have to say to me.

September 5, 1947:

Máire was waiting for me at the castle ruins today at noon, as she'd promised. I'd brought along a picnic lunch from the grocers in the square, hoping that I'd find her, and we spread out the cheeses, bread, cut meats, and beer on a small blanket. A brace of ducks flew noisily overhead to land on the lake, and Máire laughed, mockingly covering her head as they passed us, so close we could have nearly touched them. The day was another like the one before, the world displaying an exceptional warmth and beauty. Everything was emerald and jade around us: the grass on which we sat, the mossy blanket on the stones of the old castle, the hedges lining the path, the trees just beyond.

We talked of everything and nothing. Máire wanted to know why I was here in Roscommon, and I told her how my feet had become impatient with being in one place, and how on my sixteenth birthday, I'd left Wicklow where I'd been born and raised, left my parents and my siblings and started my long trek, first south into Cork, Kerry, Limerick, and Clare to see the sights there, then following the River Shannon north until I reached the very heart of our country in Roscommon. I even showed her this journal, where I've been writing down my little adventures, though I wouldn't let her read it.

I told her that I intend to continue walking north into Donegal, then wander down through Sligo and Mayo until I reach Galway, and from there, having put as much of Éire as I could hold into my heart and memories, I plan to take ship to America to see what might await me there.

I asked Máire about her own past, but she was strangely coy and shy about that. Instead, we talked mostly about Éire and the old ways and how things had changed slowly over the centuries. It was then that I felt a deeper sadness inside Máire, and she seemed far older than she was. "So many have left the country," she said. "The west, especially, is desolate, with empty villages everywhere, the houses all roofless and ruined, just like the old beliefs that the people there once held. And now yeh talk of leaving, just like the rest of 'em. 'Tis sad that makes me."

I asked her if she ever thought of leaving Ireland herself and she shook her head, her hair swirling around her like a storm cloud. "I will stay here forever in Éire," she answered me, "and one day I'll fall asleep and never wake up."

"Like the fairy folk under their mounds," I ventured, and she smiled.

"Aye, very like them," she responded.

We spent the afternoon like that until she said that she had to go. I once more offered to escort her back to her family, but again she refused. But when we packed up our lunch and were ready to part, she pressed herself against me and kissed me so deeply that I could hardly breathe for the sweetness of her lips. That, let me say here, was grand. "So tell me, Rory O'Callaghan," she asked when the kiss ended, still smiling. "In all yer travels, how many young lasses have done the same for yeh, or perhaps even have lain with yeh among the soft grass and flowers?"

I could feel meself blush at that. "There were a few," I admitted—which was the case, as I've noted before in this journal. There were some who found romantic my story of traveling, and I'll confess that I didn't stop their advances, even if I also continued on without the lass the next day. I was thinking that perhaps this time it might be different. "But the vision of any of 'em is gone from me now. Yeh stole it from me entire, and now I can't even recall what they looked like."

She gave me that laugh of silver and gold again. "Ah, and yeh've the gift of the devil's tongue, too, Rory O'Callaghan. I want to know—when will yeh be leaving here?"

"I've no plans a'tall," I told her, which was only the truth, especially now.

"Yeh said yeh wanted to go north," she said. "Yeh've heard of Rathcroghan, near the village of Tulsk?" I nodded that I did. "In three days, yeh'll find me there close to the mound. Will yeh be there?"

I nodded again, and she gave me another kiss. "Then I'll be waiting for yeh there, me Rory, and there I might lay with yeh like those other lasses," she said.

I think it's to Rathcroghan, then, that I'll be going next.

September 8, 1947:

Rathcroghan looms large in Irish history, despite being rather neglected out in County Roscommon as it is, and hardly as well-known or well-visited as Tara or Newgrange in the east. Rathcroghan is said to be where the king and queen of the Connachta, Ailill and Medb from the Ulster Cycle, ruled—at least that's what the locals all say. If so, the splendor of their ancient home has been much diminished by the centuries.

Even before I'd met Máire, I'd thought of passing by Rathcroghan just to see it. Truthfully, this morning I was regretting that impulse and the promise I'd made Máire.

When I first saw it, the great mound of Rathcroghan was standing forlorn in a gray rain under a low gray sky. It was hardly impressive, a dull green bulge in the midst of an equally dull pasture bordered by the ubiquitous stone fences. Whatever glorious structures had once stood there back in ancient times, they've all vanished now, erased by time and the relentless Irish rain until only the elevation itself was left.

I swear that the rain was trying to erase me as well. All the morning, I'd biked along the road in foul dirty weather that managed to trickle through every crevice and cranny in the oilcloth I wore, and there'd even once been a flash of distant lightning accompanied by a grumble of thunder—a true rarity in Ireland, I must say. My pants were soaked from the knees down, the socks in my boots were sodden, and my woolen cap was as wet as the hair underneath it. I was beginning to despair at ever having agreed to this meeting as I leaned my bike against the fence and began walking through the muck toward the mound, my head down against the wind-blown pellets of water that were as hard as handfuls of thrown pebbles. I was sneezing already, the cold settling into my chest.

No lass could possibly be worth this, I'll admit I muttered to myself. I was thinking I should have found a lodging in town, spent the night, and been on my way in the morning, traveling still farther north. I should have left her like I left all the others.

I was certain that Máire wouldn't be here, not in this damnable weather. For all I knew, she'd sent me on a fool's chase and was chuckling at the thought of me looking for her out in this bucketing.

I vowed that I'd go to the mound so that I could say I fulfilled my promise, and that unless Máire appeared there within a few minutes, I'd return to the bike and find myself a place for the night, preferably with a pub close by where a few drams of whiskey would burn away the chill.

I trudged over the field, where sheep regarded me as if I were some mad creature which, no doubt, I certainly appeared to be. They lurched away startled and glared at me with reproachful eyes as I came near. My feet seemed to weigh several stone more by the time I reached the foot of the mound, my boots caked with grassy mud, though at least I couldn't get significantly wetter than I was already. I stopped there, sniffing, and wondering if I should climb the grassy slope so I could survey the area for Máire (undoubtedly involving slipping and having to go to hands and knees to finish the climb), when I saw movement to my left. She was there, her feet somehow unencumbered by the clumps of mud I'd dredged from the field, and her cloak and clothing mostly dry under a large umbrella. "And how are yeh this fine day, Rory O'Callaghan?" she called out to me.

"Oh, I'm just grand," I told her. I lifted my foot to show her the new, thick sole of mud I'd acquired. "I suppose it could be worse. The roads could have been flooded entirely, or I could have been struck down by the lightning I saw."

"Aye," she laughed. "It could be worse. Yeh kept yer promise, though, and that pleases me wonderfully."

"I'm glad to hear it. I'd hate to have traveled all this way for nothing. 'Tis lashing out here."

"'Tis indeed," she agreed. "Come with me, then. I've found us a place out of the weather." With that, she turned and starting walking, leading me southwest away from the mound, and going slowly enough that I caught up to her quickly. She lifted her umbrella in invitation, and we walked that way together, her arm through mine. We walked for perhaps half a kilometer, and I noticed that she walked so lightly that her feet barely made an impression on the muddy ground at all, while I left behind a trail of watery depressions in the soil. Near a gravel road, she turned slightly aside, leading me down a steep hollow to a souterrain—the entrance to an underground structure—so cleverly hidden under a tree that the casual passerby would miss it. The entranceway was made of two lintels, carved with faded ogham letters and holding up a horizontal slab of limestone.

Máire collapsed the umbrella and entered by nearly sliding in. I followed less gracefully, grateful to at least be out of the rain for the time being. Inside, the space was tight and low; we could sit, but little more. I glanced into the darkness farther back, which looked to be a deep cave, and there I saw a glittering like a guttering torch. Máire was already moving back toward the darkness. "What is this place?" I asked Máire as I followed her deeper in.

"It's called the Cave of the Cats: Oweynagat," she said as she continued deeper in. The cave widened as we descended, the roof now higher overhead so we could stand. I could see the torch, a bundle of sticks lashed together with string, topped with pitch, and jammed into a crevice in the rock; Máire must have placed it there earlier. The cave passage continued on into darkness, and I could not tell how far back it went.

Máire must have noticed my curiosity, for she pointed with her chin to the black night past our torch. "They say these caves connect with another system," she whispered, though her voice was loud in the bare circle of torchlight around us. "The locals have all sorts of lovely stories about Oweynagat, like how one woman's cow ran into here and came out again near Keshcorran in County Sligo."

Taking the crude torch from the crevice in the rock, she moved farther back in the cave, and I had no choice but to follow her or be left in the dark. She continued to talk as we walked. She told me how the first priests to enter the region called the cave the "hell-mouth of Ireland," how in the ancient days the three-headed monster called the Ellén Trechend flew from its mouth and plundered the land until Amergin killed it, how later a flock of tiny red birds flew out from the cave, their breath causing all the plants to wither, and how finally, in the days of Ailill and Medb, the cave vomited forth herds of pigs who could cause everything around them to decay. "And there's yet another legend," she said. "'Tis said that the Morrígan herself emerges from Oweynagat every Saimhain."

I laughed at that, but Máire only looked at me strangely. "Do yeh not believe in the Morrígan?" she asked.

"Believe?" I answered. "Do I think the Morrígan's real? Of course not." I laughed, but her face remained serious.

"That's too bad," she said. "No one can survive without belief."

It was a strange statement to make, but Máire didn't give me a chance to ask her to elaborate. We walked on for a time in silence; it was impossible for me to guess for how long it was in that unending darkness, nor to know how many turns we made or how many passages we passed. Eventually we came to a room where the torchlight could no longer touch the walls of the passage and I could feel moving air and hear the sound of running water. There, Máire crouched and thrust the torch into a pile of sticks and peat set in a small ring of stones, rekindling what I realized was a banked fire. The flames stirred and took hold, the light seeming to push back the eternal night here, and I imagined that I half-glimpsed forms moving away with it, rustling and murmuring. Ghosts and shadows. I saw a bed of thick rushes close to the fire, covered with a soft cotton blanket. There was a basket with a loaf of bread sticking out from beneath a lace napkin draped over it, and a kettle hung from an improvised stand over the fire, with a teapot set near it.

I shivered—though maybe that was only my soaked clothes. The heat of the fire felt wonderful, and I moved closer to its warmth. "Yeh might want ta' get out of those wet things," Máire said, again seeming to know what I was feeling. She sat on the edge of the bed, the blankets rumpling under her, and her eyes were on me. "G'wan," she said, "an' I'll do the same." With that, she let her cloak fall from her shoulders, and began to unbutton the dress she wore underneath, her lovely moss-green eyes regarding me all the while.

And the rest I won't relate here as I write this in the Cave of the Cats, but I will always remember it, and I can look at her now in the firelight, sleeping near me . . .

September 10 (?), 1947:

I write this while still in the cavern near Rathcroghan. Here, under the earth, I confess to not being certain what day it is. I can say that late on that first day, Máire led me back to the mouth of the cave. It had stopped raining, and I ran across the fields over the road to where I'd left my bike, with its cardboard suitcase of my clothes and belongings strapped to it under a tarp. I brought the bike back to Oweynagat. With Máire's help, we hid my bicycle in the brush under the tree over the entrance, then carried my suitcase back into the cave, following Máire again through the darkness until we reached her room again.

Which is where we've stayed since . . . but for how long, I can't tell now. I suppose I won't know until I see a paper somewhere or can ask someone— who will undoubtedly look at me as if I'm daft—what day it might be. Máire doesn't seem to care. We spent much of our time talking, though I still think I know too little about her or about the truth of her past.

I don't know how much to believe of what she said, or whether I've found myself infatuated with a madwoman or am just bewitched entire. I feel like I should be frightened, but I'm not. When I'm with Máire, everything feels *right*, as if I were destined to meet her, that there was a purpose to our finding each other. I've never felt this way about another person before . . .

I don't even know how to write any of this down here, but if I'm to do so, now is the time since I can write privately and not have to worry about Máire reading this over my shoulder. Máire has gone deeper into the caverns—to see after others in her care, she says, though she refuses to let me come with her or help her or even to explain much about who these mysterious others might be—and so I'm alone here with the fire near the bed. *Our* bed.

No one can survive without belief, she told me, and she says the old gods and the creatures of myth still live, though they diminish with each passing year. *In the old times, those who followed the black-robed priests of the crucified god still also believed in the Old Ones, but now too many of them follow only the newer god. That's why I'm here. If Oweynagat is truly an opening to the Otherworld, then maybe here I can find a way in, a path some of the Old Ones have already taken to another world where they are known and remembered, and where they live again. I'm here to help those who were left behind find that way themselves.* That's what she told me. I thought it a tale like many of those I'd heard in my travels, and I asked her why someone as young as her would help these mythical Old Ones and why they would even follow her, and she gave that laugh again. "I'm older than yeh might believe," she told me, but I knew that couldn't be true, looking at her face.

Yet . . . What she says is unbelievable, but I can't hear a lie in her voice. I think *she* at least believes it.

And she's told me more, words that I thrill to hear when she whispers them in my ears as we lay together. *I love you.* She says that I'm the one she's waited for, that I was sent by the old gods themselves to help her. In the passion of our nights, I've repeated that same promise to her. *I love you.* But I don't know yet what that means . . .

I can hear her footsteps away in the darkness and see the guttering light of her torch, and so I should stop and write no more for now.

September ?, 1947

Máire tells me that she's forgotten too much of what she once knew, and that's why she can't be certain that the twisting passages of Oweynagat are where she can find this mysterious portal for which she's searching. She tells me that she needs me, that she knows that I was sent to help her, and she now lets me accompany her on her walks into the dark recesses of the caverns. She tells me that she can't open this portal without my help. *How* she knows this or what help it is that I'm to give her, she can't say. "I just *feel* it," she says. "An' I know yeh feel it as well."

Maybe I do—and that frightens me most of all. I know that when I'm with her, I don't wish to leave. I don't know that I *could* leave her.

We sleep. We eat. We make love. We're alone down here, but we're also not alone. I sometimes hear other whispering voices or footsteps, or the rustling of someone's clothing in the dark, or even the clanking of arms and armor. I catch a glimpse of a fleeing shadow as we move along or see movement from the corner of my eyes; I smell a peat fire, the pungent fragrance of pipe smoke, or the foul droppings of some creature. Time passes at an uncertain pace in the world outside. I feel as if we left here, I wouldn't be surprised to find it to be the same day that we entered or a hundred years later. Máire and I walk the passages, searching for . . . what? I don't know.

When we did that today—whatever day today might be—everything suddenly changed. Always before, I wandered with Máire, who seems to be able to negotiate these twisting passages without becoming lost, glad to be with her but blind and deaf to whatever force drew her along. We'd already passed several branchings of the passageway—I've become able to sense them: a greater darkness off to one side or another, accompanied by the touch of moving air and a subtle change in the sound of our footsteps on the uneven floor. We were passing one such branch, when a sudden impulse that I still don't understand made me grasp Máire's arm.

"Wait a moment," I said to her, and she turned, her face puzzled in the warm yellow light of the torch. I pointed to the left. "We need to go that way," I said.

She didn't ask the question that I might have asked if our positions had been reversed, the same question I was asking myself. *Why?* Máire only nodded, and silently turned in the direction that I'd indicated. We stepped carefully over a jumble of fallen rock and into a narrow archway that appeared to have been carved from the living rock. The room beyond was small, the roof so low that we had to walk stooped over for fear of striking our heads against rock, but after a time, the low passage ended and we stepped out into a larger chamber. We both immediately noticed that the walls here were squared, polished, and carved with ornate swirls, like the stones of the passage graves I'd seen at Newgrange, in County Meath north of Dublin, and that the floor was flagstoned and level. Our torchlight struck fire from quartz-flecked granite, and I noticed that the carved lines in the walls had been painted the blue of a deep sky. Another stone, almost like an altar, stood in the middle of the room, held up by two smaller, low plinths. We approached it, half-expecting to see a body or skeleton laid out there, but the altar stone was vacant.

Máire started to walk away again, perhaps to explore the farther recesses of the room, but the same impulse that had led me here kept me rooted to the spot. I crouched down, and under the altar, I saw something. "Máire," I called out. "Bring the light here."

She returned, and together we crouched down at the altar stone. Underneath, on the flags of the room, lay a crystalline stone. The color was difficult to discern in the torchlight, but I thought it, even then, to be a vivid green like an emerald, like Máire's eyes. The stone wasn't large—one could easily hide it in the palm of a hand—and it was polished and smooth. Máire reached for it; as she took it up, she gasped as if in alarm and dropped the torch on the flags, where it hissed and fumed.

"What's the matter?" I asked. Her eyes were open, but she was staring at something past me, transfixed. I turned to see, looking over my shoulder, but there was nothing there. I turned back to Máire and called her name. There was no response; I called again, and she seemed to rouse herself as if from a trance, still clutching the stone in her hand.

"Yeh di'nah see?" she asked. "The light? The place beyond?"

I shook my head. Máire released a long, shuddering breath. "I saw it," she said. "'Tis a place beyond here, but yet right beside us. I could hear voices in the cloch, the voices of those who have held this stone before me, calling to me, beckoning . . ." She shook her head. "'Tis gone now. But I saw it. I heard it." She looked directly at me then, and I could see the wonder and relief in her face. "This stone—'tis the key, and yeh were the one I needed t'find it." She picked up the torch from where it was sputtering against the floor. "We can go now," she said. "This is what I came for."

I wonder now why I agreed with her so quickly. I wonder what other treasures or artifacts we might have found in the place, which I knew I could never find again on my own. Still, I asked no questions of her then, but followed her back out, and through the passages until we were back in our comfortable cave again—what I thought of now as "home."

There, Máire sat down on our bed, holding the stone and staring at it. I sat next to her; the stone looked to be a crystal and it was indeed a deep green, but when I reached for the stone to take it from her for a moment, her fingers closed around it. She must have seen the puzzled look I gave her then, for she sighed and opened her fingers again so that I could see the stone: the deep and rich color of it, with veins of lighter blue writhing deep inside. I also noticed that she kept the stone away from me, where I couldn't easily have snatched it from her; I kept my hands at my sides, even though part of me wanted to insist, to say "I found it; why won't you let me touch it?"

"This is the key," she said again. "I don't know how it came to be here, or who put it here, but this is the connection, the bridge we need."

"We?"

"Yeh and me," she said, but there was a hesitation and I knew she meant something more than that. "You're a walker of the land; with this, we could walk between *two* worlds. I just have to understand how the spell works, and how to place the power in the cloch."

"Spell? Power?" I could hardly keep the skeptical laughter from my voice.

She didn't seem to hear me. "Do yeh sing, Rory? Do yeh know the old tunes? Tell me yeh sing."

"I can sing a bit, I suppose . . ." but she only nodded, her attention still caught by the stone, the cloch.

"There are things that yeh might not believe in, but that doesn't mean they don't exist," she told me. "All that I've told yeh before is the truth, and yeh must open yer mind to that if yeh love me as yeh say."

September ?, 1947

Máire has spent all her time with the emerald cloch. I don't know how long it's been—many hours, certainly, or perhaps a day or more. She sits with it clutched in her left hand and her eyes closed, as if she's listening to voices only she can hear, and sometimes I hear her conversing with them. She rouses herself to eat, and she sleeps. Little more. We've made love only once since then, and even then she seemed distracted and uninvolved.

While she explores her own mind, I've begun to explore Oweynagat on my own—carefully, counting the turns and drawing a crude map here in my journal as I go. It was easy enough to puzzle out the way back to the entrance, as Máire's "home" is not that far into the complex—I did that first, because I'm starting to feel that is something I may need to know. But going the other way, back into the deep labyrinthian maze where we found the cloch . . .

For that, it's as if Máire somehow walked an entirely different path than those I'm able to discover, which are without exception narrow and low limestone tunnels that all end abruptly a short distance in. None of the passages seem to be the deep and winding passages we walked together, all of them with branching corridors in which one could easily get lost. Yet

I've taken every exit from our "home" cavern that I can find by the light of my torch and our fire.

There aren't any other ways farther in. There can't be.

But that makes no sense. Or rather, it makes no sense unless I believe that Máire somehow has the ability to find pathways that simply aren't visible to me. It makes no sense unless I believe in magic and spells and the existence of the old gods and fey creatures. It makes no sense unless I believe that Máire is something more than what she appears to be.

Sometimes, I think I hear voices laughing at me as I stumble about, and I think I see people moving just outside the light of my torch.

But what else can I do while Máire is snared by her voices in the cloch except to continue to search?

So I'll explore more, and see if I can't find a more rational explanation for all of this.

Somehow, I don't think that's going to happen. I'm lost in a world that doesn't actually exist, and even though I stopped going to church a few years past, I find that I'm praying that I eventually will find the way back to my own reality.

September 24, 1947

It's been a long time since I set anything down here, and so much has happened since that I despair of ever adequately transforming it to mere words . . .

I'm currently aboard the *Mauretania*, en route from Liverpool to New York City. Where Máire might be, I no longer know, but I feel the loss of her still. I wonder if I've made the right decision, or if this is something I'll now regret for the rest of my life.

I don't know when it was or on what day that Máire finally stirred, as if awakening from a trance. "We have'ta go outside," she said, already moving even as she said the words, grabbing a torch and walking swiftly toward the passage that led to the entrance. "We must go now."

I followed her, barely able to keep up.

It was night outside, the air crisp as a winter apple, the sky lit up by the cratered face of the moon looming over the horizon while the stars shimmered, jewels on velvet between the blue-white sailing ships of clouds. Máire was standing not far from the entrance, twirling in place with her face raised to the sky as if searching for something, the cloch we'd found still in her hand.

She stopped. She lifted the stone to the sky as if it were an offering . . .

. . . and the sky answered. I witnessed a tendril of silvery green light twisting down from the zenith, like a phantom's rope attached to the clouds. The light was faint, but it brightened when it reached her, and I saw its cold fire wrap around her hand and forearm like a living thing. Máire gasped with the touch—not a sound of alarm but more like the cries I'd heard her make when we were together. The light from the sky brightened slightly, and a few curtains fled away above us, like fleeting sheets of aurora light touched with blue-and-red streaks. Faint marks appeared on Máire's arms, not unlike the swirling patterns carved on the entrance stones at Newgrange or on the walls of the room where we'd found the stone.

Then, as quickly as it had come, the aurora faded and vanished again, and Máire let her hand drop as if exhausted by the effort of holding the stone aloft, but I could see emerald light between her fingers. The cloch itself was alight: a beacon.

Then it happened . . . I was standing near the entrance to the cave, and a rush of cold air from within stirred the legs of my pants and fluttered the collar of my jacket. I felt the touch of hands on my face, plucking at my clothing, and I heard voices calling: some high and fair, others low and ominous, dozens of them calling in Gaelic and in languages that sounded older than any I'd ever heard. A dark fog seemed to surround us; in the mist, the forms of people moved. I heard the blowing of horns, the sound of hooves, the bellow of what might have been a bull. They passed by me and gathered around Máire until she was lost in the midst of them. "Máire!" I called out to her, frightened both for her and for me.

"Yeh needn't worry," I heard her answer, though I still could not see her. "'Tis only me people, awake again for a time." The black cloud continued flowing from the mouth of the cave and past us, moving westward over the fields, with the sheep running startled from the apparition and the sounds of its passage fading, until only Máire and I were left. The light from the cloch was now extinguished and Máire sagged, cradling her left arm. She let the cloch drop to the ground, as if she could no longer bear to hold it.

I went to her and held her. She leaned against me, letting me support her weight as if she'd been stricken nearly lifeless. "There's a door we can open," she told me, her voice but a husk. "The power's gone now, but the cloch and the voices of those who held it before me . . . they told me there's a gateway we can use. Yeh are part of it, too. Yeh are to be the bard," she said.

"Me, a bard? An' a gateway to what?" I asked her. With one hand, I picked up the cloch, the emerald stone. She didn't seem to notice, and I placed it in the pocket of my jacket.

She spread her hands, as if confused. "To another world, or perhaps it's only to another version of this one. But 'tis a *better* place. 'Tis where some of the Old Ones have already gone, where I should have gone long ago, had I been wiser." She looked up at me, her face illuminated by moon-glow, and hers was no longer the face of a comely young lass, but that of an old woman, her skin dry and cracked, her eyes rheumy and contained in a nest of wrinkled flesh. With the vision, I felt as if a spell had cracked and broken within me. She smiled, toothless, and I laid her on the grass, standing and stepping away from her, horrified. "I need you, m'love," she told me, her voice quavering like a hag's.

A cloud passed over the moon, hiding her face from me, and as the clouds slid away again, her face had transformed again, no longer that of the hag but the young Máire again.

I continued to step back from her. "What's wrong, m'dear?" she asked, and I thought I could hear the hag's voice overlaid with the sweet tones of the Máire I knew. She looked westward, to where the black fog filled with voices had gone. "We have to follow them. 'Twill be in the west, the portal we must open. We have'ta find it."

She stopped as I stood there, shaking my head. "I ca'nah," I told her.

"No, yeh must!" Moonshadow slid over her face: Hag/Máire/Hag/Máire. Máire's face was not only her own, but the hag's . . . It stared at me with violence and fury, a madwoman's eyes. She stared at me as if I were a thing to be devoured.

Máire lifted her arms toward me, like she wanted to clasp me to her again, but now fear clutched me harder than any love I had, chasing away the infatuation and the lust. I didn't know what I was afraid of; I only knew that she'd become someone—or perhaps something—that I no longer understood, and for all the wanderlust in me that wanted to always see new things, I could not make myself step back into her embrace. I continued walking away, and her hands dropped. "Rory!" she called after me, but I turned my back on her. "I ca'nah do this without yeh," I heard her say, her voice pleading.

I didn't answer. I started to run, leaving behind Máire, my bike and my suitcase, the cavern, everything. "Rory!" she called again, her voice a storm wind that chased me over the fields and past the mound of Rathcroghan and even to the road. I began walking under the moonlight and the stars away from her, and with each step, I wondered about the choice I'd just made and whether it was the right one.

Part of me was still there with her. Part of me will always be, I think.

It wasn't until I was far from her that I realized that I still had the stone in my pocket. I took it out, looking at it. It was now nothing more than a polished stone, and I put it in my pocket again as I continued to flee.

I still hear her, in my dreams. I think I hear her call my name. I hear her say that she's waiting for me, that she needs me, that she loves me still, that I must come back to her and I must bring the stone.

And I wake wanting to follow where she's gone: toward the west coast of Éire.

But I don't, and I find that I also can't stay here, not when Máire haunts the land for me. I won't—I can't—walk the west coast as I planned, because she's going there. Instead, I traveled back to Dublin, and from there went across the Irish Sea to Liverpool and booked passage for America. I'll go farther west than Máire, and I'll hope that with the sea between us, I'll stop hearing her call.

I'll hope that she can discover the path she so desperately wants to find without me.

I'll hope that I'll forget her.

12

Toss the Feathers

IT HAD BEEN WELL INTO the early morning hours when Colin finally stopped reading the journal, and the implications still rang in his head. He'd taken the jeweled pendant Aunt Patty had given him and held it for a long time; he'd gone to sleep with it in his hand, but what little sleep he'd managed was racked by dreams where he and his grandfather were together, and the dark-haired Máire was there also, and he and his grandfather were sometimes one person and sometimes two.

The next morning, he woke and showered, then picked up the journal again, reading earlier and later entries, and going back and rereading the section that talked about Máire. He wondered what Aunt Patty had thought of the journal, and if she somehow *knew* the resonance that shook him as he read his grandfather's tale. The description of Máire, the description of the cloch and what she'd done with it . . .

The entire tale was unbelievable, yet the words had grabbed him by the throat and shaken him. He wondered if it was all some elaborate fiction his grandfather had made up, a fanciful tale that had never happened, a story that Rory had written for some reason. Colin found that he couldn't believe that. He'd paged through the earlier sections of the journal, and those were the entries of a young man wandering the land, carefree and wide-eyed, and enjoying whatever his journey gave him. And after that entry aboard the *Mauretania*, Daiddeó Rory never mentioned Máire, the stone, or the strange events again. It was as if he refused to even think about it, and once again the journal was filled only with the mundane minutiae of his travels: his arrival in New York City, his wonder at the sights, and—eventually—his meeting the woman he'd marry, a second-generation Irish immigrant.

Daiddeó Rory continued to wander throughout his life. Colin remembered that his grandfather always seemed to be somewhere else, that it was rare that he and his grandmother were home for more than a few months. But he'd never gone back to visit Ireland again.

Daiddeó Rory never went back because he was afraid that if he did, he'd meet her again . . .

Without any evidence, without any proof, Colin was certain of that.

He stared at the journal, now closed on the bedspread next to him. He lifted his glasses from his nose and rubbed at his eyes. At the same time, he heard a horrified cry from the kitchen: Jen's voice.

"Aaron! Colin! Get in here!"

Colin rushed into the kitchen as Aaron came hurrying in from the other bedroom. They saw Jen standing by the sink with a horrified look on her face, pointing to the kitchen table. A crow was sprawled unmoving, its wings outspread as if it were making one last attempt to fly. Finnigan the cat was also on the table, sniffing the bird and tapping it with a quick paw. A few feathers were scattered around the table. Colin grabbed a dirty fork from the sink, pushing Finnigan back from the bird as he approached, and prodded the crow with the fork. There was no reaction from the animal.

"It's dead," Colin said, pushing up his glasses.

Aaron shook his head. "Finnigan probably got it while we were out grocery shopping earlier, Jen," he said. "The damn thing must have got in then somehow."

"I came in to get lunch ready, and that thing was just lying there," Jen said. "Though I could swear I glanced in here when we got back and didn't see it or Finnigan. Jesus, that's creepy!" She inhaled deeply, and let it out again. She glanced at the window where the crow had appeared earlier, and Colin followed her gaze. The window was shut, the catch engaged and the glass intact. "How the hell did a crow get in here? Who put it in on the table, and why? The door was locked, and it didn't come in through the window. Jesus . . ." She ran her fingers through her hair.

"You want me to call the cops?" Aaron asked, but Jen shook her head.

"And tell them what? That my cat killed a bird on the kitchen table? There's nothing missing in the apartment that I can tell, there's no note with the bird and no obvious threat, and no sign that anyone's been in here. I can't figure out how the damn bird got in here, but . . . Colin?"

Colin realized that he'd been staring at the bird the whole time that Jen and Aaron had been talking. He found himself shaking his head. "You got a garbage bag?" he asked Jen. "I'll go put it in the dumpster out back."

Jen handed him a plastic bag; Colin and Aaron, both grimacing, maneuvered the body into it while Finnigan mewled in protest. Several black feathers were left on the table. Colin cinched the bag shut. "I'll be back in a few," he said.

Carrying his burden, he made his way outside and around the side of the building to the dumpster. "Look," he said to the air, still holding the bag, "if this is all supposed to be some kind of sign, I wish you'd be a lot more obvious about what it means. What are you trying to say? Are you telling me I'm making a mistake, or that I should be leaving or going or finishing my doctorate, or what?" He opened the garbage bag and peered in. The bird's dead eyes stared back at him, the beak slightly open as if in a perpetual, silent *caw*. After staring at it for a moment, Colin resealed the bag. "Okay," he said to the sky, feeling rather foolish. "You had your chance."

He tossed the crow into the dumpster and went back inside, where Jen was scrubbing the table. The feathers were gone. Aaron was padding around the apartment, looking to see that nothing was missing and evidently trying to figure out how the bird had entered the apartment. Colin went to the sink and washed his hands; Finnigan, on the floor, was doing the same with his tongue.

"Weird, huh?" Jen said.

"Yeah. Definitely on the weird side," he answered over the running water. He shook off his hands and dried them on a dishtowel. He heard Jen start to say something, stop, then start again.

"Hey, little brother, not to change the subject, but I saw Tommy talking to you at the cemetery yesterday. You have a job offer?"

The shift was jarring. He still could see the crow's dead eyes staring at him like an accusation. Colin shrugged, forcing himself to concentrate on what Jen had said. "It seems like I was the last one to know Tommy was going to ask me that," Colin said. He watched as she took the dishtowel he'd just used and wiped down the table. "I take it you know what he wanted."

"Mostly, yes." She hung the dishtowel on the rack at the side of the counter. "So, are you staying?"

"I don't know yet. I'm thinking about it."

Without saying anything, Jen went to Colin and hugged him fiercely. After a moment, his arms went around her as well. He heard her cry, muffled against his chest, and his own eyes filled sympathetically with tears, splashing on his glasses as he blinked. "I'm going to miss Dad so much," he heard her say. Finnigan came over and brushed against their feet, wrapping his tail around their legs. "I don't think I'll ever get over this. It's like there's this huge hole in my life all of a sudden, and I have to keep stepping around it or I'll fall in and be lost. Do you know what I mean?"

"Yeah. I do." Guiltily, he realized he was thinking more of himself than he was of his father. The image of the dead crow came back to him, overlaid on the memory of his grandfather's words in the journal. "You feel like you're missing a part of you that's supposed to be there." He stroked her hair, cradling her. "You'll get through this," he said. "All of us will. We'll keep going; that's what he'd want us to do."

Jen sniffed, releasing him. "Yeah, he would," she said. "It's going to be hard, though. And it'll be hardest of all on Mom."

"You'll help her. So will Tommy and Aunt Patty."

"And you?"

"I'll try," he told her.

Even as he said the words, he wondered how true they would be.

"Hey, Beth," Colin said as the door to his mother's house opened, revealing the Doyle's housekeeper behind it.

Beth was a short woman, less than five feet tall, and plump. She possessed a plain face and hair that had once been brown and was now mostly gray, pulled back into a long French braid. She wore, as always, a loose skirt and white blouse decorated with blue-and-yellow vines on the collar, and a plain, cotton apron tied over it all. Her surname, Banaszewski, screamed her ancestry. So did her first name—Elzbet—but she had always simply been "Beth" to the family. He didn't have a memory of when she hadn't been part of the household.

Her face split into a smile as she saw Colin, and she nodded approvingly as she looked him up and down. "I have no time to talk with you last night," she said. "But you look healthy." Her voice had maintained its strong accent despite decades in the States. "They feed you good there in Seattle, then."

"They treated me just fine," he told her, "but the food there doesn't hold a candle to your *pierogi*."

She beamed at that and hugged him once fiercely. "Come in, come in," she said. "Your mother, she is upstairs with your aunt, but Tommy, he's in the back room. Go see him, and I tell her you're here."

"Thanks. I'll go in and see Tommy, then."

"You want something to drink, to eat? No *pierogi*, but I have leftover *makowiec* in the fridge." She patted his stomach. "I know you like that."

"I'm just fine, Beth. I ate lunch with Jen and Aaron."

Beth gave him another quick hug and went toward the stairs. Colin went into the back room, which still smelled like a funeral home, every available flat surface holding a vase of flowers. Tommy was sitting on the couch, appearing to stare at the flatscreen TV even though it was off. "Mom could open a flower shop," Colin said.

Tommy stirred, craning his head around. He gave a short, polite laugh. "I know what you mean. The smell is pretty powerful." Tommy's smile twitched, faded. "You've made up your mind, haven't you?"

"Made up your mind about what?" a voice interrupted before Colin could answer. He turned to see his mother entering the room. "I hope that means you're taking Tommy up on his offer."

Colin looked at Tommy. "Man, nothing is secret in this family."

Tommy shrugged. "I asked Mom if she thought you'd agree."

"And I told him that you would," his mother said. "Because it's what your father would have wanted."

And there it is, the guilt ploy . . . Even Tommy realized it. "Mom," he said. "That's not fair. If Colin's going to stay, it needs to be because *he* wants to stay, not for any other reason."

"Your father's wishes don't matter now that he's gone?"

"Mom . . ." This time the protest came from both of them.

Her eyes were shining in the light coming in from the windows; she wiped at them once, a gesture that wasn't lost on Colin. He could see the pain in her face, her exhaustion in the lines drawn by the light from the windows, and she hugged herself as if cold. "I know you think it's selfish, but it's not. Your father and I have never asked any of our children for anything unless we believed it was in your own best interests, even when you didn't see it yourselves. This is no different. You're needed *here,* Colin— maybe you can put school aside for a semester. Your brother needs you, and the family needs you. *I* need you. We've just experienced a tremendous tragedy, and it's going to take all of us together to help us heal."

Colin saw Tommy's sympathetic glance toward him. "Mom," Tommy said, "I know you and Dad always tried to do what you thought best, and for me, that turned out to be the case. For Jen, too, mostly. But Colin's not me and he's not Jen. If Colin needs to do something else, then I completely understand that, and I not only won't stand in his way, I'll support him unconditionally." He paused—and Colin saw the polished, studied cadence of a public speaker in that. "And that's what you need to do as well, Mom," he finished.

His mother's eyebrows lifted and her head tilted. "That sounds as if there *is* something else that Colin is intending. Colin?" His mother's gaze hadn't left him, nor had she relaxed the arms folded over her stomach.

"Mom, I know how much everyone's hurting right now, and believe me, I am, too. And I appreciate that Tommy's going to take over Dad's path. We all miss Dad . . ."

"Colin." His mother's mouth tightened into a line, pulling the skin of her cheeks into taut, short canyons. "Just tell us what you've decided—or tell us if you haven't."

The image of the crow on the table flashed across his mind, followed by the memory of his grandfather's journal. The competing pulls of family and his earlier decision to leave school and pursue music in Ireland seemed to tear him in half, ripping down the center of his mind. His head ached, his pulse throbbing in his temples. He put his hand in the pocket of his jeans, cupping the well-polished surface of the crystal Aunt Patty had given him. The stone felt icy. He clenched it tightly, pressing the silver lace of the cage into his skin.

"Mom, you remember that I'd wanted to go to Ireland to study the music, before you and Dad convinced me that I should go for the PhD?" he said. "Well, I've left school; a couple weeks ago before I even heard about Dad—it just wasn't for me, and I haven't been happy there. It's music that calls me right now. I'm sorry."

Tommy nodded. His mother gave a cry that might have been a sob, and she turned away, fleeing the room. A few moments later, they heard her feet on the stairs and the closing of her bedroom door.

Tommy came over to Colin. He hugged him tightly. "Don't worry about this," he said into Colin's ear. "I understand—you gotta make the decision that works best for you, and say what you truly believe. It's something maybe I should have done myself, some time ago." Then he stepped back and ruffled Colin's hair as he had when Colin was a child. "But I think you'd better go talk to Mom. Without Dad . . ." He stopped. "Just go talk to her," he repeated. "She loves you, and eventually she'll understand."

Colin nodded, patting Tommy on the shoulder. "You're gonna win this race," he told him. "I know it."

"I hope you're right. And I hope you're right about your own choice."

"Yeah. So do I. I'll go talk to Mom."

Aunt Patty was waiting for him at the top of the stairs. She inclined her head toward his parents' bedroom. "She's in there," she said softly. "I knew you were going to follow your music. I knew it all along."

"I didn't."

"You would've if you'd listened inside," Aunt Patty told him, tapping her own forehead with a bright red fingernail. "You've read the journal?"

"Yeah." He didn't elaborate, and Aunt Patty simply nodded.

"You're doing what I think he always wanted to do himself, but he couldn't bring himself to make the journey. I think he always wanted to know the truth behind it all. Maybe you'll find that somewhere."

He managed a shrug, her comment igniting a smoldering in his stomach. He had to admit that now that he'd committed to going, a fear trembled through him. He didn't know what he was going toward, didn't know what was expected of him or understand it, didn't know what was going to happen.

The crow, dead on the table . . . That still felt as if it were sent as a sign to him. His stomach churned.

"Maybe," he said. "If there's any truth to it at all."

Patty laughed. "Your grandfather told some entertaining tales, and I know he sometimes elaborated on them to make them better ones. So who knows."

He chuckled with her; the amusement tore away some of the tension in his stomach. "I remember a few of those tall tales, though I wonder why he never talked about the one in the journal." He glanced toward at the closed door down the hall. "I worry about Mom."

"Don't," Aunt Patty told him. "Rebecca and I and the rest of the family will take care of her when you're gone. You only have to take care of yourself." She went to him, pulling his head down to her and kissing his cheek. "Promise me you'll do that."

"I will," he told her. He hoped it wasn't a lie.

"Good," Aunt Patty answered. "Now go tell your Mom how much you love her and how much you'll miss her."

PART TWO

NEMAIN

⟡ 13 ⟡

The Black-Haired Lass

"**D**'YEH KNOW 'The Ghost Lover,' Colin?" Lucas Flaherty asked, turning away from his mic.

Colin pressed his lips together, tapping long fingers on the top of his Gibson. He pushed his glasses up his nose; with the sweat from the stage lights, they'd slid halfway down. "I remember it well enough, I think," he said. "What key?"

"G, but the song starts on the five, remember." With that, Lucas nodded to Padraig, Bridget, and John, the other musicians on the little stage, and gave his attention back to the mic and the audience in the pub. "Right, then," he said. "We're endin' this set with another of those lovely little necrophilia songs: a woman pining for a lover lost at sea, his ghost visiting her at night and she wishing that the night would never end. Here we go, then. One, two, three, and . . ."

They launched into the song, first an instrumental verse with Padraig's concertina taking the melody while Lucas' fiddle added musical filigrees to the tune and John's bodhran drove the beat. The second time through, Colin began singing, with Lucas—also playing mandolin—and Bridget adding occasional harmonies.

> *Johnny, he promised to marry me*
> *But I fear he's with some fair one and gone*
> *There's something bewails a man, I don't know what it is*
> *And I'm weary of lying alone.*
>
> *Well, Johnny he came there at the appointed hour*
> *He tapped on the window so low*

93

This fair maid arose and she hurried on her clothes
And she bid her true love welcome home.

She took him by the hand and she lay him down
She felt he was as cold as the clay
She said, My dearest dear, if I only had my wish
This long night would never turn to day.

The audience was clapping along by the second verse, and there was applause and a few shouts as he finished the verse and Lucas launched into a fiddle solo. Colin grinned into the glare of the stage lights, buoyed by the energy of the band and the crowd.

As Lucas played, Colin took the time to scan the audience. Regan's, one of several pubs situated around and near the main square of Ballemór, was fairly well-packed on a Friday night, the crowd a mixture of locals and tourists. Ballemór was one of the larger towns in the Connemara district, attracting a large share of those visiting the region. The main road linking the mountains called the Twelve Bens to scenic Ceomhar Head ran through the town, and there were ample inns and B&Bs all vying for the tourist trade. The "Sky Road" led out from Ballemór in a loop along the head, giving scenic panoramas of the Atlantic and some of the nearby islands.

The locals were mostly belly to the bar or ensconced at their usual tables. The booths nearest the stage were full now, though they hadn't been when they'd first started playing. Through the stage lights' smeared haze on his glasses, Colin noticed one particular booth a few down from the stage. There were six people crowded into the wooden confines: two women and four men. A woman with long black hair was seated at the edge of the booth, facing him, and she was the one that Colin fixed on. She was watching the band; no, she was watching *him*, because he suddenly felt the shock of eye contact. He smiled, but looked quickly away. When he glanced that way again, she was still watching him, and this time it was she who smiled and seemed to nod once in his direction, raising her hands in silent applause.

For him. He knew it, somehow.

The person sitting next to her, a burly, dark-haired young man, seemed to notice her attention to Colin as well. He scowled, and leaned over to her as Colin began to sing again.

Oh, crow up, crow up my little bird
And don't crow before it is day
And you'll keep shielding made of the glittering gold
And your door of silver so gay.

And where is your soft bed of down, my love?
And where is your white hall and sheet?
And where is the fair maid who watches over you
As you lie in your long, dreamless sleep?

Colin's gaze kept returning to the woman in the booth through the rest of the song, and she watched him in turn, nodding her head slightly in time to the music. She wasn't exceptionally pretty—there were a dozen women in the pub that Colin found far more physically attractive—but there was a presence about her that compelled his attention. Every time he noticed her, he could see her laughing, grass-green eyes.

Oh, the sea is my soft bed of down, my love
And the sand is my white hall and sheet
The long, hungry worms they do feed off of me
As I lie every night in the deep.

Oh, when shall I see you my love? she cried
Oh, when shall I see you again?
When little fishes fly and the seas they do run dry
And the hard rocks do melt with the sun.

When little fishes fly and the seas they do run dry
And the hard rocks do melt with the sun.

With the reprise of the last two lines and a flourish, the song came to an end. "T'anks all," Lucas called into the applause. "We'll be taking a wee bit here to wet our throats, and if any of yeh would care to buy a thirsty band member a pint or a dram or both, well, we wouldn't be saying no." He put his fiddle in the case; Colin slid the strap of his guitar over his head, put the Gibson on its stand, and adjusted his glasses. The jukebox began to drone over the crowd noise—American country music; something by Blake Shelton judging by the voice, though country wasn't a genre Colin knew well at all. Colin let Bridget slide by him ("Yeh sounded grand, Colin. Just grand.") then stepped down from the stage.

He immediately looked toward the booth and the dark-haired woman. He thought she gave him the slightest incline of her head, as if beckoning him. He sidled slowly through the crowd until he was standing next to her. Up close, her eyes were even more extraordinary; the green of a shallow sea with swirls of aquamarine lurking around the iris, large enough to drown in. The color of her eyes struck him—they matched that of the stone of the pendant he kept in his pocket, the stone that his Aunt Patty had given him, his grandfather Rory's stone. They also matched a stone around her own neck, a polished green pebble caged in silver wire that looked similar to his stone. Her hair was so dark that it seemed to swallow the little light the pub afforded. He ran fingers through his own sweat-damp locks, pushing the strands back from his forehead. *Start with music; it's all you have, and it works often enough.*

"Hope you liked the set," he said. "I noticed you listening."

Her eyebrows lifted a bit, and the man next to her snorted. "Yer American," she said. "I'm surprised at that, yeh playing with the locals." Her voice was lower than he'd expected, with a growl to it that he found interesting, and her own brogue was more pronounced than most of those in Ballemór: *yeh playin' wit' da lahcols* . . . He wondered if the gravel would be in her singing voice as well, and what that might sound like. The voice sounded tantalizingly familiar to him somehow, though he couldn't place it.

"Yeah, you pegged it," he told her. "I'm American, from Chicago originally, though I've been in Ireland for almost a month now, playing here and there. Just got to Ballemór a few days ago, actually, but Lucas—he's the fiddler—was nice enough to let me sit in with his group; he heard me playing up in Galway a few weeks ago with some other friends of his, and he lost his guitar player last week and said he liked my playing and my voice, so—" She seemed amused as the man next to her rolled his eyes, and Colin realized he was babbling. "Sorry," he said. "My name's . . ."

She shook her head as he started to tell her, and stopped. "No, let me guess," she said. "Yer name starts with . . ." She paused, fingers spidering on her chin. " . . . an R," she finished.

Colin laughed at that. "Not bad, but wrong. My grandfather's name was Rory, Rory O'Callaghan; he was born in Ireland. I'm Colin. Colin Doyle." He put out his hand.

She shook the proffered hand with a smile. "Maeve Gallagher," she said.

"Maeve," he said. "Good to meet you." He glanced at the others in the booth, and Maeve chuckled.

"Ah, me mates . . ." She went around the circle, starting with the dark-haired man next to her. "Niall Tierney, Dolan Connor, Aiden Nolan, Keara Shea, Liam Doherty." They each nodded in turn, though none of them offered a hand. Niall, especially, favored him only with a scowl, and Colin wondered, again, if he and Maeve were together.

"I thought you sounded wonderful," Keara, the other woman, who looked to be no more than nineteen or twenty, said to Colin. Niall snorted.

"'Tis jus' bloody tourist crap," he said. "Next set they'll be doing feckin'

'Danny Boy.'" He stared at Colin with pupils the color of oak and just as hard. "Won't you, Yankee boy?"

Colin smiled, trying to blunt the edge of Niall's animosity, looking at him over the top of his glasses. "Hell, if I started that one, Lucas'd pull out wire cutters and snip the strings right off my guitar," he answered. "And I wouldn't blame him, myself. But yeah, for most Americans, if you say 'Irish music,' that's the first song they think of. That's a shame, ain't it?"

Colin wasn't certain still if Maeve and Niall were actually a couple, but it was obvious that Niall was territorial with her, even if Maeve didn't share that opinion. A couple of the others chuckled at Colin's comment, but Niall just shook his head. Colin could see that the man wanted to retort, and the belligerence that colored his cheeks and balled his fists on the booth's table made Colin decide that Niall was going to pick a fight. He'd seen such behavior before in pubs: alcohol-fueled confrontations, but Maeve managed to defuse the fight that Niall seemed to want. She placed her hand on Niall's arm and smiled up at Colin.

"How about I buy yeh a pint, Colin?" she said, rising from the booth and linking her arm with Colin's. *Okay, maybe they're not a couple* . . . There was a musky, earthy smell around her that he thought might be perfume. She led him away before he could answer, though he heard Keara and the others talking heatedly to Niall as they made their way toward the bar. "Just shut the feck up, Niall. You know why Maeve . . ."

He wondered just how well Niall knew Maeve, and if that was going to cause problems for him. But he walked with her to the bar. The regulars in the pub—easy to tell from the tourists, who were wearing new Aran Islands sweaters and were in general too well and too warmly dressed for the evening—glanced at Maeve and slid aside to let her approach the bar. The expressions on their faces weren't particularly appreciative or friendly, however, and Colin found himself wondering at that. If Maeve noticed, she said nothing, just lifted a hand to the bartender with two fingers up in a "V." The bartender lifted his chin in understanding and set two pint glasses under the Guinness tap, filing them and setting them aside to settle.

As they waited, Maeve turned to face him. The crowd pressed them together; Colin found that he didn't mind that at all. "No, Niall and I aren't an item," she said. "At least not in the way yer thinkin'."

He laughed nervously. "Umm, was I being that obvious?" She didn't answer, just raised an eyebrow. "Okay, so I probably was. But I don't think your Niall likes me much."

"Niall's being a wee overprotective, 'tis all. Yeh have a sister?"

"As it happens, I do."

"Wouldn't yeh be watching who she talked to if yeh were out with her?"

Colin shrugged. The comment made him think of Jen, and he wondered how she and Aaron were doing. It had been a week since they'd last talked. "I guess so. Niall's your brother, then?"

"Not m'brother." The answer was short and clipped, and she grinned at him as she turned back to the bar. Her jeans were pleasantly fitted. Colin glanced down as she leaned over to take the two Guinnesses the bartender slid down to her. She showed the bartender a 10-euro note and placed it on the bar, then turned back to Colin, who lifted his gaze too slowly. "Enjoying the view, are yeh?" she asked as she handed him his pint.

"Obvious again?"

She smiled and changed the subject. "So yer a bare month in Ireland. Pardon m'saying, but yer looking too old to be a student and most tourists don't take that kind of time. And yeh wear glasses . . . Yeh a prof a' some sort?"

He laughed again. "No. Well, not anymore, anyway. I'm a musician with an interest in traditional music. My family's Irish on both sides—my grandfather Rory, remember?—and so I've always been interested in Ireland and its music. I studied a lot of Irish history and culture in college and took plenty of lessons with people in Chicago and Seattle who played traditional music. Now I've come over to soak it all up and learn what I can here."

"So yeh think yeh know Ireland from all this soaking, do yeh?" Her smile took out the sting that the bare words might have had. The crowd kept them tightly together. Colin knew that "personal space" was closer here than it was at home, but he could feel her hip graze him as they moved a few steps from the bar.

He shook his head. "I know mostly how little I actually know. But I've managed to learn a bit. For instance, I can tell you that 'Maeve' is the Anglicized form of 'Medb' or 'Meadhbh,' so your parents named you after the great Queen of Connacht."

She laughed at that, a silvery sound that seemed to wrap around him and pull him even closer. "Now that sounds like a prof to me. So have yeh actually read the *Táin*, or did yeh just look that up on Wikipedia?"

He grinned. "Nope. I've actually read it a few times. Not in the original—my Gaelic's mediocre, and my Old and Middle Irish are nonexistent. But I've studied Celtic mythology with the idea that I could better understand where the traditional songs were coming from." He shrugged. "I'm not sure it helped much, honestly." He took a sip from his pint, licking away the foam that clung to his upper lip. "What about you? Have you been in Ireland all your life?"

She nodded. "That I have, and I don't intend to ever leave, as much as some might want me to." She leaned even closer to him, enough that he could smell her perfume again. She looked up at him with those extraordinary eyes. "Which means I need to be thinking carefully about Americans who'll be leaving soon enough, doesn't it? And yeh should be thinking about whether yeh want to get involved with someone like me."

Colin raised his eyebrows at that, and she continued. "After all, since yeh've read all those old Irish tales, yeh know that even the good ones always end sad. Take the 'The Children of Lir'—those poor children cursed to be swans for three hundred years, and when the happy day comes that they're finally released and returned to their human form, well, they're three-hundred-year-old people and immediately die. 'Tis a lovely ending. Yeh would'nah want something like that to happen, now would yeh?"

She grinned at him, and Colin was saved from having to answer by the sound of a fiddle: Lucas was back on the stage and tuning up. Colin took another long sip of the Guinness and lifted the glass in Lucas' direction. "Looks like we're starting up again," he said. "Hey, I'd love to talk to you some more, Maeve. Stick around after the set, why don't you? It's our last one of the night."

Her lips pursed. "Maybe," she said. "We'll see. I ca'nah make promises; we just stopped in for a pint."

"And now I owe you one," Colin answered, nodding to his own glass. "I always believe in paying my debts—so if not tonight, then some other time?"

"I'm around here sometimes," she said. "So we'll just have to see, won't we?"

Somewhere during the middle of the next set, Maeve and her friends left the pub. Colin wasn't entirely certain when that was; she was there when they started a song, he turned to pay attention to Lucas' fiddle solo, and when he glanced around again, the booth was empty.

When the set ended, Colin put his guitar in the case, wiping down the neck and strings before he closed the latches. He took off his glasses, cleaning them on the hem of his sweater. "That was a grand time tonight," Lucas said behind him. "Yeh were even better than I expected. Nicely done, and yeh've a powerful voice—I saw everyone turns to listen to yeh really let loose with those pipes, and most of 'em stayed the night. So 'tis glad I am that I asked yeh to sit in."

"So am I," Colin told him. "The gig was a blast."

Lucas nodded. He handed Colin forty euros in small bills and coins. "Here's yer portion of the take. T'ain't much, but we play three or four times a week, and the private gigs pay a lot better than the pubs. Bridget, Padraig, and John all said they loved your addition. So . . . would yeh be willing to do this again tomorrow?"

Colin grinned. "Absolutely."

"Brilliant. Then maybe we can talk about yeh staying around Ballemór for a bit, eh? I could introduce yeh to all the local musicians—some of 'em go way back, and they have songs in their heads that no one's ever bothered to write down, especially the older ones. They'd play them for yeh, and teach yeh what they know. That something yer interested in?"

Colin's grin widened at the thought. He patted the guitar case and thought of the notebook in his rented room, already stuffed with centuries-old songs and fragments of half-forgotten lyrics. "Yeah, that could convince me to stick around here for a while." Involuntarily, Colin glanced over at the empty booth where Maeve had been sitting. When he looked back, Lucas was giving him an odd look. "What?" Colin asked.

"'Tis nothing yeh'd be knowing as a newcomer, but around here, 'tis not the best idea to be talking up the Oileánach."

"The Oileánach?" Colin repeated.

"The Islanders—that's who you were chatting up during the break, and that Maeve woman's chief among 'em. They all live out on Inishcorr off Ceomhar Head—just came here outta nowhere one morning and took over the island like 'twas their own, without asking no one. They're a strange bunch that keeps together and don't mix with the townsfolk. No one trusts them."

"Why not?"

Lucas gave a shrug in reply. "Don't matter. Just take my word for it. Yeh ca'nah trust 'em, and that's the end of it. They won't be out there for much longer anyway: the NPWS wants to take over Inishcorr as a national park, so all the Oileánach are to be removed and relocated. Good riddance to 'em, too, I say."

For Colin, that explained a lot about the evening. *"I don't intend to ever leave, as much as some want me to,"* Maeve had said. "Don't worry," he told Lucas. "It doesn't look like she was that interested, anyway."

Maeve stepped into the boat, but she was looking back down Beach Road toward the lights of Ballemór.

"Damn it, Maeve, you ca'nah be serious. That's him? That's the bard yeh've been telling us we need? The man's not even Irish. He's just a leamh, like all the others. He sings well enough, I'll grant yeh, but that don'nah make him the bard."

She glanced back. Niall's face was in half-shadow, illuminated only by the starboard running light; most of the others were already getting ready to cast off from the quay. They were all pretending not to listen. Their boat, the name *Grainne Ni Mhaille* painted on her bow, was a battered Galway hooker that they'd found beached on Inishcorr, near the abandoned cluster of cottages there. They'd patched and repitched the hull, stitched the holes in the blood-red sails, and added a decrepit, sputtering outboard motor for when the winds failed or were too strong. The boat rocked in the tidal swell, the single mast and rigging creaking, the sails furled at the moment and looking black rather than red in the night.

Maeve shook her head at Niall. "The man might not be from here, but he has an old soul, and he's more than just a leamh," she retorted. "He's Rory O'Callaghan's grandson, as well. Tell me you didn't feel it yourself, Niall Tierney. I did."

"And the cloch? He has that?"

"He does. I felt that, too."

"Yeh *want* to feel it," Niall answered. "And more besides. I heard about yeh and this O'Callaghan. Yeh allowed yerself to think of him as more than just a tool. That turned out well, didn't it?"

Had Niall not added the last comment, she might have admitted that there was a shred of truth in what he said. Instead, she scowled. "If you're thinking I'd jeopardize all'a us for something as trivial as a bit of a tumble, then yeh don't know me at all, no matter what yeh've been told about that time. 'Tis really what yeh believe?"

He had the grace to look away. She wondered whether his cheeks flushed with embarrassment, but it was too dark to see. "Neh," he admitted.

"Good. Then we won't be having problems. There's no reason to decide about this now. We still have time."

Niall sniffed. "Not much, I'm thinking."

"Enough for now. Do'nah forget; he has to come to us willingly an' give me the cloch and himself the same way, or I ca'nah open the portal."

"Yer wrong about him, Maeve. I don't care if he has an old soul or not. Yer reading this one wrong, and he's nah going to do as he must. I tell yeh that because yer blind to it and I don't care if that makes yeh angry with me for pressing yer nose in the shite. Yeh've made a mistake. Like the last time."

She glanced back again at the town, its lights glittering up on the steep hills bordering the inlet. She wouldn't let Niall be right. She couldn't let him be right, or it was all lost. "Yer wrong, Niall, and yeh'll see that soon enough. Right now, let's get back to the island. The rest can wait for the time being."

◄ 14 ►

Two Conversations

THE NEXT DAY was a blustery April morning, with a cold, arrogant wind off the Atlantic that tore the gray-black clouds and threw down rain so hard that the drops stung. The gale shrieked and whistled through the chimney and drafty windows of the little bed and breakfast where he was staying, waking Colin earlier than he wanted. He fumbled for his glasses on the dresser next to the bed and put them on, blinking as he glanced out the window to gray-black clouds rolling past.

After taking a shower and dressing, he wandered downstairs to find Mrs. Egan, the house's owner, in the small kitchen. "Quite the morning, Mr. Doyle," she said. "I swear yeh can hear the very devil in this wind. Would yeh like some tea? The kettle's about to boil. There's fresh soda bread and butter on the table, and I'll be cooking up eggs, sausages, and bacon. There's black pudding, too, if yeh like. T'other guests haven't come down yet. Yer an early riser for Ireland, and for a musician, especially."

Colin shook his head. "You needn't go to any trouble for me, Mrs. Egan."

"'Tis no trouble; it's part of what yer paying for, and a good breakfast sustains a young man for the whole of the day, especially if yer going to be walking about in this weather. G'wan into the dining room and I'll bring yeh out a bite."

"Thank you, then," Colin told her. "Though you can skip the black pudding for me."

"Not to yer taste, eh?" she asked, coming out the kitchen with a platter. "None of the Americans I've had here much cared for it, though the Germans, they love it. Why, my brother Darcy, God rest his soul—that's his picture there on the mantel behind yeh—used to make the best black

103

pudding yeh can imagine, but then he had his farm. 'Margaret,' he used to say to me, 'we were meant to use everything that the good animals can provide us and not waste their noble sacrifice.' The day he died, oh 'twas much like this one: a beastly, nasty day when I would swear the very creatures of hell were about . . ."

Mrs. Egan rattled on in that vein for some time with Colin adding the occasional "uh-huh" and "you don't say," though he'd mostly stopped listening to her story about her brother's death as he poured himself some tea and buttered a slice of the brown bread. Mrs. Egan placed a plate laden with three eggs, several sausages, and thick Irish back bacon in front of Colin. She sat across from him, watching as he ate and sipping her tea.

"I hear from Mr. O'Malley that yeh were playing at Regan's with that Lucas Flaherty's band last night," she said as he sopped up yolk with his bread.

"Yes. Lucas is quite the fiddler, and he knows the old songs better than most."

"Aye, an' his father knew 'em as well, which is how Lucas learned 'em, and he from his father before that, who came down here from up Sligo way. The Flahertys have always been a musical family. Their first cousin John Flaherty married my second cousin Mary McBride. She lives up in Roscommon, but came here one summer and there were sparks just a'flying between her and John. Before yeh know it, they were calling the banns for 'em, though the little babe came a wee bit early, if yeh take my meaning . . ." The conversation devolved into a genealogical discussion that rapidly lost Colin's interest, about how the Flaherty and various other Ballemór families were related. He listened politely, then let Mrs. Egan take his plate into the kitchen.

"I think I'll take a walk," he called out to Mrs. Egan.

"On a blustery day like this? Och, I want nothing more than to sit at the hearth and drink some tea and maybe read a book. But yer young and the damp don't get into yer bones the way it does me, I suppose. Take a good sweater and scarf, and your cap. There's a macintosh in the front closet yeh can borrow if yeh care to; Mr. Finch, he stayed here a few years ago, left it behind. I suspect it would be fitting yeh. A strange man, was Mr. Finch. Now he was one of the McGinnis' by his mother's side . . ."

"Thank you, Mrs. Egan," Colin said loudly, knowing he'd be in for the full tale of Mr. Finch's ancestors if he let her continue. He slipped on his jacket and cap from the stand near the door, picked up his blackthorn staff, and stepped outside.

The weather had moderated a bit, the wind no longer quite so angry and fierce and the rain dwindling to a drizzle, though low, slate-gray shreds of mist were still sliding rapidly eastward under a more ominous-looking and dark cloud cover. Mrs. Egan's house was on the Sky Road well up from the main square of Ballemór and a good half-mile walk from the nearest neighbors. Going west out of the house led along the Sky Road and eventually out onto Ceomhar Head proper, overlooking first the small inlet that Beach Road—well down the green slope of the hills—followed, then the great vista of the nearest islands and the open Atlantic.

Colin turned west, but rather than staying on the road, he climbed even higher, following a winding trail through the rhododendron, purple moor grass, and heather, toward a small stand of mountain ash trees and a few scraggly oaks and hawthorns on the summit of the bluffs. There, by the trees, stood the gray-black, pocked face of a standing stone along the high sea cliff. The stone leaned forward, as if readying itself to leap over the edge. Colin had glimpsed the stone before on his walks; he imagined how it must have looked to some other ancient wanderer walking the Head when the stone was new and the carvings on it not yet blurred by the relentless efforts of wind and rain and time. As Colin moved toward the stand of trees and the stone, stooped over so as not to fall and using his staff to keep his balance, a startled rabbit jumped away as he thrashed along. A few gulls circled in the high wind, diving low over him before descending further toward the sea, and he thought he saw a large crow lift heavily from the branches of the nearest oak before flapping deeper into the stand. The only sounds were those of his own making, along with the faint calls of the gulls and the wind rustling the gorse. It was almost possible to conceive of himself being alone in an ancient world, and he found that thought almost comforting.

He'd spent his first few weeks in Dublin, and while that had been fine and he'd learned more than he'd hoped playing with the musicians in the pubs there, Dublin was a city first and foremost: an urban environment not all that different from Chicago. It hadn't been until he'd left Dublin and come to the west of Ireland that the sense of truly being in a foreign country finally struck him. He'd been in Connemara National Park, standing high on the summit of Diamond Hill and looking westward toward Tully Mountain rising over Ballynakill Harbor. It was then that the gorgeous landscape sprawled out below struck him, a nearly physical blow in the gut that left him gasping momentarily. It was as if some ancestral part of him had risen up from his DNA at the sight, crooning the words "this is your home" inside him.

He'd told himself that it was ridiculous to feel that way, that it was only a bit of unconscious serendipity and he was just indulging himself, but he'd never forgotten that moment. He couldn't. It hit him too often while walking around this part of the country.

Now, he reached the stand of trees atop Cemohar Head and paused for a moment, leaning against the trunk of an oak to catch his breath as he looked down toward the standing stone at the cliff's edge. His glasses were speckled with rain; he wiped them off on his sweater. From this height, he thought that, out toward the sea, he could faintly glimpse the darker shoulders of the islands through the mist, and he wondered.

"No, you ca'nah see Inishcorr from here."

The woman's voice spun him around, the blackthorn staff thumping hard against the trunk of the oak. Maeve was grinning at him, leaning against one of the ashes with a reed basket balanced on her hip, half-filled with green stems and flowers. She wore a long woolen cloak that was dyed a dark, earthy red, and rather than jeans, was wearing a long, loose broomstick skirt. The shoulder of the cloak and her hair were adorned with beads of water from the drizzle: against the midnight of her hair, the droplets shimmered like fleeting jewels. With the sight, too, the crystal in his pocket seemed to pulse with heat, and he plunged a hand into his pocket in alarm, but the stone felt ordinary to his touch, wrapped in its silver prison and chain. "Jesus, Maeve," he said. "You damn near sent me tumbling back down the hill. I thought I was alone up here."

"As did I," she answered. "Seems we were both wrong." She shifted the basket on her hip. "I was gathering herbs. This is one of the few good places left anymore." She turned her head to look back into the shadowed depths of the stand. "So why are yeh here?"

"I don't know," he answered. "It's just . . ." He shrugged under his jacket and pulled down his cap to the rim of his glasses. "This place *feels* right, that's all. I have a sense that here's a little patch of Ireland that hasn't been touched—or maybe it's been touched a lot, if you know what I mean." He nodded toward the standing stone a few yards away.

"I think that I do," she said. "And 'tis interesting that yeh'd put it that way. I feel the same. Yeh've an interesting way of thinking, Colin Doyle; a rather Irish way of thinking, which is unusual in a Yank." She smiled at him. "But good, I think," she finished.

"Thanks," he said. "I think."

"And yeh still owe me that pint, y'know. I haven't forgotten yer promise."

"Well, then let's walk down into Ballemór and I'll buy it for you now."

She shook her head quickly. "Ca'nah. I need to be getting back. But I'll take yeh up on it later, an' that's a promise." She pushed herself away from the tree with a shove of her hip. The basket swayed. She walked past him, closely enough that again he thought he could smell a trace of perfume, or perhaps it was the shampoo she'd used that morning. He imagined himself reaching out to her: *He put his hand on her cloak just at the shoulder, and she turned. Her face was very close to his. "What is it that yer wanting, Colin?" she asked, with a mischievous smile. Her eyes sparkled like true emeralds, beckoning . . .*

But he seemed to be caught in a stasis, unable to speak or act. She was already past him, whistling an air that he vaguely recognized as she walked northward along the stony and heather-clad frozen waves of the summit, away from the stand of trees and away from the standing stone. She stopped as she was about to descend into one of the shallow valleys, fifty yards away. "So," she called back to him, "have they told yeh yet in the village that yeh shouldnah be talkin' to me?"

He didn't answer immediately, and the sound of her laughter trailed back to him, bright in the soughing of the wind. "I make up my own mind as to who I talk to and who I don't," he answered finally, raising his voice to be heard over the distance between them.

"Do yeh now?" she replied. "We'll see about that, won't we?"

She waved once with her free hand, and began walking, the lip of the rise quickly cutting her off from view. That seemed to break Colin's stasis. He followed her: slowly at first, then hurrying a bit to try to catch up with her. When he reached the top of the rise, he looked down, but she wasn't there; it was as if the land had swallowed her up. There was a faint trail at the bottom of the slope that led toward the steep fall down to the Sky Road, and another that led into another stand of wind-twisted trees and tall shrubs—she must have taken one of those.

"Maeve!" he called into the wind.

There was no answer.

Later in the day, Colin descended from the Head and walked back into Ballemór and down to the main part of the town. Entering Regan's, he slid into an empty booth and ordered a pint and a basket of fish and chips. As he waited for the meal, he took out his phone. It was 1:30 in the afternoon here; early morning back in Chicago. He touched the link for his sister Jennifer. He heard the click of the connection, a long hiss of static, and finally a ring. A second ring. A third.

"Hey, Colin," a sleepy voice answered finally. "At least you've learned to call later in the day on a weekend."

He laughed at that. "Long night last night?"

"I'm still not discussing my sex life with you, little brother." He heard a masculine chuckle in the background, the sound of Jen covering the mouthpiece, though not quite successfully. "Quit that," he heard Jen say, her voice muffled. "Save it for later."

"Later, eh?"

"You just be quiet. I can't wait until I can harass you the same way."

"Not much chance of that at the moment, I'm afraid, although . . ." He stopped, and he could almost hear her eyebrows climbing.

"Although. . . ?"

"Don't worry about it. It's nothing. Not for the moment, anyway. Thanks." That last was to the waitress who slid the plate of fish and chips in front of him. On the other side of the phone, he heard sheets rustling, and Jen padding into the kitchen. He heard the beep of the coffeemaker. "So how's Mom? How's Tommy doing with the election? Has he come out publicly yet?"

"Tommy made the announcement last week, and promptly dropped ten points in the latest poll, so his lead has pretty much vanished. Carl says it's temporary, and the polls will rebound over the next few weeks. I think Tommy's just glad it's done and over and he doesn't have to be concerned about it anymore. Mom is Mom, and doing okay, though I know she still misses Dad terribly, like we all do. You'd know that too if you'd call her."

The accusation was broad in Jen's voice. "I will, I promise. Soon."

"Right," Jen answered. He heard coffee being poured and a cautious, loud sip. "And you'll be swimming home, too. Speaking of which, *are* you coming home anytime soon?"

" 'Fraid not. I just got to Ballemór on the west coast and hooked up with one of the bands here. Lots to learn. Figure I'll be here for a while yet. I'm making enough money to get by."

"And your 'although' girl is there, too? There *is* an although girl, I take it?"

He laughed. "Yeah, she's here, but she's still very 'although,' I'm afraid— we haven't gotten past small talk yet, and there seems to be some local social issue I'd have to deal with, too. So how're things with you, Jen? You still liking the academic life?"

He heard the toaster ding on her side, and imagined her taking out a bagel and smearing cream cheese on it. "Getting tenure's a bitch right now, I can tell you that. But you know I have the grant to go to China early next year on a research trip . . ."

He listened to her tell him about the trip as he ate his fish and chips; listening to her enthusiasm and drive reminded him how much he missed his sister and being able to talk face-to-face with her—and, he had to admit grudgingly, he missed the rest of his family as well. Yes, he knew that if he were home, there'd be the inevitable arguments with his mother, a firestorm that would die quickly enough yet leave behind the taste of ash, but . . .

". . . but listen, this is costing you a fortune I know you don't have," Jen was saying on the other end. "We should Skype next time, if you can get a decent Internet connection. It was good to hear from you, Colin."

"Even on Saturday morning?"

She laughed. "Yeah, even then. Listen, stay in touch. And you really should call Mom, too. She'd like that. Tommy, too. And Aunt Patty."

"Yeah, I will. Take care, Jen. Love ya."

"Love you, too, Colin. Bye."

He heard the click and he brought the phone down from his ear. He took off his glasses and rubbed his temples. His favorites screen was still up, and there in the middle was his mother's number. His forefinger hovered over it for a few seconds.

Instead, he clicked off the phone and put it back in his jacket pocket.

15

Petting the Seals

"**L**ET ME KNOW if you come across that O'Neill book, then, will you? I've been looking for an original copy of one of the early editions for a long time, and it'd be terrific if you can dredge one up for me. You have my cell number, or you can just ring up Mrs. Egan on the Sky Road if you come across it and leave a message."

The proprietor of Mullins' Used Books—Colin had no idea if the elderly man to whom he was talking was actually Mr. Mullins or not—waved to Colin in acknowledgment from behind the dusty stacks of books on the front counter and pushed his glasses back up his long nose, a gesture that Colin knew all too well. The bell above the door chimed as Colin stepped out onto the street.

He was in the warren of twisting, narrow streets lined with little shops that bloomed just off the south end of the town's main square. Lucas, after their last gig, had directed him toward Mullins' shop. "I've picked up some old sheet music from him, and if yer looking for something particular, they have lots of contacts," Lucas had said. Frances O'Neill's *Music of Ireland* was a collection of old Irish airs and ballads, the volume itself dating from 1903. Colin hadn't expected to actually find it, especially since it had been originally published in America, but if Mullins could do the legwork and scour the rest of County Galway for him, well, it might be worth the effort.

It was one of those gorgeous days that only the west coast of Ireland could provide: a sky of deep sapphire at the zenith, adorned with white strands of clouds drifting above in the hint of a breeze, the temperature a balmy 60 degrees Fahrenheit. Colin unzipped his jacket and stuffed his woolen cap in his pocket. The locals seemed to regard this as a too-early harbinger of summer—most of them were walking around in shirtsleeves and complaining about the oppressive heat. Colin trudged up the hill of the main square, heading vaguely toward Mrs. Egan's but thinking that he might try tramping out along the Head, given the day.

He saw Maeve coming out from the grocers on the corner, pulling a two-wheeled cart laden with cardboard boxes and paper sacks. She still had on her red cloak despite the heat of the day, though her dark hair was pulled back and tied in a rough pony. "Maeve!" he called, but she'd already stopped, as if she felt his presence behind her. She turned.

"Colin," she said. He couldn't quite decide if she was smiling or not. She was squinting into the sunlight, with a hand shading her eyes.

"Missed you at Regan's over the weekend," he said. "Thought maybe I could buy you that pint. You got time now? I know it's early, but . . ."

She rolled the cart back and forth. "Not at the moment," she said. "I'd like to get this back to the boat, actually."

"Where are you moored? Out along Beach Road?" She nodded. "Mind if I stroll along with you? Thought I'd take a walk out that way anyway, since it's such a nice day."

Her shrug was hardly inviting, and Colin hesitated, wondering if maybe the attraction he'd thought he'd felt between them had faded for her. "Yer certain yeh want to?" she asked.

"Why wouldn't I . . . ?" he began, but realized what she meant before he'd finished the question. No one was precisely staring at the two of them, but the locals were definitely glancing their way, and most of the faces carried sour expressions. An older woman emerged from the grocers where Maeve had just been and—head down—nearly ran into Maeve's cart. She glared at Maeve, who made a gesture with her free hand: first and last fingers out along with the thumb, twisting the hand so it pointed to the ground. The woman literally hissed in response, but her eyes widened and she backed away hurriedly, retreating down the sidewalk in the other direction.

"Did you just give her some kind of hex sign?" Colin asked, almost laughing at the reaction of the woman.

"Nah, but she thinks I did and that's what matters," Maeve answered. "So, yeh still sure yeh want to be seen in public with the witch woman?" she repeated.

"I told you the other day that I make up my own mind about people," he told her.

Her chin lifted and fell in a single, slow nod. "Do yeh really now?" The corners of her mouth twitched as if she wanted to smile, and her eyes glistened in the sunlight. She grabbed the handle of the wire cart and started walking up the street, the wheels of the carts rattling behind her. He fell in alongside. "Is that the way it is with all Yanks?"

"No," he answered. "We generally aren't any better at it than the Irish and are maybe actually worse, from what I've seen. I've been particularly bad at it for most of my life, but I finally realized that I had to stand up for what I wanted, no matter the cost." *And I just wish I'd been able to talk to Dad and get his blessing, no matter how grudging it might have been.* That didn't seem to be something that he should tell Maeve, though. "Call it a family trait," he finished.

She nodded at that. "I'll accept that."

"But I'm curious to know *why* you're getting those looks," Colin continued.

From the side, he could see the muscles of her jaws tighten as she spoke. "Let's just walk," she said, "since yer willing." She said nothing for a time as they strolled slowly up toward the end of the square, then across the street toward the opening of Beach Road, which curved away from the town toward the sea inlet a quarter mile away. Finally, away from the crowds of the town, Maeve sighed.

"We came here five years ago now," she began. "And if yeh've been told that we 'stole' the island, well, to some extent 'tis true. We're not the original people of Inishcorr. We don't own the land, not in any proper or legal way. There was an old village out there once, maybe a dozen houses, but the place was abandoned almost a century ago, when many people were leaving Ireland. The island had nothing but roofless, tumbled shells; now it has real houses with good thatch on 'em. The townies and the government can say whatever they like about us not 'owning' the island, but it's ours. We *made* it ours, and ours 'twill stay."

Her vehemence surprised him; Colin shrugged as he pushed back his glasses. "No worries. That makes sense to me. I understand what you're saying," Colin told her. The sidewalk ended as the road curved hard toward the inlet, and Colin helped her place the cart on the edge of the asphalt roadway. He took the handle from her silently; she glanced at him strangely but made no comment. They could hear waves lapping at rocks and smell the salt wind, but the inlet itself was hidden by trees and the last few houses of the town. "But I don't see how that explains all the antipathy I've heard. Why should anyone in Ballemór even *care* that you're out on the island if it was so long abandoned? You'd think they'd be pleased, since your people are coming into town for supplies and the like." He gestured at the groceries.

"If that were it, maybe yeh'd be right," Maeve answered. "It started when Father Quinlan from St. Joseph's came out to the island, not long after we came. He wanted to see about our attending Mass in the town, or maybe him celebrating Mass out on the island. We told him that we didn't have any interest in him or his church's rituals, or any other church's, for that matter. We believe in the old ways and the old gods of the isle." The road curved left one last time around the last of the houses, and they were walking along the edge of the inlet itself, with only rocks and boulders between them and the water. The wind off the Atlantic, funneled between the hills on either side, discovered them as they made the slight turn, and Colin felt as if the temperature had dropped ten degrees. He zipped up his jacket. "Our attitude didn't sit too well with the priest," Maeve continued. "And—I have to admit—we Oileánach can be rather suspicious of strangers and aren't easy to know." She laughed, suddenly. "Yeh met Niall, after all."

Colin snorted. "Yeah. I met Niall."

"Then yeh know how we can be. The townies don't like us Oileánach because they think we're aloof, strange, and too fond of the old pagan ways—and they're right. We remind them of a time when everyone believed in witches and the fae, when they saw the supernatural everywhere just below the surface of the world around them. Now if anything strange happens around here, we get the blame: when someone's flowerbox withers, when a farmer's cow stops giving milk, when a house burns down, when a babe dies. Trivial or tragic, it's somehow our fault. We scare 'em, when we're the ones who should really be the most frightened."

"I did see you hex that woman back in town." Colin chuckled as he spoke, to let Maeve know that he wasn't serious, but her mouth pressed together in a grimace.

"And when she twists her ankle tomorrow coming down her back stairs, she'll be thinking she knows why."

"'When' she twists her ankle? So you know she's actually going to do that?" Maeve just glanced at him with a serious look; Colin shrugged. "That was a joke," he said. "We Yanks like to make jokes sometimes."

Maeve didn't answer, and they continued walking. He could see a small, one-masted ship just up the road, red sails lashed closed and a mooring line stretched out to a stone pillar. Between the ship and them, Colin saw a pair of gray-black humps on flat rocks a few yards out from the shore. "That your boat?" he asked, and Maeve nodded. "And look," he said to Maeve, pointing at the rocks they were approaching. The seals' heads lifted and turned in their direction as he spoke, as if they were aware of their presence. One of them let out a coughing grunt. "Seals. I haven't seen too many of them this far in."

"Neh, yeh don't," Maeve said. As they came abreast of the animals,

Colin let the wire cart sit upright on the roadway as Maeve walked down toward the water. Colin started to follow her—as he did, he saw both of the seals start to turn as if they were about to leave the rocks for the safety of the deeper water. Maeve held up her hand toward Colin. "Not yet," she said. "Yeh just stay there." She crossed the last of the boulders and stepped onto the narrow, pebbly fringe of a beach. The seals had stopped, watching her. Maeve crouched at the water's edge, one hand dangling in the gray-green wavelets, not seeming to care that the hems of her red cloak and her skirt were in the water. The seals looked at her, then the larger of the two—the bull, Colin assumed—wriggled and slid into the water, swimming toward Maeve. He came out of the water directly in front of her, his snout lifting up her hand. She stroked his wet fur: to Colin's eyes, there was a deep blue hue lurking in the dark fur. The bull crooned, a basso greeting.

Colin laughed. "I've *never* seen anything like that," he called out to her. "What have you been doing, Maeve—feeding them?" Colin slid his legs over the boulders lining the road's edge. At the crunch of his boots on the pebbles, the seal still out on the rocks grunted and rolled backward, splashing into the inlet's water on the far side away from the shore. The bull—if it *was* a bull—glared once at Colin, gave a nostril-flaring huff that sounded strangely like human exasperation, and left Maeve, waddling quickly back into the water. Before Colin could reach Maeve, he was already swimming away. Their heads made twin V-wakes in the water, arrowing toward the open sea.

Maeve was shaking her head. "What about 'stay there' did yeh fail to understand?" She seemed more amused than irritated, though, heaving a dramatic sigh and rising up. The bottoms of her cloak and skirt dripped water on the stones. One eyebrow lifted as she looked at him.

"I'm sorry," Colin said. "That one came right up to you, so I thought maybe they were tame."

She lifted her cloak and shook it so that droplets scattered, and that also brought the scent of her hair to Colin again. He inhaled it deeply. "Nothing that lives and breathes is ever tame," she said. "That's just a myth. Even the most obedient dog might turn and bite its owner one day. At least with a wild animal there's no pretense, no veneer: they do what instinct tells them to do. We all have that wildness within us—humans no less than animals. It's just that we like to pretend that the animal part has been burned out or contained in us." She leaned close to him. Her fingertip touched him at the hollow of his neck and slid downward a few inches before leaving him. "Which is why people are the most dangerous creatures of all," she finished. In her eyes, he could see the warped reflection of his silhouette against in the sky. Her breath was warm against his skin.

"So I shouldn't trust you?"

"Nah," she said. "Yeh really shouldn't, Colin Doyle." What happened then startled him. She rose up on her toes and kissed him: a fleeting touch of soft and gentle lips. He felt her heat all along the front of his body, and it felt strangely familiar to him, and with that sensation, he realized where he'd heard that voice before—that her voice was like that in the dreams he'd had back in Chicago, when his father had died. Strange; he'd nearly forgotten those, but now the memories flooded back, washing over him and then receding again, impossible to grasp even as he tried to hold onto them.

Then she stepped back and the moment was over. She turned, her cloak swirling like blood in water, and she crossed the fringe of beach and stepped over the boulders and back onto the roadway. She took the handle of the cart as Colin stood there, still tasting her on his lips. He didn't seem capable of moving, didn't want to move. "I need to go now, Colin," she told him. "Thanks for the walk, but yeh still owe me that drink."

"Let me help you get the groceries on the boat," Colin called out.

She shook her head. "I'm fine. Niall's there waiting for me."

"Ah, Niall," Colin said. He said the name as if it were a curse. "When will I see you again?"

"Soon," she said. "Do yeh trust me?" He nodded, and she laughed: it was sparkling silver, like the cage that held the emerald jewel in his pocket. "I told yeh that yeh should'nah trust me," she said. "But if yer going to anyway, I'll find yeh. Soon." The wheels of the cart protested as she started to walk toward the boat, but after a few steps, she stopped and looked back at him. "Oh, and that lady in Ballemór. She *will* twist her ankle, I'm afraid. But not because of anything I did."

With that, she waved to Colin and took the cart in hand again. She walked quickly away, her cloak billowing behind her and the cart of groceries squealing its helpless protest. Colin watched her, his own hand raised. He saw someone jump down from the boat as Maeve approached and come up to her—Niall, he thought. They embraced, and Niall lifted the cart onto the boat.

The stasis that surrounded Colin lifted then. He left the beach and clambered over the rocks, and began the slow walk back to Ballemór.

"Right, so now yer having him walk yeh with yer groceries down the bleedin' street. Yeh might as well been holding feckin' hands. What the hell is this, Maeve? He's not worth this, I tell yeh. He's a leamh. Nothin' more. He can't help us. Have yeh seen the cloch? Have yeh even asked him about it?"

Niall waved his arms as Maeve stared blandly at him. His accent, usually fairly thick, had only become more pronounced with his agitation. The *Grainne Ni Mhaille* rocked underneath her, its blood-colored sails cracking sharply in the wind as the ship cut through gray-green chop, heading into the harbor at Inishcorr. Thatched roofs were visible just beyond the small, heather-clad arm of land that sheltered the deep harbor, and the *Grainne Ni Mhaille* canted over as the crew handling the sails adjusted them to tack windward and into the harbor's gentler waves. Maeve steadied herself against the railing; Niall had to crouch to catch his balance on the wet boards of the deck.

"Are yeh done?" she asked Niall. "Because right now I'm not listening to yer prattling."

"Yeh planning to shag him, or have yeh done that already?"

Maeve glared at him, blinking against the salt spray. Her hair was plastered against her forehead. "'Tis not any of yer business a'tall, Niall. Never has been, never will be. I keep tellin' yeh—I will do what I need to do. Are yeh done now?"

"Nah, I'm not. And yeh'll hear more a' it till yeh know the sense I'm making. We have t'ings we have'ta take care of. What're we going to do when the gardai and the NPWS decide to try and throw us off the island by force? What then? How much of our hand do we show?"

"T'ain't yer choice, Niall. 'Tis mine. Alone."

"'Tis yeh that has to do the job, I agree."

"Aye, and I need this Colin for it. I need the bard."

Niall scoffed loudly. "That may be or it may nah. But the decision affects us all, don't it? If yeh make the wrong choice, then everything we've worked so hard to accomplish all falls apart. And I worry, Maeve—if yeh have feelings for this man, actual feelings, then are yeh going to be able to do what needs to be done a'tall? Can yeh answer me that?"

They rounded the head and the boat's swaying calmed. Maeve stood up, holding onto one of the hawsers. "Yeh know me, Niall, and so yeh know I'll do what I need to do for us. Have yeh forgotten everything? And as for feelings . . . well, the boy's a tool that I need. That *we* need. No more. Is that what yeh want to hear?"

"'Tis a tool that yeh must break when yeh use it. So I want to hear the truth as to whether yeh can do that: the person that yeh are now, not what yeh once were."

Maeve laughed. "Well, then, here 'tis: what we're hopin' to do isn't easy, or yeh or some of the others could just do it yerselves, but yeh can't and yeh know it. Yeh need *me* because I'm the only one who can open the path. Not even Fionnbharr can do that. So I ask yeh: what choice do yeh have, Niall? Yeh aren't going to be able to save yerselves, whether 'tis against the gardai or the NPWS or just the leamh out there. *Yeh need me.* So shut yer bleedin' gob, why don't yeh, and let me do what I need to do without asking me stupid questions."

Niall didn't answer—not directly. He strode away from her toward the front of the boat, stripping off his shirt as he went. At the bow, he dropped his pants and kicked off his shoes, standing naked there for a moment. He glanced back at Maeve, then dove into the water. There were three or four seals who had come up to the ship as they rounded the head, swimming alongside the boat; they vanished at Niall's splash. The remaining four of the ship's crew pointedly avoiding looking at Maeve, and none of them spoke or called out after Niall. The *Grainne Ni Mhaille* sliced through the water in an awkward silence. By the time they tossed the hawsers to those waiting at the dock and tied up the red-sailed hooker, twenty minutes later, a bull seal with a blue-black coat had already clambered from the cold water and was sitting on a rock off the shore, staring outward at the water as if standing guard over the island.

Maeve was first off the ship. She passed the seal with her lips pressed tightly together, and strode up toward the village without speaking, ignoring the basso honk the seal sent her way. It wasn't until she was in her own small house with the door safely shut that she allowed the salt tears to come.

"Tell me about the Oileánach," Colin said to Mrs. Egan.

They were sitting at the table in the dining room, with the usual ample breakfast filling a plate in front of Colin. Mrs. Egan sat across from him, with a mug of black tea and a blueberry scone. Colin watched her face as he asked the question, and saw the tightening of the lines of her face as she lifted the mug and sipped. "And why are yeh wanting to know about the Oileánach now?" Mrs. Egan asked.

"I met a few of them at the pub last week, but Lucas didn't seem to like that I was talking to them."

"'Tis a fine young man, that Lucas is. A good head on his shoulders, even if he is a musician," Mrs. Egan remarked, then glanced at Colin. "Meaning no offense to yeh personally, Mr. Doyle, of course."

"None taken," Colin answered, trying not to smile. "Believe me, I understand the sentiment—I've heard it often enough from my parents and family, I'm afraid. But what is it about the Islanders that makes everyone here seem to dislike them?"

Mrs. Egan sniffed as she tore off a bit of the scone and put it in her mouth. "Ah, they've gone too dry, they have," she said. "I'll be needing to make up a new batch." Colin waited. Mrs. Egan swallowed and put her hands around the steaming mug. "The Oileánach stole that island, first of all. 'Twasn't theirs, but they just came and took it, wit'out asking."

"I thought Inishcorr had been abandoned."

"Indeed, it had," Mrs Egan admitted. "But that still doesn't change the fact that those people just stole the place when they had no right to do so." Her voice added an audible sneer to "those people." "They're not *normal* people a'tall, Mr. Doyle. Not normal a'tall."

"What do you mean, Mrs. Egan?"

The woman leaned back in her chair. The cane backing creaked and complained. "Ever since they've come, all manner of odd things have happened. Things that can't be explained. I already told yeh what happened with my poor Darcy." She pointed to his picture on the mantel. Darcy smiled back at them: white-haired and wiry, his eyes surrounded by wrinkles and his thatched farmhouse behind him as a backdrop. "And t'ain't all. People have been seeing creatures that shouldn't be there, the very devil's beasts, I tell yeh: great hounds with glowing eyes and fur like orange fire, fog haunts that wrap around yeh in the mist and suck yer very breath away; and people have tales of seein' the ghosts of their dead loved ones walkin' the roads of a moonlit night, as if those who are buried now are restless in the cold ground. That's the Oileánach's doing. They've stirred up things best forgotten."

Colin couldn't stop his head from shaking, and Mrs. Egan's eyes narrowed.

"Sure, and yeh can scoff at that as yeh like, young man," she said. "But I remember my grandmother saying that in her own grandmother's time, the little people and the good folk were always about, as well as things that one wouldn't want to meet: ghosts and spirits and bewitched creatures. The fey folk would come out of their mounds at night and ride about. There were witches and sorcerers who could take on the appearance of animals, and the night was a time when sane folk stayed inside. Since these Oileánach have come, there are tales that make it seem like those times might be comin' back again with them."

"The Islanders I've met just seem like people to me," Colin told her. "They didn't seem *fey* at all."

Mrs Egan had lifted the mug to take a sip of the tea. She set it down again, hard enough to shiver the cutlery on the table. "Well, fey they are," she said emphatically. "Why, just yesterday Mrs. Brennan was telling me that one of 'em gave her the evil eye down near the greengrocers and hexed her as she was coming out with her sacks, and that evening at home she twisted her ankle something terrible on her back stairs."

"Anyone can twist their ankle," Colin answered, but he remembered Maeve's comment: " . . . *that lady in Ballemór. She* will *twist her ankle.*"

"That may be, and I know it. But I also know what I've seen with my own eyes. When my brother Darcy died, God rest his soul, I was there, and saw everything with my own two eyes, I did. The sky was a'stormin that night, and the spirits, the Old Ones, they came calling for Darcy's soul, howling and shrieking outside. One of the Oileánach, that dark-haired witch woman, she just appeared in Darcy's house like she'd come down the chimney and made herself out of the smoke, and in the meantime the denizens of hell were shaking and tearing at the windows and door, shrieking like mad things. Even the good Father, who I brought out to bless Darcy on his way, was in a desperate state. Then the fiends tore open the door and they rushed inside, and it was only our prayers that saved us then, I tell yeh. I still worry that they took Darcy's soul with them, since he wasn't a believer as I am and hadn't been inside the church in a donkey's years, but the good Father, he tells me not to fret and that the holy water would'a stopped them from taking Darcy away to eternal damnation."

Mrs. Egan picked up her mug again, and Colin saw that her hands were trembling with the memory. "You said there was a storm that night," Colin began skeptically, but Mrs. Egan's eyes over the rim of her mug stopped him from going further.

"I know the difference between a common wind and something unnatural, Mr. Doyle," she told him firmly. " 'Twas no mere gale. It nearly put me heart crossways in me, it did."

"I believe you," Colin said, though frankly a storm combined with whiskey-lubricated imaginations seemed more likely to him—he'd seen Mrs. Egan tipping the bottle in the dining room cabinet of an evening. But the remark seemed to mollify Mrs. Egan, who settled back in her chair once more. She tapped with a fingernail the plate on which her scone sat.

"Yeh should stay away from 'em, Mr. Doyle," she declared firmly. "No good will come of it, and yeh can take my word as pure gospel. Those Oileánach don't come to church, they stay to themselves, and they cause nothing but trouble when they come to town. Yeh just ask the gardai how many fights they'd had to break up because of 'em. They're the devil's spawn, and 'tis true that they can curse people and give the evil eye."

"Mrs. Egan—"

" 'Tis *true*," she insisted. "Yeh don't want to believe that because yer soft on that black-haired beauty that leads 'em—yes, I've heard all about her *and* yeh—but she's just bewitched yeh, Mr. Doyle, so yeh can't see the real face she wears. Well, one day you'll see it in truth, and yeh'll be wishing yeh'd paid more attention to what I'm telling yeh." She pushed her chair away from the table and stood up, wagging a forefinger in Colin's direction. "Yer caught in her charms, Mr. Doyle, but in the end, she means no good to yeh. None of 'em mean any good to any good Christian person."

Her lips pursed together in a moue of disgust, and—mug and plate clattering—she strode off into the kitchen. He heard the china rattle hard in the sink and the water begin to run. Colin decided that further argument would be both useless and counterproductive on his part.

He stared at his breakfast, but his appetite was gone.

16

Learning New Music

COLIN'S CELL PHONE RANG a few afternoons later as he was leaving a practice session with Lucas and his group at Regan's. "Mr. Doyle, this is Joseph Mullins from Mullins' Used Books—yeh asked me t'other day to keep me eye out for that O'Neill book? Well, I've found a copy—an early edition, though not the first printing, from 1903."

Colin caught his breath at the news. "That's fantastic, Mr. Mullins," Colin answered. "I'd really like to see it." He didn't dare ask "How much?" because he was afraid that the answer would deflate the excitement of seeing the book. His checking account was already looking terribly thin in just the month he'd been here. He shouldered the guitar in its gig bag and waved to Lucas as he headed out of the bar. The wind was blustery, and he could hear it in his cell phone's speaker. Even though the morning's weather report had called for a partly cloudy day, it seemed that rain was threatening from off the coast. "I'm just leaving Regan's, as it turns out. Is the book at your store? I could drop down there in a few minutes to take a look."

"'Tis," Mr. Mullins replied. "I'll see yeh in a moment, then."

Mr. Mullins was waiting as Colin stepped into the dark shop, the bell atop the door jingling as he entered. He appeared from the back of the store with a battered book clad in scratched and faded brown leather. He patted the worn cover as he set it on the counter. "Here yeh are, then, Mr. Doyle," he said. "There are cheaper reproductions of the book out there, I know, but I thought yeh'd appreciate the genuine article."

Colin picked up the book, feeling the embossed cover with its Celtic cross patterns around the lettering and the central image of a harp entwined in a tree. The book had seen better days, certainly—the cover's edges were blunted and frayed, and someone had scrawled the name

"Samuel" in pencil across the edges of the yellowed pages. When he opened the book, the smell of musty old paper filled his nostrils; a concentrated burst of the odor that filled the entire shop with its stuffed shelves of old volumes. The paper itself was brittle and fragile, with flyspecks and water stains, but the music was readable. Colin adjusted his glasses and hummed one of the melodies to himself as he traced the staff with a forefinger. "The University of Notre Dame has all the O'Neill books and sheet music in their Rare Books and Special Collections section," he told Mr. Mullins. "I got to examine this one once when I was there; their copy's in much better shape, but this one"—he tapped the book—"this one's been read and used and loved, I can tell."

Mr. Mullins shoved his own glasses up the slope of his long nose. "Don't know about that," he said. " 'Twas in an estate collection that a colleague of mine in Knocknacarra bought. I had him send it over. So, 'tis what yeh wanted?" The proprietor paused; Colin knew what he was waiting for.

He took a breath. "I'd love to have it," he said. "But . . ." He shrugged, feeling the weight of his guitar strapped to his shoulders. He saw Mr. Mullins' gaze go to the covered instrument. "My funds are rather limited. How much are you asking for it, Mr. Mullins?"

The man's mustard-brown teeth bit at his lower lip for a moment. He had a bad case of receding gum lines. "Well, 'tis a rare one, yeh have to admit, and nah easy to find. But 'twas part of the estate bundle, so my friend didn't pay full market rate. Still, he knows what it should go for, and I have to pay his costs and a bit of profit on top . . ." He sighed. "I couldn't let it go for less than €250," he said, "and that's with me making very little, and that's God's very truth. Again, yeh know there are reproductions out there yeh could get for much less—why, Mel Bay has a paperback edition that I could sell yeh for €30. I could have one of those here in a few days . . ."

"I have that one already," Colin answered. "Can't really be a traditional musician without it. I guess I was just hoping . . ."

"Hoping what?" a new, familiar voice intruded. Colin glanced over his shoulder, then turned completely, grinning.

"Maeve!" he said. "I didn't hear you come in."

She smiled back at him. Her long cloak hung open, caught only at the collar. She was wearing a long, plaid skirt and a red blouse with a small raven embroidered on it; a silver chain glistened on the red, with a stone caught in silver wire, much like the one in his pocket. "The two of yeh were talking so intently yeh must not have heard the bell." She stepped up to the counter next to Colin and glanced down at the book. "Yeh buying this?" she asked Colin. " 'Tis a grand book, I'm told."

"You know it? I was hoping to, but I'm afraid it's a little rich for my blood," he said. He glanced at Mr. Mullins, who was not looking at him but scowling at Maeve. "Thanks for letting me see this," he told the man. "I appreciate the effort to find it and you've given me a fair price, I know, but I just can't afford it."

"How much?" Maeve asked Mr. Mullins. She was still smiling, as if she hadn't noticed the proprietor's reaction to her. Colin started to answer, but Mr. Mullins jumped in before he could speak.

"If the lady's interested in the book, the price is €300." He looked at Colin then, and his voice had gone distant. Behind his glasses, his magnified eyes were pale blue, the white laced with pale red lines. "Which would be the same price I'd be charging yeh, Mr. Doyle. I misspoke a moment ago. I forgot for a moment just how much m'friend was charging me."

"I'll take it," Maeve said. "Yeh'll accept a cheque?"

Mr. Mullins' eyes had widened behind the spectacles. His fingers tapped the leather cover of the book on the counter. "A cheque? I don't know that I . . ."

"How much do yeh have on yeh in cash?" Maeve asked Colin before the man could finish, wheeling around to face him.

Startled, Colin patted the wallet in his back pocket as if he could tell from the touch. "Umm, maybe €75, or a little less."

"That'll do. Get it out."

"Maeve—" he started to protest.

"Get it out," she repeated, "before Mr. Mullins here tells us that he's forgotten that he had to pay shipping and the price is actually €350."

The proprietor flushed red with that and started to open his mouth. Maeve raised a hand. "Don't yeh dare say anything," she said. "Yer selling us that book." She reached into an inside pocket of her cloak, producing a small wallet from which she extracted a sheaf of bills. She took the money that Colin had pulled from his wallet, and counted out the currency. "€275," she said as she laid a final note on the pile, holding it down with a forefinger. She stared at Mr. Mullins. "And yeh'll take that, since 'tis more than the €250 yeh were asking from Colin just a minute ago. Yeh won't mind, either. 'Tis a lovely bookstore yeh have here, but books be fragile things. Why, water or fire . . ." She shook her head. "I'd hate for yer precious stock to be damaged, Mr. Mullins, an' there be so many ways that can happen."

Maeve lifted her finger. Colin glanced from her, smiling darkly, to Mr. Mullins, who stared back at Maeve, owl-eyed behind his glasses. Colin thought for a moment that the man might speak, but he only grabbed the money and scuttled away, disappearing into the back room of the store. "There," Maeve said. " 'Tis yer book now. Take it, and we'll go."

"You threatened him, Maeve."

Maeve shook her head. "I di'nah," she answered. "I only told him what a lovely establishment he has, 'tis all. If he heard a threat in that compliment, then 'tis on his own head."

Colin glanced back toward where Mr. Mullins had disappeared. He thought he could hear paper rustling. "Umm, thanks," he said. "I'll consider what you paid as a loan to me. I won't be able to do it all at once or even that soon, but I'll pay you back."

"Aye, yeh will," she answered.

Outside the shop, the sky was still dark and threatening, clouds as gray as slate stretching from horizon to horizon, and Colin tucked the book carefully into the pouch of his gig bag, looking at the sky. The gig bag was now heavy on his back. "I'd better get this to Mrs. Egan's before it rains," he said to Maeve. "Like you told Mr. Mullins, books are fragile things—and so are guitars."

Maeve laughed at that. They were walking along the main street of Ballemór, with Maeve's arm linked in his. Colin thought he could feel the townsfolk occasionally staring at the two of them. Whispers trailed after them like wisps of fog. "It won't rain for a few hours yet," she told him. "Would yeh be interested in a short stroll out along the Head? I feel like walking."

"Ah, so now you can predict the weather?"

"I can," she told him. There seemed to be no irony in her voice at all.

"If it rains and ruins the book, I'm not going to pay you back that money I owe you."

He could feel her shrug on his arm. "'Tis just paper," she said. "It's not paper that I want from yeh, Colin Doyle."

"That sounds ominous."

"Does it now?" She pulled him closer, leaning into him as they walked. He could feel the warmth of her body along his side. "So are yeh as frightened of me as poor Mr. Mullins?"

"I don't think frightened is quite the right word."

"An' what would that right word be?" she asked.

It was his turn to shrug. "I guess I'm more curious. Or maybe 'intrigued' would be a better word." One of the villagers—an older man that Colin remembered seeing in Regan's several nights—had stopped on the sidewalk across the street from them in front of the grocer, his head turning as he watched them. Colin nodded toward him, and the man seemed to

snort and walked into the grocer's. "The way the people here seem to regard you Oileánach; the way you hold yourselves apart . . . I don't understand it, and nobody seems to be able to explain it very well for me."

Maeve's fingers stroked the stone on her necklace, and Colin found
himself wanting to mention his grandfather's journal, and how he had
come across a strange young woman once who had captured his heart, but
some caution held him back, and how there was a stone very like hers in
his pocket now. But that tale hadn't ended well. Instead, he put his hand
in the pocket with grandfather Rory's crystal, cupping it in his palm.

"'Tis very simple," Maeve told him. "People are always afraid of what
they don't understand, and we Oileánach are different. If anything bad
happens, we're the ones who are blamed for it, whether we're actually responsible or not. 'Tis a common thing. From what I've heard of the States,
you should'nah have any trouble understanding that."

They were walking along the Beach Road, with the steep, green slopes
of the Head looming to their right and the sea inlet to the left. There were
seals on the rocks ahead of them again; they slid quietly into the water as
they approached. "Your boat's moored here?" Colin asked.

"Up ahead a bit."

"What were you in town for? It doesn't look like you've been shop—"
Colin stopped, suddenly guilty. "I hope that you paying for the book didn't
mean that you couldn't get whatever you came to town for. If that's the
case, then let's take the book back to Mr. Mullins . . ."

She leaned her head on his shoulder. "No worries," she told him. "Some
of the others are doing the shopping for the island. Not me. I found what
I came for."

"You did?"

"Did."

He didn't want to ask the question, but it seemed to slip from his mouth
before he could stop it. "And what was that?"

"A linen stole," she said, and Colin had to fight to keep the disappointment from showing in his face. "It had such lovely embroidery and
needlework. I saw it in a window the last time in and I decided I had to
have it. I gave the stole to Keara to take back to the boat for me." She
paused; they continued to walk along, the hush of small waves lapping at
the rocks the loudest sound. "I was hoping to see yeh also," she said. "Does
that help?"

She was smiling at him, and he had no idea how to answer that. "You
showed up at just the right time," he told her.

"It's a gift I have," she answered.

"Like twisting someone's ankle?"

She grinned. "Think of what I could do to yer guitar playing if yeh get on me bad side."

He laughed at that. Out in the water, the seals answered. "I guess I'd better stay in your good graces, then." He glanced up at the sky again. The clouds had gotten darker and lower, and the wind was picking up. "Listen, how about we head back to Regan's and I buy you that pint I owe? We can talk there without worrying about getting wet."

She released his arm as she shook her head. "Not right now," she told him. "I'm going to head on to the boat, and yeh should get back to your place. Yeh have about twenty minutes before the rain, so yeh can just about make it."

"If you can be that precise, you *really* missed your calling."

She laughed again, and again he was struck by her amusement, which was so free and enchanting. It made him want to laugh with her, to pull her into an embrace, and . . .

. . . And he *was* in her embrace. She kissed him hard, her mouth opening under his. When she pulled away again, she kept her arms around him, speaking into his ear. "When do yeh play at Regan's again?" she asked.

"Tomorrow night."

She kissed the side of his neck. "I'll be there. Promise. And yeh can buy me that pint then."

With that, she released him, squeezing his hands with her own before striding off down the Beach Road. She waved to him without looking back, her hair lifting in the breeze. "Tomorrow, then!" he called after her, and she waved again. He watched her until she vanished around a curve in the road. The seals out in the water had disappeared with her.

Colin hefted the gig bag on his shoulders, and started back the other way toward Ballemór and Mrs. Egan's.

The first drops of rain began to fall just as he opened the door to her house.

◄ 17 ►

At Regan's

HE WONDERED WHETHER MAEVE had forgotten her promise. When Lucas led the band onto the stage to start the first set, Maeve hadn't yet arrived at Regan's.

Colin went through the first few songs feeling significantly disappointed and out of sorts. He played and sang desultorily, doing what he had to do but forcing the smile he gave Lucas and his fellow bandmates and mostly keeping his head down. The crowds had been growing steadily during his stint with Lucas' group, and it was obvious his performance was off—their applause was thin, and people seemed more interested in drinking than in listening. The rest of the band noticed, too; the group was loose and the rapport they'd established over the last few weeks was missing.

During the third song, he saw Maeve, Niall, Keara, and Aiden enter the pub and slide into one of the booths near the door. Maeve waved to Colin; she was wearing a long, loose skirt over a pair of high boots, a peasant-type white blouse, and her blood-red cloak around her shoulders, though she was taking that off as he watched. He nodded back to her, smiling. Lucas had seen the wave as well; his glance at Colin seemed tinged with either irritation or disappointment, or perhaps both, but Colin could feel the energy return to him, and when he ended the next song, a ballad that showcased his range and ended on a long high note, the audience broke into loud applause and whistling approval.

When Lucas finally announced their break, Colin put the Gibson on its stand as Lucas laid his fiddle in its case and the pub's jukebox kicked on in mid-song, drowning out the conversations around the tables and booths. Bridget and John were already stepping down from the stage and heading to friends' tables. "I t'ought that you knew to be careful with the

Oileánach," Lucas said, grabbing at Colin's arm as he passed, hard enough to turn him.

"C'mon, Lucas," Colin said. He blinked at Lucas through his glasses. "They're no worse than anyone else. And that Maeve, you have to admit she's attractive . . ."

Lucas was shaking his head. "I swear to yeh, Colin, the woman's a literal witch—a damned fine-looking one who looks like she'd be lovely to shag, I'll admit, but still a witch. She's hexed yeh, boyo."

Colin had to suppress a surge of irritation at Lucas' assessment. He glanced down at Lucas' hand on his arm, but the man didn't let go. "You can't believe that."

"Oh, I can," Lucas answered. "And so can lots of others around here. I tell yeh, the lot of 'em are no good and dangerous besides." Colin was still shaking his head, and Lucas released his arm with a gesture of disgust. "I like yeh, Colin. Yer a good person, a damn fine musician and singer, and I know yer the reason most of the seats out there are filled. Yer the best addition to the group we coulda made, and that's why I'm saying this to yeh now. Be careful with those yeh hang about, and keep yer head alert. Both heads, if yeh take me drift. Yer not the first person that one's hexed."

"Oh?" Colin felt his eyes widen slightly with that. "Who else? Was it you?"

But Lucas only shook his head. "Yeh'd best be very careful, 'tis all," he repeated. With that, he waved at someone out in the crowd and left the stage. Colin stepped down himself and gestured toward Maeve, but went first to the bar and ordered two Guinnesses. When the bartender slid the pints over to him, he made his way toward Maeve's booth. She was sitting next to Niall, with Keara and Aiden on the other side. Colin noticed that Keara's and Aiden's hands were intertwined on the table between their pints—they were a couple, then. Niall also had a pint cradled in his hands. Significantly, Maeve did not; Colin set down one of the pints in his hand in front of her. She grinned.

"Yeh remembered. That's sweet." She slid over in the booth to make room for him. His leg, jean-clad, pressed against hers as he sat, though he knew that he was also moving Maeve closer to Niall.

"I always pay my debts," he told her.

Niall snickered at that, as if the comment fulfilled some private joke for him. Colin glanced over to him. "That's funny?" he asked.

"'Tis when yeh don't know what yeh are being asked to pay," Niall retorted.

"Shut it, Niall," Maeve snapped suddenly. "Next time, yeh can stay back on Inishcorr. I can take care of meself." Colin watched the two glare at each other, then Niall looked away with a huff and took a long swallow of his stout. Aiden and Keara glanced at each and began talking as if nothing had happened, discussing a broken line on their boat that they felt needed to be replaced.

"'Tis a little crowded here." Maeve leaned against Colin. Her voice was very soft against the roar of the jukebox. "Why don't we step away for a few minutes for a little privacy?"

"Sounds good," Colin told her. He picked up his pint and slid from the booth; Maeve did the same. As he paused, she walked away from the booth toward the bar area, the skirt billowing out from the fury of her walk. He followed her. He could feel Niall's gaze on his back, as well as that of some of the other patrons. They found a corner of the bar that wasn't too crowded, and Maeve leaned against the wall with her pint. Colin could see her glaring over his shoulder toward the booth where the Oileánach were sitting. "You're not responsible for him," he said.

"Ah, but I am," she half-muttered, then she seemed to shake herself and managed a wan smile at him. "So—is that book yeh bought everything yeh hoped it would be?"

"And more," he told her. "I mean, I have one of the reproductions of the book, and so I knew what was in it, but having this old edition and seeing how some of the pages are creased down, like the person who had it before me was marking their favorite songs, well, it makes me see the whole thing in a different light, and I'm finding myself going back over the tunes in there and somehow playing them differently. Better. It's almost like hearing them again the first time. I suppose the age of the thing is what makes it more attractive to me."

"'Tis a good thing, that," she said. "'Tis one of the problems in the world—no one giving proper attention to the old things. They want to discard them, like they mean nothing, like they were never there before all the rest. Like they're either dead or aren't important anymore, an' neither of those is true."

There was more heat in her voice than Colin expected. He found his eyes widening. "Okay, then," he said. "Yeah, I guess that's true."

She reached out with her free hand for his, her fingers curling into his palm, warm and soft. "Sorry," she said. "It's just . . ." She shook her head, her long, dark hair swaying. "I'm happy to see yeh again. So I'm not going to let anything else bother me. How late yeh playing?"

"Till eleven. Then there may be an open session after closing if other musicians show up." He watched her nod slowly at that. "I wouldn't nec-essarily have to stay for that," he finished.

"But yeh'd want to." She pressed the hand she was holding. "'Tis fine. I understand. Kayla, Aiden, and Niall will be going back to Inishcorr before then. I thought maybe I might take one of the rooms above Regan's here for the night instead." She tilted her head, staring at him. Her emerald eyes held him captive. "Sound good?" she asked. "If the session doesn't go *too* late and yer not too fluthered after." Her smile seemed to harden. "An' if yer not taking all the warnings about the terrible Oileánach too literally. I saw that Lucas talking' to yeh and looking our way."

A small coal seemed to burn low inside him. He pushed his glasses back. He could feel his stomach tightening with a strange pressure—the same feeling he sometimes had when he was auditioning in front of someone, a volatile combination of eagerness and uncertainty. "Are you telling me you don't eat your dead and steal children away in the middle of the night for horrible purposes?"

"Och, we do, but only if absolutely necessary," she answered. She tugged him closer, rising up on her toes to kiss him, a fleeting but promising touch of lips. She stayed pressed against him, their entwined hands placed on the rise of her hip. Then her hands left his, she leaned back against the wall again, and took a sip of the Guinness. She nodded toward the stage. "Looks like Lucas is about ready to start up again."

Lucas had opened his fiddle case, tucked the instrument under his chin, and was beginning to tune up. "Guess so," Colin said. "Let's talk some more after the set."

"Good," she said. She lifted her glass and tapped the rim against his. "I'll have another pint waiting for yeh."

"You just want me to owe you again."

"Ah, I see you've figured out my evil plan," she answered. "G'wan. Sing something good for me. 'Tis a fine, fine voice yeh have."

"I'll do that," he told her. He hesitated, their gazes still locked. Then he lifted his glass in salute and went to the stage.

"What's up first?" he asked Lucas.

The set started off well, from "Behind The Haystack" to "Maid Behind The Bar," then into "Monaghan's Gig." From time to time, Colin snuck glances out into the audience toward the booth where Maeve and her companions sat.

Those frequent glances meant that he witnessed the start of the altercation, though he wasn't quite sure how it all got started. Playing in pubs and bars in both the States and Ireland, Colin had been a spectator for (and the occasional reluctant combatant in) several bar fights. It was only in movies that these were epic battles dragging on for long minutes, with the two fighters careening from one end of the bar to the other or being tossed through windows and out through splintered doors. *Real* fights ended in a minute or less, with one or the other combatant down or the two quickly separated by their friends and other patrons. Such clashes were generally more bluster than actual blows, with insults hurled along with some pushing and shoving. Usually, the companions of one group or the other would separate the eager combatants, or they might—with the ungentle encouragement of the bouncers of the establishment—take the argument outside to be finished one way or another.

That was the usual situation. This wasn't.

A trio of local young men were passing by Maeve's booth on the way to the bar as the band went into "Rocky Road To Dublin" with Colin taking the vocal. Colin assumed one or more of the youths had made some inappropriate remark, as he saw Niall rise in his seat, point a stubby forefinger at one of them, and shout something that Colin couldn't hear over the music.

There were angry shouts in return from the trio; Colin caught the shouted insult ". . . nothing but a skinful of shite!" above Lucas' fiddle solo, and saw Niall heave his pint at the man. Beer and blood flowed as the heavy glassware slammed into the young man's forehead, and Niall came leaping after him in the same motion. "Feckin' leamh!" Colin heard Niall shout.

With the crash of the pint glass on the floor and the shouting, the attention of everyone in Regan's went quickly away from the music to the fight. Niall threw a punch as Aiden struggled to get out of the booth and Maeve and Keara shouted something toward the two of them. One of the trio struck back, a fist landing directly on Niall's nose and knocking him backward. Colin had already stopped playing; Lucas' fiddle solo was severed in midbeat though John's bodhran and Bridget's mandolin staggered on for another bar or two. There was a surging of patrons all around the bar, and a duo of Regan's burly bouncers were already pushing their way toward the uproar. Colin thought he saw the flash of steel in one of the trio's hand, but Niall—with blood smeared across his face and drooling from his nostrils—shoved the man with both hands; the knife went flying from the attacker's hand and he went staggering backward toward the stage, his arms flailing. His feet hit the edge of the stage, and he continued falling, tripping over the edge of the stage and plowing into John on his stool: Colin, next to John, had to leap away holding his guitar to avoid it being smashed, and so he didn't see much of the next few moments as he scrambled away, as Bridget shouted and slid to the back of the stage clutching her mandolin and Lucas glared as if the fight were a direct insult to him.

As Colin tried to escape the chaos on the stage, as he tried to decide where to put his guitar, he also attempted to locate Maeve in the fray. He caught a glimpse of black hair moving toward the knot of combatants. Everything was confusion out in the pub. Colin would have sworn that he heard an animal's raw howl in the midst of the shouting.

"Stop!" Maeve's shout thundered above the noise. A flash erupted from the upraised hand, and three or four bodies went sliding away from Maeve, thrown by some invisible giant's hand as Colin tried to blink away the blinding afterimages. At the same time, the club bouncers hit the mob and starting pushing people away from each other. Colin saw Niall ready to swing at one of the men, and Maeve was there alongside him, grabbing his arm. Colin couldn't hear the word, but he could read it in her lips, her scowl, and the shaking of her head: "*Neh!*" Niall's hand dropped, then one of the bouncers grabbed his shirt from behind, propelling him toward the door.

"Yer out—and yeh bastards had better scatter fast, 'cuz we've called the gardai," the bouncer shouted as the noise level began to drop and the floor started to clear. Aiden and Keara, with Keara supporting a bloody-faced Aiden, were following behind Niall. Maeve was still standing in a strangely clear space, her hair wild and disheveled, beer splashed over the front of her blouse, a bloody, long scratch on her arm. She looked back to Colin and spread her hands wide. "*I'm sorry,*" she mouthed. With that, she grabbed her red cloak from the booth, flung it around her shoulders, and followed after the others.

"All right," Colin heard Lucas say, as if from a distance. "That's over, then. Let's pick up the tune at the fiddle solo. John, yeh okay? Get us going, if yeh would . . ."

As the bodhran began its insistent beat, Colin stared outward. "Colin!" Lucas barked. "Yeh with us or not?"

Colin started, hesitated. Maeve had left; he was certain that after this the Oileánach would be heading back to Inishcorr, Maeve with them. *I'm sorry,* she'd said. So was he. He adjusted his glasses, then grabbed the strap of his Gibson and brought it around. He nodded to Lucas, and began strumming the chords to the song.

He hit the strings viciously, as if they were responsible for ruining this night.

"Miss Gallagher, a moment, if yeh please."

Maeve saw the garda Superintendent Dunn beckon to her. He was standing in the yellow pool of light from the streetlight across from Regan's, with the blue strobe of one of the garda cruisers providing a stormy second illumination. Two uniformed gardai were standing outside the cruiser, hands on truncheons, watching as Keara and Aiden attended to Niall, sitting on the curb. The trio of young men who'd started the ruckus, also ejected from Regan's, walked slowly away down Market Street, with glances and gestures back toward Maeve and the others, still shouting half-heard insults. From inside Regan's, Maeve heard the music start again, Colin's guitar loud in the mix. Maeve took a long, slow breath and went to Dunn.

"Superintendent," she said as she approached. "Things must be slow in the district if they're calling yeh out at night for a little pub brawl and a few bloodied noses."

He smiled—a long, slow amusement. His gaze drifted from Maeve to the cluster around Niall and back again. "We need to talk," he said. "Yeh know how many of the people around here feel about yer people."

"And how do yeh feel yerself, Superintendent? The same as that lot you just let walk away after attacking us, all unprovoked?"

Dunn glanced at the retreating trio. "They had a different story."

"No doubt."

"Would yeh rather I arrested them and had yeh come to court to testify?"

Maeve laughed at that, and Dunn gave a tight-lipped smile. "So," he asked, "when can I expect yeh to vacate Inishcorr?"

"I thought I gave yeh that answer when we last spoke, Superintendent. We're not vacating a'tall."

Dunn gave an audible sigh. In the light of the streetlamps and storefronts, his face looked tired. "Miss Gallagher, the fact is that I'm getting pressure from above that I ca'nah ignore much longer. I've stalled for months now, hoping that the issue of Inishcorr might get lost in the NPWS bureaucracy, but it hasn't—I suspect because of contact from the Ballemór council. They don't like yeh much, but then yeh already know that." He nodded toward Niall and the others. "T'ings like this tend not to help yer cause."

"'Twas nothin' we started," Maeve said.

Dunn nodded. "Isn't it just? An' I believe yeh, though yeh just being here seems to start things—like yeh being on Inishcorr. I wanted to tell yeh; I ca'nah ignore the warrants yeh've been given much longer. I'll have to take action, and I do'nah want to do that."

"Then do'nah," Maeve told him. "We're not leaving, Superintendent. That's final."

She saw his shoulders sag, and his face did the same with near-sadness. "I wish yeh'd change yer mind, Miss Gallagher. It's nah trouble I'm wanting, and I wish none of yeh any harm."

"Neither do we," she told him. "We just want to be left alone."

"Unfortunately, that's nah going to be possible." He heaved another sigh and inclined his head toward Niall. "D'yeh need that one to go to the clinic? I can have him taken there."

Aiden and Keara had lifted Niall to his feet; he was shaking their hands away, almost angrily. Maeve shook her head. "Nah. 'Tis mostly his pride that's hurt, and we take care of our own."

A nod. "I'll wish you a good night then, and safe travel back to yer island. I hope yeh think about what I said. When I come out there next—and I *will* be coming out very soon—I'd like to see the island empty."

"Tell me when yer coming, and I'll make certain we have dinner waiting for yeh," Maeve answered.

With that, the Superintendent gave a final exhalation and moved away from the streetlamp. One of the garda opened the passenger door of the cruiser for him. A few moments later, the cruiser turned off its light bar and pulled away from the curb. Dunn's face swiveled to watch Maeve and the others as the car passed them.

◄ 18 ►

The Fairies' Lamentation

THERE WAS NO INTERNET CONNECTION at Mrs. Egan's B&B. *"I do'nah have interest in wasting me life in front of a computer screen, and neither should yeh,"* she'd said when Colin had inquired about that, back when he'd first arrived. *"Yeh should be out looking at the real Ireland all around yeh, not at pictures of God knows what from these Internets of yers. 'Tis the real world yeh should be paying' attention to, Mr. Doyle."*

The best wireless signal that Colin could tap into was the Ballemór library's network. It was Sunday and the library was closed, but in any case, the library staff frowned on people holding conversations inside the building. Colin had discovered a week earlier that if he sat on the stone bench just outside the southwest corner of the building, he could snag a strong enough signal and just enough bandwidth to use Skype. He took a seat on the bench, glancing up at the library as he did so—a raven was staring back down at him from the gutter well above him. He kicked up Skype, saw that Jennifer was logged in, and called her. After a few rings, his sister's face suddenly appeared in the screen window: brown hair touched with red highlights, cropped short and frothy; full lips on a wide mouth, adorned with a red that was a little too bright for Colin's taste; blue-green eyes that crinkled at the corners whenever she smiled—the "Doyle family eyes" that both of them shared with their father, though Tommy had his mother's dark, rounder eyes. "Hey," she said. "How's my little brother?"

"He's fine at the moment, but getting hungry for dinner," Colin answered. "It's late afternoon here. Look, here's Ballemór town center . . ." He swung the laptop around, letting the camera capture the scene. As he did so, the raven cawed and flew away above him.

"It's not raining," he heard Jennifer say. "Thought you were supposed to be in Ireland."

"Hah," he answered. "Anyway, it rained earlier this morning, and I'm sure it'll rain tonight yet. Hopefully not before I get the laptop back to my place, though." He settled the laptop on his knees again, adjusting the screen so that his face was centered in the camera view. Jennifer grinned back at him—he saw the kitchen of her apartment in the background and Finnigan, the orange-and-white cat, prowling along the edge of the counter. "So how's Aaron? You two set a date yet?"

"We're not there yet, but things have been good." He saw a grin slide over her face. "I'm not ruling that out someday. And what about you? How's your 'although' girl?"

Colin returned the grin. "Maeve? Still in the 'although' stage, but there's hope." After the debacle at Regan's the previous night, though, he wondered when he'd see her again.

"'Maeve,' eh? What's her last name?"

"Umm . . ." Colin glanced away, as if the answer were written somewhere farther down the square. He seemed to remember her telling him, the first time they met, but he couldn't conjure up the name in his memory. "Uh, C-something or other, I think."

"C-something or other," Jen repeated. Her eyebrows climbed her forehead once more. She clasped her hands mockingly to her breast. "That's so touching, Colin. So romantic. I'm sure Mom would be happy to know that you really get to know someone first before you commit."

"I haven't committed anything yet, I'll have you know. We're just . . . friends at the moment." *But if that damned Niall hadn't ruined things last night . . .*

"You're such good friends that you still don't remember her last name. I know *my* boyfriend's last name." Jen took a long breath. Her image stuttered, and he thought he was going to lose the connection. "When's the last time you called Mom? She asked about you just last night." Her static-laden face froze, then moved belatedly with the words.

It was Colin's turn to sigh now. He shook his head. "I haven't called her in a bit. I just haven't—"

The image settled once more. "Uh-uh. Don't say you haven't had time, Colin," Jen interrupted. "We both know better. You're a musician; you don't have anything to do but practice during the day. You could take ten minutes out of your day to call her."

"If it were just ten minutes, I might," he answered. "But it would be thirty seconds of hellos followed by twenty minutes of lecture on how I'm wasting my life and should be back home doing something productive and useful, like helping Tommy."

"Call her, Colin. She's your mother, she loves you, and she isn't going to be around forever. We both know that, now more than ever." Jen's words struck him like a hammer blow. Colin remembered his father, remembered those last days with him and the funeral. When Jen spoke again, her voice trembled, and he knew she'd been affected in the same way. "Look, just do it."

"You know, you can sound awfully like Mom sometimes. I pity your and Mr. Goldman's eventual children."

Jennifer sniffed. "And *you* have Dad's idiotic stubbornness, and so I pity your and Ms. C-Something's offspring, too. Call Mom."

Colin started to retort, then realized that someone was standing next to him. He glanced up to see Maeve. He wondered how long she'd been there. He grinned helplessly up at her. "Hey, Maeve! I was hoping I'd see you."

"Yeh always have conversations with yer computer screen on the sidewalk?" she asked him.

"I'm talking to my sister," he said. He shifted the laptop so that Maeve could see—and so that the camera saw Maeve. "Jennifer, this is Maeve."

"Oh, hi!" he heard Jennifer say. "I'm Jennifer Doyle, Colin's sister. I didn't catch your last name. . . ?"

"Gallagher. And it's good to meet you, even through a computer. Yeh have his eyes—or himself has yers."

"Good to meet you, too, and I love your accent. Gallagher . . . That's a nice name. Starts with a 'G,' doesn't it?" Jennifer laughed then. "I'm sorry, Maeve—you can make Colin explain why that's so funny. It was good meeting you: virtually, anyway. Colin's mentioned you a few times now. Be kind to my brother—he's a lovely, gentle, and talented person, even if he's not exactly the sharpest tool in the shed. He's somehow managed to keep his naiveté despite his age. Don't take advantage of that."

"Jen—" Colin said warningly.

She laughed. "Okay, okay. I need to leave you two anyway; I have to be off for an appointment. Colin, don't forget what I said: *call her*."

Colin turned the screen back to him. "I'm calling *you* at 6:00 in the morning next time. On a Saturday. Unless you'll be at temple then."

Jennifer stuck out her tongue at Colin and laughed again. "Hey, someone has to help you with these things," she said. "At least I have a name to give Mom when she asks. Maeve, I don't know what you see in him, but please be good to him; he's the only little brother I have and I love him dearly." Her hand waved in front of the screen. "Call me soon," she said, and the window collapsed as she cut the connection.

Colin closed the laptop.

"Starts with a G?" Maeve asked.

"It's a long story," Colin answered; then, as Maeve continued to look at him: "It was a private joke, and it's not that funny anyway. Trust me."

"Hmm." Maeve didn't seem entirely convinced, but she shrugged as Colin packed up the laptop, slid it back into its case, and stood up. "I came looking for yeh," she told him.

"And how did you know to come here?" he asked her.

She didn't answer. Instead, she nodded her head westward. "I wondered if yeh'd want to come out to Inishcorr and see the place, especially after everything fell apart for us last night. Yeh could stay overnight, since we wouldn't get there until late. That is, if yer not playing tonight, because I don't think that it'd be a good idea for me or the others to come back in Regan's any time soon."

"Probably not," he agreed. "But it's Sunday, so no, I'm not playing," he told her. "And I'd love to see the island." *And you.* He could feel the anticipatory stirring in the pit of his stomach again. "I'd have to cancel a practice and pack a couple things . . ."

"Ah. If it's too much trouble for yeh . . ."

"No, no," Colin hurried to say. "It's no problem at all. I just have to get hold of Lucas and let him know I won't make practice, and if it's an overnight stay, I need to get a few things together."

"G'wan," she told him. "I've some shopping to do in town anyway. Meet me back here in two hours; the boat's moored up in the usual place on Beach Road, and yeh can help me carry the supplies. Bring yer guitar, too—yeh can play a few of those songs in the book, and do some singing for those who haven't heard yeh yet." With that, she leaned forward toward him. The kiss lingered. He closed his eyes, losing himself in the moment, and only opening them again when he felt the warmth of her lips leave his. There was almost a sadness in her eyes when he saw them, regarding him steadily, then she blinked and the moment was gone. "Two hours," she said, "or Niall will happily sail without yeh."

"How *is* Niall?" Colin asked.

"Wait till yeh see his face. Looks like a horse stepped on it." She shook her head into Colin's helpless smile, as if amused by it. "Two hours," she repeated.

"I'll be here," he told her.

Niall said nothing to him during the entire trip, though Colin noticed that both his eyes were slitted under purpling bruises, his nose was swollen, and his voice, when he called out orders to the crew of the Galway hooker, was distinctly nasal. As the *Grainne Ni Mhaille* docked at Inishcorr's small quay, Colin didn't even see Niall, who seemed to have entirely vanished.

Some of the islanders glanced at him as he and Maeve walked onto the pier to which they were moored. He had a backpack stuffed with clothing and toiletries, and a guitar—his Seagull rather than the more expensive Gibson—was slung over one arm in a gig bag.

His grandfather Rory's crystal was around his neck, though hidden under his sweater. Somehow, that felt right.

A seal stood on a rock near pilings crusted with black barnacles, the waves lapping against the rock and splashing the creature's smooth, glistening, blue-black fur. The seal snorted in their direction, its head swiveling as they walked past. The islanders, for their part, stared for a moment then nodded—mostly to Maeve, he noticed—before moving on about their business. He recognized Keara, the young woman who'd been with Maeve in Regan's. The others were all strangers. Keara came up to Maeve as they came to the end of the pier. She nodded to Colin, and handed Maeve a paper. Colin caught a glimpse of a gold-trimmed official-looking letterhead. Maeve scanned the paper, grunted, then crumpled it as she handed it back to Keara. "We ignore it," she said to Keara. "There's still time."

Colin heard a splash behind them: the seal had slid from the rock into green-gray waves; he could see its dark head for a moment near the end of the quay before it dove underneath the water with a nearly silent flick of its tail.

"Ignore what?" Colin asked Maeve as Keara walked away. He wiped his glasses—spattered with salt spray from the trip over—on his shirt and settled them on his face again.

"Nothing," Maeve told him. "Come on, let me show you around . . ."

Stepping onto Inishcorr was stepping backward a century into Ireland's past.

The "village" was a cluster of shops and houses near the pier in the island's small bay. On the shore a few currachs were beached with their hulls up. Several storefronts lined the area back from the water, but few of the shops seemed to be occupied—those that were seemed to be necessary for the upkeep of the community: a fishmonger, a smithy, a small dry goods store, a leather-worker, a carpenter, a small pub.

All were the type of shops that might have existed in Ireland for centuries. Nothing new; nothing modern.

Colin saw few signs of modernity in the port area. A trio of diesel oil drums near the wharf seemed to be the only concession that motors existed. There weren't any cars in the few slots along the unpaved street, though there were three bicycles leaning unchained against a post near the head of the quay, and another near the carpenter's shop. There'd been an attempt to cobble the narrow street in front of the storefront, though the cobbles were rough and uneven, with scattered pools of dark water. The ghosts of muddy footprints marked the passage of the islanders over the cobbles, while not a hundred strides to Colin's right, the cobblestones gave way to bare, rutted dirt, with weeds and grass growing unbothered in the high center, the narrow lane hemmed in by waist-high drystone walls and winding away into grassy pastureland in which sheep wandered. There was no traffic visible anywhere; it seemed that if you wanted to go somewhere on the island, you were expected to either walk or bike.

The place even smelled old: Colin could nearly taste the distinct scent of burning peat, mingling with the salt wind from the sea, the earthy smell of mud and turf and wet stone, and an underlying whiff of old, rotting fish here by the shore.

"So what do yeh think?" Maeve asked as they reached the shore. "T'ain't much, but 'tis ours. Yeh should have seen it when we came—the houses all empty shells going back to earth. The island had been deserted since the 1930s when the last family left."

"If there was no one here, why is everyone back in Ballemór so upset that your group took it over?"

"They'll tell yeh that it's all about the legality," Maeve answered. "'Tis not the truth, though." She took his hand and smiled at him.

"What's the truth? I've seen the way the locals look at all of you. Mrs. Egan thinks you—well, 'you' in the general sense of the Oileánach—are responsible for all sorts of strange goings-on in the Ballemór area."

"Does she now?" Maeve's smile widened. "Let's do some traipsing," she said, taking his hand. She led him away from the harbor and the village, following the dirt path between the stone walls, which looked like it had been laid out by a wandering sheep. The fields were being actively worked; Colin saw more sheep and a few cows grazing, and there were crops planted in the tiny fields, all of them marked off with stone walls. Around a one-room farmhouse just off the path on a small hill, he could see chickens scratching at the bare dirt. Peat smoke drifted from the chimney of the farmhouse, and someone waved at them from the doorway. Maeve waved back and they continued on, her skirt billowing in the wind, her hair tousled, the red woolen sweater she wore over her blouse half-buttoned. To Colin, she looked like a figure from an old painting. *Woman Walking in the Country.*

"I feel like I've dropped back a century. Maybe two or more," Colin commented as the lane led them around a curve and a small stand of trees. They couldn't see the village anymore, though out past the fields were the gray waves of the island channel, and beyond that, the green, steep slopes of Ceomhar Head, hazed blue with distance. Dark, fast clouds were playing with the sun, shafts of bright light sweeping over the landscape only to vanish in shadow again.

"Yeh have, in a way," Maeve answered. She was still holding his hand, swinging their clasped fingers between them as they walked. "We keep to the old ways here. At least, mostly." He saw her look at the direction of his gaze, then glance that way herself. "The west of Ireland never was tamed as much as the east. 'Tis still that way. Here in the western counties, there remain pockets of strange places where the Old Ones might still walk."

"Like this island?" he asked.

She shrugged and laughed. "Maybe. Keep yer eyes open; who knows what yeh might see."

"To listen to Mrs. Egan talk, you'd think the sidhe were hiding in every corner of the town and behind every tree on the Head." He laughed. "You should hear her talk about the day her brother Darcy died."

"Maybe she's right," Maeve said, and when Colin laughed, she let go of his hand, though she continued to walk along the rutted lane. "Yeh know, there are two tales about how Inishcorr came to be abandoned," she said. "The first is the one the mainlanders would tell yeh, about how the economy failed and most of the people here just moved away to better places. That's a plain tale and boring, but believable."

"And the second?"

"That's the one yeh likely wouldn't believe."

"Try me."

"I will at that," she answered. She jogged a little farther up the lane, then swung around to him. "Come on, laggard. There's something I want to show yeh, then."

She took his hand again as he caught up to her, and began talking.

The first family that came out here was the Coffeys. They were Catholics, though John Coffey was also someone who kept one foot in the church and the other set on older, pagan paths. It was John Coffey who led his family to Inishcorr to settle the place in 1846. The family was originally from County Roscommon, where *an Gorta Mór*, the Great Famine, hit hardest of all. John Coffey's parents were poor Irish, and they'd fallen first to the famine. But John had heard the blight that was killing the potatoes wasn't affecting the west as much yet, and they had cousins near Ballemór, so John took his wife and five children west, to the Connemara region.

The Ballemór relations weren't particularly happy to have John show up with his family in tow. But it was through them that John was told that he might be permitted to settle his family on Inishcorr, since the British lord who actually held title to the island never came this far west nor did he care about the place, and so John did exactly that. He thought they could establish a viable farm on the small, deserted island and raise sheep and cattle, maybe do some fishing as well, and being on an island maybe the blight wouldn't ever reach the potatoes in their lazybeds. They could be self-sufficient there, John declared, and his family believed him. He wrote to his two younger brothers and his sister—all of them married and with their own families back in Roscommon—and they all came west as well.

For a time, everything was good here. Certainly life was hard for them, as hard as it was for any poor family in Ireland at the time, but the Coffeys did indeed manage to scrape a living from the stony soil of Inishcorr, and between their fields and the bounty of the sea, they managed to have enough to feed their growing families. The sons and daughters of the Coffey family left the island when they were old enough, but some few stayed behind, and some of those who left returned again with new wives or husbands to add to the settlement. The cluster of houses became a true village, and they were doing well enough to trade and barter with those on the mainland. Inishcorr was flourishing as well as it could.

The highest point on Inishcorr was a large earthen mound on the western side of the island, where the wind sliced in unfettered from off the gray, stormy North Atlantic. A withered, bedraggled hawthorn tree stood near the mound's summit, and a strange ring of dark stones surrounded the hillock. John Coffey had found the place when he'd first come to Inishcorr, and he'd forbade anyone to wander there or to disturb the mound or stones because of what he'd claimed to have seen there on dark Inishcorr nights. He told the Inishcorr families that when he'd first come to the island, he could *feel* the presence of the sidhe in and around the ring of stones and the mound behind them, and sailors who had passed that way in the dark or during storms talked of strange lights and sounds around the hill, and said that the *sluagh sídhe*, the fairy host, sometimes whirled madly from the mound, even coming over the channel to Ceomhar Head and the mainland.

"Yeh don't be diggin' there or knockin' o'er the stones, y'hear?" he'd told his own children and all the rest. "That place is na' for us, but for the *aos sí*: the fey folk, the people of the mounds. 'Tis their place, not ours. I've talked to Fionnbharr, the king of the fey ones, here on this very spot, an' a bargain we made, him and meself. They will let us be, if we do the same to them. So yeh best leave them well alone, for alla our sakes."

During his lifetime, everyone heeded John Coffey's words, but John died in 1900 at age 82, and those on Inishcorr began to forget his admonitions and warnings. In 1911, one of John's grandsons—Padraig Coffey—decided that the hawthorn tree looked already half dead and he needed some fuel for his fireplace anyway and it was too far to the mainland for him to go and dig peat, since there wasn't a proper bog on the island. Wood would work just as well.

Padraig said afterward that the first blow of his ax sent what felt like an electrical shock all up his arms, and he had to let go of the ax with the head still embedded in the trunk. A superstitious man, Padraig said he thought he heard laughter as he stood there shaking the tingling from his fingers, and he ran off. That night, in the tavern down in the village, he told his tale to several of the Coffeys and their relations; with the courage of whiskey circulating in their bodies, Padraig and several of the Coffey men went off to the mound where they pushed down the ring of stones, singing and laughing. That's when they saw someone standing near the hawthorn at the top of the mound. One by one, the men went silent as the figure glared at them, his eyes glowing under the cowl over his head, and the heat of the whiskey went cold in their stomachs. The apparition was tall and fair-skinned, a sword girt at his side on a golden chain, and another fine, heavy chain with gilded links draped over his shoulders. He wore a fur cloak and underneath it, silver chainmail studded with jewels glittered in the moonlight.

"I am Fionnbharr, an' yeh have broken the promise that was made to me," the figure rumbled, his voice as deep and dark as the rumble of a storm. "Now yeh will pay the price. A curse on yer family and yer land. Yeh will nah stay here long. Yer families will be scattered and broken for what yeh've done here this night."

And with that pronouncement, there was a flash of light from the cloudless sky and when the sparks had faded from their eyes, the man was gone. Padraig and his crowd fled back to the tavern, where they drowned their fear in yet more drams and pints, and let the tale grow more with each retelling until it was said that the entire fey horde had erupted from the mounds and chased them back every step of the way, howling and screaming.

But in the cold light of day, they could begin to laugh at the night's doing, and started to believe that it was only a dream. That is, until over the next several months the milk cows stopped giving, the lambs began to die, and the women of the island delivered stillborn sons and daughters while the crops withered and rotted in the ground. One by one, the Coffeys and their relations left Inishcorr, none of them saying aloud that it was the curse that drove them off, but all of them knowing. By the time the Irish Republic declared its independence from Great Britain in 1922, there were only a few left on the island, Padraig Coffey among them. By the mid-1930s, even the aging and penitent Padraig had left, and the island was entirely deserted once again . . . or so those back in Ballemór said.

It remained that way, the rumor of its haunting keeping any other would-be settlers from the land, until we finally came to claim it for ourselves . . .

19

Come to the Dance

"**S**O YOU'RE TELLING ME that Inishcorr was abandoned because of a sidhe curse?"

Maeve shrugged as they walked along the lane; they were on the seaward, higher side of the island now, the Atlantic waves tearing at the tumbled rocks of a tall cliff a few yards away to the right. Inishcorr was tilted like a plate in the water. Looking to the east, they could see much of the small island laid out below them, and beyond that, the strip of sea between them and the steep landscape of the Connemara headlands, blue in the haze. The air was laden with the smell of brine, and sprays of white occasionally lifted above the cliff edge. The sound of the surf was a low rhythmic grumble.

She had heard the disbelief bordering on scorn in his voice, and it tore at her. *Maybe yeh've made the wrong choice. Maybe Niall's right about him after all . . .* She shook away the skepticism, tugging her sweater tighter around her, hugging herself as they walked. "I'm telling yeh what some have said, and what I've heard. Yeh can believe whatever yeh like."

"Are you familiar with the concept of Occam's Razor?" Colin asked, and Maeve felt heat rising to her face.

"And now yer going to explain it to me because no uneducated Irish lass would know such sophisticated principles, eh?"

She was pleased to see his cheeks color immediately as he stopped walking. "No," he said quickly. His hands spread wide in apology. Near them, a wave crashed into the shore, sending spray high behind him. "Not at all. I wasn't implying that. I just—"

"Yer saying there's no reason to complicate an explanation with fecking leprechauns," she interrupted. "Yer saying that yeh should be thinking 'tis much more likely that the land here just could'nah sustain the Coffey clan rather than that they were chased away by the fey folk."

"Ah, c'mon, Maeve," Colin said. He was trying to laugh, to make it a joke. "You have to admit that's more likely."

She stared at him. "'Tis what I have to admit, is it?"

She started walking again. The lane veered away from the sea and began a slow, meandering descent, leaving a large swath of land between them and the cliffs. Maeve pointed. "Look. There yeh can see the very mound with its ring of stones, and on top, the hawthorn."

The sight still made her heart thrill, as it had since they'd come here. Against the sky, the mound and the tree made their silhouette. The standing stones were the height of a man, the rock darker and smoother than any on the island, brought here, she knew, from a sacred quarry in the Connemara hills barely visible on the horizon. Musical stones these were, though few knew or remembered that now; if you struck them in just the right place with a hammerstone, they would sound a pure note, like someone had struck a bell or gong. The stones leaned in the ground in a rough circle around the base of the mound.

"Those stones are still standing upright," Colin commented. "I thought you said Padraig and his crew pushed them over."

More disbelief . . . "An' they put them back up again as well, a few years later, trying to placate the ones who had cursed them. It did'nah work. Leave your pack and guitar here for the moment—there's no one here to bother them. Come on, climb with me, and . . . well, please try to *feel* this place."

She took his hand again when he shed the pack and gig bag. She led them through a small gate in the drystone fence and out to the field with the mound and stones. She felt Colin shiver involuntarily as they passed between two of the stones and started up the slope toward the summit of the mound, and she allowed herself a small smile at the realization. *Yeh see, Niall; he feels it. He does* . . . Underneath their feet, the high grass was dotted with red clover, dog violets, and St. John's Wort. The hawthorn tree was storm-battered and weary; it leaned heavily to the east, as if the sea winds had forced it that way over the centuries of its life, but the life within it was tenacious, unrelenting, and strong. The feel of the tree's stubborn energy surrounded the mound, as solid as the ring of stones.

The climb up the mound wasn't strenuous: the mound was less than a hundred feet high and the slope was gentle. Still, when they stood at the top under the spread of the low hawthorn canopy, they could see the open sea thrashing against the rocks of the shore a few hundred yards from the encircling stones on that side down a steep cliff, and they were high enough that the roofs of the village and the small harbor were visible—in their walk, they'd already nearly circled the island back to the village. "Look here, will yeh," Maeve said. She touched the trunk of the hawthorn near where they stood. A rusty axhead stuck there, bark growing black around it as if to seal up the wound, the handle rotted away but for a few lingering fragments.

She saw Colin's eyes widen as he realized what it was. He ran his fingers along the edge, the rust staining his fingertips. She could nearly hear his thoughts. "Someone took a chop at the tree. That's certain," he said.

"But?" she prodded.

"But that doesn't prove anything except that someone once took a swing at the tree. The rest of the story . . ." She heard his breath shudder with a deep inhale. He looked at the tree and the blade, not at her. "Maeve, I was raised Catholic, but I don't practice that faith anymore—which, believe me, has caused me no end of trouble with my family. I stopped believing in gods, religions, and mythologies all the way back in high school." Now he looked at her, and she wasn't sure what she saw in his face. "I stopped believing in fairy tales long before that," he added.

"I'm not asking yeh to have faith in yer Holy Trinity again, Colin. I'm actually not asking yeh to believe in *anything* unless yeh want to. I'll let yeh make up yer own mind when it comes to it. I promise."

"Make up my own mind about what?"

She only smiled at that. "Yer daiddeó, your grandfather, did yeh learn nothing from him about belief?"

"I don't know what you mean," he answered, but she saw his hand touch his sweater as he spoke, and she saw the outline of something underneath the wool. She felt it then: with his touch, the cloch's energy flared up, so strong that she nearly gasped with it. She wanted nothing more than to snatch it from him, to hold it again herself, to use it to open up a window into that other world, the Talamh an Ghlas, where she could have once gone herself.

But she could not. *For this to work, he must use the cloch on his own. Freely. As his daiddeó might have, had he not fled from me.* So instead, she smiled at him, and touched the arm of that hand so she could feel the tingling of the power through him. She leaned against him.

"'Tis cold here," she said, "and warmer in my house."

Maeve's house was nearest to the mound of any in the village—a four-room, thatch-roofed cottage with freshly whitewashed stone walls. She led him there as the sun was easing down below the Atlantic horizon. Keara was inside, setting food on a dining table in the front room. Colin seemed startled to see her, and even more puzzled when Keara gave a curtsy to Maeve as she entered. Maeve stopped her and brought her up again with a slight shake of her head as Colin stared. Maeve glanced over the table as Colin set down his backpack and guitar, leaning them against the wall near the door.

"This all looks lovely, Keara," Maeve said. "Thank you so much."

"'Tis my pleasure," Keara answered, and Maeve was pleased that Keara remembered not to use her title. "Would yeh like me to serve?"

"No, but thanks. We'll be fine. G'wan back to the village; we'll join yeh later at the tavern. I'm sure Colin will be interested in the music and hearing yeh play."

"I'll let the others know," Keara answered. She started to curtsy again, then stopped herself, glanced at Colin with a hint of a knowing smile. "I'll be leaving, then. Enjoy the evening, both of yeh. I'll just get my things from the kitchen and let meself out." Keara went into the kitchen. Maeve could hear the quick clatter of metal and the rustling of cloth, and a moment later a door opened and closed at the back of the cottage. Maeve saw Colin watching Keara from the small window at the front of the house, as she strode toward the lane leading into the village, a basket under her arm and her cloak billowing in the wind.

"Yeh'll be making me jealous, staring at Keara like that," Maeve said to Colin's back, amused. He turned. "Though she is very attractive," she added. "But already spoken for."

"No, it wasn't that," Colin said, hurriedly. He turned back to Maeve, habitually pushing his glasses back up his nose. She smiled at the unthinking gesture, so much a part of him. "You're much more . . ." he started to say, then the words trailed off. She could see his face flushing even in the dimness of the cottage. "How is it that you have someone fixing dinner for us and offering to serve? I thought Keara was going to call you 'm'Lady' or something at one point."

So he could hear it without it being said. "I asked her if she'd mind doing it, 'tis all. Wouldn't yer sister Jennifer do the same for yeh?" As Maeve spoke, she went to the desk against one wall and plucked a wax taper from a glass, lighting the wick from the kerosene lantern there. She cupped the flame in one hand as she went to the table and lit the candles Keara had set on the tablecloth. Colin watched her, and she knew he had noticed that there was no electricity in the cottage at all.

"Jen *might* do that," he admitted, "but you can bet I'd hear about it—and there wouldn't be any curtsying and I can flat-out guarantee she wouldn't be offering to wait on us at our table. So is Keara *your* sister?"

Maeve blew out the taper and gently shook her head as the wisps of smoke curled away. "We're very close, but she's nah my sister." She didn't elucidate any further, only gestured toward the table. "Let's talk while we're eating. I'd hate to have Keara's hard work going cold." She sat at the table herself, watching as Colin took the seat across from her. She passed him plates. Keara had outdone herself: the bread was fresh-baked and hot, and the potatoes were soft and steamed with white clouds when opened. The fresh-churned butter melted into a golden puddle on the potatoes. The lamb was done to a medium-rare perfection with the juices still slightly bloody, and the meat seemed to simply dissolve on the tongue. The red wine was dry and deliciously tart, leaving the palate with a splash of undertones.

"This is fantastic," Colin managed around bites; she watched him stab another slice of the lamb with his fork. "I haven't had a meal like this in . . . well, a long time. If the Coffeys had eaten this way on Inishcorr, they'd still—" He seemed to realize what he was saying, and stopped abruptly. "—be here," he finished lamely. Maeve laughed.

"The Coffeys could have had suppers like this—and likely did at first," she told him. "The land and the sea provided enough for all for 'em, and would have continued to do so. All they needed was to pay attention to the right things."

"Like not bother the sidhe under the mound?"

She didn't answer directly. "Colin, whether yeh believe it or nah, there are places around Ireland where the connection to old beliefs and that almost-forgotten world before Christianity came to Eire is still strong, though those places are fewer and fewer each year. Inishcorr is one of 'em."

"Is that why *you* came here? Because you believe this is one of those places?"

"Aye," she answered simply. "Tell me honest now, did yeh feel *nothing* while we were standing on the mound under the hawthorn? Nothing a'tall?"

"I . . ." He shook his head, looking toward the window. The sky had grown dark; Maeve knew he could see little in the window but their own reflections, the two of them at the table. "I don't know how to answer that," he said finally, turning back to her. "I felt strange there, but after your tale about the Coffey family, that might have just been the power of suggestion."

"Or it might have been real."

"Maybe. What about Rathcroghan? Is that one of your 'places,' too?"

Rathcroghan . . . The stone remembers, even if he doesn't. "Why would yeh ask about Rathcroghan?"

Colin shrugged as if it had just been a coincidence, and Maeve nearly laughed at the poor deflection. "Just wondering," Colin said. "Have you ever been there?"

She nodded. "I have. Some time ago. And yes, it's another place like Inishcorr, or at least it was. If 'tis now, I do'nah know."

He seemed to consider that for a long time, his fork scraping the plate. "Sometimes it's hard to tell what's real or not. Every once in a while, if I went to church with my parents at Christmas, there'd be this fleeting moment when I'd feel what I used to feel when I was a kid and still believed, like there was some *presence* there watching, but that moment never lasted more than an instant and I knew it was just the incense and sounds and sights dragging back some ghost of a memory."

"Is that what it was now?" Maeve asked him, keeping her voice carefully dry and noncommittal. "And at the mound what did yeh think yeh felt?"

"At the mound . . ." He shrugged. "I don't know *what* I felt. There was a moment, when we entered the ring of stones . . . But Maeve, you set it all up for me, with that spooky story of yours. You made me all ready to feel something even if there was nothing there but a mound and a tree with an ax in it. Don't you see?"

"I do'nah, though I thought I did," she told him. She placed her fork and knife carefully on her plate and took a sip of the wine. "So yeh don't believe any of those old songs yeh say yeh love so much and yeh sing so well? To yeh, they're just words spouting nonsense and blather?"

"No," he said. She could see the confusion on his face. "It's . . . I love those songs. I like . . ." He looked down. "I like to imagine what it would have been like to live back then, to imagine that you could see mysterious beings in the mists and fogs, that sometimes the ones who died lingered here with the living . . ." As Maeve watched, he bit at his lower lip, glancing at the guitar in its gig bag, leaning against the whitewashed wall near the door.

"What would it take for yeh to believe in something, Colin?" she asked, and that brought his head around again.

"I have to *feel* it," he said. "Here." He tapped his chest where the cloch still lay hidden. "I have to be able to see it and hold it and feel it. It has to be solid and real."

"Like the pendant yer wearing?"

Behind the lenses of his glasses, she saw him blink. "How . . . ?"

Maeve laughed. "I can see the silver chain around yer neck, and the outline of something under yer sweater. Let me see it." She watched him pull it out slowly from underneath the sweater and lay it there. She felt the possessive need inside her again, as she had in Rothcroghan. She remember the voices inside the cloch and the instructions they'd given her. She had to resist the impulse to lean across the table and snatch it from his neck. "That's very nice," she said instead. "I've a necklace with a green crystal very like that." *It's not time yet. But soon enough, now that I know the cloch is here . . .*

"I know. I saw you wearing it the first night at Regan's. I almost showed this to you then."

Which is why I wore it. "But yeh di'nah. Yeh di'nah trust me?"

"No, that wasn't it. It's just . . . This was my grandfather's. He brought it over from Ireland when he left."

"Did he now? Was there a tale with that as well?"

"Yeah, there was, but . . ."

"But 'twas another thing yeh had trouble believing."

He nodded in silent answer.

Maeve pushed her chair back from the table. She stood and walked over to him. He watched her, not moving. She leaned down, tilting her head so she could kiss him, her lips parting after the first tentative brush of lips, her hand going around his head to draw him closer to her, tasting his breath and the rising urgency with which he kissed her in return, his hands stroking the sides of her body. She took his hand in her own as she drew back from him and placed it gently on her breast.

"I'm solid and real enough," she said softly. "Will yeh believe in me?"

A few hours later, walking from Maeve's house into the village, Colin would have sworn that Inishcorr was abandoned once more. It was a pleasant night, but no one was walking out along the single main street. A few of the houses had lanterns throwing yellow light against curtained windows, and peat smoke curled from the chimneys, but otherwise Colin and Maeve had the lane to themselves. Across the street at the harbor, Colin could see the *Grainne Ni Mhaille* still tied up at the wharf: rising, falling, and rolling with the slow pattern of the waves.

Twinned wedges of lamplight spilled across the uneven stone flags of the square from the pub, just up the cobbled street. The establishment was fragrant with the aromatic smoke of cigarettes and pipes. Colin could smell it before they even opened the door—it seemed that the ban on smoking in public places wasn't followed here. Through the half-opened windows on either side of the door—Colin assumed they were trying to keep the air inside semi-breathable—he could hear voices in conversation and occasional laughter, along with the dull clink of glasses on wood. Someone was playing a fiddle, noodling with the melody of "Come to the Dance" while a mandolin strummed quiet chords behind.

This, then, was where most of the Oileánach had gathered. Colin shrugged at the strap of his guitar case, feeling his stomach flutter a bit. He pressed his glasses against the top of his nose. Maeve must have sensed his unease; she squeezed his hand once and pushed open the unlocked door with her other hand.

The room went silent, as if a hidden switch had been shut off with the movement of the hinges. Over Maeve's shoulder, Colin could see dim, shadowed faces staring toward the door. "Maeve!" a female voice called from the smoke-hazed shadows. He thought it might be Keara. "*Cen chaoi bhfuil tú?*"

"*Tá mé togha,*" Maeve answered. From the smattering of Gaelic that Colin had managed to pick up, he knew that one: *I'm grand.* Maeve started to enter the tavern; Colin would have released her hand, but she only gripped his fingers tighter. "No reason to hide anything," she whispered to him as he ducked his head under the low wooden lintel. "They're going to know anyway."

He could feel them watching, could feel their speculation as he and Maeve stood there with hands intertwined, but it lasted only an instant. Heads turned away, conversations started up again, if a shade too heartily. In the back corner on a small stage, the fiddler—Keara, he noted—started up again. Two men rose from the nearest table and moved off to the bar; one of them gesturing to Maeve to take the vacated seats. She inclined her head toward the table. "G'wan with yeh," she said to Colin. "I'll get us a couple of pints." She let go of his hand and headed toward the bar, talking to some of those gathered there. Colin unslung the gig bag from his shoulder and went to the table. Both chair and table were crude but sturdy, looking as if they'd been hewn from ancient timbers a century or more ago, the marks of an adze still visible along the thick legs; he wondered if perhaps one of the Coffeys had made them.

As he sat, he glanced around the room. The tavern was deceptively deep, and there must have been three dozen or more adults, male and female, gathered here, sitting at tables or on benches along the walls, standing at the bar or in small groups in the corners of the room or gathered near where Keara and two men were playing music. A few children ran among the tables or were sitting on parents' laps. The conversations flowed around Colin—mostly in Gaelic rather than English, he noted. Though no one addressed him directly, he saw many quick glances toward Maeve or himself, adorned with shrugs or conspiratorial nods toward their companions.

And Niall was there as well. As Colin scanned the room, he found himself making eye contact with the man, who was standing near one of the front windows. Niall pushed himself off the wall and, pint in hand, came over to Colin's table. The black-brown stout inside the glass shivered as Niall set it down hard on the table. His face looked well-battered and almost certainly sore to the touch, the bruises from the fight at Regan's turning green and purple. "Havin' a good visit, are yeh?" Niall asked. His slitted eyes behind the thick swellings appraised Colin; there was no smile on his face.

"It's been good enough so far," Colin answered. He forced himself to hold Niall's unblinking stare.

Niall was leaning on his hands, fisted on the table in front of Colin. "Maeve fancies yeh, and that's plain," he said in a low growl of a voice, sounding like he had a horrible cold and couldn't breathe through his broken nose at all. "'Tis her choice. I don't care for it and I don't trust yeh, but I ca'nah go against her. I tell yeh now, though, between us, that if she casts yeh aside, yeh'll find no sympathy in me. And if yeh hurt her, then it's more than just me you'll have to answer to. Do we have an understanding?"

"I hear you," Colin told him. *And right now, if I punched you on that broken nose, I think you'd go down hard*, he thought.

"And what is it yer hearing, Colin?" Maeve interrupted, coming up behind Niall. She set two pints on the table. "Niall, I hope yer not bothering me houseguest."

Niall straightened, still staring at Colin. He picked up his glass again and took a swallow. "Nah," he said. "We was just having a bit of a chinwag like old chums." With that, he nodded to Maeve—nearly a bow, Colin thought—and went to join those standing near the door. Maeve sat next to Colin. Her hand covered his. If they'd been in a tavern in Ballemór, Colin might have turned his hand over to lace his fingers with hers, and he might have pulled her close enough to kiss her. But here . . . He was too aware of the eyes watching them.

"Niall thinks he got the worst of the fight at Regan's," she told him. "That's why he seems so angry. That, and he's afraid."

"Afraid of what?"

She didn't answer, only gave him a smile that was almost shy. Her fingers stroked the skin of his arm. "I told Keara yeh'd play music with her and sing a few songs. How about it? Show me some of what yeh've learned in yer time here, and from that book yeh bought." She leaned toward him, her face close to his, her eyes large and dark and smiling. "And after yeh've done that, we'll go back to my place and we can continue what we started, if yeh've a mind."

Her lips touched his, soft and inviting, and their kiss was slow and gentle. For that moment, the room vanished. Then Maeve pulled back, and the noise of the room returned. Her hand touched his cheek. "G'wan," she said. "Sing something for me. Show me people what a gift yeh have."

Colin grabbed his Guinness and his gig bag, sliding between the tables toward the back of the room. Keara saw him coming and lifted her fiddle bow in salute, giving him a smile and a beckoning nod. One of the people sitting next to her vacated his stool as Colin approached. He set his stout there and unzipped the bag, pulling out his Seagull acoustic. He took a drink of the stout and set the glass on the floor beside him, sitting on the stool and quickly checking his tuning. "What'dya want to play?" he asked Keara.

"Yeh can pick," she said.

"How about 'Mháire Bhruinneall' in E?" Keara nodded, and Colin looked out at the crowd. They were nearly all watching him, the room quiet. He concentrated on Maeve's grin rather than the dour face of Niall. He strummed an open E, adjusted the tuning, and ran his fingers across the strings again. "I have to sing this one in Gaelic," he said to the room, using what his sister Jenn always called his "teacher" voice. "Hope you forgive my poor pronunciation." He glanced over at Keara. "Ready, then?" She nodded, and he played the opening chords, running through a verse with Keara playing the melody line above him. The next time around, he began to sing:

> *Órú 'Mháire bhruinneall, 'bhláth na Finne (Oh, Maire Bruinneal, flower of the Finn)*
> *I ndiaidh mé do leanúint aniar anall, (I followed you here and there)*
> *Ó, ba bhinne liom do bhéal ná na cuacha a' seinm (Your mouth was sweeter to me than the cuckoo's singing)*
> *Is tú 'd'fhág mise i ndealraidh 'n bháis (And it's you who has left me at death's door)*
>
> *'Á mhéad é mo thuirse ní léir domh an choinneal (I am so grieved I couldn't keep her)*
> *'S deir siad gur mise a mheallas na mná (They said I was one who deceives women)*
> *Mharaigh tú go deo mé, lagaigh tú go mór mé (I never killed you; I wanted you weakened)*
> *Is gach a bhfuil beo domh, bhris tú mo chroí (And all that's alive in me, you broke my heart)*

All the talk in the pub had died entirely, everyone listening. He nodded to Keara, and they went through a verse and chorus with her improvising, leaning heavily into the strings with her bow, her eyes closed as she played. He began singing again, more confidently now.

> *Tá a trí phointe óir léi síos go troigh (Her golden trident points down at her feet)*
> *'Gus iad á gcarnadh ar gach taobh (and they are piled on every side)*
> *Mharaigh tú go deo mé, lagaigh tú go mór mé (I never killed you; I wanted you weakened)*
> *Is gach a bhfuil beo domh, bhris tú mo chroí (And all that's alive in me, you broke my heart)*

> *Bhí mé lá go ceolmhar ins an ród (One day I was singing in the road)*
> *Tharla domhsa an óigbhean chiúin (And I met that quiet young woman)*
> *Mharaigh tú go deo mé, lagaigh tú go mór mé (I never killed you; I wanted you weakened)*
> *Is gach a bhfuil beo domh, bhris tú mo chroí (And all that's alive in me, you broke my heart)*

He nodded to Keara, and as he launched into the repetition of the first verse, she played along with him, her fiddle harmonizing with his voice and curling grace notes around his words.

> *Órú 'Mháire bhruinneall, 'bhláth na Finne (Oh Maire Bruinneal, flower of the Finn)*
> *I ndiaidh mé do leanúint aniar anall, (I followed you here and there)*
> *Ó, ba bhinne liom do bhéal ná na cuacha a' seinm (Your mouth was sweeter to me than the cuckoo's singing)*
> *Is tú 'd'fhág mise i ndealraidh 'n bháis (And it's you who has left me at death's door)*

As he struck the ending chord, the applause broke over them, appreciative, and he grinned at Keara, at Maeve, at the crowd. He saw Keara look toward Maeve, tilt her head toward Colin, and nod, as if she was confirming something that Meave had said. "Come on, then," someone called from the crowd. "Give us another!"

Colin shrugged. "Your turn," he said to Keara.

"'Ghost Lover'?" she suggested. "Yeh played that one at the pub."

"Sure . . ." They played that, then a few instrumental reels and jigs with Keara playing the melody as Colin accompanied her. Whenever he looked for Maeve, she waved to him from a different location in the room. She'd left the table, moving around and speaking softly to one group or another as they played, smiling and laughing. Someone came up with a bodhran, and the mandolin player returned, and Colin sang a few more songs. Someone brought the musicians a round, then another, and another. The alcohol dispersed the last of his inhibitions; he played a few American songs, and even one of his own modeled on an old Irish melody he'd once heard. No one seemed to mind; unlike Niall, the crowd gathered around the musicians treated him as one of their own—or rather, they treated him as the centerpiece of the group, and the crowd in the pub grew as other of the Oileánach came in and stayed. Colin could feel them watching him and listening carefully as he sang, sometimes nudging one another with an elbow and applauding loudly at the conclusion of each song.

When he finally snuck a glance at his phone—there was no service out here, but at least he could check the time—it was already nearly midnight. He blinked, trying to clear away the alcoholic fog. He played one more song, then made his excuses to the players, putting his guitar back in the gig bag. There were protests from the crowd as he prepared to leave the musicians: "Nah. Play some more. 'Tis early yet. That's a lovely voice yeh have; give us more of it!" Maeve came up to him as he was slowly zipping up the bag.

"How'd I do?" he asked her.

"Do'nah know yet," she answered. "Maybe we'll find out, if yeh aren't too bolloxed. How many pints have yeh had?"

"Four," he answered. The word sounded strange to his ear. He made certain to pronounce the rest distinctly. "Or five. I may have lost count." Maeve was shaking her head, though she was smiling at the same time.

"Indeed. And how many shots along with 'em, or have yeh lost count of those as well?" She shook her head at him some more.

"I've had a bit more than I probably should have had, I'll admit," he said, "but I'm not drunk." He shouldered his gig bag. It seemed heavier than usual, and the room spun a little with the motion. *"Oh!"* he said suddenly, stopping. "You 'don't know yet.' Does that mean . . ." He took a long breath to steady the room. ". . . what I think it means?"

"It might," she answered. She laced her arm through his. "I'm thinking it depends on how the night air and a stroll up the hill works on yeh. I'd hate to have yeh just fall into bed an' start snoring. 'Twould be a waste."

"Well, then, let's go," Colin said. He smiled at her. He wanted to kiss her, but everyone was watching, and he glimpsed Niall still in the pub, watching the two of them. He settled for pulling Maeve tightly to him. He thought he could feel the gazes of everyone in the room on them as they left. Together.

He knew that Niall, if no one else, watched their exit carefully.

As they walked down the grassy lane, as they reached the gate in the dry-stone wall outlining the yard of Maeve's cottage, Maeve stopped suddenly. When Colin tried to stop with her, he wheeled about clumsily and had to put his hand on the gate to stop the world from whirling around him. "What's the matter?" he asked Maeve. He could hear that he slurred the words—"Wassamattah?"—but decided against trying to repeat the words more distinctly. He blinked heavily, and glanced upward into the night sky. "Wow," he said. Distinctly.

The night sky would have been stunning all on its own: stars dusted like multicolored salt on black velvet, and the dusty sweep of the Milky Way arcing overhead. Colin had seen night skies like this in Ireland before, in country villages far away from any city lights. But what made him gape were the curtains of light and color washing across the sky.

He'd seen the aurora borealis before. This was similar, yet very much *not* a common aurora. This display was too small: too localized and far too low in the sky. It was as if a miniature aurora hung over Inishcorr and especially over Maeve's cottage and them like a glowing, rippling cloud, and the colors were intense and unusual. The auroras Colin had seen before were mostly a pale green, with occasional reddish curtains. This one . . . the colors were far more saturated, and seemed to contain flashes of every possible color. Through his smudged glasses, they shimmered with bright halos.

His grandfather's stone, now in his pocket again, seemed to respond, or maybe that was just his inebriation. It felt cold against his thigh and he slid his hand to put his fingers around it. He gasped at the touch: it *was* cold, as if it had been sitting in snow. The lights in the sky seemed to be dancing for him, and coming closer.

He thought he could hear the whisper of voices in his head as he held the stone.

"Pretty," was all he could manage in response, and he heard Maeve's silvery laugh answer. She seemed to be looking at his hand, and he guiltily pulled it from his pocket, reluctantly letting go of the stone. The ghostly voices in his head faded.

"Aye, pretty indeed, 'tis," she said. "Here, let's put yeh inside so yeh can sit, and I'll be right in behind yeh . . ." With that, Maeve took his arm, opened the gate, and escorted him to the door. She pushed it open. "G'wan in. I'll be with yeh in just a bit. Why not start some water for tea, and have a bit of the bread and jam that Keara brought? That'd be good." She hugged him, kissed him fleetingly, then gave him a little shove inward. "G'wan," she said, and closed the door behind him.

He yawned and used the poker to stir the banked fire in the kitchen hearth, checked that there was water in the kettle, and put another piece of dried turf on the fire before swinging the crane over it. He sliced two pieces of bread and put tea in the pot. Maeve still hadn't come in; he went to the window and glanced out. She was standing in the yard, staring upward with her hands raised as though she wanted to touch the aurora's glow. As Colin watched, the impossible aurora seemed to respond to her gesture, but not in the way Maeve seemed to wish. The tendrils of the light curled away from her, fading now, though they were brightest just above the window where Colin stood.

The kettle over the hearth began to whistle, and Colin glanced back at the white steam flowing from the spout. When he looked back at the window, Maeve was no longer there and the aurora light had faded entirely. He heard the door open, saw her walk in. She was grimacing, as if something pained her. "That tea ready?" she asked.

Colin shivered, the alcoholic fog returning to his head. She sounded so . . . distant. He went to the kettle and swung the crane away from the fire so that the whistling slowly faded. He took the kettle by its wooden handle and poured the steaming water into the waiting teapot, and set the kettle back on the crane. He straightened . . . and found Maeve facing him, very close. She took off his glasses and her lips found his, sweet and yet oddly passive. "Are yeh too tired?" she asked, pulling back slightly from him. He shook his head; the alcohol fumes had cleared entirely from his head.

"No," he answered. Then: "Maeve, that aurora . . ."

"'Tis vanished now," she said. "Sorry." Her hands were still cupped around his neck, his glasses dangling from her fingers.

"I thought I saw yeh trying to touch the lights."

"Yeh'll see many things on Inishcorr," she told him. "An' I know the place for yeh to see more." She inclined her head toward the bedroom. She put his glasses back on. "Bring the tea and bread in there. I'll be waiting for yeh."

The *Grainne Ni Mhaille* ducked her head into the waves as it left the shelter of the harbor in Inishcorr, sending salt spray flying over her bow. Maeve laughed as the cold water drenched them. "It makes yeh feel alive," she said to Colin, shaking the folds of her red woolen cloak.

Colin wiped futilely at the front of his sweater, beaded with water, holding onto the railing as the Galway hooker pitched and rolled in the long swells coming in from the southwest. He peered through the water-speckled lenses of his glasses. They were alone in the bow, with the crew farther aft handling the sails. Niall wasn't among them this time. Looking down at the water, Colin saw two seals carving paths through the gray-green, heaving sea alongside the boat. He shivered. "It makes you feel damp and cold," he answered, "if that's what you mean by alive. Glad my guitar's back in the boat's cabin."

Maeve laughed again and came over to him. Her arms went around either side of him, her hands on the rail, pressing him against the side of the boat and holding him captive. She smiled up at him, the cowl of her cloak falling back; he leaned down to kiss her, letting go of the rail and holding onto her instead.

"So did yeh enjoy yer visit to m'island?"

"I had a wonderful time." He could feel the hunger for her again, but also the guilt. He glanced over the prow of the boat and beyond the bright red foresail, where the steep landscape of Ceomhar Head, maybe two miles away, was half-hidden in mist. "Maeve," he said. "We should talk."

She cocked her head slightly toward him. "Now?"

"Yeah, well . . ." His voice trailed off. He'd tried to speak with her this morning, after they'd awakened, but Keara had come to the door with breakfast, staying in the house while they'd dressed. After that, they'd walked into town, and it seemed they hadn't been alone long enough for him to broach anything personal. "I just wonder . . . After last night . . . When I'm back in Ballemór . . ."

She laughed, though the amusement didn't quite touch her eyes. "G'wan and pick a sentence," she said. "Any sentence."

"I just don't know where we stand right now," he said finally, still holding her, her arms still binding him to the rail. "I didn't come out here with the idea . . ."

"That we'd end up in bed?" she finished. "Oh, yeh knew when I asked yeh to the island, did yeh not? 'Tis a wee bit late now for regrets, I'm thinking." She lifted her hands from the rail and took a step back from him. He dropped his hands from around her and reached behind to hold the railing as the *Grainne Ni Mhaille* rolled again; Maeve simply shifted her weight easily, not seeming to notice.

"No," Colin said hurriedly. "I don't have any regrets. None at all. I'm just—" He stopped again.

"Are yeh worried about what yer friends back there—" she nodded toward the shoreline ahead of them, "—are going to think, yeh involved with one of the Oileánach women?"

He shook his head. His woolen cap sprayed droplets with the motion. "They can think whatever they want."

"Then *what*, Colin?" He thought he saw pain in her gaze, which she tried to hide by looking away, blinking into the salt spray. "What is it yer wanting to know? Are yeh thinking this was a mistake, that it's better not to see each other again?"

"God, no." He released the rail to make a gesture of denial, and the deck tilted underneath him. He had to catch himself again. "No, Maeve. You've the wrong idea about what I'm trying to say."

Her chin lifted. "Then tell me what the right one is, because I'm flummoxed right now."

"I'm saying that even though we've made love, I feel like I really don't know you as well as I should."

"So yeh *do* have regrets."

"No," he insisted. "It's just that, well, I've never been the guy who goes easily from bed to bed, no matter how things might appear to you right now. I'm wondering where we go from here, wondering what happens now, wondering what it *means*. Do you understand?"

Her face gentled, and he saw the hint of a smile touch her lips. "Aye," she said. "I think I do." She stepped toward him again, hugging him with her head against his chest before looking up at him with such open vulnerability in her face that it pained him. "I know what Niall told yeh," she said. "He claims it was me that made a choice, but he's wrong. 'Tis always been *yer* choice to make, Colin. Always yers. Always will be. It *must* be that way. Once yer back there, in *that* world . . ." She put a strange emphasis on the phrase. "Well, yeh think about me and my people. If 'tis me yeh still want, then we'll make that work. And if not . . ." He felt more than saw her shrug under the cloak. "Then I'll deal with that as well. I put no claim on yeh for last night. None at all. If 'twas just the one night, then it was a very nice one, and I'll remember the time and yeh fondly. If it happens to be more, then . . ." Her voice quieted so that he could barely hear it over the wind and the sea. "Yeh need to know *all* of what that means, and I'll tell yeh then. But I'd like that. Very much."

"I already—" he began.

She wouldn't let him finish the sentence, putting a finger on his lips. "No," she said. "'Tis enough said for now. I'll see yeh again in two days, an' we'll talk more then. Right now, let's just be here, together, for the wee bit of time we have."

20

Blow the Candle Out

INISHCORR SEEMED LIKE a fading dream.

Mrs. Egan gave Colin a sour, sidewise glance from the kitchen when he walked into her house that morning, wet from the passage over from Inishcorr and lugging his guitar and backpack. He'd told her only that he'd be staying with a friend for a few days. From her look, it was apparent that she knew—or at least suspected—where he'd actually been.

"'Morning, Mrs. Egan," he called to her through the intervening dining room. He heard a sniff as an answer. The dirtied dishes and crumbs on the table told him that the other guests at the bed and breakfast had already eaten and gone about their day. "I'll be taking my things up to my room. Is there still breakfast, or should I get something in town? I don't want to put you out."

Another sniff. "Them Oileánach didn't feed yeh, eh? 'Tis too like 'em." There was a clatter of dishes. "Put your things away, then. I'll cook yeh up some eggs and a bit of toast and jam."

Ten minutes later, Mrs. Egan plunked down in front of him a large plate of eggs, toast, and bacon, as well as a pot of tea. She sat across the table, watching as he ate. "I told yeh before," she said after a long silence. "There's no good to come from the Oileánach. But yeh would'nah listen to me."

"I can tell you that the Oileánach are just people, Mrs. Egan," Colin responded. "No worse and no better than anyone else. They're not bothering anyone here, out on their island as they are."

"That shows how little yeh know," Mrs Egan insisted. "Patrick Davies was saying that his cows haven't given milk in a week, not since one a' them was haggling with him over his prices. Mrs. Naughton said that after an Oileánach walked past her house one evening, there were lights twinkling all around the fairy mound in her field for the whole night, and she could hear the wee folk making music and singing. The next morning, all the flowers had been pulled from her window boxes. Her cats were cowering in the shed and wouldn't come out, and when they did, they looked all bedraggled like they'd been ridden all night long. Then there's poor Mrs. Brennan—"

Her face was so serious that Colin forced down the laugh that threatened. "I know," he said instead. "Mrs. Brennan twisted her ankle. Mrs. Egan, begging your pardon, but I happened to be there when Mrs. Brennan ran into Maeve, and Maeve never cursed her, only made a meaningless gesture to make her *think* she'd been hexed. The fact she twisted her ankle was entirely an accident, nothing more than that." He stopped, remembering that Maeve had also told him that Mrs. Brennan *would* twist her ankle. That didn't seem something to mention.

"So 'tis 'Maeve'? Yeh know her so well now?"

"I know her better than I did before, yes. And I have to say I like her."

"That may be," Mrs. Egan answered with another sniff. "An' yeh might be hexed just like Mrs. Brennan. I know what I hear, and there are plenty folks hereabout who have tales about strange things since the Oileánach have shown up. Things out of old tales, things that shouldn't be walking." She pressed her lips together as she shook her head. "Yeh like the old songs," she added. "Do yeh never think of what they say about those who sleep with the fey?"

To that, he had no answer.

"I'm not sure I can use yeh tonight, Colin," Lucas said. "Sorry for the late notice."

Lucas had stopped Colin the following morning as he walked down from Mrs. Egan's to where her drive met the Sky Road, which wound from Ceomhar Head to the main square of Ballemór. Given the distance of the Egan house from its neighbors and the main section of Ballemór, Colin suspected that this was no casual meeting, that Lucas had been coming up to Mrs. Egan's with the intention of talking to him. "Is there a problem?" Colin asked him. "I thought things were working out pretty well with me in the group."

"Nah problem," Lucas answered, but his gaze was fixed somewhere past Colin's left shoulder. "Yeh sounded grand. In fact, I have to admit that it's true magic when yeh sing. The audience notices, and I hate to give that up." He rubbed his head, as if trying to scratch away the last comment.

"It's just that . . . well, Regan's is wantin' a smaller group with the size of the stage and all, and I've been playing with the others longer, so . . ." He shrugged. "Yeh see how 'tis."

"Yeah. I'm pretty sure I do," Colin told him.

Lucas didn't seem to notice the sarcasm Colin couldn't hold back, or he chose to ignore it. He extended his hand. "Well, good, then. Yeh'll have a fine career with that gift yeh have. I'll give yeh a call when something else comes up. Promise."

"You do that," Colin told him. He gave Lucas' hand a brief shake. Afterward, Lucas rubbed his palm on his jeans, tugged at the sleeves of his sweater and pulled his cap farther down on his head. He gave Coin a lukewarm, uncertain smile and walked away, heading back down the hill toward the town. Colin decided he no longer wanted to go that way. He turned back and instead headed up the slope, his hands jammed into his pockets, a slow anger burning in his stomach, and a dozen unspoken rejoinders to Lucas ringing in his head.

After Mrs. Egan's comments and getting sacked by Lucas, he was beginning to wonder whether his trip to Inishcorr hadn't been a terrific mistake. Maybe it was simply time to move on; after all, he'd been in Ballemór for a few weeks now, and there were still a hundred places in Ireland he'd like to see. He could go on up the coast to Mayo, Sligo, and Donegal, or down the other way to Clare, Limerick, and Kerry, or, he thought as he put his hand in his pocket and felt the stone with its silver cage and chain there, he could retrace the steps his grandfather Rory had taken and see the places he'd mentioned in his journal. There were pubs everywhere where he could hear music and play along with the local folk—it seemed that you couldn't throw a pebble in Ireland without hitting a pub. There were a thousand people out there whose memories he could dredge for old tunes and lyrics. He could start writing that paper he'd been thinking about for a few years now, exploring the linkage between Celtic music and Appalachian folk songs.

He didn't *have* to stay here. If his welcome had been worn out, it would take him less than half an hour to pack his things at Mrs. Egan's and move on. He could run away from Ballemór and the Oileánach and Maeve . . . as his father might have said that he'd run away from his obligations and his future at home.

A raven cawed at him from the branch of a nearby tree, a hulking black presence on a branch of a weather-bent and stunted oak. The bird's harsh cry shook him from his reverie, and he realized he was walking in the heather-laden grass high above the Sky Road near the standing stone on the cliffs of Ceomhar Head, with the lower slopes stretched out below him, hazy and bleeding into the cold gray-blue of the ocean. Strong gusts were coming in off the sea, pushing ragged clouds with them that tossed down a cold drizzle. His jeans were damp nearly to the knees, his sneakers and socks sodden. The wind plucked at his cap and sweater, making him squint. The raven cawed again, as if trying to get his attention, and he turned to glare back at the bird. "You just shut the hell up," he said.

The bird shivered and flapped its wings, its long, thick beak clacking. Then it dropped heavily from the branch, its wings pumping once to gather air before turning in the wind. As it passed over Colin, it dropped a splatter of thick white excrement on his shoulder. Colin cursed again as the bird cawed and glided down the slope toward a stand of trees. He saw it settle there. *"Fuck you!"* he shouted into the wind. He grabbed a clump of the heather and rubbed at his sweater; it only spread out the stain. He thought he heard a muffled laugh behind him, but when he turned, there was no one there.

I'll see you again in two days, Maeve had said. It didn't matter—she'd also told him that she felt no claim on him. Fine. He was free to leave. He *should* leave. He'd become caught up in a stupid local feud, and he didn't need the drama or the indigestion. Maybe the bird was trying to tell him something.

The oak groaned, as if in pain, and Colin glanced back at it. The lower branches were swaying in the rising wind, creaking. "It hurts, doesn't it?" he said to the tree. "I can understand that. But I haven't put down roots here. I'm free to leave. I am. I don't have to stay. I shouldn't stay."

The words did nothing to convince him. The oak groaned again. Colin could see sheets of rain approaching, marching toward the land like gray curtains; already the islands closest to the shore and the end of the peninsula were lost in them. He shivered and tugged his cap tighter against his head. He started back down, wondering if he could reach Mrs. Egan's before the storm found him.

As it turned out, he couldn't.

He was well-drenched by the time he reached Mrs. Egan's porch, though at least the rain had scrubbed away the worst of the raven droppings. He could barely see through his glasses, which were running with water. His sweater seemed to weigh nearly as much as himself, hanging in sad folds and weeping from the bottom hem. His socks squelched noisily with every step. The rain was still pelting down hard, driven by gales so vicious that rain sometimes appeared to be falling horizontally. The planks of the porch were wet all the way to the side of the house. "Och!" Mrs. Egan said, opening the door as he ran up the steps, trying to shake off the worst of it. "Jus' a moment, dear . . ." Colin saw someone behind her—not one of the other residents that he recognized: a thin scarecrow of a man, with a flash of white at his collar.

Mrs. Egan came bustling out with two large towels, which he took gratefully, taking off his cap and glasses and rubbing his head and face. "The weather caught yeh, did it? I should'a warned yeh; I felt it coming in me joints. Well, come in, come in. I already have the kettle on for tea . . ."

Colin took off his shoes and socks on the porch, wrapped the towels around himself, and entered the narrow entranceway. The man he'd glimpsed behind Mrs. Egan was there, smiling sympathetically at the sight of the drenched Colin: a priest, he noted—middle-aged, with brown hair liberally touched with white and beginning to thin at the crown. Mrs. Egan was sliding past him toward the kitchen. "Colin, this is Father James Quinlan, from St. Joseph's," she said. "He stopped by and was caught in the weather, too."

"Good to meet you, Father," Colin said, taking the hand the man extended; it was like shaking a bone-infested piece of fresh cod, and Colin released it quickly. "Give me a few minutes and I'll be back down . . ."

"Certainly," the priest said. "It wouldn't do to get Mrs. Egan's rugs all damp."

By the time Colin came back down, Father Quinlan and Mrs. Egan were ensconced at the dining room table drinking tea. She'd lit several candles on the table against the gloom of the day. "Sit," Mrs. Egan said, pouring a steaming cup in front of one of the empty seats. "A rain like this just seeps into yer very bones." As Colin sat, Mrs. Egan shot a glance at Father Quinlan, then her attention wandered to the window of the room, where sheets of water were being tossed at the rattling panes. She pointed to the picture of her brother on the mantel of the fireplace. "It was storming just like this the night that Darcy died," she said, and shivered.

"Indeed 'twas," the priest agreed. Colin decided not to mention that Mrs. Egan said that every time it stormed. He lifted his cup to his lips, sipped, and set it down again. "So, Colin," Father Quinlan continued. "Mrs. Egan tells me that yer Catholic, but I ca'nah say I've seen yeh at Mass."

Colin could feel both of them staring at him. He felt like a child ambushed by his parents after receiving a bad report card. "I was raised Catholic," he told the priest. "St. Ann's parish in Chicago. Went to parochial schools all the way through high school. But I've kind of lost the habit of going to church over the years."

"But yeh still believe, don't yeh?" the man persisted.

"I suppose so. Honestly, Father, I haven't given church much thought over the last several years." That wasn't precisely true. As he'd told Maeve, he'd lost his faith in high school and had never found it again. He wasn't certain he could call himself a complete atheist, but he was certainly agnostic. His father had brought up Colin's lack of church attendance regularly since that time, and he'd (somewhat grudgingly) been a "C&E Catholic" while living in Chicago, going to Mass with the family on Christmas and Easter because it was expected and because that's what the family did; once he moved out to Seattle for school, he gave up even that pretense.

He could imagine poor Father Quinlan on Inishcorr, trying to convince Maeve and the Oileánach that they should come to church. It wasn't a pretty image.

The priest was nodding as if deciding what to say next; Mrs. Egan clucked once reproachfully. "That's why the Oileánach are especially dangerous for yeh," she said. "Why, 'twas only our faith that saved the good Father and me that night at Darcy's, with the very hounds of hell carousing 'round the house."

With Mrs. Egan's comment, the shutters all slammed hard against the west side windows of the house. Broken glass chimed against hardwood floors as rain and the wind blew freely into the dining room, toppling over the china figurines Mrs. Egan had placed on a buffet table underneath the window and blowing out the candles. The lace curtains flapped and fluttered like white, grasping hands. The hissing of the gale through the broken panes almost sounded like laughter.

Mrs. Egan cried out in distress as Father Quinlan and Colin lurched from their chairs. Colin rushed outside with Father Quinlan to help resecure the agitated, swaying shutters. The rain cut off as if a celestial faucet had been turned, though the wind still screamed through the trees surrounding the house, making them bend and sway. "Look here," Father Quinlan half-shouted against the din. "The wind's torn loose the clamps. Help me close the shutters over the window for the time being, Colin, and we'll get something to cover the broken windows until Mrs. Egan can get them repaired. Then we can help her clean up the mess."

But Mrs. Egan wasn't cleaning. When they went back into the house after securing the outside, they found Mrs. Egan standing in the midst of shards of broken glass and china. She was staring at the center of the table with her hands to her face. "Father . . ." she said, pointing with a finger that trembled visibly.

In the middle of the table was the photograph of Darcy in its frame, sitting perfectly centered as if someone had carefully placed it there, facing the window. "I was watching the two of yeh dealin' with the shutters. I started to go get me broom, an' I turned around and there was Darcy a'smiling at me."

Father Quinlan crossed himself. "'Tis only the wind," he said. "A gust toppled it from the mantle, and an angel was looking out for your dear departed Darcy and made sure the picture landed there safely, that's all, 'tis all." Father Quinlan glanced at Colin. "Would yeh not agree, Colin?"

Colin stared at the picture, at Darcy's smiling face. The man seemed almost to be laughing at him. "Yeah," he said. "That must be it."

✦ 21 ✦

The Fairy Ring

"**H**EY."

The call was so soft that Colin thought he might have imagined it. He turned, and saw Maeve leaning against an oak tree at the edge of Mrs. Egan's property, wearing a long skirt and a loose, red sweater, her dark hair down and falling over the shoulders. He grinned, seeing her, then glanced back toward the house. "Hey, yourself," Colin answered.

"I see yeh haven't left yet."

He felt his cheeks growing hot, as if she'd somehow overheard his musings of the other day. "Did you think I was going to do that?" he asked her, and she shrugged without answering. She took a step forward out of the shadows. "Y'know, if Mrs. Egan sees you here on her property, she's going to have a fit. She'll be calling the gardai on you."

Maeve's laugh was quicksilver. It wrapped around him and drew him toward her. She hugged him, giving him a fleeting peck on the cheek, but turned her head when he tried to make it more. She held him nearly at arm's length, then released him entirely. "Yer Mrs. Egan doesn't worry me a'tall," she said. "Besides, her dining room window's boarded up at the moment, ain't it? She won't be looking out it."

The comment brought Colin back to yesterday's storm, and the strange occurrence with Darcy's picture. He felt a roiling in his gut as he looked at her. "How'd you know that?"

"Why d'yeh ask?" she answered. She gazed at him coyly. "Yeh think I had something to do with it?"

"Did you?"

Her smile came and vanished, like the sun slipping behind fast-racing

169

clouds. "Someone who believes in the Papist God wouldn't believe that possible—or they'd attribute it to the devil or something equally gacky."

"You're not answering my question."

"I'm thinking yeh already know the answer, but yer asking only because yeh need to pretend yeh don't." She held out her hand to him. "Come on. I promised yeh a talk. Let's take a stroll, the two of us, and we can have that chat."

He hesitated, then took her hand. She led him away from the house and farther up the slopes into a tangle of trees and brush, moving along winding, narrow trails that he couldn't see himself but that she seemed to find easily. They crossed two quick streams running down the headland, nearly hidden underneath the heather. He was panting as he followed her, though the climb didn't seem to bother Maeve. Finally, she paused in a small open glade sheltered by oaks and hawthorns; there, he saw a small earthen mound, an outcropping of gray rocks speckled with moss thrusting through the loam blanketing it. Around the mound was a ring of slightly-raised earth, as if there'd once been a low wall surrounding the hillock, now pressed down and cushioned with centuries of loam and grass. Maeve sat on one of the boulders, waiting as he straggled after her. "Yer fierce slow," she said.

"You're fierce fast," he answered. "And I think I stepped in the stream back there."

"Ah, yer a fine, fine singer, Colin Doyle, but a poor tramper." She laughed again and patted the rock next to her. "Come and sit. The sun's nice."

He sat beside her and she leaned into him. The sun dappled the ground, and the stone was surprisingly warm. He was nearly sweating after the climb, despite the chill of the day. He put his arm around Maeve's shoulder, enjoying the feel of her against his side. It felt right; it felt natural. "Where are we?" he asked. She raised an eyebrow. "I mean, where's this place? It feels old, somehow. I thought I'd explored most of the Head, but I've never seen this before."

"Yeh don't know how to look for it," she answered. "I do. But it's interesting what yeh say, that this place feels old. I like that." She moved away from him so that his arm dropped, leaving his side cold. She shaded her eyes from the sun. "It's been two days. So have yeh been thinking about yer visit to Inishcorr?" she asked.

"I have, and it seems everyone else has as well," he told her. "The entire damn town has been giving me their opinion."

One shoulder lifted under the sweater, then fell. "I care nah about the town's opinion. Only yers."

"Maeve, I still don't *know* where we stand. I've enjoyed being with you, I've loved the time we spent together, and yeah, maybe there could be more between us if things keep going. Being with you was wonderful, and I'd *like* it if things kept going between us. But right now, I don't think I really know you well enough to give you more of an answer than that. I *want* to know you better. I feel like we could share more. I guess . . ." He hesitated, feeling guilty over what he'd actually been thinking the last few days. His hand reached into the pocket for his grandfather's stone, as if the answer might be there; her gaze followed. "I guess I'm willing to stick around to find out what's possible with us. Is that good enough?"

"*Are* yeh willing to stick around?" she asked. "Even if it means yeh have to deal with the crap the locals are going to give yeh?"

She was staring at him, and he had to look away, remembering how he tried to convince himself to do exactly the opposite, with nearly the same words. "I thought about leaving," he admitted. "But I haven't."

"Not yet yeh haven't." She said it flatly, so that he couldn't tell what she meant by the comment.

"What about *your* people?" The rejoinder was reflex. "Some of them seemed less than thrilled about me."

"Like Niall?" She leaned closer to him again, her arm sliding between his arm and side. She laid her head on his shoulder. "Niall doesn't hate *you* specifically. He would hate anyone I chose to be with. An' he's just one person. The other night—well, yeh saw how m'people responded to yeh in the pub. I remember hearing lots of applause, and seeing everyone watching yeh, all mesmerized. Yer quite the bard, Colin, and Niall . . . he's jealous of yeh more than anything."

"Of me?"

"It's more complicated than yer thinkin'," she told him, and shook her head. "'T'ain't just the relationship. He's afraid I've made a wrong choice with yeh, but I know I haven't. Yeh see, sometimes two people care about the same thing deeply, and yet differ completely on what needs to be done about it."

"And what is it the two of you care about?"

"Inishcorr," she said, "or rather, not the island but the people there: Niall for his people and me for mine. We're the Last." Her voice capitalized the noun.

"The last of what?"

She didn't answer. Instead, she lifted her head to his and gave him a long and lingering kiss. When it ended, she stood. From a leather pouch tied to the belt she wore over her skirt, she took a small metal flask. She unscrewed the top, then poured a small amount on the mound behind the rocks. "For the fairy folk," she said. She took a small sip from the flask herself. He watched her face. There might have been a small grimace, but she licked her lips afterward and extended the flask to him. "Here, have a drink."

He took the flask and sniffed at it, then drew back, his eyes widening. "Wow," he said. "That's got a kick. Potcheen?" She nodded. He put the lip of the flask to his mouth and tilted it, listening to the gurgle of liquid inside. The swig was larger than intended, and he swallowed fire that burned all the way down to his stomach, making him gasp for air. "That's smooth," he said in a strangled voice. He drew in another breath. "Just a little stronger than I expected."

Maeve laughed at that, and the sound seemed to linger in the air, reverberating like the strike of a gong. He thought he could almost *see* her amusement, like a winding line of fireflies emerging from her mouth, except that he'd never seen fireflies in Ireland, and certainly never ones bright enough to be seen in the daylight. The light about them had changed as well; the sunlight was the rich gold of late afternoon, and the grass under his feet was a saturated emerald that throbbed and ached in his vision. "Maeve?" he called out, trying to find her in the dazzling vision. His voice sounded too low, and he saw *his* voice as well, an umber wave that rippled out from him, foaming white at the edges like a great sea wave. "Maeve?"

He couldn't see her, though he swept his gaze around the glade, but heard her call back to him. "Don't worry," her voice said. "Just let it happen."

"Let *what* happen?" he asked. The umber swell crashed and broke around her.

Dark laughter answered him, coming from unseen dozens of throats all about him. The light dimmed, as if storm clouds had hidden the sun. He looked up, but everything was confused and fuzzy, and he felt as if he were falling. His arms flailed, and hands grasped at him while low voices murmured words he couldn't understand. He could feel his body being pulled, dragged along the ground by his feet as the world went abruptly dark around him. He tried to kick at those pulling him, but his legs refused to work. Stones and dirt scoured his back, and his head bumped against something hard and solid, like he'd been taken down a series of steps. Yellow lights flickered across his vision and more voices filled the darkness, deep and laughing. They spoke in Gaelic, not English, so fast that he could understand none of the words. A face—the face of an old hag—looked down at him, and he felt her hands sliding across his face, the dry, scaled skin of her hands like fine sandpaper. "He was born with a blue caul," the old woman said to someone. "An' the voice is the one that's needed. 'Tis good, that."

Voices answered her, and he squinted, trying to see them. "So what?" a male voice shouted back. "That doesn't mean shite. Not with him. His grandfather was much the same, and that di'nah work."

"Niall?" Colin called out. He tried to focus on the shapes in front of him and failed. Behind them, he glimpsed a huge room lit fitfully by guttering, smoking torches, the spots of light receding well into the distance. The walls were rough stone, though with gleaming and polished half-pillars carved into them at a separation of several strides. The ceiling was lost in darkness above. The room could have easily held thousands of people, but Colin could only see a few dozen gathered here, moving in the twilight darkness, though perhaps more were lurking in the shadows further out in the hall. "Maeve, where are you?" Colin called, but there was no immediate answer except for a susurrus of laughter from those around him, as if he'd said something amusing.

"You *dare* call for Her in that manner?" the hag said. "That's not her name. That's a *new* name, and t'ain't hers. T'ain't her *true* name." She stood at his feet as he struggled to sit up. She spat on the tiles between them. But a shadow moved behind the hag, and she glanced over her shoulder. The hag bowed to someone in the shadows and slid away. There was a fluttering of wings, and he thought he saw a huge raven descend from the air into the misty shadows of the hall, but even as Colin pushed at his glasses to see more clearly, from the mist a human figure emerged: tall, spectral, its face hidden by the hood of a cloak that might have been red, but appeared black in the dimness. Behind the figure, a white-horned bull stamped its feet in shadow, snorting and angry.

"So yeh can hear us, mortal?" he was asked. It was a woman's voice, and he thought at first it might be Maeve's except that this voice sounded older and deeper, as if time and a hard life had roughened and scrubbed away any lightness it had once held.

"Of course I can. I'm not deaf." More of the sinister laughter billowed from the shadows in response.

"Do yeh know who I am?" The figure swept back her hood, and he was looking at Maeve-but-not-Maeve. This face was much older and more careworn, and other visages seemed to cross her face like clouds chased by winds.

"The Morrígan," he said. The name came to him; he spoke it without thinking, without knowing why.

She seemed to taste the sound of that, as if she'd taken a sip of whiskey and was rolling the liquid around her tongue. The bull behind her stamped its feet, its hooves drawing sparks from the stone tiles. "Aye," she said finally. "The Morrígan, Morrígu, Mór-ríoghain . . . Some say that I'm actually three people: Badb, Macha, and Anand. I'm sometimes seen as a young woman, as an old hag, as a crow. Many names, and many forms. I was loved." She smiled at him, but there was no affection in that gesture. "And feared. Once."

"But not now?" Colin asked. His mouth was dry; the words tasted like ash and dust on his tongue.

"Now?" she repeated. "Now there are so few of us left, and 'tis my fault. I convinced them to stay when the others left." She waved an arm at the hall behind her, and where her hand pointed, a beam of cloudy light swept across the creatures there. He saw them and knew them somehow as they drifted in and out of the light: Selkies, the seal-changelings. Pucá, the goblins. Failinis, the war-hound. The fear-forta, the emaciated "man of hunger." Abcan, the dwarf poet. The merrow, human above the waist and fish below. The sluagh, the spirits of the evil dead. The neamh-mairbh, the "walking dead."

And dozens more. The gods and demigods: Danu, Dagda, Cromm Cruaich, Brigit, Boann, Aengus, Lugh, Epona, more . . . Their names came to him as the Morrígan's light swept over them. They were others as well, but nearly all of them seemed to be slumbering in niches in the hall.

They were with him here, all the creatures of myth and legend and tales. He glimpsed them in the sweep of light from the Morrígan, and they were gone as quickly. "We are the Last," the Morrígan said. "We are the remnants, and we are dying."

"Dying? Why?"

The Morrígan didn't answer. She closed her hand and the light died, leaving purple-and-green ghosts chasing themselves across Colin's eyes. Her hand reached out, and though he drew back, she was quicker. Her skin felt cold and dry; the caress of a dead lover. "Yeh might open the door again for us," she said.

He shook his head. "I don't understand. What door?"

"Yeh have the cloch," she told him. "The cloch that Rory took. Yeh have it, and now yer the one who must use it."

Involuntarily, his hand went to his jean pocket, and he felt the lump of his grandfather's stone there. The touch of it was icy, and it seemed to throb. The Morrígan's gaze was on his hand, and she nodded.

She was turning from him even as he guiltily took his hand away from the stone, and all was fading with the sound of soft earth falling like rain. The creatures had all left. Only the Morrígan was still there, her cloaked back to him as she, too, started to leave. She stopped, her hand lifted again, and she spoke without turning. "Yeh have to believe me, Colin. Yeh have to *believe* in me, and yeh have to give me what yeh have freely." The Morrígan's voice was fading like the cavern. "Do yeh believe?" she asked, but her voice trailed off into the soughing of the wind and the rustling of leaves.

The wind had picked up; the tops of the trees around the glade in which they were sitting were swaying as if in time to some unheard music. Colin rubbed at his eyes; the flask from which he'd drunk the potcheen was lying on the grass beside him, and Maeve was sitting next to him, her quiet gaze on him. His eyes burned; his head was pounding as he rubbed his temples. The dream was already fading, more distant and unreal with every passing second. He couldn't seem to hold onto the images; already he was forgetting what he'd glimpsed. "Damn, what did you give me?" he asked. "One little drink put me out. That's never happened before."

"I thought Yanks could hold their liquor better," Maeve answered gently. "Good thing there was nobody here who wanted to take advantage of yeh." He couldn't read her expression, whether that was a smile that touched her lips and crinkled the lines at the corner of her grass-green eyes, or something else entirely.

"I've been drunk, I'll admit, but I've never passed out before, and certainly not from one little swig. What was in there?"

A shrug. "A dream," she said.

"Well, it worked. I had the weirdest dream ever. Sorry, I didn't mean to fall asleep on you . . ." He blinked; his eyelids felt terribly heavy, and his pulse throbbed in his head.

"So what was weird about yer dream?"

Colin shook his head and sat up; the movement caused his head to pound more, and he groaned. Maeve leaned over and rubbed his temples; he closed his eyes at the touch and let it drain away the pulsing of the headache. "Thanks. That feels good . . ." Colin tried to remember the dream: *the Hall, the Morrígan, the others* . . . "I don't know. It must be this place—I *think* I was under the fairy mound, and I was talking to the Morrígan. At least I think I was." He opened his eyes and stared hard at Maeve. "She looked like you."

"Did she now?"

"Yeah. And there was something about a caul," Colin added. "Some old woman in the dream said I was born with one. I've heard about cauls— something to do with the amniotic sac?"

"A caul is real enough," Maeve told him, still massaging his temples. "Sometimes a babe is born with what looks like extra flesh draped over his or her face and body—and aye, it's actually part of the amniotic sac. A long time ago, being born with a caul was supposed to signify that the child had the gift of being able to access the Otherworld. Those born with one were thought to be especially blessed by the old gods. Not all that long ago, here in Ireland, yer caul might have been preserved as a charm, though in the States, they'd just dispose of it. Ask yer mother or someone who witnessed yer birth; she might know if yeh had a caul." She lifted her hands away from his head. "There; does that feel better now?"

Colin titled his head from side to side, listening to his neck cracking at the motion. The headache had receded to a distant tidal pulse. "Yeah. Much better." He found her hands and clasped them in his. "I don't know why I'd have someone talking about a caul in a dream considering I haven't thought about the term in forever. I must have dredged it out of my subconscious."

Maeve tilted her head. "That's one possibility."

He closed his eyes again. Opened them. He was beginning to feel somewhat normal, though he vowed never to take another shot of that potcheen if Maeve offered him one. "Listen, we haven't talked much about . . ." He lifted a shoulder. ". . . us," he finished. "I've been thinking about that a lot, though. Lucas kicked me out of his group because of it, I think."

"Did he now? I'm sorry, Colin. I know how much yeh enjoy playing music; I know that's the reason yeh came here. But I'm not particularly surprised." Her hands squeezed his. "Out on Inishcorr, yeh could play all yeh want. They'd be happy to have yeh there, and Keara and the others know most of the old songs—more of 'em than Lucas. Our memories are long out there, and deep. There are plenty of houses there for yeh to take and fix up, if yeh want." She paused. Began again. "Or yeh could stay with me, if yeh'd like."

He pulled his hands away from hers; she seemed to let go only reluctantly. "I appreciate that. I do. It's just . . . It feels like you're saying I have to make a choice between Ballemór or Inishcorr, that if I'm with you, I can't be here, too."

She held his gaze, unblinking. "Yeh know what they're like here. Do yeh think that's a wrong assessment?"

"Maybe not," he admitted. "But I don't have to like it. I don't like being told there's only one way, and that's the way I have to do things. I like being with you, Maeve. You know that, right? But . . . I don't know . . ." He exhaled, hard, and with the next breath, the world seemed to snap back into focus around him again. The glade was just another glade on the

Head, no longer imbued with strange, saturated colors. The stones around the mound were just stones, and the mound itself just a frost-upheaval in the sod. "Look, give me another few days. Let me talk to Lucas again, and think about what's best for me right now. Is that fair?"

Maeve rose to her feet, her skirt swaying. She brushed her hair back from her face as she looked down at him. "It's fair; in fact, I'll give yeh over the weekend. I'll have the *Grainne Ni Mhaille* moored on Beach Road next Monday morn when we come over for supplies. We'll stay there until noon. If yeh want to come back to Inishcorr with me, then be there. An' if yer not, then I'll just wish yeh well." She turned and started walking back down the trail, not waiting for him as he rose, brushing dirt from his jeans. She turned back to him. "I thought yeh might be the one for me from that first night I saw yeh," she told him. "Yeh have to believe me. Yeh have to believe *in* me. Do yeh?"

Her last words seemed overlaid with another voice, and with that the last moments of the dream returned to him, the Morrígan speaking the same words, in the same tone. He seemed to feel the resonance of the voice in his grandfather's stone as well. In the pocket of his jeans, it vibrated against his skin like a cell phone.

"Maeve," he started to say, but she shook her head and half-ran from the glade and into the trees. He stayed there, wanting to chase after her, but his legs refused to cooperate.

She had disappeared into the trees before he could manage his first steps.

22

Mothers and Brothers

"IT'S GOOD TO HEAR YOUR VOICE, too, Mom. Sorry I didn't call earlier. Things have been a little crazy here, and some of the places I've been there just wasn't any service at all."

Colin wondered if his mother could hear the excuses in his voice. He could imagine her in the living room of their house in Chicago; he could hear the TV on in the background, thin voices scratching at the speaker of his cell phone accompanied by equally tinny music. His mother's breath obliterated them. "Jen told me *she's* talked to you several times." The accusation was implicit, with just a hint of guilt-inducing *"You'll call your sister, but you won't call me"* underneath it.

"Yeah, sorry, Mom. *Mea culpa*, and all that." He pressed his lips together. Downstairs, he could hear Mrs. Egan puttering around in the kitchen, and the smell of baking bread wafted through the house. "I'll try to be better about that. I promise." *But if I move to Inishcorr, there'll be no phone service at all . . .*

"Jen says you've met someone?" The bald statement had a dozen conversational hooks dangling from it. Silently, he cursed Jen for giving Mom the bait, and he wondered how he was going to avoid getting dragged into a conversation he didn't want to have. He decided that a lie would be the best course for the moment. *It's no coincidence that Mom's named Mary*, he and Jen used to joke in their teenage years. *She's intent on making sure we stay virgins.*

"Her name's Maeve, but right now we're just friends. Nothing more. So there's really not much to say. She lives on one of the islands around Ballemór; I don't see her all that much."

"Ah." He heard a click and the voice on the TV changed to Ellen DeGeneres' distinctive voice. He imagined his mother, sitting on the couch with the remote in one hand and the phone in the other, her coffee steaming on the table in front of her. "Jen made it sound like this was something serious," she said. *Dangling the hooks again . . .*

"Well, Maeve's five months pregnant, though I'm not entirely sure I'm the father. Still, I married her last week just in case, but, nah, it's not serious."

From the other end of the connection came a gasp, then a shaking laugh. "Oh, you! You're awful, you know that?" He heard the laughter die away quickly. "So . . . when are you going to be back, Colin? We miss you so much, and Tommy could use your help with the campaign."

"I'm sure Harris will do everything that Tommy needs," he told his mother. "I'm managing to keep myself afloat financially playing music, my visa's still good, and I'm learning a lot. I'm really not planning to leave anytime soon."

"Yes, but what *good* is all this music stuff going to do for you? Colin, someday you're going to have a wife and family; how is music going to provide for them? Why, you'll need medical benefits and a house in a decent neighborhood, and a down payment for that is going to be tens of thousands of dollars, and—"

"Mom," he said into the rush of her objections, the same litany he'd heard for the last several years, "it's the twenty-first century. Maybe that wife of mine will be the one with the good job and benefits. Or maybe folk music will come back into favor again and I'll be giving concerts in stadiums. I don't know what the future holds, and neither do you. In any case, I'll worry about a wife and family when the time comes." Then, simply because he knew it would annoy her: "Or maybe I'll just stay here in Ireland. Things are relatively cheap over here, and they *like* musicians. Maybe I'll just settle down with Maeve, become an Irish citizen. I won't have to worry about the high cost of living over there, and Ireland has free public health care, so I won't have to worry about that, either. You'd just have to fly over here to visit your grandkids."

There was silence on the other end for a moment, though he heard her intake of breath. He imagined her sitting there, staring at the TV and trying to decide if that was another joke. "Well," she said, drawing out the word over a long breath, "I'm sure you'll do what's right in the end." He knew that in Mom-speak, that translated as *And you'd damned well better do what I think is right.*

"Sure, Mom," he said. "I'm sure I will. Listen, I have a silly question. Do you know what a caul is?" She didn't, and he explained. "Anyway, was I born with one?"

She gave a cough of surprise. "Why on Earth would you ask that?"

"Someone said that she could tell that I had been. Something about it being considered lucky."

"What kind of people are you hanging around with there, Colin? Gypsies and fortune tellers? Is this Maeve of yours one of them? Of all the ridiculous things to ask—"

"Mom. Just answer the question. Was I born with a caul?"

Television voices chattered beneath his mother's breaths. "I . . . I don't know—they told me they had to clean you up before they gave you to me, and I couldn't see what they were doing. Your Aunt Patty might remember. She was there, since your father was stuck in Indianapolis at some meeting. You could ask her, if you really want to know. It seems silly to me, and rather gross, honestly. All I cared about was that you were healthy. Yours was the easiest birth of all of you. I was in labor with Tommy for twelve hours, and eight with Jennifer . . ."

He was half-listening now, having heard these stories too many times over the years: *Tommy was breech and they almost went to an emergency C-section but the doctor managed to turn him at the last minute. I swore I'd never have another child after that horrible experience. But a woman forgets these things, dear, and Jennifer was a sweet, even-tempered child from the moment she emerged. Now you—you squalled with colic for the entire first two months and the only thing that would sooth you was riding in the car, and your father or I would put you in the car seat and drive you around for hours . . .*

Colin allowed their conversation to drift into polite niceties. He heard all about Tommy's progress with the campaign and how his "coming-out" hadn't seemed to affect the polls too badly, and how well Jen was doing (though his mother somehow neglected any mention of Aaron), and how her knees were hurting and the doctor was thinking it was incipient arthritis and at some point she'd probably have to have knee replacement surgery ("You see, it's things like that that countries with public health care just won't provide until you're practically crippled . . .").

He finally made his excuses and disconnected with the promise that he'd call again soon.

He suspected that their definitions of "soon" would be wildly divergent.

After the conversation with his mother, he hesitated, sitting on his bed as he listened to Mrs. Egan puttering around downstairs, but he finally pulled up the contact list on his phone and pressed the number for Aunt Patty's cell phone. There was the hiss of the overseas connection, a long pause, then he heard the phone ring on the other end. After four rings, he thought he would need to leave a message, but he heard a click and then Aunt Patty's voice, a little breathless.

"Colin! I'm at the mall; my phone was in my purse and so I didn't hear it right away. How are you? I've been hoping you'd call so we could catch up."

"Sorry, Aunt Patty. I've been busy here, and some of the places I've been just don't have cell service."

"Oh, I understand. Have you called your mom, though? She calls me at least every other day to see if I've heard anything from you."

"I just talked to her. Which is actually why I'm calling you now." He took a breath, running his tongue over his lips. "Listen, I've a strange question to ask you. I asked Mom, and she said you might know. When I was born. . . . Well, do you know what a caul is?"

Aunt Patty laughed. "As a matter of fact, I do. And yes, when you were born you had a caul, if that's what you're wondering. You looked like someone had plastered a really ugly, pale blue, splotchy wet cloth over your face. Took the doc a few moments to get it off so you could start breathing. There were a few anxious moments for me watching them, but I don't think your mom really noticed, and it was easy to forget about once everyone knew you were all right. God, I haven't thought about that in *years*, Colin. Why in the world are you asking?"

"Believe it or not, the subject came up here in Ireland."

"Really? How odd. I mentioned it to my mom—your Maimeó— afterward. She was the one told me what a caul was. She said that, back home, there were tales about children born with cauls and that supposedly Daiddeó Rory was born with one, too, so maybe it runs in families. It's supposed to mark the child for something special, according to Maimeó. I can't remember if I ever told your mom that or not. If I did, she probably didn't think much of it."

"No, it seems she didn't. She wasn't even sure what a caul was. But thanks, Aunt Patty; that's what I wanted to know."

"Glad I could help. So tell me, how are you?"

"I'm fine."

"Uh-huh," he heard through the speaker. "That's the answer someone gives when they don't want to actually answer the question. I know you better than that, Colin. Let's try again. How are you?"

He didn't respond immediately. On the other side of the line, he heard the tinny blandness of mall music over the speakers, and fragments of people passing his aunt, who waited patiently for his response. "All right," he said at last, "things have been somewhat strange. This is going to sound bizarre, but I'm wondering if I'm not caught up in part of the same impossible tale that Daiddeó Rory wrote down—all that nonsense he talked about in the journal you gave me. I thought that was just some tale he was making up, but now . . ." There was nothing but the hiss of the connection in his ear. "Aunt Patty?"

"I heard," she said. "Is that why you were asking about the caul?"

"Yeah. Maeve, the woman I've been seeing here, she said she could tell I was born with one. And . . . Well, I'm not sure exactly *how* she knows some of the things she tells me or does some of what she does. I'm even starting to wonder . . ." He stopped.

"Do you trust this Maeve?" Aunt Patty asked. "What does your heart tell you, Colin? Dad—your grandfather—always told us that if we followed our hearts, we couldn't be led astray, no matter where we ended up. That was always good advice for me."

"I'll remember it. Aunt Patty, please don't tell Mom any of this. Not even Jen or Tommy. I don't want anyone worrying. Or thinking I've gone off the deep end, either."

"What about me?" she said, though he heard a laugh riding under the words.

"I figure you can handle it," he told her. "Listen, I'll let you get back to your shopping. You've given me a lot to think about, and that's what I'm going to do."

"You do that, dear," she told him. "And listen to that heart of yours most of all. Of the whole family, you're the most like your Daiddeó. Maybe more than any of us thought. Take care," she said, "and call me if you need to talk more. I'll be here."

"I appreciate that. Bye, Aunt Patty."

He pressed the End Call button. He dropped the phone to the bedspread, then took off his glasses, placed them alongside the phone, and rubbed his eyes. He put his hand in his pocket, pulling out his grandfather's stone. He rubbed the polished facets between his fingers as he sat there.

Lucas wouldn't answer Colin's repeated calls and messages. Mrs. Egan's attitude toward Colin had turned decidedly frosty; when she did deign to talk to him, it was with short, clipped sentences. The story of the storm and Darcy's picture standing in the middle of the table was now, with embellishments, a part of local lore. The tale of how Maeve had "threatened and nearly put a curse" on Mr. Mullins seemed to be all the gossip in town, and the fight at Regan's between the Oileánach and the townsfolk had taken on mythic proportions.

When Colin walked into town, he could feel the stares and hear the whispers. When he looked at them, they'd look quickly away; when he came close enough to possibly overhear, conversations would abruptly cease. He tried to tell himself that it was only paranoia, that they weren't paying any more attention to him than they would any stranger on the street, but he knew better.

To the people of Ballemór, Colin realized, his decision had already been made. He was now just another Oileánach, whether that was what he wished or not.

On Sunday, after dinner, he remained at the table after the other residents of the bed and breakfast had left. Mrs. Egan bustled in with her cart to take the dishes into the kitchen. She didn't look at him as he watched her. "Mrs. Egan, I'll be settling my bill tonight. I'm planning on leaving in the morning."

"Oh, is that so?" He could see her struggling to keep a smile from her face. "So . . . tell me that it's not to that dark witch woman yer going." She put his plate on the cart with a crash. "Yeh risk your very soul with that 'un," she told him sternly, the wrinkles deepening in her face. Her forefinger wagged at his nose. " 'Tis what Father Quinlan says, and he's a man of the cloth so he'd know."

"I'm sorry, Mrs. Egan, but I don't believe that."

"That's the trouble with yeh, if yeh don't mind my sayin'," she told him. "Yeh *don't* believe in the proper things." The finger looked in danger of wagging again, and her face had soured.

"Well, it doesn't matter. Actually, I'm thinking of heading farther up the coast—maybe toward Sligo."

Her lips pursed hard at that, and she nodded once firmly. "That'd be good for yeh. I'll put together a nice breakfast for yeh tomorrow morning, and a sandwich to take for lunch. Yeh'll be taking the bus, then?"

"Don't know. I might check at Regan's to see if someone's heading up that way and wouldn't mind a rider."

"Well, just yeh be careful. And if yeh come back this way, give me a few days' notice and I'll make sure yer room's still available."

He ventured a smile. "Thanks, Mrs. Egan. I appreciate that. I'll certainly recommend your place to anyone coming to Ballemór."

Her lips might have twitched. She took his plate and pushed the cart of dirty dishes into the kitchen. A few minutes later, with the sound of dishes rattling in the sink, Colin went upstairs to pack.

"Yeh still think he's worth yer time? Worth *our* time? Maeve, if yer wrong, yeh've doomed us."

"Are yeh speaking for all yer kind, or just for yerself, Niall?"

Niall scowled, but he lowered his gaze. "For me, mostly," he admitted.

They were standing on the battered quay jutting into Inishcorr's harbor. Maeve could feel the boards shifting under her feet as the waves lapped at the pilings. The *Grainne Ni Mhaille* was tied up at the end of the quay, bobbing gently in the swells; Keara and four others of the Inishcorr villagers were already on board, working on the lines and sail.

Niall had climbed up from the water as Maeve approached, discarding his seal's skin even as she saw him. His hair was plastered to his skull, dripping saltwater from the long ends, and his face still bore the fading bruises of the fight at Regan's. He was also entirely naked, seemingly unconcerned about the chill wind on his sea-soaked body. Maeve was certain that was deliberate; he could have chosen to stay in seal form, knowing that she was planning to take the hooker to the mainland.

"Then why are yeh still carrying on with me, Niall?" she asked. "Are yeh disputing that this is my decision to make? Are yeh questioning my authority on Inishcorr? Do yeh think yer better prepared than me to do what's necessary? Yeh think yeh have even a tithe the power that I have, that yeh can open the way to Talamh an Ghlas on yer own and without the bard and the cloch?"

"Yeh do'nah know if that man even *has* the cloch."

"But I do," Maeve insisted. "I know that. I held it once, and I've seen it with Colin; the same one. I saw it call down the mage-lights t'other night."

Niall's head shook, scattering cold droplets: a rain of denial. "I'm not questioning yer authority, Maeve, only the choice yeh've made with the man."

"Why?" She nearly spat out the question. "Yeh heard the Crone same as I did: Colin's caul-born, like his grandfather. He could hear and see us in our true forms, even if he di'nah understand what he saw. He fits our needs. He's the one was sent to us."

"'Tis possible. I'm not sayin' the man's a total wanker, only 'tis also possible that there could be another just as well suited, or better—someone who means less to yeh. Maeve, everyone can see that yeh also *like* the man, and maybe more than like him, if yeh take me drift. That's what's got everything all bolloxed. I wonder if yer still goin' to be able to do what has to be done when the time comes—and I'm nah the only one wondering."

He nodded his head back toward the village. "Yer the Eldest. We follow yeh because of that. But are yeh lettin' yer feelings take yeh down the wrong path—one that has consequences for us all?"

In truth, she'd wondered that herself, more than once, but that was nothing she was willing to admit to him. She scowled, and drew herself up, allowing him to see a glimpse of her true face. He stepped back.

"Yeh needn't do that," he said.

"I think yeh need the reminder," she answered. "Yeh forget yourself, Niall. Yeh forget how we're connected, and who rules here."

"I've forgotten none a' that, and 'tis only my concern for all of us that makes me speak out now. To me, 'tis loyalty to speak out when I see something that threatens us, and unfaithfulness to remain silent. If yeh feel different, then maybe *that's* a problem as well."

Maeve sighed. She let the power flow unused from her, let her current face return. She reached out and touched his bare forearm. "Yer right in that, Niall. I want yer honesty. I *need* yer honesty. I'll never fault yeh for that, I promise. I'm sorry." She took another breath and let her hand fall away. "But I've not changed my mind. 'Tis Colin we need. Nah other."

Niall pressed his lips together. "Then I hope yer right, for all our sakes," he said. He bowed to her then. Without another word, he plucked his abandoned skin from the deck, turned, and dove into the water.

A breath later, she saw the form of a bull seal making its way through the harbor waves toward the ocean. "Cast off," she called to the others. "'Tis time to sail."

His bill settled with Mrs. Egan, the morning sun warm on his head, a bulging pack and two guitar cases heavy on his back, Colin walked down the hill toward the town center. He took a few pictures of Ballemór with his phone as he walked, just so he'd have the view to look back on: *Panorama of Ballemór Square in Morning Sun.*

At the bottom of the hill, he reached the intersection where Beach Road ran off to the right, while the Sky Road changed its name to the unimaginative "Main Street" and curved off left toward the square. He paused there, looking at the top of the monument in the square and the roofs of the buildings. A crow sat on the top of the street sign. As he glanced at the bird, it cawed harshly and flew off over his head, flying west along Beach Road.

Away from where he probably should go. Down beyond the square, the bus to Sligo was already idling.

He also noticed a garda cruiser idling across the street. As he looked at it, the passenger door opened and an older man with graying hair, wearing a suit that looked like it might have fit him several pounds ago, got out. The man gestured casually to Colin; with a sigh, Colin walked across the street to him. "Superintendent Cedric Dunn," the man said as Colin approached, holding up a leather wallet with a badge and identification. He let Colin glance at it, then snapped it shut and put it in his suit pocket. "Yer Colin Doyle." It was a statement rather than a question.

"Guilty," Colin said. He cocked his head quizzically. "Though I don't know why you'd care, Superintendent."

"American?"

"Guilty again."

"Mind if I see yer passport and visa?"

Colin shrugged off his backpack and rummaged in one of the zippered pockets, pulling out his papers. He handed them to Dunn. "Have I done something?" he asked.

The man smiled; Colin actually liked the smile—the gesture seemed genuine as it pulled the wrinkles deeper around the man's eyes. "Not that I know of," Dunn answered. He glanced at the passport, then at Colin, and handed the identification back to Colin. "Unless yeh'd like to confess to something, of course." He laughed, then his face collapsed into serious lines. "Yer going out to the island, are yeh?"

Dunn didn't have to name the island; Colin knew which one he meant. "As a matter of fact, I'm not," he told Dunn, which was the truth. After wrestling with everything in his head for the last few days and without the presence of Maeve to muddy the waters, he'd thought his mind was finally made up: it would be best and easiest for him to abandon the whole mess. Colin nodded his head in the direction of the bus. "I'm thinking of heading up to Sligo. I'm a musician, and there are places to play there. I might even head up toward Donegal before my visa expires." Colin hesitated, then: "Are you saying I wouldn't be allowed to go to Inishcorr?"

Dunn shrugged, his suit coat pulling dangerously at its buttons with the movement. "'Tis a free country, and I ca'nah stop yeh if that's where yeh want to go. Though yer friends won't be there long. They've been told they must leave; 'tis my job to make sure a'that."

"They've told me they won't be leaving voluntarily. I assume they've told you the same, Superintendent."

"They have, indeed. But we all have duties and obligations we must attend to, no matter what we might think ourselves. I'd be telling yer friends that, should yeh see 'em."

"As I said, I'm heading to Sligo."

"So yeh say." Dunn shrugged again. "Then I'll leave yeh to it, Mr. Doyle. As the saying goes, may the wind be at yer back." With that, Dunn got back into the cruiser and spoke briefly to the garda behind the wheel. The cruiser lurched into gear, and drove away. Colin watched it until it turned the corner at the bottom of Main Street, sliding past the waiting Sligo bus. Colin put his backpack on again, pondering the Superintendent's conversation.

It was easier to leave than to stay, and he tried to convince himself that also meant it was the right decision. Part of him still rebelled at that decision, believing that he was just demonstrating again that he'd rather run away than deal with a problem, and he had to admit there was truth in that as well.

But now here he was, and his feet didn't want to move in the right direction. He glanced down Beach Road, but if the *Grainne Ni Mhaille* was there, it was moored past the curve where the bulk of Ceomhar Head hid it from easy view of Ballemór.

"I'm sure you'll do what's right in the end." His mother's words, but he knew that she didn't expect that of him. He was the one who never did the "right" thing, at least not by his parents' reasoning. He was the one who followed his heart, not his head.

Listen to your heart, Aunt Patty had told him. She knew him.

He was also the one who fled rather than confront those who disagreed with him. He'd proven that more than once before, as well.

Sligo would be the right thing. In Sligo, there'd be no distractions. In Sligo, or in Donegal, or even back in Dublin, he could continue to work on his music, run out his remaining months, and go home to Chicago without encumbrance.

Sligo would be fleeing from the conflict. Fleeing from the drama. But Sligo would also mean he'd be without Maeve. He hated the thought of that.

The crow was still visible, high up in the brilliant, cloud-studded sky, circling well down Beach Road as if it had been watching him talking to Superintendent Dunn the whole time.

Colin tried to take the step onto Main Street toward the bus. Instead, he found his foot turning the other way, and that way simply *felt* right. He looked back over his shoulder toward Ballemór, but he couldn't make himself step that way at all. His whole being resisted the effort.

He took his grandfather's pendant from his pocket. He held it in his hand, staring at it. For a brief second, he thought he heard his grandfather's voice, faint but recognizable. *Go to her. Do what I should have done.* Then the voice was gone.

"Shit," he muttered. With that, he put his back to the town and started down Beach Road. The knot of uncertainty in his belly loosened with every step.

Ten minutes later, as he rounded the curve in the road, he saw the *Grainne Ni Mhaille* tied up a quarter mile farther down. On the road in front of the boat, he saw Maeve standing. She waved at him; he waved back.

He tried to convince himself that he was still doing the right thing. He didn't quite manage it, but in his heart it felt right.

◄ 23 ►

Revelations

HE COULD FEEL MAEVE WATCHING HIM as he put his belongings away in the bedroom of her house, leaning his two guitars against the wall, placing the O'Neill book reverently on top of the dresser, and arranging his clothes into a single long drawer. "Yeh travel light," she said as he closed the drawer. "Except for the guitars."

"Don't need much beyond them. A couple pairs of jeans, a few sweaters and T-shirts, a pair of shoes . . ." He shrugged. "I think I told you that my grandfather—Rory O' Callaghan, my mother's dad—emigrated from Ireland. I remember him saying many times that the more possessions you have, the more they weigh you down. He always told me that once you owned too much stuff, you'd find yourself too heavy to move and grow. He was supposedly quite a wanderer himself through his whole life: always restless, always taking off even after he was married, even into his seventies. He and my grandmother didn't settle down in Chicago until late in life, and even then I remember their house being bare and spartan compared to ours. Mom says I'm a lot like him—which, by the way, isn't a compliment, coming from her."

"I'm very certain yer like yer Daiddeó," Maeve commented. The undertone in her voice made him glance at her; she gave him a smile. "And what about yer Maimeó? How she'd like his wanderlust?" Maeve had moved across the room, standing close in front of him. Her hands went around him and she laid her head on his chest.

"He met her after he got to the States. I remember the two of them well: it was obvious she loved him, and he her. She enjoyed traveling, too, if not quite as much as he did. They'd go off on trips together two or three times a year as long as I knew them."

"But they never came back here?"

Colin shrugged. "No, they never did. I always thought that a little strange, since my grandfather was born here, and my grandmother's parents had come over as well. I asked him once, and he said there too many new places he'd never been to, so going back to one he already knew would be useless. They were the same with houses. Every few years, they'd pack up and move to some new city or state; my mom didn't like that much growing up, changing schools every few years, but she said they both claimed moving was what kept them young. And Daiddeó—you're right; that's what we called him, and my grandmother was Maimeó—might go off somewhere on his own for a few weeks now and then. My sister Jen would tell you that Maimeó always said that a good husband doesn't need a leash any more than a good dog does: he knows what he should and shouldn't do, knows where he belongs, and he always comes home."

Maeve laughed, the sound muffled against him. "She's a wise woman, then."

"She was."

"She's gone now?"

"Yeah, they both are. He died about a decade ago of a heart attack; Maimeó followed him a year later. Said the devil had probably had enough of him by then, and she needed to go steal him away."

Maeve chuckled at that. "I think the both of 'em would have fit in well here." She lifted her head up, raised up on her toes, and kissed him. "I hope yeh will, too."

"So far I like it." He smiled at her. "You're sure it's not a problem, my staying with you? I could take one of the empty houses, maybe fix it up . . ."

"Have yeh not lived with a lover before?"

He could feel his face reddening. "I did. Once. For about a year before we decided we liked each other more as friends."

He felt her nod against his chest. "I've done the same, an' more than once. The last time was a long time ago, though." Her arms tightened around him, then she stepped back, her head cocked so that her long hair fell over one shoulder. Her eyes, in this light, were the color of the sea under overcast skies. "It's yer choice, Colin. If it would make yeh more comfortable, yeh can live on yer own. Or yeh can stay here. Yer choice, and I promise I'll take no offense either way."

"No," he told her. "I'm fine if you are. This feels . . . right." And it did. Even as he said the words, a calmness settled around him. He opened his arms and she slid back into his embrace.

"Yeah," he said. "This is definitely good."

The next morning, Keara, carrying a plate of freshly-baked blueberry scones, entered the house with no more warning than a soft knock, startling Colin who was sitting in the living room gently strumming the Gibson. Maeve was still in the bedroom.

"You're damned lucky I was dressed," he said to Keara.

She gave a short, bright laugh. "Oh, I dunno. That depends on yer point of view, I'd say. Want one?" she asked Colin, proffering the plate to him. "I'll put water on for tea. Is herself up yet?"

Keara nodded her head in the direction of the bedroom. "Herself?" Colin laughed. "She was stirring a bit when I left. You always bring her breakfast?"

She shrugged, a little shyly. "Often enough. She likes my baking and cooking, so . . ."

"So what *is* Maeve to all of you? Everyone seems to defer to her like she's royalty."

"She is," Keara answered. "T'us, anyway."

"What do you mean?"

Keara gave a shrug. "Yeh should ask her, though I should think by this time yeh already have yer suspicions."

"Meaning what?"

"Meaning that yer nah stupid, and it's right in front of yeh t'see." She lifted the plate of scones again. "Sure yeh don't want one? They're good, I promise. Let me get the tea going, and I'll set the table in the nook for the two of yeh. Why don't yeh go tell her that things will be ready in a few minutes?"

Colin watched Keara go into the kitchen, her long dress swaying. He leaned the Gibson against the arm of the chair, tilting it so the headstock rested safely against the back, and went to the bedroom. He knocked softly on the open door, but Maeve was already sitting up, the coverlet pooled around her waist. She yawned. "I heard Keara come in," she said.

"Yeah. She said that tea and scones will be ready in a few minutes." He leaned against the door, watching her as she ran fingers through her hair, threw the covers aside, and put on a robe. "You always get this kind of service, Maeve? I thought the way everyone waited on us last time was something unusual, but evidently it's not."

"Does it bother yeh?"

"I guess not. It's just . . . not something I expected."

She gave a laugh at that. "Expectations get yeh into trouble. In the meantime, I really need to pee and brush my teeth, so if yeh don't mind, tell Keara I'll be out in a few. Yeh can go ahead and start, if yer hungry. G'wan with yeh now."

With that, she went into the tiny bathroom off the bedroom and closed the door: as Colin had seen the night before, there was little there but a chamber pot and a little sink with a hand pump to pull a thin stream of water from the cistern. As far as Colin knew, there was no indoor plumbing on Inishcorr, and every cottage also had an outhouse in the rear.

Colin padded into the kitchen, where Keara had filled the teapot from the hand pump in the kitchen sink, and was setting it over a wood fire in the hearth. He sat at the table. "Y'know, at the very least, you people could bring propane from the mainland for the stoves," he said.

Keara grinned over her shoulder at him. "We have all the ancient conveniences here. I don't miss the modern ones much, though I must say that flush toilets have their good qualities." Keara grinned. "In general, things take longer here, if we do have to get the water from the town well and rain barrels. Yeh have to be more patient; that's nah a bad thing, all told. I like the pace, and I like the quiet. Same with music—I prefer the old tunes. Yeh too, right?"

He nodded. Maeve came in then, still wearing her robe. "Would yeh like me to cook up some eggs and bacon?" Keara asked. Colin couldn't avoid noticing that the question was directed at Maeve, not himself.

"No, the scones look lovely, dear," Maeve replied. "I'm sure they'll be enough." The teapot rumbled and whistled on its hook; Keara swung out the crane, wrapped a hand towel around the handle and moved the pot to the table, dropping in a ball infuser. The aroma of mint and spice rose from the boiling water.

"If there's nothing else, I'll be on me way," Keara said, with a faint inclination of her head to Maeve.

"Thank you, Keara. We'll see yeh later, then." Maeve took the seat across from Colin and plucked a scone from the plate, taking a bite. "These are delicious."

Keara nearly curtsied at the comment. "Thank you, ma'am. I'll be going, then. Will yeh need me for lunch?"

"No, we'll manage here."

"I'll see yeh at supper, then." With a quick nod of her head, Keara was gone. Colin raised an eyebrow toward Maeve.

"So you're royalty," he said.

"Maybe to those of us here, in a way," she said. "Not to anyone else beyond this island. Tea?" She poured a cup for herself, then filled the cup in front of him. He stared at it.

"That day in the woods, the dream I had in the fairy ring. Are you saying that you're . . ." He couldn't finish the statement, but she nodded.

"Aye. 'Twas real, in a manner of speaking."

"How am I supposed to believe that?"

She smiled at him as a forefinger stroked the rim of her teacup. "Yeh already do, mostly, or yeh wouldn't be here. Yeh'd still be in Ballemór playing with Lucas, or yeh'd have gone on yer way up to Sligo and beyond." Still smiling, she took a long breath. "Rory believed it. 'Tis what frightened him, I think."

"Rory . . . My grandfather?"

"Aye," Maeve said to his implied question. "Drink yer tea and have a scone. I'll go get dressed. I have things to show yeh."

"Haven't yeh ever been somewhere, somewhere old, and felt like there was a *presence* around yeh—like the people who had once been there hadn't entirely left?"

Maeve spoke as they walked. Colin had been silent since they'd left the cottage, seemingly lost in his own thoughts. She could see the confusion in his face, the visible sign of what she knew was an internal struggle to make sense of things. *Yeh can't make sense of this until yer willing to give up yer old ways of thinking,* she wanted to tell him. She hoped he was ready for that, because he would need to be.

"You're talking ghosts?" Maeve shrugged, and watched as Colin waited for her to say more. "I guess I have," Colin said finally, when it was apparent she wasn't going to say more. They were standing near the mound of the hawthorn tree, on the small cliff edge with the cold water of the Atlantic crashing into the rocks below them. A briny scent from the spray filled their nostrils. To their right, a faint, steep path led down to a rocky beach, and a quartet of seals cavorted in the water below them, diving and honking at each other. "Sometimes, in old houses, I've heard creaks and groans or felt cold air, or had the classic shiver down my spine like someone's behind me. Sure. But I've never actually *seen* any apparitions or anything supernatural."

"Maybe you just didn't listen or look hard enough. Come on." Maeve took Colin's hand and led him to the path to the beach. "Be careful. If you slip here, you won't be stopping until you hit the stones at the bottom."

That was true enough: the stones were wet with spray and moss covered, but Maeve had traversed them often enough to know where to walk. Behind her, Colin took his time, using his hands often to steady himself and at times half-sliding downward. She reached the beach long before he did, laughing as she looked back up the slope to him. "Are yeh asleep up there, Colin?" she called out.

"Very funny. You'd probably find it hilarious if I ended up on the rocks with a broken leg or arm." It took him several minutes more to clamber down the path until he stood, panting, next to her. His glasses had slipped down his nose during the descent; she watched him adjust them. The beach was pebbled and coarse, little more than a few feet of shelf littered with broken mussel shells and small rocks at the foot of the cliff, and perhaps only twenty yards long before it vanished entirely. The seals had stopped swimming; they stared at the two of them from boulders a few yards out from the beach, wet in the green-gray waves. One of them honked curiously in their direction, and Maeve beckoned with a curve of her arm.

The seal barked in response, and slid from the rock into the sea. Colin watched it swim toward the end of the beach, behind a tumble of boulders. The seal vanished for several moments, long enough that Colin started to look away. "No," Maeve told him. She put her hand on his arm. "Keep watching."

She watched his face as a man rose up from behind the rock, entirely naked, his hair plastered wet from the sea. He carried a black pelt draped over one arm, and Maeve saw Colin's moment of recognition: it was Liam, one of the people he'd met that first evening in Regan's. As Liam approached them, stepping carefully on the rocks and shells, he held out to them a seal's pelt, also dripping wet, the skin whole. "This what you wanted him to see, Maeve?" Liam asked, holding out the pelt. Despite the nudity, his attitude was as casual as if they'd just met in the pub.

"Show him, Liam," Maeve told Liam. Then, to Colin: "G'wan. Touch it."

Liam held out the pelt, and Maeve nodded to Colin. He glanced from Maeve to Liam, then reached out and stroked the skin, though Liam held tightly to the pelt as if he were afraid that Colin might snatch it from him. The fur was soft and damp, with blue highlights glinting from the dark fur. "That's me," Liam said. "At least, most of the time. The skin of my true form."

Maeve saw Colin's eyes widen behind his glasses. "I . . ." Colin began to say, but his voice faltered. "You're saying you're a selkie?"

He sniffed and shivered. "Aye. As are some of the others here: Niall, for instance," he answered. "And if yeh don't mind, it's fierce cold out here without clothes an' in this form, so I'll be changin' back now." With that, he opened the pelt as if it were a cloak, placing it around his shoulders. As Colin watched, the skin seemed to writhe and envelop Liam's human form: as he hunched down, first to his knees, then lying down entirely. The seal's head opened like a mouth along its throat, swallowing Liam's head and pulling down tightly. Maeve had heard the accompanying sounds from the transformation a thousand times in the past, but she still wasn't certain how to describe it, like the crunching of small bones under a boot or the crackling of a fire against damp wood. The sealskin fully covered Liam's body now, muscles and hidden forms wriggling under the fur. With a shudder, the seal suddenly lifted its head, its black eyes like polished jet staring at Colin, the whiskered muzzle lifting, the mouth opening. The seal barked once, then waddled over the beach toward the water, its flippers raking the beach. It pushed into a wave and started swimming back toward the rocks.

To Maeve, Colin looked slightly sick, as if someone had just punched him hard in the stomach. He was shaking his head. "Are you saying you're one of . . . *them*?" he asked Maeve.

"I'm nah one of them," she answered. "I'm something else entirely. *Someone* else."

That made him feel slightly more comfortable. "So what are you to them? What's going on here?"

"Yeh already know, my love," she answered. "Yeh just haven't wanted to admit it aloud because it threatens the entire way yeh view the world." Her chin lifted. The wind from the sea lifted her dark hair as she stared at him, her gaze tinged with sadness. She closed her eyes momentarily, letting the spell that held her appearance relax and taking on her old form, her true form. As she did so, a glow kindled around her, brightening so that it was visible even in the wan daylight, as if a floodlight the color of the late afternoon sun had sparked deep within her, its radiance shimmering through skin gone translucent. Shadows shifting along the beach in response as the seals on their rocks barked raucously.

Her hands spread wide. Her voice was a trumpet, her breath was spice and blood. The seals howled into the storm of her words. "Oh, my dear one . . . I'm what yeh thought I might be, what yeh've seen once already, what yer grandfather knew. Back when we first met, Colin, yeh said that I was named after Queen Medb of the *Tain*, but I was never her friend even if I've used her name. I've had so many names and guises in the past that I've forgotten most of them. As the hag told yeh under the mound on Ceomhar Head, I am the Morrígan. I am the Phantom Queen."

In that moment, the radiance of her was so bright that she saw Colin shade his eyes. He staggered back, cold waves lapping at his ankles as mussel shells cracked under his sneakered feet. "No, that isn't possible."

Through the brilliance, she smiled toward him, understanding his confusion and denial. "Yeh say that, my love, even when all your senses insist that yer wrong. Listen to yer heart and believe this. I am the Queen, we are going to war, and you, Colin of the Caul, are to be my Cúchulainn."

The radiance died around her as she brought the spell back around her like a cloak, and Maeve closed her eyes to take in a long breath of the sea air. "Ahh," she sighed. "That's *so* exhausting to do," she said. She opened her eyes again to see Colin still staring at her, his mouth open, almost wet to the knees from the surf in his retreat from her. "I'm sorry," she told him. "'Twas time to open yer eyes, love."

She held her hand out to him. He just stared at it. "Colin," she said gently, "I'm still the same person. I'm Maeve, the woman you slept with last night. I'm no different now than I was then."

He didn't move. On their rocks, the seals watched and listened, and she gestured at them to leave. Colin's head turned with the movement of her hand; they both watched the two selkies slide into the water, diving underneath the foam. Colin's head swiveled back to her. "The woman I slept with last night didn't function as her own nightlight. I'd've noticed that."

"Cute," she told him. "But wrong. Colin, yeh asked me to show you what I was, and now I have. But I haven't changed. I've always been this, ever since yeh knew me."

"The Morrígan? A goddess from Celtic mythology. Someone who only existed in ancient tales and stories? How am I supposed to believe that?"

She could feel his distress, and that made her want to take a step toward him, to fold him into her embrace as she had last night, to comfort him however she could. The potential inside him surged and roiled; she wondered that Colin couldn't feel it, that he couldn't take it up himself and use it, too early now.

This isn't the time or the place . . .

"Believe your eyes," she told him. "I'm a woman first. The Morrígan . . . I'm born in a new body as soon as the old one wears out—it's a weary thing, to carry the Morrígan in human form. This body—" she spread her hands out, "—is the latest of many. More than I could ever count over the centuries. I'm as human as yeh are yerself, Colin, but aye, I'm also the Morrígan, and I have always lived here in this land. I'd hoped to always be here, but 'tis not to be. One way or another."

She didn't move. She waited. *You have to trust him. He's the one you chose.*

"You said you're going to war?" he asked, his incredulity making almost a laugh of the phrase.

"Not just yet, and not war as yer thinking of it," she answered. "But that's what it feels like, to those of us who have gathered here. The world out there doesn't want us anymore; too few of 'em have any belief in us, which is all that sustains us, and so we keep losing ground. Yeats called it the 'Celtic Twilight,' this dwindling and shifting of beliefs way back at the turn of the nineteenth century into the twentieth, and 'twas true then that the old ways had already begun to die. 'Tis a long, slow, and incomplete death we face, but the pace is quickening as the centuries and decades and years go by. So many of our kind are gone now: vanished, or asleep in their barrows, or entirely dead. Those of us who are left are fighting to hold on until we can find our own place."

"Here? On Inishcorr?"

She shook her head. "No. But 'tis here that we'll find the path to that place, if we can. With yer help."

"*My* help?" His forefinger stabbed at his glasses, dewed with spray from the surf. "I'm a nearsighted guitar player and singer. You want to entertain someone with old Irish folk tunes, I'm your guy. Want me to help plant your potatoes or cut some turf or herd your sheep, I could probably manage to learn to do that, too. Beyond that, I don't see what I have to offer. I don't know what you're talking about or what to do." He stopped, his hands wide.

"Yeh might try stepping out of the water first, before yeh catch your death," she told him. She extended her hand again. He wouldn't take it, but he did step back fully onto the beach. His pants dripped; his sneakers were soaked through. He shivered. Again, she felt the impulse to embrace him; again, she held back, knowing he wouldn't accept it. Not now.

"Back on Ceomhar Head," he said, "in that dream, you . . . or the Morrígan I dreamed was you . . . said something about me being able to open a door. What's that mean?"

"Are yeh admitting that the dream was real, now?"

He shrugged. He shifted his feet on the pebbles and mussel shells, and she could hear his socks squelching. He took off his glasses and cleaned them on his T-shirt. "Dunno," he answered. "I'm just asking."

"Then let's get ourselves back up there," she said, pointing to the cliff top, "an' maybe I can answer."

Maeve turned at the top of the path; Colin was climbing up after her, on all fours and scrabbling for handholds on the mossy gray rocks. She watched him, wanting to reach down and help him but knowing that he wouldn't allow it. He finally managed to reach the top without mishap and stood, his jeans and jacket stained with mud. He wiped his hands on his jeans. She could feel the cloch there also, a simmering power. "Okay," he said, "so what—" He stopped, and she saw him looking past her shoulder, his eyes narrowed. "Who the hell's that?" he asked.

She glanced back, and her own breath slipped from her. "Yeh *see* him?" she asked Colin.

"Aye, that he does," the figure answered for Colin, though he spoke in Gaelic, not English. "What did you expect, Morrígan? One caul was taken from him at birth, and now you've ripped away the other. He sees true enough now. So this is the one t' open our path, is he?"

The speaker was a man, as tall as Colin, handsome and fair-haired, with eyes the same green that Maeve saw in the mirror each morning. He was dressed in a fine, silken cloak of blue, belted over plainer clothes, and from his side hung a long sword in its scabbard, the pommel wrapped in well-worn leather. One hand rested comfortably there; the other was on his hip as he stood at the base of the mound of the hawthorn tree. Maeve inclined her head to him. "Fionnbharr. Yeh'll be leaving Colin alone," she said, speaking also in Gaelic. "He's mine."

"The man's not a piece of furniture nor a pet, Morrígan. But I'll leave him be for now, perhaps. We'll see if yeh can manage to keep him." Fionnbharr stepped toward them, though she knew he wouldn't break the line of the standing stones ringing the base of the mound.

"What are you two saying?" Colin asked Maeve. He squinted toward Fionnbharr as if the apparition were hard to see, like a shadow glimpsed in twilight.

"Come closer, mortal," Fionnbharr answered, in heavily-accented English this time. His voice was honed steel, ringing and sharp. He gestured toward Colin, who glanced at Maeve.

"Don't step inside the ring, and yeh'll be safe," she said to Colin, nodding, and Colin moved past her to stand just outside the stones, an arm's length from Fionnbharr, who looked Colin up and down closely, leaning in almost as if to sniff him. "There's death around yeh," Fionnbharr stated. "Yeh lost someone close to yeh recently, but that's not why the stench remains."

"Fionnbharr," Maeve said warningly. There was never a certainty that the aos sí were on any side other than their own; over the long centuries, they had always made for uneasy allies. It had been that way since the aos sí had retreated into their Otherworld inside the mounds after their defeat by the mortal Sons of Míl centuries ago. She still remembered those battles and that time, and not with pleasure. Fionnbharr, as one of their leaders, was not someone Maeve entirely trusted. He glanced over to her with a leer on his face.

"What's the matter, lass?" he said. "I'm not coddlin' 'im. Yeh do'nah want yer man to know what yer about?" He gave a short, bitter laugh that the stones echoed, as if the hidden aos sí were also listening. Colin heard them, too; she saw his head lift as he looked around. "No worries. 'Tis not yer death I'm talkin' about, mortal. Not yet."

"Whose, then?" Colin asked.

Fionnbharr gave a one-shouldered shrug that rattled the scabbarded sword at his side. "Everyone of yer kind dies," he answered. He inclined his head toward Maeve. "Even the Morrígan will die—at least the body she's wearing now will, and she'll have to rob another. Death stalks yeh all. But that's not what I wished to tell yeh, mortal. Those things yeh speak of in the old songs?—they're not just tales and stories; they're real, or parts of them were, an' some a' the creatures that lived in them still walk this land. They're weak and sick, most of 'em, but they live, an' they want to keep on livin'. The Morrígan wants yeh to open a path for them, for us—a way to a safer place—but yeh should remember that doors work both ways, an' that's the problem: keeping out what's inside. The aos sí opened our own door when we fled from yeh mortals, so we *know*. She hasn't told yeh yet what the cost is to be, has she?"

"Fionnbharr," Maeve said again in warning. She raised her hand, pulling in the energy of the air around her. The wind began to blow, the hawthorn tree on the mound above them bending. Dirt and leaves flew around her, the center of a burgeoning tornado.

"Och, there's no need of violence now, Morrígan," Fionnbharr said in Gaelic to her, looking alarmed. "I'll be gone and leave yer poor fool still a fool." With that, he gestured himself, flinging a hand toward the sky. Lightning cracked from the clouds above, blinding; the following thunderclap deafened Maeve momentarily. When her vision cleared, Fionnbharr had vanished. The echo of the thunder still lingered, rebounding from Ceomhar Head three miles away, and still dinning in her ears. Grudgingly, Maeve released the energy she'd captured. The whirlwind around her dissipated, blowing off seaward. The wind diminished into the normal salt-laden breeze off the Atlantic, and the branches of the hawthorn settled once more.

She sighed, a weariness surging through her as it always did when she touched the world that way. This world was, mostly, no longer hers to affect, and it exhausted her to do so.

With the flash of lightning, Colin had scrambled backward, landing on his rump, his glasses falling off onto the ground. From his sitting position on the grass, he shook his head groggily as she went to him.

"Are yeh hurt, darlin'?" she asked, crouching alongside him. She hugged him, quickly; this time, he didn't pull away. "Fionnbharr likes dramatic exits."

He found his glasses, put them back on, and blinked at her. "Dramatic's a good word for it. So I *did* see him, then? I was talking to one of the mound-folk?"

"Aye, yeh were indeed." She hugged him again, sitting alongside him on the damp earth. The sun struggled from behind clouds, and the ring of stones cast spiked shadows around them. "I'm sorry, Colin. Yeh deserve the truth, an' that's what I've been trying to tell yeh."

He blinked again. "The truth, then. You're really the Morrígan?"

A nod. "I was, once. I still am, a part of me anyway."

"This is awfully hard to process or even believe, I have to tell you." He looked at her, and behind the glasses, his eyes were full of confusion and hurt.

"I understand. I truly do. But I don't like having to lie to . . ." She chose her next words carefully. ". . . someone I believe I love."

There. The hook is set, even if you're no longer certain that you want to land this fish and see him gutted and cleaned for the table. The words had come too easily, and the conviction in them had been too real. She wanted to take them back. She wanted to tell Colin to flee, now, before he was snared too tightly in Inishcorr's affairs, before their relationship held him fast. She wanted not to be the Morrígan, but just a mortal person—to be Maeve and no more than that. *Yeh were ensorcelled,* she wanted to tell him. *That first night, when yeh met me. I cast my spell and caught you, the same way I caught your grandfather . . .*

She smiled, plainly, despite the thoughts fighting in her mind. Once, she'd felt the same about Rory. She'd thought she'd captured him . . . and yet he'd left her. Left her and the others, back when there was still time and hope.

Now there was very little of either.

She saw Colin struggle to return her smile. "Maeve . . ."

"Nah," she told him, wagging a finger in his face. "What I just said doesn't obligate yeh to say anything in return. In fact, please don't, be-cause if what yeh say 'tis anything like what I want to hear, I won't—I could'nah—believe it now. Save it for when I can."

He nodded. "Okay, I will," he answered. He looked down at himself. "I'm soaked to the knees, my clothes are filthy with mud, and I'm sitting on my ass in a wet field. Quite the dashing figure, aren't I?"

She laughed and kissed him hard and quickly. "Yer my hero," she said. "And hey, how many men can say they made love to a goddess, even a mostly forgotten one?" She rose to her feet and extended her hand. "Come on, hero," she said. "Let's get yeh some dry clothes."

This time, he took her hand.

24

A Blindness Lifted

"**H**ERE," MAEVE SAID, handing him a sheaf of thick papers embossed with an Irish harp and foil letters across the top proclaiming *National Parks & Wildlife Services: Parks & Reserves Unit*. "Read this; it will tell yeh a lot of what's going on, and why everyone's on edge right now." She sat down at the table across from Colin. Keara, as promised, had brought supper to Maeve's cottage and set it on the table, then taken her leave once again. Colin took up the papers, leaning back in his chair and sipping from the mug of tea in front of him. He settled his glasses on his nose and scanned the words, glancing occasionally at Maeve.

She'd been strangely quiet during their walk back from Fionnbharr's mound (which she told him was named Cnoc Deireadh), deflecting his questions with promises to answer later. His own head was a whirl of confusion: the revelation of Liam, witnessing the transformation in Maeve, seeing Fionnbharr. Part of him still wanted to refuse to believe any of it. He especially wanted to disbelieve the talk of him being caught up in some mythical conflict.

Yet . . . he could still remember the Maeve of last night. He could remember the taste and smell of her, the gentle caresses and lovemaking, her sighs as they made love. That Maeve had been real and solid, and there had been nothing imaginary about his feelings for her—and, he could hope given what she'd said to him, her feelings for him.

He scanned the words on the paper, trying to make sense of them against the confusion in his heart. The words kept wanting to bleed together into an indecipherable gray. He forced his eyes to focus. "This is saying that Inishcorr is the property of the NPWS, and they are giving you two weeks to vacate the island—as of three weeks ago. One of the people who signed this is Superintendent Dunn—as it happens, I met him just before I came back here."

Maeve gave a laugh at that. "I'm not surprised. He's a decent enough man, Dunn, but he's all bound up in rules and regulations and what he thinks is his duty."

"And this is the third notice they've given you? You've not given them any response to the others?"

"I went and talked to Dunn a while back," she told him. "I told him that we weren't going to leave. He wasn't happy."

"It appears not. They're threatening to forcibly remove you this time. 'By any and all means necessary.' That doesn't sound good."

"Aye," she said finally and—to Colin's mind—far too calmly. "We won't allow them to remove us. We ca'nah. We've been pushed as far as we can be. 'Tis here we will stand, no matter what. Finally."

"Maeve, they'll put you all in jail."

She shook her head. "Neh, they won't. They ca'nah take Inishcorr if they ca'nah get to it."

"I don't understand what you mean."

"Can yeh go under Cnoc Deireadh with Fionnbharr?" she asked him.

"No. Well, not without some digging equipment. Give me a good back-hoe, and maybe . . ."

She laughed, but her amusement seemed more sad that anything else. "Even then, 'twouldn't work. The world under the mound isn't a place yeh can dig to—nor will Inishcorr be. There are other 'lost' Irish islands; Inishcorr will join them if need be. Become part of them."

"And how will that happen?"

"I don't know yet," she told him. The sadness seemed to fill her then. She looked away, closing her eyes hard, then back again. "We'll figure it out. Yeh'll help figure it out, and I'll help you."

He shook his head at that. "Maeve, I've no clue what you're talking about or what you expect me to do. None. You—everyone—seems to expect something from me and . . ." He sighed, putting the NPWS notice on the table. "Right now, all I feel is lost. I'm sorry. I'm not Cúchulainn—not anything close. I'm not a warrior and I'm not strong. I'm a decent musician and, I hope, a halfway decent person. That's all."

A smile came and vanished, like a spring snow. "Yeh are all and everything I want."

"What *you* want, or what the Morrígan wants?"

"Both," she answered. She pushed her chair back and came over to him, crouching alongside him and leaning her head on his shoulder as his arm—almost of its own accord—went around her. "And for this moment, let's just be Maeve and Colin, and forget the rest. Can we do that, for at least this evening?"

He wanted to shake his head, wanted to say "no," but he couldn't. With her touch, his mind eased and the confusion receded. "We can try," he told her, and he turned into her embrace.

The pub at Inishcorr harbor was busy that night. Maeve had wanted to go, had wanted Colin to bring his guitar. "Yeh'll be feeling more yerself if yeh play a set or two with Keara and the others," she'd insisted.

He thought she might be right. The guitar case felt familiar and comfortable in his hand as they walked toward the pub, and he heard the strains of Keara's fiddle, somebody playing bodhran, and two voices in harmony singing "Dark-Eyed Sailor." When the two entered the pub, the song was ending, and Keara waved at Colin from the little stage in front. "Colin! Get your guitar and a pint, and bring yer sorry arse up here!"

"G'wan with yeh," Maeve laughed along with several of the patrons. "I need to talk with some of the others."

"All right. Save me a seat, then."

"Promise." She gave him a quick kiss and a pat on the rump. He grinned back at her.

Colin snagged a Guinness from the bar, the foam still settling, and took his guitar up to the little stage. He put the Guinness on one of the stools there, laid his case on the stage, and took out his Gibson. He took a sip of the stout and placed it on the floor next to him as he sat on the stool, the curve of the Gibson's body comfortably over his thigh. "Give me a 'G,'" he told Keira, and tuned his guitar as she played the note. "What do you want to play first?"

"How about 'Cliffs of Dooneen'? Yeh know the verses?"

"Some, not all," Colin answered. "Enough, I'm sure."

"Then let's do it . . ." With that, Keara launched into the melody with her fiddle, and Colin followed with the guitar, and the bodhran player played softly along, accenting the beat. After a verse and chorus instrumentally, Colin began to sing:

> *You may travel far from your own native land*
> *Far away o'er the mountains, far away o'er the foam*
> *But of all the fine places that I've ever been*
> *Sure there's none can compare with the cliffs of Dooneen*

Colin felt the world shift around him before the first verse had ended. It began with a pulse from his grandfather's stone in his pocket, a lance of raw fire running through him. He drew in his breath with the next line, and it seemed that the pub around him became somehow thin and semi-transparent, and past it, he saw another land entirely: tall, rounded mountains blanketed with green bracken and girdled with oak forests, misted valleys between, a sapphire sky pillowed with clouds, and in the distance, a line of green-blue sea frothing at cliffs. With the vision, he felt a pulse of homesickness, as if this were a glimpse of a world to which he belonged, even though it was no place he'd ever seen before.

At the same time, he heard his voice swell, booming in the room, his tones as rich and colored as that of a cello played by a master hand. With each line, his voice gained depth and power, and he could see everyone in the pub turning to him, their conversations dying forgotten, leaving only the song and his voice.

> *Take a view o'er the mountains, fine sights you'll see there*
> *You'll see the high rocky mountains o'er the west coast of Clare*
> *Oh, the towns of Kilkee and Kilrush can be seen*
> *From the high rocky slopes round the cliffs of Dooneen*

When the song ended, two more verses along, there was a reverent silence, then a deafening roar of applause and approval. Colin grinned into the applause; the energy of their approval filling him, as nourishing as a gourmet meal. "Another!" someone shouted. "'Tis grand, that! Yeh have the gift, yeh do!"

Keara was tapping on her fiddle's body with her bow. She leaned toward Colin. "I've never heard the like. Never. An' I saw the far land. I *saw* it, even if them out there di'nah," she whispered to him. "I saw it without a spell. Maeve is right about yeh. Yer the one to help us." She ran the bow over the strings, calling forth a new melody. "So, how about 'Castlehyde'?" she asked. "Can yeh do that again with it?"

Colin lifted his shoulders in a helpless shrug, the grin still on his face. He saw Maeve watching him. She smiled as his gaze snagged hers, and she nodded to him, as if she, too, had seen what he'd seen.

"Don't know," he said to Keara.

"Then let's find out."

He found he could. Again, as he began to sing, his grandfather's stone responded with searing heat that found its way into his body and his voice, that while he was singing caused the air in the pub to shimmer and call forth another vision that slid over reality like a ghostly mask only to vanish as quickly as it had come.

He wondered if they could all see it.

The visions would come again with the next song, and the next, as well, and if those in the pub didn't seem to notice them as he did, as Keara evidently did, they could all hear the power that had been given to his voice, and to that they responded.

An hour or so later, the musicians took a break to tremendous applause and cheers for Colin. Colin was still reeling from what had happened, the applause filling him with heat and light. He put the Gibson in its case, hugged Keara, and headed for the bar to get another pint. He could see Maeve in the far corner of the pub nearest the door, now in deep conversation with Liam, Aiden, and a few others. "Another pint, thanks," he told the bartender.

"After that, yeh deserve it an' more," the bartender told him. "That was sometin'." He shook his head. "I never heard the like."

"Thanks," Colin told him, beaming. As the barkeep turned to the tap and Colin leaned against the bar, he heard a voice behind him.

"So now yeh know all about us? Yeh think that because they call out yer name when yeh sing, that because yeh can make them think of another place, that yer all special?" Colin turned to face Niall. The man was standing a little too close for Colin's comfort—though that was usual enough in Ireland. His face still bore the vestiges of the beating he'd taken at Regan's: a touch of purple under the eyes, the shadow of a bruise on his cheek. Colin could smell alcohol on the man's breath. "Liam said Maeve made him show yeh his skin," Niall continued, his words slightly slurred and his accent heavier than usual. "I would nah have done it, no matter what she said." He shook his head. "Yer just a pretty boy, and not the one we need. Maeve's made a mistake and ca'nah admit it, 'specially now that she's shagging yeh." His dark eyes looked Colin up and down. "Yeh don't look to me like yeh could beat fecking snow off a rope."

It might have been the two pints he'd already had, or perhaps the long and strange day, or perhaps the residue of the power and fire from his grandfather's stone. Colin could feel the muscles tightening in his face. "Y'know, Niall, if I ever find your sealskin on the beach, I might just take it and burn it."

Niall sniffed in disdain. "Boyo, the problem with yeh is yer all mouth and no trousers."

Colin could see Maeve over Niall's shoulder, glancing in their direction with a worried look on her face. "Look, just let me by . . ."

Niall didn't move. "Yer going to hide behind the lady's skirts? Are yeh that scared a'me that yer brickin' it?"

He knew that Niall was deliberately goading him. He knew that he shouldn't respond, that he should just press his lips together, grab his pint, and slide past him, knowing that Niall probably wouldn't do more than make another comment to his back.

He knew that. He started to move, and Niall pressed a hand against his chest, pushing him. "Niall!" Colin heard Maeve call in warning, but Niall ignored her and pushed at Colin again.

The shove seemed to click something over within Colin. He let all the anger, frustration, and confusion of the day take him.

He slammed his pint glass down on the bar, and he swung.

Colin's fist hit Niall square in the nose. He heard a distinct crack and saw blood smear across Niall's cheek as the man staggered back. Niall howled and threw a wild roundhouse punch in Colin's direction. Colin blocked Niall's fist with left forearm, though he winced with the force of the contact, and struck again, this time sweeping his fisted right hand across Niall's chin. He felt the contact, jarring his arm and splitting open the skin of his knuckles. Niall went down, suddenly, to his knees, his eyes glazed and his mouth open, his bottom lip drooling red.

By that time, hands had grabbed Colin from behind, and another of the islanders stepped between Niall and Colin as two other patrons helped Niall to his feet. Niall was cursing, spitting blood, and trying to lunge at Colin, but the others held him and dragged him away. "C'mon," one of them said. "Yer bloody bolloxed, Niall. Let's take the air . . ." The door to the pub opened, and they escorted him outside, with Niall still shouting obscenities and fighting their restraining hands.

The hands around Colin relaxed, one of them slapping him affectionately on the back as he looked at his right fist. Blood was smeared over it, his own and Niall's. His knuckles throbbed. His left forearm was going to have a nasty bruise tomorrow. He saw Maeve making her way through the crowd around him. In front of him, she put her hands on her hips, shaking her head. "I hope yer feeling proud of yerself now," she said, but a smile lurked in the corners of her lips.

"Actually, I am," he told her. "Niall's done nothing but act like an ass toward me, and he deserved that."

"And yeh think that come tomorrow he'll come up and give yeh a big hug all friendly-like, now that yeh've shown him what a real man you are?" Sarcasm rode heavily on her words.

"No," he admitted sheepishly, then added with a smile: "But it still felt good."

Maeve shook her head again. "Boys," she said. She took his hand in hers. "Let's get yeh cleaned up. Why don't yeh get yer guitar and we'll walk back to the house? There's been enough excitement tonight." She hugged him then, lifting on her toes to whisper in his ear. "I thought yeh did just grand, all around."

He grinned at her.

He didn't sleep well that night. His dreams were wild and touched with violence and strange mythical characters. He awoke as false dawn was painting the horizon, slid from bed without waking Maeve, and left the house. He walked up the path toward Fionnbharr's mound. The air was still; mist-ghosts writhed and rose from the dewed ground. He strode through them, the cold wetness leaving droplets on his woolen pullover and beading his glasses so that he had to wipe them clean more than once. The mist seemed to cling to him with insistent fingers that didn't wish to let him pass. He thought he could hear a constant whispering around him, words in Gaelic that drifted just on the edge of comprehension.

It seemed he couldn't leave his dreams behind.

He shivered.

He half-expected to see Fionnbharr standing inside the circle of stone around Croc Deireadh, but the hawthorn stood lonely, its branches swaying in the ocean breeze, the leaves rustling softly. He remained carefully outside the ring of stone, walking uphill around them until he stood at the sea cliff, at the head of the path down to the beach. Fifty feet or more below him, waves battered at the rocks there, foam making lacy patterns on the gray-green water as it surged away, then in again.

Colin sat on a mossy rock at the top of the cliff, his thoughts as chaotic and torn as the waves below him.

The previous day . . . it had been nearly too much to process. Seeing Liam transform from seal to human and back; the blubbery soft fur of his sealskin; Maeve's insistence that she was the Morrígan or at least some shadow of that ancient goddess; the way she'd changed her appearance; Fionnbharr of the aos sí and his hints of death and violence; the way his grandfather's stone had reacted to the music last night; the way his voice had morphed into something he'd never heard before; the glimpses of another world he'd seen as he sang; his fight with Niall . . .

Now that the alcohol had worn off, here in the unrelenting light of a new day, all of it seemed distant and impossible.

He put his right hand in his pocket, wincing a bit as his bruised knuckles slid along the denim, and took out Rory's stone—his cloch, as he'd called it. He held it in his fingers, looking at it from all sides, staring into its emerald-hued depths as if it might hold the answers he sought.

Yes, maybe Maeve could have set all of this up, performed some elaborate deception involving special effects, sleight of hand, smoke and mirrors, whatever—but *why?* Why go to all that trouble to convince him that what she was saying was true? He had nothing to offer the Oileánach; he wasn't rich, and while his family wasn't poor, they were solidly middle class and entirely lacking influence in Irish affairs. He couldn't change anything for them. There wasn't any *reason* for such a complex hoax.

Why him? Why?

"Have I given yeh too much to think about, darlin'?" The voice made him start, standing abruptly and turning. Maeve was there, dressed in a red robe over her nightgown, her hands on her hips as she smiled at him. Her gaze slid from him to the stone he held, in its cage of silver; Colin closed his fingers around it.

"That's the cloch Rory took with him." Maeve nodded toward Colin's fisted hand. "I remember it."

"*You* remember it? That's not . . ." Colin began. He stopped.

"Aye," she said. "'Twas me, or rather, me in another body. I knew yeh had the cloch. I could feel it, all along, and 'twas the cloch that called down the lights t'other night. When Rory found it, I thought it was for me and I took it, but I was wrong. 'Tis the bard it gives its power to, and yeh are the bard."

Colin kept his hand fisted around the cloch. He could feel the wires of its cage pressing into his skin.

"I woke and yeh were gone," Maeve continued. "I figured yeh might come here; the place does pull at one." She nodded to the mound and the hawthorn. "'Tis them under there does it. Their sleep is restless lately, just like yers and mine. They can feel the storm a'coming." She came up to him, standing so close that he could see the flecks of color in her irises. "How's the hand?"

He glanced down at the swollen knuckles of his hand. He flexed the fingers, revealing the cloch in its silver prison, grimacing slightly as the scabs on the two middle fingers pulled. "At least it won't hurt my guitar playing," he said.

Her lips pulled upward. She touched his cheek, then took a step back from him. "Yeh still don't understand?"

He shook his head mutely.

"Give me yer hand," she said. "The one with the cloch." He held it out to her, and she clasped his hand between her own.

She closed her eyes and gave a long, slow exhalation. As she drew in the next breath, he saw the emerald began to glow between their fingers. The glow intensified, streams of greenish-white light streaming westward over the waves below. The radiance coalesced a few strides out, over thin air, an aerial whirlpool that slowly thinned and spread out, and in the growing vacant center framed by the light from the stone, Colin saw it—not misty and translucent, as it had been in the pub the night before, but solid and genuine, another landscape over which they seemed to be suspended.

He felt again that pull of the land, both familiar and strange to him: rolling hills like those he'd walked here in Ireland, alive with heather and gorse, the grass a lush, saturated green, the white dots of sheep punctuating the fields. There was a village, with turf smoke curling from the chimneys, so real he thought he could smell the burning peat, and among the cottages, people strolled a grassy lane. A dark forest lurked beyond the cleared fields, a forest like those that had once graced Ireland before they were all chopped down and destroyed; beyond the forest were taller, pine-clad mountains, old hills that reminded Colin of the Appalachians. It was either early dawn or evening there, and in the darkening sky, he could see the colorful sheets of an aurora like the one he'd seen above Inishcorr the last time he'd been here: low in the sky, and brighter and more saturated in color than the other aurora he'd seen.

There was a gasp and a moan behind him, and even as he turned, he saw the radiance from his grandfather's stone diminish and the phantom landscape disappeared into the brightening sky. "Maeve?" She was kneeling on the ground, hunched over, her arms wrapped around her waist as if she were sick. He crouched down in front of her, worried. "What's wrong?"

"Nothing," she breathed, the word a husk. She lifted her head, lines of weariness in the corners of her eyes and mouth. She still cradled herself, but whatever pain she felt seemed to be fading. "Yeh saw it?"

He nodded. "I saw another place. Maybe another time. How did you do that?"

"'Twas Talamh an Ghlas, the Green Land—'tis where I intend to take my people, since it's clear we ca'nah stay here and survive much longer."

"Okay . . ." Colin said tentatively. "Then why. . . ?"

Maeve was shaking her head even as he spoke, sitting on the rock he'd sat on before. "I opened a wee window, that's all. I could let us look in, but even that was exhausting. It *hurts* to handle the power in the cloch, yer stone—hurts more than I care to tell yeh. To actually open a door into that place, a portal . . ." Her sigh trembled. He watched her fingertips slide over the emerald in his hand, like a priest touching a sacred relic. "I ca'nah do that. Not alone." She was staring at him, and he found himself backing away from her and closing his fist around the cloch again, shaking his head.

"I can't help you with that," he heard himself saying.

"Yeh can," she answered. "Yeh just don't realize it. Though doing so will hurt yeh far more than doing this much hurts me."

"Why?"

She laughed, a brief amusement, and held out her right hand. "Yeh can help me stand up, first. Then yeh can help me walk back to our house, and yeh can help me eat some of Keara's lovely scones and drink her tea until I recover my strength. Can yeh manage that?"

He was still shaking his head, still trying to believe what she'd told him, but he took her hand and helped her to stand. She *was* weak; he had to support her. "Thank yeh, love," she told him. She leaned her head on his shoulder, embracing him. "I *do* love yeh, Colin," she whispered. "I want yeh to know that and believe it, because yeh'll need the truth of it. I know all this confuses and worries yeh, but do yeh at least feel that much? Do yeh believe me?"

Colin took a breath. He kissed the top of her head, inhaling the scent of her hair, and he could feel the certainty inside him, solid and unyielding. He knew what Mrs. Egan would say, that she'd ensorcelled him, worked a spell on him to make him feel that way, but he couldn't deny the growing affection he had for her, despite the impossibilities she'd shown him. Part of him still denied what he'd seen here, still refused to believe the evidence of his senses. *She can't be what she says she is. She can't be the Morrígan, she can't be the Máire my grandfather met. The Irish gods are myth and legend and dust.*

Yet he couldn't deny that he felt more drawn to this strange woman— no matter what she claimed to be—than any of the other women he'd been involved with. He tightened his hold on Maeve.

"Yeah," he told her. "I do. Come on, let's go back to the house."

Still supporting her, his arm around her waist, he led the way down the path.

🐦 25 🐦

A Summoning

MAEVE SAW KEARA walking up the lane toward her house; she walked slowly to the gate in the stone fence that bordered the narrow path and met her there. "M'Lady," Keara said, holding out a basket to her; the scent of newly baked bread wafted from underneath the towel draped over it. "I didn't expect you to be out."

Maeve inclined her head toward the house. "Colin's sleeping," she said. "I thought I'd take the air." She lifted the towel and peered into the basket at the brown-topped loaf. "Thanks. That smells delicious."

"I made an extra loaf; I thought you'd appreciate it."

"I do. 'Twill make a good lunch sandwich when Colin wakes up."

"How's his hand? I saw Niall earlier, and he has a lovely fat lip and bruise."

"He'll live to play again," Maeve told her, smiling.

"And did yeh tell Niall to make that fuss, an' to take the punch? Because from where I sat, it seemed Niall went down on the quick side."

Maeve shrugged at that, trying half-successfully to keep a grin from her face. "He might have. 'Tis possible."

Keara laughed at that, then her face went serious again. "He's genuine, that Colin. He's definitely the one we need; not even Niall can deny it after last night. We all saw it; we all heard it." Keara's hand reached out to touch Maeve's, holding the basket. "I worry about you, m'Lady. I worry about how this is going to affect you."

Maeve glanced down at their hands. The old Morrigan would have pulled her hand away, affronted by the familiarity of the gesture; she would have narrowed her eyes and scowled, and her next words would have been a harsh rebuke. *The years, the centuries have softened yeh. They've worn yeh down and made yeh at least half-mortal yerself.* Maeve forced her-self to look at Keara, to hold the young woman's gaze. "Are yeh asking me whether or not I can do what needs to be done, like Niall? Is that what yer saying?"

But Keara was already shaking her head before Maeve finished. "No, m'Lady. It's just . . . I know when I look at Colin that he's caught up in yeh, that there's no doubt about how he feels about yeh. Yeh've snared him well. But I've also looked at yeh, m'Lady, and if yeh'll forgive me sayin', I see some of Colin's enchantment in yer own eyes when yeh look at him. I do'nah doubt that yeh'll do as yeh must, but I wonder at the cost to yeh when it happens, and I do'nah want yeh hurt, either."

She knew what Keara wanted to hear her admit, but she refused to say the words. Instead, she answered the other, unasked question. "There's no way around that pain," Maeve answered. "Yeh know the cost as well as I do. We all know it. The path opens with blood and sacrifice, an' no other way."

"He'll be willing?"

Maeve nodded. "He will, when the time comes. He will."

"'Tis a waste, though. That talent . . ." Keara's fingers tightened around Maeve's. She shook her head again and found Maeve's eyes with her own. "If 'twas me Aiden the one, an' t'were me who had to strike him, I do'nah think I could do it, even if Aiden were willing and even though 'twould save us all."

"'Tis not Aiden, so yeh needn't worry," Maeve answered. "Colin and me . . . 'tis not the same way."

"Yer certain?"

"Aye," Maeve answered, though she knew she answered too quickly and with too much heat. She took a step back from the gate and Keara's hand slipped away from hers. She lifted the basket toward Keara. "T'anks, Keara. We'll enjoy this."

Keara ducked her head at the obvious dismissal. "Yer welcome, m'Lady. I'm sorry if I—" she left the rest hanging in the air unsaid.

"Yeh've no reason to apologize, Keara. Yer my cailleach and have yer own role to play. When the time comes, yeh know yeh'll be as vital to this as any of the rest. More, I suspect."

Keara ducked her head again. "M'Lady," she said, and turned. Maeve watched until she reached the turn in the lane and vanished. Then she hugged the basket to herself, closing her eyes.

I feel every year in my bones. I feel like I could turn to dust any moment and blow away. It would be a relief.

She took a breath, inhaling the scent of the grass, the salt air, and new-baked bread. She went back into the cottage.

Colin was awake and in the kitchen, sitting with a cup of tea steaming between his hands, as she entered the cottage. She could see the bruise on his right hand, the one he'd used to strike Niall. Maeve wondered if Colin had overheard any of the conversation she'd just had with Keara, but the half-asleep look in the eyes behind his glasses indicated he hadn't. "That smells good," Colin said as she set the basket down on the table.

"Keara baked some bread. Want some? I'm going to have a piece with a bit of butter; 'tis still hot from the oven." Maeve lifted the golden loaf out of the basket and set it on a cutting board, taking a serrated knife from a drawer and opening the cold box to take out the butter.

"I'm certainly not going to refuse," he said. "I made you tea as well. It's there on the table waiting for you."

"Thanks, love." Maeve cut two thick slices of the bread, put them on small plates, and slid one over to him. She set the butter and a butter knife down in the center of the table. She took a sip from the mug of tea Colin had made for her, then sat down across from him, watching as he buttered his bread. He took a bite, and she smiled as she saw his pleased expression. "Good?"

"Delicious," he answered.

She took her time buttering her own slice, wondering what she should say, wanting this comfortable moment to last and knowing that it couldn't. "How's yer hand?"

He lifted it, opening and closing the fingers. "A little stiff, but it'll be okay." His lips curled upward in a quick smile, and she wondered if he was remembering the fight. "I heard you talking to Keara out here."

"Ah. And what is it yeh thought yeh heard?" She took a bite of the bread. It *was* delicious, the bread itself perfection, the butter golden and sweet. She watched him as she chewed. He seemed confused by the question, finally shrugging.

"I don't know . . ." His voice trailed off and he shrugged again. "I guess I'm still processing things. Maeve, what is it that you want of me? You keep hinting about what I'm supposed to do and what you're supposed to do, and the things you've shown me here—" He stopped, taking a long breath and looking away from her, as if the answer to his question could be found through the window of the kitchen. "My God, I still have trouble believing that what I've seen was real."

"I know yeh do," Maeve began, "and—" She stopped, her head coming up. She could feel the prickle of unease passing through her, a ghost's presence sliding through her body.

"What?" Colin said as she paused, and she didn't know if he felt it himself or if he was only responding to her silence. She held up her hand to quiet him. It came a few breaths later: a bell ringing urgently from the direction of Inishcorr's little harbor.

"Something's wrong," she said. "Come on; we need to see." Without waiting to see if he'd follow, Maeve pushed her chair back from the table and rose, hurrying from the cottage and into the open air. She pushed open the gate and turned right, heading toward the harbor.

She heard the gunshot then, and began to run.

Colin had caught up with her before she reached the harbor. The lane opened out onto the square before the harbor, and there Maeve saw the knot of Islanders shouting at the ranks of blue-suited policemen near the police boat pulled up to the quay. The smell of cordite still hung in the air, a film of blue smoke dissipating as they approached. Maeve felt a quick wave of relief, realizing that the shot had evidently been fired into the air: there was no one down, no one running from the confrontation, and through the press of people, Maeve could hear Superintendent Dunn bellowing and gesticulating angrily at a garda. "Yeh idjit! All a'yeh get yer fingers where they should be. The next man who fires a shot without provocation will be sacked, d'yeh hear?"

Maeve pushed her way through the islanders. Niall was there in front, as she expected he would be. She could feel Colin following in her wake. "Superintendent," Maeve said as she came to the front of the crowd. She did a quick count of the men with him: fifteen to twenty gardai, all of them looking uncomfortable, armed with automatic weapons and trussed with bulky bulletproof vests. Even Dunn wore one, making him look like an angry black bear. "If yeh'd given me notice of yer visit, I'd have arranged some refreshments for yeh and yer men. What's the trouble here, and why is someone firing their weapon in the middle of an unarmed crowd?"

Dunn glanced behind him at a shame-faced young garda, then turned back to Maeve. "Miss Gallagher, let's not pretend yeh don't know why I'm here. Yeh've been given enough warnings, and I've been as patient as I can be, but I have duties I must perform." She saw his gaze slip past her and behind. "Mr. Doyle," he said. "I see yer here as well."

"I am," Colin said, and he took a step forward to stand alongside Maeve. "Is that a problem, Superintendent?" His arm went around her waist. She wondered whether that was a possessive gesture or a protective one, but she allowed it, remaining where she was. She heard a derisive sniff from Niall on her other side.

"Yeh ignored the warning I gave yeh," Dunn answered, "but yeh've done nothing illegal that I know of, other than displaying rather poor judgment." He turned back to Maeve then. "'Tis time for yeh to leave Inishcorr," he said bluntly. "All a'yeh. The NPWS is wanting to move forward with their plans."

"And yer the NPWS' goons?" Niall burst out before Maeve could answer. "Yeh think yeh frighten us, with yer guns and black vests and shiny helmets? Yeh think yeh can take us all out before we smash yer faces in?"

"*Niall!*" Maeve snapped, and Niall scowled but went silent. She turned to Dunn. "Are yeh so afraid that I'll put a curse on each and every one of yeh for this that yeh needed to bring guns and armor? Are yeh waiting for the sí to come with their ghostly horses and spears? Do we scare yeh so much?"

A few of the gardai made a furtive sign of the cross behind Dunn. But the Superintendent merely stared blandly at Maeve. "I'm just doing me job, Miss Gallagher, as I told yeh I would. 'Tis all."

"An' yer job involves taking us off at gunpoint? Yer not going to cram us all on that little boat yeh brought with yeh, I hope?"

Dunn glanced back at the boat. He shrugged. "I do'nah want trouble, Miss Gallagher."

"It's trouble yeh'll be gettin'," Niall spat. "Yer nasty guns or no. The first of yeh that tries to lay a hand on me . . ."

Maeve put her hand on Niall's, shaking her head. She closed her eyes, forming her thoughts as she had with Colin when he'd been in Chicago, and sending them into Dunn's head. *The man on your left, Superintendent. Did you know he has a bad heart? Why, just the tiniest squeeze . . .* The garda to Dunn's immediate left suddenly groaned, bending forward. One hand left the stock of his weapon to clutch at right arm and chest. *You see, perhaps we don't need weapons . . .*

Maeve opened her eyes again. The garda took a deep breath and straightened as Dunn stared at him. "Sorry, sir," he said. Dunn grunted, his gaze flicking back to Maeve.

She wondered if he knew her trick for the bluff it was.

Dunn was staring at her still, his head shaking slightly as if in disbelief. "I understand yer duty, Superintendent," Maeve told him. "We all have duties and obligations, me no less than you. But I'm telling' yeh: this isn't the time to carry yers out. Not yet."

Dunn was still hesitating. Maeve saw him glance again to his left. "This isn't over," he said.

"No," she answered. "It's not."

"Next time, it won't be just me that's coming. I've already been told that the Naval Service has dispatched two vessels at the request of the NPWS. I came out here today hoping to avoid that, because the Naval Service . . . well, they won't be as accommodating as the gardai."

"I believe yeh," Maeve told him. "But we're still not leavin'."

Dunn nodded. "If that's what yeh want, then . . ." He turned to his men, and nodded his head in the direction of the gardai's launch. "We're done here," he said. "For now."

The gardai at the rear turned, heading toward the quay.

"Mr. Doyle," Dunn said as the Oileánach crowd slowly began to dissolve and drift away, though Niall, Keara, Aiden, and Liam remained behind, clustered around Maeve and Colin. "If I could speak to yeh privately a moment . . ."

"Anything you have to say to me, Superintendent, you can say in front of my friends," Colin answered.

Dunn shrugged. "What I need to know is that these *are* yer friends, and yer not being held here against yer will. Yeh stepping away from them to talk to me would tell me that. And I spoke to yer family yesterday, and yeh might want to know what they had t'say . . ." Dunn stopped. Maeve could feel Colin looking at her, as if waiting for instruction, but she remained silent. There was something in this moment. She could feel it: a new tension, as if everything she cared about hung on what she would do now, what would happen in the next few minutes. She could feel the stone in Colin's pocket, calling to her, and she fought not to react. Colin's hand dropped from her waist, and she watched him take the steps over to Superintendent Dunn. She saw him extend his hand as if offering it to Colin, but when Colin responded in kind, Dunn grabbed Colin's wrist and twisted it suddenly, turning Colin with his hand behind his back.

The click of handcuffs was loud even over Colin's shouted protest. "What the fuck—"

Niall and the other started to move forward, but the muzzles of the gardai's weapons came up at the same moment. "No," Maeve said, and the single word held them.

"As I said, I do'nah want trouble here," Dunn said loudly. "Mr. Doyle here's a foreign national, and I've been especially instructed to make sure that only the Oileánach are left here on Inishcorr. I'll be taking him with us, per me orders and his family's wishes, whether Mr. Doyle wishes to stay or not."

"You can't do this!" Colin shouted. He was staring at Maeve, his glasses askew on his face, as if expecting her to do something. She stared back, keeping her face impassive.

"I can," Doyle answered, "and I am. And I expect Miss Gallagher and her people to cooperate that far at least." He paused, and his gaze stayed steady on Maeve. "For everyone's safety," he added. "I truly do'nah want anyone hurt. Anyone." His eyes, kindly despite the sternness of his expression, seemed to plead with her.

"Morrígan . . ." Niall whispered the name, like an incantation.

Morrígan . . . Once, she would have flown into a rage. The Morrígan of the ancient past would have endured none of this. She would have called her power around herself, wrapped herself in it, and sent it hurtling at this pitiful, arrogant mortal without concern for who it might kill or maim or hurt, because all that mattered was the insult to her. Even a bare few hundred years back, six or seven bodies ago . . .

She still felt the urge, the black rage boiling deep in the pit of her stomach. It would be easy to let it vomit forth, and there would be enough power still within her anger to send several of these men screaming and flailing into the sea. But not all . . . and her people had no protection against the bullets that might follow. And even if her fury caused them to flee, she knew what that would mean: the next time, they would come with a force and power that she would not be able to resist, and though many of the unbelievers would die, so would too many of those in her charge. Maybe all. Maybe they would be able to raze even the mound of Fionnbharr and slay those who slumbered beneath the hawthorn tree, and she could not bear that loss. Not now. Not when the promise was so close to being fulfilled.

This wasn't the time. They had to have more time to prepare.

She swallowed the bile instead.

He's yers, and there's a bit of time yet. There's still another way, and yeh'll get him back.

"Yeh won't harm him. Yeh promise," she said, and Dunn nodded.

"He's not under arrest, though I'm sure someone will be talking to him about his visa when we get back. I'm only removing him from the island for his own safety."

Maeve nodded. "Maeve . . ." Colin said. "What about—" He clamped his mouth shut then, and she wondered what he was going to say. *What about us?* Or: *What about the gateway you said I would open?* Maybe both, or neither.

"There's time for that," she called out to him. "No worries." Then, to Dunn: "Yeh harm him in any way, and yeh'll pay."

He simply nodded. He turned and made his way with the gardai toward their boat, pulling Colin along with them. Colin looked back over his shoulder toward her.

"It'll be fine," she told him. "Yeh'll see."

She hoped she was right.

Niall was already complaining to her before Colin was even off the quay.

"Are yeh daft, Maeve?"

She didn't answer, watching as Colin was escorted up the ramp and into the police launch. The motor began its full-throated song and water spewed behind it as the launch pushed away from the quay. She could feel Niall's consternation even through the pain in her arm and the feeling that she'd just ripped away a vital piece of herself.

The need for the cloch tore at her mind, an addiction that boiled red and black inside her, touching sparks in her own uncertainty. She wanted to scream, wanted to run after Colin and snatch the stone away from him. *Mine! It's mine! I need it!*

But she also needed Colin: his voice, his ability.

And the part of her that had become more human than god just wanted his love.

Niall's denunciation matched that in her own head.

"Yeh can't let him go, not with the cloch," Niall continued to rant as the others watched, silent. "By all that's sacred, woman, place a binding on the man now before it's too late. Bring him back. Yeh can do that. Yeh ca'nah let him go—not like this, not with the cloch, not with his voice. Yeh said we must have the bard; yeh can't let him be taken."

She clamped her jaws against the inchoate fury and agony. "Nah," she managed to say between gritted teeth.

His hand on her shoulder spun her around. His face was close to hers, his features twisted with fury. "*Nah?*" he shouted at her. "How can yeh say nah?"

"Take yer bloody hands off me, Niall," she spat back at him. Aiden put his hand on Niall's shoulder, and Niall angrily shrugged it away.

"Or what?" he raged. "Are yeh going to use one of yer fecking spells on *me* when yeh won't do it on those that need it?" She glared at him, and his hand dropped away in a gesture of disgust, or perhaps he saw the pain that racked her. "Don't be a fecking gobshite, Maeve. This is *all* our bloody lives yer playing with. Yeh told us that we need the cloch and yer damned singer to open the portal, and that yeh'd bring him here. Fine. Yeh did.

Yeh told me to let him hit me at the pub t'other night so he could think that he'd whipped me. Fine. I did what yeh asked even though I don't think he's what yeh believe him t'be. Well, if yer right, then we ca'nah let him go and have the cloch go with him. Not now. 'Tis too dangerous. What if he don't come back? Yeh'll have doomed us all."

He gestured at the boat, already turning its bow toward the mainland and the open sea at the mouth of the little harbor. She could see Colin, standing at the railing with Superintendent Dunn alongside him.

She wanted to agree, wanted to take Niall's advice and force the police launch to turn back, but she shook her head at the thought and at Niall. *There would be death if that happens, and yeh can't control whose 'twould be.* "There's another way, I tell yeh."

"To open the portal? Yer blowing smoke. Yeh don't know that for certain, an' we both know that if there *is* another way, the cost would be terrible. That's why yeh snared yer little friend in the first place, so it was *him* would pay for us." She saw him look past her toward Colin. "Damn it, Morrígan! You ca'nah go soft now. Bring him back."

She took the pain and self-doubt and used it as a lash against Niall. "Yeh forget who I am. Yeh don't give me orders, Niall. 'Tis the other way 'round, and if yeh want out, well, yeh can take those who want to go with yeh an' find your own way. See how long yeh last. How many of yer kind have been born in the last decade or the last half-century? How long before yer all gone and dead, like the others we've known? 'Tis what yeh want?"

"Damn it, Maeve, yeh know it ain't. But I lead my kind, and I have to make sure what's done is best for us. Yeh made a promise to the selkies— and to all the others—and the man who can keep yer promise for us is bein' taken away right now." He gestured again in the direction of the police launch, which had nearly reached the breakwater at the harbor's mouth. She could no longer see Colin or Dunn at all. "Why are you lettin' him go? Have yeh actually fallen for him? Is that it?"

"Shut the feck up, Niall!" That was Keira, pushing between the two of them. "Yer the one spouting shite. The Morrígan knows what's best."

Niall scowled at her. "An' yer her cailleach. Yeh do her bidding. Yeh'd clean her arse if she asked."

"Aye, I am her cailleach," Keira responded. "Would yeh like me to prove it again? I could burn yer feckin' sealskin to ash with just a few words—"

"Enough, both of yeh!" Maeve interjected. She turned her back on them, watching as the police launch vanished beyond the curve of the island. She could feel the cloch vanish with Colin. Maeve couldn't stop the cry that the loss drew from her, a wail of anguish, though she wasn't sure which loss hurt the most. "'Tis my choice to make, and I've made it," she told him. Then, softly enough that none of the others could hear: " . . . *an' I hope 'tis the right one.*"

"He'll come back," she told Niall firmly. "We'll bring the cloch and his voice back here to Inishcorr. We will."

PART THREE

BADB

26

An American Exiled

IN HIS DREAMS, he thought himself back home in Chicago, staring at the image of the dead crow on Jen's table, or lying in his bed in Jen's apartment, reading his grandfather's journal. The images of a dead black bird and of Maeve/Máire dominated his sleep, and he worried about the meaning of them. He needed desperately to see Maeve again, to know that she was all right. The absence of her was like a bloody and terrible wound in his chest that refused to heal.

He'd thought—naively, he realized—that Superintendent Dunn would release him as soon as the launch landed back at Ballemór in the same way that he'd taken off the handcuffs as soon as the boat cleared Inishcorr's harbor, that he'd brush off Colin with another warning and that would be the end of it. He'd imaged that Maeve would come after him with the *Grainne Ni Mhaille* as well, that she'd embrace him and kiss him, then the two of them would return to the island despite Dunn's protestations.

But the fantasies had dissolved quickly. He'd been taken to the gardai station in the town, and incarcerated in the small gaol there for three days, while official-looking people in suits and somber, unsmiling faces had come and visited him, asking him questions that he mostly couldn't answer, and vaguely threatening to revoke his visa and send him home if he didn't cooperate. They asked about what defenses the Oileánach had erected on the island, what kind of armaments and weaponry they had, and they looked at him unbelievingly when he told them that as far as he knew, they had no weapons at all unless they wanted to count pocket knives.

On the third day, Superintendent Dunn had Colin brought to his office. The officer escorting him knocked on Dunn's door, opened it at the Superintendent's "Enter," gestured to Colin to go in, then closed the door behind him.

Colin could see his passport sitting on Dunn's keyboard, off to the side of the desk. He sat in the chair on the other side of the desk. "Tea?" asked Dunn. "I just made a pot."

Colin shrugged. Dunn swiveled in his chair to the credenza behind him, and poured out two mugs of tea. He put one in front of himself and slid the other across the desk toward Colin. "Sugar?"

Colin shook his head. "Me neither," Dunn said. "I prefer it black." He took a long sip before setting the mug down. "I suppose yer wondering what we're intending to do with yeh."

"It's crossed my mind a few times."

"I've talked to the authorities, and told them that I think yeh were just an innocent caught up in something yeh didn't fully understand. I told them that I thought yeh were no threat to anyone, just a musician wanting to learn some of the old tunes."

Colin nodded. "That's true enough, especially the last. I mean, I understand that the Oileánach took a deserted island that the NPWS wants to turn into a park, but . . ." Colin shrugged. "When I came here, I didn't intend to get involved in anything political."

Dunn plucked Colin's passport from the keyboard. As he watched, the Superintendent tapped the edge of the booklet softly against the top of his desk. "Yet that's what yeh did."

"I can't help that I like Maeve. And I won't apologize for it either."

Dunn nodded slowly. "I like the woman as well, Mr. Doyle—if not in the same way. I admire her passion, but I also have the law to uphold and the Oileánach have broken several. Yeh ca'nah go back there, Mr. Doyle."

"My guitars are still there, and so are my clothes."

"Those are just things, an' they can all be replaced."

Colin gave a short laugh. "You're evidently not a musician, Superintendent. The Gibson I had out there alone is worth a few thousand dollars. It's from the 1960s, and I've had it for a decade now. It's not just a 'thing' to me."

"That's unfortunate, then. Yeh still ca'nah go back there."

"If I do, would I be arrested? Would I be breaking a law?"

"Yeh'd be knowingly trespassing. That would be enough to have your visa revoked."

"Even if all I'm doing is recovering my property?"

Dunn sighed. "Mr. Doyle, at any moment, the government is likely to take any decisions completely out of me hands. They do'nah want a foreign national there when they come—an' they *will* come, sooner than later now. If yeh were to be there when they do, 'twould be them making the decisions, not me. Yeh do'nah want to go back out there, possessions or nah. Am I making meself clear?"

"Abundantly."

Dunn nodded again. He laid the passport down on the desk and slid it toward Colin, then opened his desk drawer. From it, he brought a large plastic ziplock bag, containing the rest of what had been confiscated from Colin when he'd been held: his belt, his wallet, tissues, a few guitar picks, a pen . . . and his grandfather's stone, the cloch. He could feel Dunn watching him as he took the stone from the bag and cradled it for a moment in his hand. Holding it, he thought he heard the whisper of Maeve's voice: *I love yeh, Colin. I need yeh. Come back. Come back.*

"Pretty stone. What is it?"

Colin opened his fingers slightly; the voice faded. "I don't know. It was my grandfather's, who brought it over to America from here. My aunt gave it to me just before I came here."

Dunn's chin lifted and fell again. "There's a lot of Ireland yeh haven't yet seen."

"Is that a suggestion?"

Dunn almost seemed to smile. "'Tis," he answered. "But I understand that Mrs. Egan has a room for you tonight, at least."

Ten minutes later and finally freed, Colin trudged up the road toward the main streets of Ballemór and the hill toward Mrs. Egan's. He could feel the stares of some of the town's residents on him; when he waved to those he recognized, they smiled hesitantly and waved back, then turned quickly away. No one seemed to want to stop and talk to him—which told him more than any words could have.

The Irish *love* to talk.

Late that afternoon, Colin walked back down from Mrs. Egan's to the town center. For the first time, he noticed the presence of many strangers in the town. There were faces he didn't recognize, too well-dressed and too oblivious to the streets and shops around them to be tourists. Also walking in the main part of town were several sailors in uniform, both men and women. Colin turned away from the square, walking toward Beach Road with the mist fogging his glasses.

Despite Superintendent Dunn's caution, he still wanted to go back out to Inishcorr, if only—he told himself—to get his guitars.

About a kilometer down Beach Road, he came to the small marina where the *Grainne Ni Mhaille* usually tied up when Maeve and her people came to Ballemór, which was also where most of the Galway hookers and other small craft in the area docked. He paused at the end of the main jetty, cleaning his glasses on his sweater as he looked at the pebbled beach and scanning the piers and jetties for the *Grainne Ni Mhaille*, as if nothing had changed and Maeve would be there, waiting for him. The bright red sails of a few other Galway hookers caught his attention, but none of them had the lines of the Oileánach's boat.

He walked up the steps and out along the dock toward the small office building. Behind the counter there, in front of a wall displaying a large chart of nautical knots and a display of embroidered tea towels of Irish linen with nautical themes, a bored-looking young woman was texting on her phone. She glanced up from the phone as Colin entered; then, with an audible sigh and a distinct frown of irritation, set the phone down. "'Morning to yeh," she said. "Fine weather we're having today." Her gaze traveled over him; he could see her sizing him up. She nodded. "Looking for a ride around the Head? How many would it be? 'Tis a couple tourist charter boats in dock yeh can hire . . ."

She stopped as Colin shook his head. "I need to get out to Inishcorr," he told her, and was rewarded with a laugh.

"Tiz me berries," she said, and at the confused look on Colin's face, shook her head. "Yer joking around with me, right?" She laughed again. "Goin' to Inishcorr, are yeh? Hope yeh can swim, then."

"No, I'm serious. I'll pay whatever I need to pay, but I need to get out there."

The mocking, abbreviated laugh was repeated. She glanced down at her phone on the counter. "Mister, have yeh not been listenin' to the news? The Naval Service is stopping any ships from gettin' to the island, but that's nah the worst of it."

Colin heard the tone in her voice, and his eyes narrowed. "I've . . . been away for a few days," he told her. "What do you mean?"

"Yeh really don't know? It's all bolloxed up out there. There's been a fog around Inishcorr for the last three days. Yeh can't even see the bloody island well enough to get close. The fog just sits there: all day, all night, thick as an old London Particular with no wind blowing it away. It's feckin' weird and unnatural, if yeh don't mind my sayin' so. People are saying 'tis the devil's work." She shrugged and picked up her phone. "So yer outta luck, Mister. No one here's gonna take yeh out that way."

"I can pay well," Colin countered. "Whatever it takes." *Or my credit card can do that . . .*

"Yeh can offer to pay whatever yeh want. Still won't happen." She looked at him, raising her eyebrows, and returned her attention to the phone's screen, obviously dismissing him.

"You're certain there's no one? No one at all?"

"That's the craic." She raised her eyebrows to him again. "Sorry, mate."

Colin lifted his hands in defeat. "Well, thanks anyway. Look, if you hear of someone, I'm staying up at Mrs. Egan's for the next few days. You could send word there."

"Sure, and I'll do just that," she told him without looking at him, her attention back on her phone. Colin knew that she'd forget him and his request before he made it back to the Beach Road. He left her and walked out onto the pier again. He glanced west, toward where the inlet widened as it met the open Atlantic. He could see a few of the islands beyond that hugging the coast, gray and faint in the mist, but Inishcorr couldn't be seen from here.

He made his way back down to the Beach Road.

Before Colin reached the intersection for the town center, he turned and made the long, slow climb up a walking path winding through the heather and brush from Beach Road to the Sky Road that ran around Ceomhar Head, knowing that farther out around the Head, he would normally be able to glimpse Inishcorr. At least he might be able to see if what the young woman at the marina had told him was true.

Gray streams of clouds rolled by overhead and a misty, erratic drizzle had started as he made the long walk. A few cars, their tire treads hissing on the wet blacktop, slid past him: tourists out to gaze at the lovely vistas the headland afforded. After an hour's walk, Colin reached a turnout beyond which the lower reaches of Ceomhar Head spread out toward the sea, with the closest islands hugging the coast. Beyond, gray waves rolled in to thrash white and foaming against the unyielding, stolid granite of Connemara.

He should have been able to glimpse Inishcorr from here—a low hump nearly on the horizon, on a good day blued with distance but clearly visible. Today, there was nothing. Out where Inishcorr lurked, he could make out two coastal patrol vessels, one of them a large "Róisín" class ship. Between them there was a white smudge, a cloud that appeared to have abandoned the sky and come to rest on the ocean's surface. Colin stared outward as if the intensity of his gaze could manage to pierce the fog and reveal the contours of Inishcorr, as if he expected that because *he* was there that the mists would part and the island reappear. Magically, like the mythical Hy-Brasil suddenly revealed behind its misty blanket once every seven years.

The fog remained stubbornly opaque.

Colin sat on the wooden railing at the edge of the turnoff. A steep slope ran down to a farm where distant sheep were grazing, a thin trail of smoke coming from the farmhouse chimney. A tiny form—the husband? the wife?—moved from the back door toward a barn. The landscape was bucolic, belying the presence of the patrol vessels. He watched the white dots of the sheep moving against the deep green of the field, glancing out past the shore to the implacable fog.

Out there was his lover. Out there were his guitars, his laptop, his clothes. Out there was the place he had been told needed his presence. Out there, he could feel deep in his gut, was where he was supposed to be. His destiny. He reached into his pocket and dragged out the cloch. He held it in his hand, gazing into its milky, green depths before draping the chain over his neck.

Maeve, talk to me. Show me that you're still there. Damn it, you said you needed me. Show me that I haven't done something really stupid. Again.

The stone was terribly cold in his hand, and again he thought he could hear faint whispers of voices in his head as he held it. *Maeve,* he thought silently, as if he could project his mind to hers. *I'm here. Give me a sign that you can hear me. Tell me how I can get to you. Help me.*

If Maeve heard his internal plea, she didn't reply.

He stood there watching the play of clouds and sea until another quick shower curtained the view in rain, then he slid the pendant under the collar of his sweater as he turned to walk back toward Ballemór and Mrs. Egan's, still wondering how he could reach Inishcorr and Maeve.

A garda's car passed him as he was walking back toward the village, heading in the same direction. Colin gave it little notice until he saw the car stop just beyond him and back up with a whine of its transmission. The car stopped alongside him; the garda who was driving remained in the car but two passengers in the rear seat got out, a man wearing a naval uniform and Superintendent Dunn. They approached Colin, who felt a sense of trepidation.

"Identification," the officer said without preamble, holding out his hand. Under his officer's cap, his blue eyes were cold and unsympathetic. Dunn said nothing. Colin reached in his pocket for the passport Dunn had just given back to him this morning, handing it to the man.

"Is there some kind of problem, Officer, Superintendent?" he asked, but neither answered. The officer snapped open the passport and scanned it. Colin saw the driver reach for the radio microphone. The officer gazed steadily and impassively at Colin's face before glancing once at Dunn.

"Colin Doyle," he said, as if tasting the name. As Colin watched, he handed the passport to the garda driving the car, who picked up his radio and began relaying his passport number to someone. "You were just en-quiring at the Beach Road Marina about hiring a boat to take you to Inish-corr." There was no question in the man's tone. "Superintendent Dunn informs me that he'd already warned you about going back out to Inish-corr."

"Yeah," Colin told them. "I was warned."

"Inishcorr is currently under naval interdiction," the officer responded. "Going there would be a crime. For someone like yeh, here on a visa, that would mean immediate deportation."

"I don't recall Superintendent Dunn mentioning anything about an in-terdiction."

"The interdiction order was just issued a few hours ago," the officer answered. "But the Superintendent advised yeh not go there, regardless, did he not?"

Colin could feel the heat of his cheeks reddening. "He did. I also told him I wanted to get the guitars and laptop I left out there. I was just seeing if that were possible." He could feel Dunn staring at him, and he stared back. "From what I've been told, it appears it's not."

"'Tis not," Dunn agreed, and the naval officer nodded.

"Yer a friend of these Oileánach, Mr. Doyle?"

Colin shook his head and shrugged at the same time. "Yeah, I'm . . ." He paused. ". . . a friend of one of them," he finished. "I went out to play music with them, to learn the songs they know. That's the reason I'm here in Ireland—to study music." He had the sense that he was rambling, giv-ing too much information and speaking too fast. The officer continued to stare, impassive, then turned away and leaned into the open window of the car, speaking to the garda who was driving. Colin couldn't hear what they were saying. Finally, the officer stood up again. He had Colin's pass-port in his hand, and extended it back to Colin. As Colin took it, the offi-cer's fingers continued to grip the blue cloth.

"As the Superintendent told yeh, yeh ca'nah go out there, sir," he said. "Those ones on the island, they've broken the law and taken land that isn't theirs, and they'll be made to leave one way or t'other. Yeh can't be there when that happens. Do we have an understanding, Mr. Doyle? I don't ex-pect to hear yer name again in connection with trying to find a way out there. In fact, I'd advise yeh to leave the Connemara area entirely, just so there aren't any . . . mistakes. Go study yer music somewhere else in Ireland, why don't yeh? There's music a'plenty elsewhere in the other counties. Would yeh like a ride back to Ballemór with us, then?"

Colin shook his head. "No, I prefer to walk. You've given me a lot to think about."

The officer let go of the passport, nodded to Colin once, and got back into the cruiser. Superintendent Dunn remained outside. He took Colin's arm and moved him a few steps away from the car. "Yeh understand the man, then," he said to Colin.

"I do, Superintendent."

"Good. Between the two of us, Mr. Doyle, I di'nah give a bollocks when the Oileánach took the island. I'da been satisfied to let 'em have it—and I di'nah push it until I had to. Same with yeh—if yeh'd been able to get yerself out there, whether to get yer instruments or to stay, I would'nah have cared. 'Tis yer business. But now it's all a pain in the hole with the Naval Services involved, and there's nothing either one of us can do." Colin saw him glance back at the car. "Do yeh understand me, Mr. Doyle? The Oileánach will have to deal with others now, not me, and if yeh want to stay in Ireland, then yeh ca'nah go back out. Yeh see that?"

"I do," Colin told him.

"Good. I hope yer as smart as yeh sound, then." Dunn released Colin's arm and nodded once to him. The man's face nearly crinkled into a smile, then he turned and went back to the car. He opened the door and slid into the back seat with the naval officer.

Colin watched the driver start the car, swing it around on the narrow road, and head back toward Ballemór. Colin watched them, standing at the side of the road. When the cruiser vanished around a curve, he glanced back toward the sea, but even if the fog around Inishcorr had vanished, he could no longer have seen the island.

He began walking again.

◀ 27 ▶

The Gray Daylight

THE WHITE SHROUD covered the island, masking Inishcorr from the patrol vessels around it but also making it difficult for the residents to move around easily. The fog was at its thickest about Keara's house, so much so that Maeve found herself stepping carefully, looking down at her feet because the ground even two strides away was hidden and indistinct. It would be easy to trip over a hidden clump and twist an ankle. She breathed in the fog, exhaled it, and her movements caused tendrils to writhe and snake around her. Reaching the door, she knocked; Niall opened the door. Beyond him, the small cottage was stuffed with fog in which shadows moved slowly, speaking in mist-hushed voices. "How is she?" Maeve asked quietly.

"Nah good. The girl's failing," Niall answered, and she could hear the accusation in his voice and see it in the lines of his face. *It's your fault. She's doing what you commanded her to do, and it's slowly killing her. It's your fault.* Niall stood stolidly in the doorway, blocking her entrance.

"Then yeh'll let me see her," Maeve said, and Niall, ponderously, stepped back to let her into the room. She could see a few others of the Oileánach there in the front room, as if holding vigil. They nodded to her as she passed into the bedroom where Keara lay—nodded with respect, but also with the shadow of the same accusation that had been in Niall's voice.

Keara's breathing was a hoarse rasp, and her voice a husk as she intoned the repetitive words of the endless chant that held the fog in place. Her eyes were closed, and the fog vomited from her mouth with every word, white and thick. Aiden, her lover, sat in a chair next to the bed, leaning over to wipe her brow with a cool cloth. He glanced up at Maeve as she entered. "How much longer does she have to do this, Maeve?" he asked.

"Not too long, I hope," she answered. "I've felt Colin. He's free again and on the mainland. I'll be bringing him over now."

Aiden nodded. His face was worried as he glanced at Keara, chanting on the bed. Niall had followed Maeve to the bedroom, leaning against the open doorway. "She ca'nah continue this much longer," Aiden said. "I won't allow it. Three days now she's been at this without sleep, and 'tis burning her up. If we end up having t' fight to keep the island, Maeve, then we have t' fight. I'd rather it come to that. I won't be letting Keara kill herself just to keep 'em away for another day."

"I don't want that either, Aiden."

"She'd do it, though," he answered. "Because it's yeh who asked, she'd do it without thinkin' about the cost. She loves and respects yeh that much. If yeh told her that she had to keep going, had to keep this up, she would do it until her last breath." His eyes shimmered with threatening tears, and he sniffed almost angrily, blinking them back. "Yeh need to tell me that yeh won't ask that of her. Tell me yeh won't."

When Maeve didn't answer, Aiden nodded with a frown. "That's what I thought," he said.

"I still believe it won't come to that," Maeve said. "Once Colin's back, once I have the cloch, we can start the process and Keara can rest. The others can hold off the leamh while we get the gateway opened."

"So he's coming?"

"He is," Maeve answered. "I know this. Very soon." Aiden nodded, and Maeve moved to the bed. She caressed Keara's sweating face, brushed the damp hair back from her brow. Keara gave no indication that she was aware of Maeve's presence. She continued to chant with her eyes closed, her voice a barely audible mumbling, the white clouds billowing from her mouth, smelling strangely of the sea. "Colin will be on his way this evening," Maeve repeated, leaning close to her ear, "and once he arrives, you'll be able to stop, Keara. You're giving us the time we need, my dear, and we all owe you everything. We'll remember this—your name will be forever part of the tales we'll tell when all this is over."

She glanced at Aiden, at Niall.

"Soon," she told them. "He'll be here soon."

Outside, the air was cold and damp with the fog. Maeve pulled her cloak tight around her as she looked around the mist-curtained landscape.

"An' if he doesn't arrive?" Maeve turned around at the voice. Niall had followed her from the cottage. "If he changes his mind now that he's free and just leaves to go home? What then? Yeh'll let Keara die waitin' on him when we could be trying another way? When we could just let the leamh come and fight them? I thought you old gods and heroes loved a glorious death, even one in vain."

"That way will cost far more lives than just Keara's," she answered. "Yeh know that."

"Aye. But it wouldn't cost Keara's, would it?"

"Her life is more important than anyone else's?" Maeve retorted. "She understands the issues and the danger, and she was willing, Niall. She was'nah forced. We're at war with the modern world, and she's a soldier. Soldiers sometimes die. That's the way of things, ain't it? She'd be one of yer heroes, eh?"

"'Tis easy for the queen to say, ain't it, when it ain't her life that's at stake."

His words stung her as sharply as if he'd slapped her across the cheek. Maeve took a backward step. "If 'tis what you think, then yeh really don't know me a'tall." She felt anger dispel the sympathetic tears that had filled her eyes while talking to Keara and Aiden. "Go and dry your arse, Niall, until yeh know what yer jabberin' about."

She saw Niall press his lips together, looking off across the island toward the fog-hidden harbor. She watched his shoulders slowly relax. "Sorry, Maeve," he grunted. "Yer right. 'Tis just . . ." He waved a hand, and tendrils of the mist moved with him. "I don't mind dyin' meself, if that's what it must come to. There are others feel the same. Watchin' Keara wasting away while I'm just doing nothing—'tis the hardest thing of all. I understand what you're saying, and yer right: if that fool of a leamh bard would come back so we could use him, that's what would be best. But yeh don't *know* that he will. Yeh *ca'nah* know that."

"I can, and I do," Maeve answered, tightly. "An' he's no fool, Niall, no matter what you believe. Colin's no fool a'tall. You'll see."

Niall shrugged. "Then I hope you're right." He paused, his gaze finally finding her eyes. "I *am* sorry, Maeve. Truly."

She nodded. "'Tis fine," she told him. "I know it was yer heart speakin', and that's all I can ask of anyone. Now, if yeh'll let me go, I need to talk to Fionnbharr. 'Tis time to push things forward, and he can do that, if I can convince him."

As soon as she crossed the line of stones that marked the hill of the hawthorn tree, Fionnbharr appeared, leaning against the trunk as if he'd expected her. The mound of the hawthorn stood in an airy pocket free of Keara's fog, as if someone had poked a hole in the mist. Sunshine poured down on Fionnbharr, the tree, and the heather, although a circular gray wall of dense fog surrounded them, boiling and twisting as if angry at being held back.

"'Tis a lovely day," Fionnbharr remarked. "At least locally." He gestured to indicate the mound and the fog-free air about them.

"And if it weren't for Keara's fog charm, that lovely day would consist of Naval Services ships in the harbor and the invasion of Inishcorr. People would be dying, both theirs and ours."

Fionnbharr grinned at her. "Och! Such a stop-the-clock grouch the Morrígan is. And are the Tuatha de Danann supposed to be afraid of leamh in uniforms? Are they going to find the path under the tree when I have it all warded and hidden?" He gestured back to the trunk behind him. "I'm not worried about leamh soldiers."

Maeve gave him a round of mock applause, her handclaps dead in the still air. "Such a grand lord is the great Fionnbharr and such a warrior. Perhaps yeh can hide from the leamh, but the rest of us don't have such a refuge, and if we did, I'm tired of hiding away and waiting for the end to come—because the end is coming for all of us if we don't take the path to Talamh an Ghlas. Consider this: I would'nah be surprised if after the leamh took those of us in the village away, that the leamh would also knock down the stones and cut down the tree, and then where will yeh and yers be, trapped under the ground forever? We all have a stake in this, and yeh know it. Don't act like yeh and the rest of the sí have no cares a'tall."

Fionnbharr sniffed. His booted foot stomped on the ground, and the earth shook underneath Maeve.

"Your little lamb hasn't come in for the slaughter yet, nor has he brought yeh back the stone that holds the light. I've heard the others complaining about the foolishness of yeh letting the man go, and the worse foolishness of letting him keep the cloch when we need it. So, were they right?"

"No," Maeve answered immediately, her chin lifting. "I did what I needed to do, and he hasn't betrayed us. He's nearly here. I can *feel* him and the cloch across the channel, over on the Head."

Fionnbharr nodded. He seemed to sniff the air to the east. "I'll give yeh that; I feel him also. Which tells me why yer here, Morrígan: yer magic can't reach out to him through the spell of Keara's fog, the leamh won't let him return here, and yeh want me to do the work for yeh."

"Ultimately we're on the same side, Fionnbharr, are we not?"

He laughed again, his feet tapping the ground so it shook underneath

Maeve as if a hundred horses were galloping below. "We're on the same side *for the moment*, not to put too delicate a point on things. That may quite likely change once this gateway is opened and we're through. My people never worshiped you, Morrígan, and we were here first. *If* we go to Talamh an Ghlas, everything changes. We don't know what will happen there or how we'll be looked at by those who live there. Ultimately, we're *not* on the same side a'things."

"I'm not asking for worship. I'm asking for yer help while we have a common enemy."

"Does it taste like ashes in yer mouth to come begging like this?" he asked her, then shrugged. "No matter," he said before she could answer. "What 'tis it yeh need, Morrígan, seeing as we be temporary allies? What are yeh thinkin'?"

"It's been a long time since the aos sí rode across the water to the Head. Maybe it's time now."

"That'll stir up the residents. Was'nah it yeh who told me over the last several years not to let the host ride, just to keep the leamh quiet? If we do this, they'll be howlin' for the Naval Services to take out the island, fog or nah. Maybe just bomb the village to rubble from above. This could cause yer war to come quicker, before yer ready for 'em."

"It's a risk I'll take. It may also serve as a warning to them that we're not powerless and they're best leaving us be."

He laughed. "And if we happen to pick up a certain stray mortal during our ride?"

"Then I'd certainly appreciate it if yeh also happen to bring him here."

"Yer a devious one, Morrígan."

Now it was Maeve who laughed, a sharp, abrupt sound as she showed her teeth. "'Tis a fact," she said. "And more."

⟨ 28 ⟩

The Night Ride

"**H**EY, JEN," Colin said as soon as he heard the click of her cell accepting his call. "How're things?"

"Colin!" His sister's near-shout rattled the speaker of his cell phone, temporarily overriding the loud conversation in Regan's Pub and the sound of Lucas' band tuning up before their set. "That's what I should be asking you. We haven't heard from you in *days* now, and Mom was about ready to call the gardai there to roust you. I think she'd half-convinced Tommy that he needed to get hold of someone in the State Department to notify the embassy in Ireland."

He could hear the relief in her voice. Colin tried to chuckle and mostly succeeded. With his free hand, he cupped the pint glass in front of him, dark with a half-finished Guinness. "You can tell her that she doesn't need to do that. I'm alive and still here. I was out on Maeve's island, and there's no cell phone reception out there. In fact, there's no phones at all, of any sort, or electricity. I just . . . well, I'm back on the mainland right now."

"Colin, what's wrong? You can't hide anything from me; I can hear it in your voice. What's the problem? Did you and Maeve already split up?"

Colin sighed, not knowing where to start or even whether he should try. "No. It's more complicated than that. A lot more complicated. In fact, I'm pretty sure most of it you wouldn't believe at all."

"Try me."

Colin did laugh at that. "Not yet," he said. "But here's the part you'll understand, in a nutshell. Maeve and her people, they took over an abandoned island, and now the state wants it back and they don't want to leave. The gardai came, and there was a bit of confrontation." He heard her gasp at that, and he hurried to add: "No one was hurt. But they pulled me off the island because they didn't want a foreigner caught up in it. Now the Naval Service has blockaded the island and I can't get back."

"Oh." Colin couldn't decipher the emotions behind Jen's single word. He waited. Lucas' fiddle skirled a bit of a tune. "I'm sorry to hear that, but honestly I'm glad you're out of the way, Colin. Mom will be, too. Maybe . . ." Another pause. "Maybe it's better this way. Maybe you and Maeve just weren't meant to be together."

"That sounds like Mom talking."

"Thanks," Jen answered with heavy irony. "That makes me feel *so* loved." Static hissed in Colin's ear and he missed the opening of her next sentence. ". . . what you're going to do?"

"I don't know," he told her. "I really don't, at this point. I'd go back out there, but that doesn't look possible."

"I'm just as glad—if you don't mind me sounding like Mom again. But you wanting to . . . that I can understand, I guess. If it were Aaron stuck on the island, I'd be trying to do the same thing."

"Thanks, Jen. I appreciate you saying that."

"Just . . . just promise me that you'll be careful, little brother. Do you hear me?"

"I hear you, and I will." Lucas counted off "Connolly's Jig," and the band launched into the tune. Colin raised his voice into the phone. "Listen, Jen, I'll give you a call tomorrow. Right now, I'm going to listen to some music and drink a pint or three. Love ya. Tell Mom and Tommy the same, and give Aaron my best, too."

"I'll do that. Why don't you call Mom? She wants to hear your voice."

"All right," he told her. "I will." It was a promise he wasn't certain he would keep, but he knew it was what she wanted to hear. "Talk to you later."

"Bye, Colin. Love ya." He heard the phone disconnect. He sighed and slid his phone in his jeans pocket. He picked up the glass on the table in front of him and drained it.

Sliding out of the booth, he went to the bar to order another pint. As he passed the band, he nodded to Lucas.

Lucas either didn't see him or pretended not to. Colin shook his head and continued on to the bar.

A thick tendril of mist snaked away from the greater cloud around Inishcorr.

In the moonlight, from an airplane flying over the area, it might have appeared to be a twisting rope of silver-white smoke, curling and slithering over the surface of a preternaturally calm and flat ocean. Leading Seaman Kieran Martin, on midnight watch on the offshore patrol vessel *LÉ Aisling,* saw the foggy arm detach from the bank covering the island, moving impossibly against the wind and heading directly toward the ship. Kieran unclipped the mic from his uniform, calling the rating who was manning the ship's radar scan. "Sean, are yeh seeing anything out by that island right now?"

"Neh. All quiet. What 'tis it yeh think yeh have?"

"I'm not sure yet. Maybe nothing."

Kieran stared out over the bow rail, blinking his eyes as he lifted binoculars to his face and tried to focus the lenses, not certain what it was he was seeing. He pondered whether to alert the ensign in charge of the watch, when the foggy limb flexed and advanced suddenly and rapidly, growing in size until it was nearly level with the *Aisling's* deck, the single coil splitting in two as it rushed toward the ship, as if a hurricane were whipping it into motion.

Kieran fumbled with the mic on his lapel, starting to call an alarm and backing away from the rail and the strange mist. The smoky murk was riddled with strange twinkling lights like torches glimpsed on a foggy night, and it was full of noise as well: thin voices shouting in ancient Gaelic, the sound of pounding horses' hooves, and the blare of shrill trumpets and pipes. The apparition flanked the ship before Kieran could find his voice, a cold wind like the air from a grave flowing outward from it. The mist surrounded the ship, and voices called to him from within the sparkling gray. A hand seemed to whip from the cloud with a laugh, pulling the cap from Kieran's head and flinging it past the cannon mounted on the foredeck. More hands plucked at him, knocking him to the deck, tearing away his uniform jacket and tossing it after the cap. Other hands grabbed him as voices whispered around him. *"Come with us! Join us, mortal!"* they called as they pulled at him, trying to drag him over the rail. He felt his body scraping over the deck plates. He clutched at a stanchion as the spectral hands pulled harder. The frigid white fog roared past him; streaks of blurred light from torches flaring within. As it engulfed him, he thought he glimpsed armored warriors riding horses with men and women running impossibly alongside.

"No!" Kieran cried, holding hard. "Leave me be!" The voices laughed, but the hands released him as the eerie fog swept past, moving beyond the *Aisling* toward the mainland, the twin strands recombining into one once more as they passed the ship's stern. As the last bit of the fog passed, the ship canted over before righting itself sluggishly, as if a giant swell had struck it from the side. From the rail, Kieran watched the mist dwindle, the clamor of it fading as alarms rang over the ship and spotlights flared wildly and belatedly.

"Kieran!" his earpiece rattled. "What the bloody hell is going on out there, man?"

Kieran shook his head. "'Tis nothing of this world, I'm thinkin'," he said.

The mist would have laughed with the comment. The line of wild fog continued to rush eastward, far faster than any speed the *Aisling* was capable of matching. As it neared Ceomhar Head, the fog flowed over a low island hugging the rugged coastline. A farmhouse stood there; the misty river of the wild ride flowed around and past it, trumpets blaring and riders howling. The sheep bleated in terror, the cows lowed in alarm. When the family within the farmhouse emerged, the turmoil having rousted them from their sleep, the riders were already gone, leaving behind ocean fish flopping open-mouthed in the pasture, in the yard, and on their windowsills. Their best milk cow perched precariously on the roof of the barn. Their tractor had been plucked from the barn and was buried nose-first in the hayfield, its two huge rear tires still spinning slowly. Several of the sheep had strips of their thick wool sheared from them so closely their pink skin showed, and they would find two ewes and a ram missing entirely.

The husband and wife shivered, clutching each other and looking toward the headland where a line of glowing, rushing nothingness flowed along the Beach Road toward Ballemór.

In the office of the marina along Beach Road, a security guard sat snoring in a chair with his feet up on the desk. The first indication that something might be amiss was the rattling of windows in the office, a tidal rolling of the marina dock and the slamming of boat hulls against their fenders. The harsh report of snapping nylon dock lines—sounding like automatic pistol shots—was finally enough to rouse the guard from his sleep. Bleary-eyed and frightened, wondering if the marina were somehow under attack, he ran to the door and opened it. He was immediately confronted by cold fog and wind, the marina lights cocooned and haloed in a white cotton blanket. Strange sounds assaulted his ears: not just the sounds of the restless boats, but muffled trumpets and strange, hoarse shouts. Hands from the fog fondled him as voices laughed. His hat was taken from his head and flung into the breeze; the long, hefty weight of his torch left his belt as the flashlight's beam seared his eyes, then it, too, was gone. More hands were at his belt buckle and his pants went down to his ankles as high voices giggled. Someone pushed at him from behind as he bent to bring his pants back up, and suddenly he was flailing in cold water with a forest of hazy pilings around him. His feet could just touch the rocky bottom, and he sputtered, coughing up oily saltwater. He could hear the boats striking into each other along the marina pier, and saw one of the black-hulled hookers sailing past with ghostly figures clinging to the rigging of the red sails.

The fog whipped by him, loud with hidden creatures, then was gone. As he climbed a rope ladder back onto the docks, the moonlight revealed a tangled mess of boats and lines around the marina, and—most strangely—what appeared to be a startled ram staggering out of the office door on unsteady hooves, its wool dyed a bilious and garish pink.

The guard cursed aloud, shaking his fist at the departing mist, which was moving rapidly down the Beach Road, and only mocking laughter answered him.

The mist advanced toward Ballemór proper. It being a Friday midnight, the main square there was still crowded, and those out on the streets turned in alarm as the wall of fog advanced on them without warning, with its blaring of ethereal trumpets, hooves, and voices and glimpses of strange, martial figures inside. The fog overran the moon and blurred the streetlamps, filling the main square before squatting stolid, heavy, and unmoving there. The residents of Ballemór ran aimlessly about, shouting their alarm and confusion: as the trumpets blared once, then stopped; as the clamor of hooves on the road faded to the breathy whinnying and stamping of horses reined in after a long gallop; as the sound of clinking armor rose around them; as mocking voices and unseen hands assailed the people from seemingly every side. The residents fled in any direction they could. They thought they glimpsed a squadron of ghostly, ancient warriors marching down the road through the mist, moving purposefully and steadily, the rapping of their spears on the ground terrible and frightening.

The squadron sang an old tune as they marched: "Come away with me . . ." Their massed voices were like a gale wind whistling through bending trees.

They headed for Regan's Pub with a mission.

Colin paid the bartender for the pint and went into a shadowed corner of the bar to sulk and think.

The phone call to Jen and the way Lucas was steadfastly ignoring him left a taste in his mouth more bitter than the Guinness. He'd come to Regan's both to listen to Lucas' group and think over the paths he could take. Despite Superintendent Dunn's admonitions, he was still considering ways to get to Inishcorr. Perhaps he could bribe a local fishing boat to take him out, but it was even more probable that any attempt to do that would result in the locals sending word to the authorities about this American trying to reach Inishcorr, and *that* could only be a disaster, leading to questions, possibly arrest, and even revocation of his visa and deportation—not to mention that even if some boat captain would do that, they would be as blind as the patrol vessels in the fog around the island.

He could steal a boat and make the attempt himself, but he wasn't a sailor and didn't know how to handle anything beyond a simple rowboat— even if he could manage the long row out to Inishcorr, he doubted that a rowboat or one of the local currachs would be able to handle ocean waves with a rank amateur such as himself at the oars. He would more likely end up drowning than reaching Inishcorr.

And staying in Ballemór was looking more and more like an unpleasant experience. Mrs. Egan had made her suspicion and distrust of him plain, and as Lucas aptly demonstrated, all the locals looked at him as if he were already branded an Oileánach. The fiddler had made it obvious that he didn't want to talk to Colin and that there was going to be no offer to play with the group again.

He felt like a novice chess player playing against a skilled and relentless Fate, who blocked all his strategies. Rooks, knights, and bishops hemmed him in while the queen lurked ominously behind the ranks of pawns. There were no good moves, only less-bad ones, and checkmate was inevitable.

Then, it seemed, a storm broke in the street outside . . .

"What the feck. . . ?" someone shouted from a table near the door. Colin glanced up, startled, the foamy tan head of Guinness at his lips. Patrons were already rising from their seats as the door of the pub rattled loudly in its frame, as if a hurricane were blowing in the square outside. The sound boomed. Lucas' group stopped playing in mid-song, and the muffled shouts from outside became audible, as well as the brittle sound of calling trumpets. There was a new, metallic sound as well, like screws and bolts being shaken in a giant tin can.

An ethereal chorus of low voices seemed to be singing "Come Away With Me" somewhere close by.

Colin set down his pint. He pushed his glasses up his nose.

The door blew open, the planks splintering as if kicked in by a massive giant's foot. A cold, thick mist blew into the pub, scattering napkins, place mats, and the sheet music on the bandstand, overturning pint glasses that crashed and broke on the floor, and causing those still seated to duck away from the flying debris. Curses and disoriented shouts erupted from all around the tavern. Colin shivered at the chill as his pint spilled over the tabletop and his lap. The mist wrapped around him; he could no longer see anything more than an arm's length away. He heard voices in the fog, voices that called his name.

"Colin Doyle, 'tis yerself we've come for. Colin Doyle . . ."

He backed away, his spine against a wall of the pub. Ghostly hands plucked at his sweater. "Colin Doyle, yeh ride with us . . ."

"Let me go!" he shouted back at the voice, flailing at the invisible hands. The mist in front of him cleared momentarily, and in the clear space, he saw a face he knew, though the man was clad in armor and a helm covered his hair. "Fionnbharr?" he managed to croak out.

"Aye. The same." Fionnbharr leaned forward, his nose crinkling under the helm. "Yeh still have the smell of death around yeh. 'Tis fainter now, but never mind." Fionnbharr held out his hand, the arm clad in mail, the hand gloved in leather. "Come! The Morrígan wants yeh."

"Maeve—she's all right?"

"'Tis fine she is, but let herself tell yeh. Take me hand . . ."

Colin took Fionnbharr's hand in his own, and with the touch, reality did a reel and jig around him. Where the mist had once concealed everything, he now saw clearly within it, while it was the pub's interior that seemed to be clad in fog and shadow. The fairy host was all around him: fair and tall men and women clad in armor and bearing shields and spears, while the patrons of Regan's became pale and ghostly; on the bandstand, Lucas was but a specter holding a fiddle in dead hands. With Colin still clasping Fionnbharr's fingers, the lord of the aos sí gestured with his head and the host turned as one, leaving the pub.

Outside, in the square, the moon seemed nearly as bright as the sun, and there were more of the aos sí, who cheered as Fionnbharr emerged from the building. Colin blinked. A monument to the soldiers of the Irish Revolution stood at the top of Ballemór Square—a stone obelisk inscribed with the names of the locals who had taken part—but now a Galway hooker had been impaled upon it, the top of the plinth jammed into its hull so the boat hung at an awkward angle atop it. The red sails flapped uselessly in the night breeze, and a chain ran down over the railing of the ship to an anchor halfway embedded in the pavement of the street.

Fionnbharr's grip on his arm remained tight. "Yeh stay wit' us," the man intoned as he gestured with his free hand to the others. "We've done as we promised. The Tuatha de Danann ride back now!" he shouted to the company. "Back to the mound! Back to Cnoc Deireadh!"

With that, the outside world seemed to shift and boil around them, the lines of the houses and buildings of Ballemór bending as if fluid and streaking away from them. A fierce gale wind blew from behind the host, taking them up as Colin saw the soldiers of the Tuatha de Danann leap into the saddles of their ghostly horses. Fionnbharr mounted as well, still holding onto Colin's arm. Colin thought he'd pull him up into the saddle, but Fionnbharr called out something in Gaelic and horns blared again. In the next moment, the host was moving, with Colin drifting weightlessly alongside Fionnbharr's steed even as he struggled in fright and called out to Fionnbharr. "Don't let go of me! And for God's sake, lift me up!"

"For which god's sake?" Fionnbharr laughed in reply. "If 'tis yers, I should let yeh drop, since it's the crucified bastard who's caused all our troubles."

But Fionnbharr didn't drop him. Instead, the host swept over the land faster than any earthly horse or any car, rushing above the streets and out into the heather-blanketed hills, a spectral cloud of silver that rippled through the valleys and was gone again. With Colin gaping at the landscape below, the host flowed over the Connemara escarpments and out over the gray, moonlight-glimmering water. They passed phosphorescent whitecaps, dipping so low that Colin thought he could hear the hooves of their ghostly horses splashing the sea underneath them. A white wall slowly rose on the horizon, a storm cloud resting on the ocean with a patrol boat slicing the water before it. The host—clamoring, shouting, singing, the trumpets blaring, swept over and around the ship in a moment. With a shout of triumph, the host pierced the dense wall of fog that surrounded Inishcorr.

And it was then that Fionnbharr released Colin's arm and let him fall.

✦ 29 ✦

If the Sea Were Ink

COLIN HEARD FIONNBHARR'S LOW, sinister laugh even as he felt the sidhe lord's fingers loosen around his arm. Then, abruptly, Colin felt himself falling, flailing in the gray tendrils of the fog as he shouted in mingled alarm, fear, and confusion. He had no idea how far he was going to fall, nor what he'd hit at the end of it. He wasn't sure how long he fell— it seemed an eternity, but it might have been but a moment. He waited for Fionnbharr to swoop down and grab him again; he waited for the ground to rise up and smash him.

His scream filled his ears, a wail that gashed the fog-hidden night sky.

The impact of intensely cold water shocked the breath from him and stung his back. He lost his glasses, torn from his face by the violence of the fall and the jarring impact with the sea. He gasped and inhaled saltwater as he sank under the waves even as he desperately tried to reach the surface again to tread water. He came up coughing, desperate for air. Waves came out of the moon-touched fog, lifting and tossing him, then leaving him in a trough while the sea seemed to heave itself into dark gray-green and shifting cliffs around him, harrowing in his myopic sight. Somewhere close at hand, he could hear waves breaking savagely on rocks, the direction confused and muffled by the fog. Colin's clothing was soaked, the weight of it dragging him down again even as he kicked frantically to keep his head above water. His thoughts raced: should he try to shed the woolen sweater and sodden jeans, his sneakers? But no, wouldn't the frigid water then just sap his strength even faster?

Panic made his heart a hammer thrashing frantically against his ribs.

He was going to die here, just off Inishcorr's shore, and he suspected that death would come quickly. He wondered what it would feel like to go under that last time, his lungs burning as he fought not to take that inevitable breath, and finally, helpless, opening his mouth and gulping in sea water and drowning, the world fading away . . .

Something touched his foot, nudging it, and he reacted in terror, imagining a shark's snout bumping him and circling away, only to return with its enormous jaws opening to rip and tear at his legs. Another nudge, and then a shape emerged from the water: slick dark fur, polished eyes blacker than the darkness around him, a whiskered snout regarding him: a bull seal. It barked once at him, almost angrily, swimming under Colin's outstretched arm. Another bull surfaced with a flip of its tail, shook water from its head, and slid quickly under Colin's other arm. "Okay," Colin said, but the effort of speaking started him coughing. He clung to the seals desperately, hoping that he understood their intentions. They began swimming hard through the surging water, with Colin kicking weakly in an effort to help them, and his cold-numbed fingers hanging on to them as best he could.

It seemed an eternity, this slow progress. The waves were starting to overwhelm him, and he could barely keep his grip on the slippery fur of the seals when the sound of the crashing surf grew louder. The larger of the bull seals gave another coughing bark, and the next wave broke white over Colin. He felt himself tumbling, lost and gasping for breath in the chaos of the water, but then realized that his body was scraping against rocky sand. He put his feet down hard and found himself standing chest-deep in surging water. He blinked, squinting as he tried to see through the fog and the faint moonlight that filtered through. He thought he glimpsed a rock-strewn beach as the receding wave attempted to suck him back into the sea.

The seals had vanished, and his confused mind wondered if they'd ever really been there in the first place. Colin staggered, trying to hold his position, then the next wave hit him noisily from behind, taking him briefly underwater again as he thrashed at the tan foam, kicking and paddling until his sneakered feet found the pebbled bottom once more. He pushed forward against the surf as it rushed back out again, stiff-legged against the pull of the waves and staggering toward the beach. He gasped with the effort, the cold, and the water-filled anchor of his clothing. He was waist-deep, then knee-deep, then he had collapsed onto the shingle, pulling himself on his belly out of the reach of the waves. He lay there, taking in great gulps of spray-wet air.

He felt hands on his arms on either side, and he let them pull him up and support him. He shook his head, doglike, drops of water splashing. He squinted at his rescuers as they stepped away from him. Both men were entirely naked. "Niall? Liam?"

"Aye," Liam answered. "And here—yeh might be wanting these." He handed Colin his glasses. Colin took them gratefully. The frames were bent and a bit awry, but at least he could see again. Colin blinked away the burn of the saltwater. "Thanks," he said. "To both of you. You saved my life. How did you know. . . ?"

"We were told to wait for yeh here," Liam said, "when we heard that bastard Fionnbharr rush toward us, laughing. 'Yeh'd best change form,' he told us as he passed. 'I dropped the fool on the way in.' So Niall and I changed and came after yeh."

"And it was easy enough to find yeh—hollerin' out there like a feckin' sow stuck under the garden fence," Niall added. He'd gone to a large rock up the beach, placing a folded seal's pelt atop it along with his clothes. He yanked a sweater over his wet hair. "And as a swimmer, yeh do an excellent imitation of a rock."

Liam chuckled—he was dressing also, his seal pelt placed carefully in a shoulder bag—but Colin was too busy shivering to care much. Liam evidently noticed Colin's condition. "Niall, the man's going to freeze to death. We need to get him up to the village. Besides, Maeve's waiting for us."

Niall scowled at that. "No doubt. All right, can yeh leg it?" he asked Colin, who shivered again, but nodded. "We'll get yeh in front of a fire ninety to the dozen. C'mon."

He'd imagined their reunion a few thousand times since Superintendent Dunn had removed him from the island. In those imaginings—at least the ones that weren't more private—Maeve would run to him and hold him tenderly. She would kiss him with fevered, urgent lips, whispering to him how much she had missed him, how she hadn't felt complete since he left the island, how she'd longed for him to be with her, how she loved him . . .

It was massively evident that his imagination was terribly defective. Maeve did rush over to him as he was half-carried into her house in the village, but the rain of kisses weren't forthcoming nor were the whispered endearments. His imagination hadn't included the worry lines creasing her face and the nearly-angry tone of her voice, nor the crowd of Oileánach that filled the room beyond the door. "Jaysus, 'tis about time," he heard her say. "An' look, the poor dear's half-drowned and positively foundered."

"Maeve. God, I've been trying . . ." he started to say through chattering teeth, and she shook her head.

"Nah. Do'nah talk. Niall, get him into the bedroom. Someone bring him hot tea and something to eat. Put some more turves on the fire and get it going good. The first thing we need to do is get these wet things off him . . ."

Colin blinked, shivering helplessly. Someone had his arm, leading him into the bedroom and letting him fall on the bed. He heard a drawer opening in Maeve's dresser, and a pair of blue jeans and a sweater that he recognized landed on the bed near him. His imaginings had included losing his clothes—at least some of them had—but not quite so roughly and perfunctorily, and not with Niall doing half the undressing. He started to push away Niall's hand as he pulled Colin's soaked sweater over his head, but his hands didn't seem to want to cooperate; Maeve tugged at his belt and unzipped his jeans; that at least he didn't mind, though when she started to roll his underwear down his legs, he shivered again. "It's the cold water, Maeve," he gritted out, forcing his lower jaw to stop shivering. "Sorry."

At the head of the bed, Niall laughed mirthlessly. "Niall," Maeve barked warningly.

"Aye, I hear yeh, Maeve. Here, put yer arms through the sleeves, boyo . . ."

Maeve pulled away his jeans . . . and Colin suddenly felt sick, as if she'd torn away a part of him. He forced the gorge down. "The cloch's in my pocket . . ." he managed to croak out. He held out his hand to Maeve. "Give it back."

She cocked her head at him strangely. "Yeh'll have it," she told him. "Just wait a mo'."

That didn't comfort him. The discomfort grew, even when a few minutes later, he was dressed in dry clothes—the clothes he'd left here, he realized—and was wrapped in a blanket in front of the hearth in the front room, his hands cupped around a steaming cup of black tea. The fire in the hearth curled greedy blue fingers around the turves, throwing out welcome heat and the distinctive scent of burning peat. He sipped at the bitter brew, relishing the heat as it flowed down his throat. His hands had stopped shaking from the cold, but there was a burning need inside him now.

Maeve crouched alongside him, one hand cupping his neck, her face still worried. He saw his grandfather's stone in her hand, the silver chain falling between her fingers. A quick surge of intense jealousy went through him at the sight; he nearly reached out to snatch it back again, a desire to hold the stone, to put the cloch back in his pocket. *It's mine.* The impulse was difficult to ignore; his fingers, unbidden, had bent into claws. *Give it back! You can't have it!*

She seemed to understand his distress. "Here," she told him, holding the stone out to him. He opened his hand underneath hers, and she dropped the pendant there. "I believe this is yours."

Holding it, he felt the anger and distress dissolve. He closed his fingers around the stone, protectively.

"Here. I believe this is yours."

She saw Colin stare at the cloch in his hand, and she wondered if he knew how important the stone was and what it meant to all of them. She believed his grandfather had at least suspected it, when he'd taken it away. "Yeh want the cloch, but yer not worried about yer wallet or cell phone?"

He looked up at her, then, blinking. "That's stupid, I guess . . ."

"'Tis fine," she told him. "It tells me yeh know what's important and what's nah. Yeh might as well put it around yer neck now; there's no need to hide it any longer." She smiled at him, and watched his face relax. "I'm glad t'have yeh back, love." *Yeh and the cloch both . . .*

"This wasn't exactly the way I expected to return," Colin told her. He put the chain of the pendant over his head and let the stone fall on his chest.

"'Twas the *only* way, I'm afraid," she told him. "Feeling better now?"

"A bit. When I hit the water, it was so cold that I could hardly take a breath. Fionnbharr . . ."

"Aye, Fionnbharr," she interrupted gently, her voice suddenly harsh. She could feel anger rising up inside her. *The fool could have ruined everything, just for the sake of what he probably thought of as a fine little jest.* "I believe we need to have words with the Lord of the Mound."

"I thought all of you were on the same side," Colin said.

Niall, standing with an arm draped on the shelf above the hearth, sniffed. "We have a common problem. It do'nah mean we're on the same side, nor that we all want the same thing. Not that you'd understand. Yer just a leamh, no matter what Maeve thinks."

"Niall, not now," Maeve said warningly. "*Especially* not now."

She stood, drawing herself up. In the firelit dimness of the room, clad in her red cloak, she saw her shadow against the far wall, and it seemed almost spectral. Colin stared at her, then at the cloch in his hand. She smiled at him, reassuringly. *Yeh will need to tell him all soon. There's nah time to waste. Not now.*

"Maeve, it's time," Niall said, as if he'd read her thoughts. "We have to do what we need to do, and we need to do it quickly." Maeve heard mutterings of agreement from the others in the room.

"Yeh don't tell me what I do or I don't do," Maeve answered. "Not any of yeh. I am the Morrígan. If yeh want me to open the path, then let me do it. If not . . ." Maeve shrugged. "Then go tell Keara to stop her chant, and let the leamh come here. Yeh can fight them, or yeh can just surrender to them. Either way, yeh will die. Which way do yeh want it?"

Niall hadn't moved; he glared at Maeve. "Yer not me mum, Maeve, so treat us like adults, not fecking children yeh can scold."

"Feckin' act like an adult, and I might," Maeve spat back. "Everything is delicate right now, and it all has to be done carefully. We can't rush this or it *will* all fail, and as far as I know, I'm the only one who can open the path—except maybe Fionnbharr, and only the Ancient Ones know what he intends or who he would help. Am I wrong?" She flung an arm wide to encompass all those in the room. "Anyone here with the power, the knowledge, the skill, or the energy to create the gateway? Anyone want to take this task from me? I'll be happy to step aside if one of yeh can."

Most of them stared at the floor, as if the worn planks there were somehow fascinating. Niall was shaking his head, but he wouldn't make eye contact with her.

"That's what I thought," Maeve finished. "Now—I need to talk to Colin, and I need privacy for that. Niall, go see Aiden and tell him that we have Colin and the cloch, and that Keara only has to hold on for a bit more. Liam, go down to the harbor and get your people ready. Dolan, I want you to go to the mound and tell Fionnbharr that I'll be coming out to talk to him, and that I'm not pleased with his little joke. The rest of yeh, there's work to be done; yeh know what 'tis, so go do it. Get yerselves ready to leave. G'wan now—the time's nearly on us."

Niall pushed away from the hearth with cheeks ruddy with blood, looking as if he wanted to say more but pressing his mouth tightly shut. Slowly, with nods and murmured apologies, the others followed him from the house. When the last one had shut the door, Maeve give a sigh that even to her sounded more like a sob. Her shoulders drooped; she covered her face with her hands. "Maeve?" she heard Colin say. She felt his hand on her shoulder. She took a long breath, then let her hands drop. When she looked at him, there was a wavering, uncertain smile on his face.

"I've missed yeh the last few days, Colin. More than I thought possible." His smile morphed into a grin. "And part of me wishes desperately that yeh'd stayed away." As she watched, the grin slowly faded.

"Because of what might happen here?"

"Aye. And other things as well. That stone yeh hold; how did yeh feel when yeh saw me holding it?" He seemed to be surprised at the harsh tone in her voice. His eyes widened at the sound.

"I felt . . ." Colin shook his head. "I wanted it back. It was like part of me went missing all of a sudden."

"Now yeh have some understanding of how hard it was for me, when yer granddad took it away from me, and now yeh know why I didn't take it from yeh when I showed yeh that glimpse of Talamh an Ghlas. I've *known* that pain yeh felt for a moment; I've borne it for a long time, since Rory took it from me." She saw Colin clamp his mouth shut against what she was saying. His look hardened as he lifted his gaze from the cloch to her eyes. "Aye. Rory . . ." She breathed the name. She looked at his face, knowing the time for lies and half-truths was gone. She could not stop the smile that touched her lips. "So now yeh know. You reminded me so much of him when I first met you. I was Máire then, as I'm Maeve now, and I knew Rory. I knew him as I know yeh."

His mouth dropped open, as if he'd expected her to lie or evade. "Jesus, Maeve. Do you know how freaking *weird* this is? I mean, you and my goddamn *grandfather* . . ." He released an exasperated huff.

"I know it's strange to yeh," Maeve told him. "But out there in your world . . ." She gestured eastward, toward Ceomhar Head and the mainland. "I've known many people's grandparents and great-grandparents, or as many 'greats' as yeh wish to add. I've been a lover to some, a friend to others, enemy to as many others. I've been around a long, long time, Colin, and so have some of the others here. Aye, I knew yer grandfather and I loved Rory, I did—but to me, that's not strange; 'tis just the way things be, and it doesn't change a whit the way I feel about yeh. When I told yeh I loved yeh, I spoke no lie. I did and still do, and that's nah weird or strange either; it just is—for this moment and for this time."

"For this moment and time," Colin repeated. "And maybe you'll be around for one of my grandsons, too."

She shook her head. "Nah. If we succeed here, I won't. And if we don't, then it's also nah, I'm thinking. I will'nah survive long enough for that." She reached out to stroke his cheek again; he started to draw his head back, then relented. He trapped her hand between his head and shoulder.

"Damn it, Maeve," he said. She saw him start to reach for the cloch again, then slowly pull his hand back.

She leaned in to kiss him. "I know," she answered. "Yeh are yerself only, my love, and that's what makes yeh precious to me. Yer not Rory, and yeh've made a choice that he wasn't willing to make. Yeh wouldn't have fled from me as he did, and when yeh had to leave, yeh came back."

He lifted his head, releasing her hand. She smoothed his damp hair back, but there was still pain in his eyes.

"Yeh read his diary, so yeh know. And now yeh know how much his leaving with the cloch hurt me, because I saw the same pain in yer eyes, only a few minutes ago, and yeh had lost the cloch only for a minute. Yeh still don't know all the power it holds or why the cloch allowed itself to be found. Neither did Rory. Neither did I, really." She allowed herself a bitter laugh. "Possessing the cloch, holding it, is an addiction that becomes part of yeh. Even for the few days I had it meself, I knew that. When I held it t'other day to show you Talamh an Ghlas, when I took it from your pocket just now, I could feel the pull of it again, and when I put it back in yer hand, I thought I might scream with the loss of it again as I had back then. But the cloch's not *for* me. Yer the one it wants, as it wanted Rory, as it made him take it from me all those decades ago."

"The stone *made* him take it? You make it sound like it's alive."

She laughed again. "I think 'tis. Do'nah yeh find yerself wanting to touch it and hold it? Don't yeh find it comforting?" She could see the answer in his face. "Aye. Yeh know. But what yeh do'nah know is what the cloch is meant to do, what it *will* do, along with the power of that voice of yers."

As she watched, he clutched the jewel on its chain. He stroked the emerald facets of the stone. "A few minutes ago," he said, "you said you wish I'd stayed away. Why?"

She turned her head, watching the flames lick away at the underside of the turves in the hearth. "Fionnbharr once told me that yeh were the one meant to open the gateway, not yer grandfather," she said, not looking back to him but at the fire. "Well, I believe he was right. Yer grandfather wasn't the bard yeh are. The cloch knew it as well, and made Rory leave so that it could be given to yeh years and years later. Yeh and the cloch together are the key we need to open the door, along with the spell I'll cast at the same time. I showed yeh the place before: Talamh an Ghlas, the Green Land. That's where those of my kind will'nah die, but can thrive instead."

"You told me once that you couldn't leave Ireland. You said that wasn't possible."

"'Tis not, but Talamh an Ghlas *is* Ireland—or what this land could be, somewhere else in another time. Colin . . ." She closed her eyes against the sudden burn of salt, her breath shallow. When she opened her eyes again, she turned to him. "We—those like me—are part of this land. What's always kept us alive is that the leamh, the mortal people, maintained their belief in us. We're the shadows of yer myths. We're what yeh made to explain how things came to be. We're what yeh believe in, deep in the core of yeh. We're the memory of ancient days, captured in the soil and stones, yes, but also in the mortals who live here. The pull of this land kept us alive, stone and bone. But that belief has faded over time, more and more in the last few centuries, and it's killed some of us and put others into a sleep that might as well be death." She lifted her hands and let them fall again. "Even those of us who aren't sleeping have been changed, slowly, over the centuries. I am the Morrígan, yes, but I'm not the same as I once was."

Nah. That Morrígan wouldn't be talking to Colin at all. That Morrígan would never have let him leave when Dunn came. That Morrígan would have already done what needs to be done, without all this yammering and hesitation. That Morrígan had no room in her for affection and love, nor for doubt.

"Yeh wouldn't have liked me then," she told Colin. "The land changes and therefore the people who live here change, and we will continue to change and dwindle and become less until no one any longer believes in us and we fade entirely. But in Talamh an Ghlas . . . those beliefs never died for the mortals there. There, we will live again as we once did."

"How do you know that?"

She smiled. She put her hand over his on top of the pendant. "I felt it in the cloch. A cloch na thintri; a stone of lightning, 'tis called. I *still* feel it, even with yeh holding it," she told him. "In Talamh an Ghlas, our kind are normal and yer kind"—she saw him wince at the implication—"are no better or numerous than any other. There, what yeh consider myths and folk tales are real. They live. *We* can live."

"So *you* can live," Colin said. "But I'm not one of you. What about me? You'll live forever. I'll die."

"Yeh will. All mortals do," she agreed, softly. She lifted her hand, looking at the cloch through his possessive fingers, watching how his eyes seemed to want to devour it. "But we can die the real death as well. The magic we have to do to open the doorway is very difficult; the power that it requires is daunting. Some of my kind have tried it before and have lost their very existence in the attempt. This is blood magic. To be successful, the spell requires a sacrifice." She saw the question in his face though he said nothing. "Aye," she told him, wishing he'd understood, but he hadn't. Not quite.

He blinked as he pushed his glasses up his nose. "Blood magic? What do you . . ." he started to say. Then, almost a breath: "Oh."

"That's why I said I wished yeh'd stayed away, because now that yer here, they all expect me to start the preparations and for us to cast the spell: if we still have time, if the others can hold off the Naval Services and the NPWS long enough." She gave a disgusted grunt. *"Feck!"*

He'd let the blanket fall from his shoulders. "So none of this was real: you coming to Regan's to hear me play, talking to me, bringing me out here, our making love . . ."

Yeh are a demigod, Morrígan. Yer above mortal things. He's just a leamh; he doesn't deserve the truth yer giving him, and yeh can't let him make the decision. Lie to him. Lie to him until it's too late for him to stop yeh. She could hear the clamoring inside her, the war-crow's voice, the voices of the sisters she'd subsumed and who were part of her, the voices of the women whose mortal bodies she'd taken as her own, the voices of those who had possessed the cloch before and were now trapped inside, the voices of legend and half-lost history and almost-forgotten memories.

"No, it wasn't real at first," she told him, the words slow and careful. "Yeh were . . ." She stopped, began again. "The spell needs a particular type of person. There aren't many leamh who fit. Yer grandfather was one, the first I'd met in a long time; yeh are, too. Yeh want to believe in the Old Ways and the ancient people; yeh were actively trying to understand us, through yer music. And yeh were marked from birth with the caul, as was Rory. But the spell also requires that the person has to be willing, even if what he believes is a lie."

"The sacrificial lamb," Colin said.

"That's mixing mythologies," Maeve told him, "but aye. A finding spell told me long ago where Rory and the cloch were, but I couldn't leave the soil here to go to him, and he never returned on his own. I think he knew I'd find him if he did, an' he was afraid of that. So I watched, and I knew yer father was born, but he didn't have the caul nor the ability Rory had, so I waited even longer, and yeh came. When it was time . . . well, yeh know that. Yeh saw me; yeh saw the green land, yeh heard my call, and yeh answered. Aye, I went to Regan's deliberately to see yeh, and aye, the flirting that night was deliberate, too."

"And you used another spell to make me infatuated with you also." Colin was scowling, looking down at the floor. "Like you did with my grandfather."

"Aye, I did that for Rory," Maeve told him. "'Twas necessary, but it di'nah last long enough, did it? But for yeh I cast no glamour at all. With yeh, 'twas genuine."

"Because I'm a sap and a fool."

"Yer neither. I couldn't love yeh if yeh were that. And I *do* love yeh, Colin. 'Tis the truth, and I wish I could make yeh believe that. I hope yeh feel it, even now." She watched him as he took in that statement. He sniffed, his fingers still prowling over the cloch as if the answers were written there. She thought his expression was snagged between hope and skepticism. The voices inside her howled in derision.

"I can't tell when you're lying and when you're telling the truth," he told her.

"I understand, and I'm sorry for it. Colin, if I'd wanted, I could have stopped yeh from ever leaving the first time yeh came to the island. 'Tis a fact, and Niall wanted me to do exactly that. A spell, a minor glamour; that's all it would have taken; yeh were infatuated with me, and just a nudge would have changed yer mind and kept yeh here—and if I had, Dunn and the NPWS wouldn't have had time to act as they have. But I waited, because . . ." Her thoughts swarmed with things she couldn't say, that she was afraid to say because she knew he wouldn't, couldn't, believe her. *Heroes have changed,* she could have told him. *In the past, it only mattered how well you fought, how many men yeh could slay and how strong yeh were. Now, courage is measured in other ways. It's in what yeh believe, and whether yer willing to stand firm in that belief and follow it, no matter what others tell yeh. I've seen yeh do that.* " . . . because as much as is possible for the Morrígan, who has lived too long and known and lost too many lovers and watched too many grand heroes die in my name, I also loved yeh, and I wasn't willing to do what I was supposed to do. Believe that, Colin. Please believe it."

Colin had started to speak, and she lifted a hand to stop him. "Nah, let me finish, now that I've started. Part of me was pleased when Dunn took yeh, because I thought he might also take the decision from my hands and send yeh home where I couldn'nah bring yeh back. I wanted the decision taken from me entirely."

"You didn't hesitate to send the aos sí after me when you found out I was still there, did you? I'm just something for you to use. A tool."

"No," she told him. She stretched her hands out to him, wanting him to take them, but he only stared at them, as if their touch might burn him, and his fingers wouldn't leave the stone. "Have yeh been listening to me? I care for yeh, Colin. 'Tis truth."

"You told Niall and the others to start getting ready to leave. How are you going to do that if I'm not willing to be your sacrifice?"

"I ca'nah do it," she told him. "I lied to them because . . ." She lifted her shoulders and let them fall. The cloak felt impossibly heavy on her body, as if she were but a specter of herself, a wisp as insubstantial as Keara's fog. She inhaled the scent of peat: an odor as old as herself. *There has to be an answer. There still has to be a way to do this.* "Come with me to see Fionn-bharr. I need to talk to him, or it all falls apart whether yeh help or nah."

◄ 30 ►

Let Sleeping Gods Lie

COLIN WALKED WITH MAEVE through the dense, cold fog up the path from her house to where the land lifted under their feet. Suddenly, the fog vanished as if they'd walked through a wall, and overhead he could see the brightening sky of dawn and the mound of Fionnbharr rising at the lip of the island: Cnoc Deireadh. "Promise me this much," Maeve said to Colin as they approached the mound. It was the first words she'd spoken since they left the house. "Just pretend that yeh agree with me, even if yeh don't. Would yeh do that much? I want Fionnbharr to think that we're a unified front, or we lose his cooperation when we need it more than ever."

"The asshole dropped me in the goddamn ocean," Colin said, glaring at the mound, standing now in quiet moonlight despite the fog that wrapped the rest of the island. "He nearly drowned me."

"I know. But the Lord of the Sidhe isn't mortal, and he doesn't think like one."

"And you do?" he asked, and Maeve stopped. She caught his gaze with her eyes; he found that he couldn't look away.

"No, I don't either, and 'tis good yeh understand that. But . . . When I gave meself to you, Colin, there was no lie at all in me. I wanted yeh as any mortal woman might want the man she desires. I *still* want that, no matter how yeh feel about me now. That hasn't changed."

"But it wasn't that way with my grandfather?"

His words stung. He saw it in her face. She gave a faint shake of her head, swaying the long strands of her hair. "'Twas nah. He was nah the same as yeh, Colin. Yer stronger and yet gentler than he ever was, and yeh know yerself better. Yer a true bard; he was an amateur. I might have come to love Rory in some way, but he left me before that could happen. I frightened him too much. I know yeh feel the same a bit, but yeh stayed when yeh could have left. He di'nah. I just hope yeh can still trust me, with all I've told yeh."

Colin blinked. He wanted to believe her, but the confusion in his mind was thicker than Keara's fog. "Maeve . . ." he started to say, but he felt the shift in the air in the same moment, and turned to see Fionnbharr, clad in armor and with a spear in his hand, standing alongside the tree at the summit of the mound.

"Morrígan," he said, nodding first to Maeve. Then he glanced at Colin, his eyes glittering. "Well, would yeh look now, the leamh's all dried off after his little swim."

"Fuck you, Fionnbharr," Colin spat back, and crystalline laughter answered him from the mound, the sound of a thousand-voiced amusement.

"So, does yer little play-toy know what's expected of 'im?" Fionnbharr boomed over the laughter.

"He does," Maeve answered. She didn't look at Colin now, and he remembered her words. *Just pretend that yeh agree with me . . .*

"An' does he know all that means? Och, nah, Morrígan," Fionnbharr said, raising his spear and thumping the shaft on a stone at the base of the hawthorn. The booming sound that followed was like the stroke of a mallet on timpani. "Let himself answer, so I can hear 'im."

Maeve waited, still not looking at Colin and her chin lifted, as if she was entirely confident and certain of his answer. Colin could hear the cold Atlantic wind sighing in the branches of the hawthorn and the faint crash of waves against the rocks below the cliff; he could smell the brine. He started to speak, then halted, taking another breath. The hesitation seemed to go on for seconds. Finally, Colin spoke, his voice sounding thin against Fionnbharr's growling bass. "I know the spell to open the Green Land to you requires blood magic. I know I was brought here for that purpose."

The words sounded ridiculous. Impossible. *Why am I going along with this? I can't trust her . . .*

"And so yer willin' to be that for the Morrígan?" Fionnbharr continued, his tone mocking. "Then yer a greater fool than any."

"*Not* for the Morrígan," Maeve answered before Colin could reply. "What Colin does, he'll do for all of us, the aos sí as much as any."

Again, many-voiced laughter echoed from the mound. "Yer the ones threatened by the leamh," Fionnbharr answered. "We aos sí are safe for now under the mound. Let them come ashore with their empty laws and their guns. They won't find *us* in our caverns under the ground."

Maeve sniffed and turned to Colin. "May I borrow the cloch? For a moment only, I promise." She held out her hand to him, palm up.

He didn't want to obey her. He didn't want to feel the pain and the loss again; he knew now what it would cost him. He wondered whether, if he gave it to her, she would give it back or if he would lose it forever, as his grandfather had done to her. He looked at Maeve's hand, then her face, trying to read what was there. *I just hope yeh can trust me . . .* Now that it came to it, he wasn't sure he could. He fisted his hand around the stone, which lay on his chest: his grandfather's stone. The Morrígan's stone. *Your stone. It's yours and no one else's.*

Reluctantly, he slipped the chain over his head and held his hands over hers. He had to fight his own fingers to loosen them. The stone fell, and Maeve's hand closed around it. Colin gave a cry, a wail that died when it hit the wall of fog around the mound. Pain racked him, as if he'd just dropped his own heart into her palm. He had to clutch his arms to himself to stop him from clawing at Maeve's hand to take back the cloch.

Fionnbharr laughed.

Maeve lifted her hand, and the wind failed in the hawthorn as Fionnbharr's amusement went silent. Movement snagged Colin's gaze, and he looked up to see yellow-green waves of lights shimmering among the stars, tendrils of that strange aurora he'd glimpsed once before stretching down toward Maeve's hands and wrapping around her arm. In her fingers, he thought she was holding his cloch, but it was no longer just a pretty crystal; it was glowing itself in response to the sky's light. Maeve spoke a single word—"Oscail!"—and the world shifted around them. She, Colin, and Fionnbharr were no longer standing on the mound, but in an immense cavern lit by thousands of torches and candles. Around the stones and through the earthen walls, the roots of the hawthorn were entwined, like the tangled base of some immense world-tree. Colin gasped, helplessly. Around them, the host of the aos sí were gathered, half-hidden in the shifting light and shadows.

Leaning over Colin, she took his hand and gave him back the stone. Colin gasped with relief, at the sense of being whole once more, but he saw pain wrinkle Maeve's face even as she released the cloch. He quickly put it around his neck once more.

She sighed, shaking her head. "That was far harder than I thought 'twould be," she whispered to Colin.

Fionnbharr's face was suffused with red, visible even in the light of the torches. He shook his spear toward Maeve. "Yer not permitted here, Morrígan." His gaze went to Colin. "Nor is any mortal, on pain of death. Yeh should nah have done this." His eyes narrowed. "Yeh should nah have been *able* to do this."

"Then send me away, Lord Fionnbharr. I've given you a glimpse of the power that my mere mortal holds. So show us yer great magic. Show me how powerful *yeh* are. Send us back."

Fionnbharr scowled; he lifted his spear as if he were about to cast it at Maeve, and she seemed to wave a casual hand, the aurora light still flickering around her fingers even though the stone was now in Colin's hand. *"Pléasc!"* she uttered, and the shaft of the spear exploded into long splinters in Fionnbharr's hands, the bronze head falling to ring impotently on the stones at his feet. Colin heard a collective gasp from the host as Fionnbharr tossed down the remnants of his weapon and spat on them. "Yer not a mortal, Morrígan. Yeh think this mortal lover of yers could'a done that? Could *he* have brought yeh down here?"

"Yeh misjudge the power of the mortals in this world, Lord Fionnbharr. Yeh always have an' that's the foolishness of *yer* kind, as it's been the foolishness of my own. I told yeh this before yeh rode: if yeh do nothing, then those mortals out there will cut down the hawthorn, dig up the sidhe, and salt the very earth, as Eithne's husband did at Cnoc Meadha. Yeh might not believe me, but 'tis fact. If yeh do nothing here on Inishcorr, then yeh and all of yer kind will die here, too. This will truly be the last mound."

Colin saw Fionnbharr scowl again. His face seemed older now, as if the centuries were marking Fionnbharr's face as they watched. "When I came here to Cnoc Deiridh, I brought the sacred earth from the heart of Cnoc Meadha, Morrígan. 'Tis that and our own spells will keep us safe."

"Scoff all yeh like, Fionnbharr. Yeh can cower here in your caverns while they turn Inishcorr into a park for the leamh and sell fairy trinkets and plastic swords in a bloody souvenir stand on top of yer precious Cnoc Deiridh. Yeh can comfort yerself with knowing that they will leech all the true magic from the earth and leave the aos sí nothing more than whispers and mist. Yeh need to have the gate open to Talamh an Ghlas as much as the rest of us, and yeh know it. If yeh fail to help us now, yeh will know the real death, eventually."

"An' why are yeh here, Morrígan? Why aren't yeh already crafting the spell to open the path? Why is the witch's fog still all about the island? Why are yeh slabberin' at me instead of acting?"

"While the fog holds, no enchantment of mine can reach outside it, and the blood spell needs to go beyond to find the gateway. Which yeh already know—'tis why I sent the wild ride to find Colin. When I tell Keara to stop her chanting, then the leamh *are* going to try to take the island and us, and the blood spell is long and difficult. I won't be able to help hold them back. We'll need the aos sí then, or it will all fail and Colin won't be the only mortal a'standin' in the sidhe caverns."

"There are more than mortals here, Morrígan." Fionnbharr chuckled, and the host laughed with him. He waved his hand toward the dark recesses of the underground, and torches flared into life there. "Can yeh wake those who sleep? Does the bard's cloch also give him that power?"

Colin took a step toward what the light had revealed, and the host parted reluctantly in front of him. Down a long passage, ornate, decorated niches had been carved into the living rock and painted brightly; there, on beds of silk-covered rushes, lay bodies. The nearest one to Colin was a stocky, muscular man, arrayed in mail and a cloak of blue. Where his arms were exposed, the jagged lines of old battle wounds were visible, as was a long scar from his chin to his temple on the left side of his face. Locks of golden hair touched with white fell around his shoulders, and a long spear, the leaf-shaped blade inscribed with the incised lines of ogham lettering, had been placed alongside him, his hand grasping the yew staff. A brown, lean grayhound slumbered at his other side, its long and narrow muzzle resting on the man's shoulder. Colin thought the man a corpse, but as he stared down at him, he saw the chest rise and fall in a slow breath.

"That's Lugh," he heard Maeve say behind him. "Son of Cian and Ethniu, grandson of Balor of the Fomorians. He's been this way for two centuries and more, though once he was vibrant and alive. Now he sleeps like the others who have been brought here, all those we could find in the old places."

"Places like Rathcroghan, where you met my grandfather?"

"Aye, there and a hundred other places as well. Now they sleep here, where we remember them." Maeve began to intone their names, and Colin heard Fionnbharr's voice join her, and those of the host as well, until the cavern swelled with the sound, the names like a litany chanted in a church, each name an echoing thunder stroke: Nuada of the silver arm, Allai, Indai, Ériu, Banba, Fodla, Aengus, Manannán mac Lir, Brigid, and dozens more—names that Colin knew from old texts: the Book of Leinster, the Lebor na hUidre, the Táin Bó Cúailnge; all the other manuscripts that comprised the three cycles of Irish myth. The syllables the aos sí intoned shivered the walls and made the flames of the torches gutter in the wind they created. With every name, one of the niches farther along the passage would erupt in shafts of gold-green light like the afternoon sun through a canopy of leaves, then fade again.

When it ended, the silence pressed down on Colin, smothering and oppressive. Maeve touched his shoulder as he stared down at Lugh's slumbering form. "It's your time," she said to Colin. "Show them what you can do."

He shook his head, confused. "I don't know how."

"Hold the cloch," she told him, "and sing."

"Sing what?"

Her lips curled into smile. "The words will come to you, love. Don't worry. Trust me, as I said."

She stepped aside and back, close to where Fionnbharr also stood. Colin glanced at the stone in his hand, standing at the foot of Lugh's bed and looking down on the sleeping god's figure. Feeling both foolish and self-conscious, he took the pendant from his neck and put it in his right hand, lifting it as he'd watched Maeve do, imagining the cloch glowing again as it had when she had held it. For a moment, nothing happened, but then his perception shifted, as if he were seeing double, and he saw the scene around him outlined in green, coruscating light as the shimmering curtains of aurora-like radiance filled the cavern above the upheld cloch, drifting downward to wrap around his arm and hand. Colin gasped at the touch of the light: frigid, burning his skin like ice. Curling lines like white, raised scars traveled down his arm to the wrist, burrowing past the cuff of his sweater. He could *feel* the cloch, he could hear voices inside it, and they gave him words and a song, and he opened his mouth, letting their words fall from his lips to become wrapped in the aurora light, his voice sounding deeper and more resonant: a stranger's voice more than his own.

> Brosdaighthear, ar Tuath Dé Danann
> doirseóir Teamhra,
> d'ionnsoighidh na craoibhe cubhra,
> aoighe Eamhna.
>
> Mása thú an tIoldánach oirrdhearc
> an airm ghlaisghéir
> is mo chean duid, ar an doirseóir,
> a bhuig bhaisréidh.
>
> Damadh é Lugh, leannán Fódla
> na bhfonn sriobhfhann,
> do bheith ann, ar Tuath Dé Danann,
> dob é a ionam.

As the last words echoed in the cavern, Colin felt he could no longer bear the bright cold that wrapped around his arm. As the scar-like lines deepened on his hand and arm, Colin saw Lugh's eyes open for a moment, startling clear and blue, and Colin's grip on the cloch loosened. He cried out as he nearly dropped the pendant. He felt more than saw Maeve move past him to bend over Lugh's body. She touched the god's face with her hand, the fading green light of the cloch still falling on Lugh's features. She spoke to him in quick, ancient Gaelic, far too fast for Colin to understand. Lugh answered in a single word in a voice that was graveled and slow: "*Tuigim.*"

But after he spoke, his eyes closed once more as the light from the cloch faded entirely. Colin brought down his arm, cradling it against his body as he went to his knees in the cavern. His arm was stiff and aching, and his fingers were clawed around the silver cage that held it.

The host of the aos sí and Fionnbharr maintained a reverent silence, while the echo of the thundering light and his own voice reverberated in Colin's memory. "What . . ." His voice sounded hoarse and broken after the song, and he licked his lips and tried again. "What did you say to him?" Colin asked.

"I told him that 'twas time for him to take up his spear once more. I told him that we needed him to come when we called, and he said that he understood." She glanced over to Fionnbharr. "Great Lugh will come," she said. "Colin the Bard has awakened him again, and he will answer the call." Maeve paused, and Colin saw her look past Fionnbharr to the gathered shadowy host. "So, what of the rest of yeh? Are yeh willin' to ride out now that it's time to do battle, or nah?"

"Aye . . ." The word came first as a whisper from one, then it was joined by other voices until it sounded like a gale off the North Sea, and finally Fionnbharr himself joined in. "Aye, Morrígan," he bellowed, and the host behind him went silent. "We will, and perhaps we can rouse others here besides Lugh. But I tell you this, Morrígan. 'Tis given to me as the Lord of the Aos Sí to glimpse the future, an' the future I see yer nah part of."

Maeve nodded. "Then so be it," she answered. She crouched down alongside Colin. "Take up the cloch and take us away from here," she said in his ear. "Yeh must do it; I do'nah think I can bear to handle it again only to give it back. Not again. So unless yeh want me to take it from yeh forever . . ."

"*No!*" He nearly shouted the word; the thought of losing the stone unbearable. He closed his fist around it, hiding it from her against his body. "It's mine."

"Aye," she told him. " 'Tis. An' yeh must use it now."

"How?"

"Hold it up as yeh did before and just think of us outside once more. It will hear you and do the rest." She put her hands under his arms, and he started to pull away again. "Let me help yeh stand," she whispered. "Yeh can't appear weak to Fionnbharr. 'Twill be easier this time, I promise."

Grimacing, Colin stood again, Maeve helping him up. With a long, shuddering sigh, he lifted his right hand once more. Using the cloch *was* easier this time: the doubled vision came quickly, and as he thought of the path leading to the mound from Maeve's cottage, it was as if the place appeared solid and complete in front of him. A word in Gaelic drifted through his consciousness: *Filleadh.* He sang/spoke the word, and the green-gold light of the stone erupted between his fingers once more, as a gust of cold air struck him so hard that he closed his eyes in response.

When he opened his eyes again, he and Maeve were once more standing on the grass at the foot of the mound. Fionnbharr and the others had vanished. Colin heard Maeve laugh even as he sagged in weariness and pain, as exhausted as if he'd run miles. His right arm ached, a cold and dead weight at his side. Maeve must have noticed, for he felt her put her arm around his waist to hold him up. He placed the hand in his jean pocket, and as he did he saw the patterns on his arm, mounded like white, angry scars but already beginning to fade. He released the cloch, letting it fall into the nest of his pocket.

"That's done, then," she said. "The host will come out when we call. Yeh did grand in there, Colin. Just grand."

"I still don't *know* what I did," he told her, "or how. It hurts, Maeve."

"I know," she told him. "But it will pass soon."

"We told Fionnbharr a lie. I haven't agreed that I was willing to be part of this spell of yours."

"Nah, yeh haven't," she agreed.

"So what happens now?"

"I don't know," she told him. "I truly don't know." The weariness overwhelmed him again; he seemed to be holding himself up only by sheer force of will and Maeve's arm. "Help me," he husked, and Maeve put both arms around him tightly as his knees buckled. She kept him upright, his arms draped over her shoulders, her body warm against his cold one, her face nestled against the curve of his neck. "Let's go home," she whispered into his ear.

Leaning against Maeve, the two of them made their way back down the path into the fog and to her cottage.

◄ 31 ►

The Twisting of the Rope

BY THE TIME THEY REACHED the cottage, Colin seemed to have largely recovered. She let go of him as he trudged—slowly—alongside her. Through the gray tendrils, faintly, Maeve could glimpse Niall leaning against the door of the cottage with his arms crossed, waiting for them. "How's Keara?" Maeve called to him as they approached.

"Exhausted," he answered, pushing himself off the doorframe and opening the door so they could step inside. He glanced at Colin once, his gaze unreadable, then back to Maeve. "Your favorite cailleach will be good for naught but rest for a long time after this. The effort is damn near killing her and might actually manage it—not that yeh'd stop her from making that sacrifice. Such things are necessary sometimes, aren't they?" With that, Niall's gaze flicked over to Colin again.

"We are all of us in Keara's debt," Maeve said calmly. She watched Colin closely in case he was about to collapse again, but he slid onto one of the chairs from the kitchen table and sat. Maeve went to the hearth and crouched down in front it. "But it's almost done now," she said as she re-kindled the banked ashes and put another turve on the fire. "Yeh can tell her and Aiden that. A few hours more, that's all."

"An' where have yeh been, Maeve?" Niall asked. His breath gusted out, gray against gray.

She stood, the iron poker still in her hand. She leaned on it as if it were a cane. "Colin and me were makin' certain that Fionbharr and the others will stand with us."

"An' will they?"

"They will."

Niall nodding, glancing sidewise toward Colin. "An' the spell to open the gate?"

"I'll be starting that as soon as I can, and that's going to require the rest of yeh keeping the Naval Service away from us while we do it. In fact, I need to talk to everyone about that: can you get those who're capable of it together at the tavern?—everyone but Keara and Aiden. We need to make plans, because as soon as the fog's gone, things are going to happen fast. Why don't yeh get the others together for me?"

Niall was still glancing toward Colin, as if he expected him to speak, but Colin only stared back at the man, his face carefully neutral. The peat fire crackled loudly behind Maeve. "Give me an hour," Niall said finally.

Colin glanced at the clock above the hearth, and his eyes widened slightly. Maeve looked as well: impossibly, it was late afternoon; they must have been hours under the mound. *Yeh know time runs differently there . . .* "Make it an hour and a half," she said. "At the pub. I'll be there by six o'clock."

Niall shrugged. "As you wish, Morrígan. Six o'clock. And then?"

"Then?" Maeve repeated, with a short laugh. "For us, we live or we die. Right here."

Niall gave a faint nod. He stood there, silent, for a moment, then slowly turned and went to the door. "Six o'clock," he said again, his hand on the handle as if waiting for Maeve to say more. She only stared placidly at him. He pushed the door open and left.

As the door closed again behind Niall, Maeve let the poker drop; it clanged against the stones of the hearth. She swung the teakettle over the fire for the water to boil, then went to the cupboard and took out black tea, two mugs, and a tea ball. She opened the ball and stuffed tea inside it, closing it again. When she heard the water began to bubble, she put the tea into the pot and brought it over to the table. Colin was watching her the entire time, but neither of them spoke. "Have some tea," Maeve said. "It'll revive you."

"And what about me?" Colin asked as Maeve sat at the small dining table in the front room. Through the haze of Keara's fog spell that had invaded the cottage, she watched him push his glasses up his nose even though they didn't seem to need the adjustment—such a familiar, habitual gesture. A mortal gesture. "What happens for me?"

"I make yeh this promise, m'love," Maeve told him, staring down at the teacup between her hands. She was weary from the pretense of displaying false confidence in front of Colin, Niall, and the others, from the confusion of not knowing what she was going to do next. "I won't ask yeh to do anything that yeh don't want to do."

"Then how are you going to open the gateway?"

"There may be another way." By far her best strategy would be to lie to Colin and use him despite the promises she'd made. The spell required a "willing victim" who would give the necessary blood and life. She had listened to the voices inside the cloch before Rory had stolen it from her, and they had told her what was needed to open the gateway. The voices insisted that the chosen sacrifice didn't have to completely understand what was required to be "willing." Lying to Colin would guarantee that she could save her people and those who had trusted her . . . at least all of them except Colin himself. The old Morrígan would have done exactly that without flinching: give Colin a comforting lie ("Just a nick to give me what little blood I need and no more . . ."), then slit his throat from ear to ear and use his gushing, dying life to complete the spell, all without any regret or guilt.

Cúchulainn and Medb would have concurred with that assessment of the Morrígan's trustworthiness. Odras, whom the Morrígan turned into a pool of water, would agree. The Dagda, whom she once loved, knew well how the Morrígan could deceive, as did Lugh himself. But that old Morrígan felt very far away at the moment, centuries away.

Maeve closed her eyes and gave a huff of exasperation. Strands of Keara's fog billowed away from her with the exhalation.

"There *may* be another way?" she heard Colin say.

She was too exhausted to do more than shrug. " 'Tis all I have now."

"Is it going to be enough?"

She tried to laugh, tried to be offhand about it. It was nearly too much of an effort. "Going to have to be, is it nah?" She sighed, pushing back from the table. "I have too little time, and you're exhausted. Why don't you lay down for a bit? I'll wake you up."

He shook his head. "I couldn't sleep, and I'm feeling better anyway. What do you want me to do? How can I help?"

His eagerness tugged at her, making her regret her thoughts. "I'd like to hear yeh sing something. Yer guitar's still in the bedroom. A song will clear my head best."

"What would you like to hear?"

"Do you ever write yer own songs? All I've ever heard yeh play are the old tunes."

He shrugged. "I've written a few. I don't think I'm much of a songwriter, though."

"I don't care. Play me one."

In the bedroom clouded with Keara's fog, she reclined on pillows piled against the headboard of her bed and watched him take the guitar from its case. Her eyes half-closed, she listened to him tune up, feeling the bed move as he sat near her feet. She remembered the voices inside the cloch, and she imagined them mocking her now, railing at her, giving her suggestions that she wasn't certain she could use. "Okay," Colin said finally. "This is something I jotted down not long after I met you. I call it 'Slip Away'— let me see if I can remember it . . ."

Colin strummed a few chords in a minor key, then started to sing. The voice . . . She could still hear the bard's energy underneath the melody, but it was mostly just Colin's own voice.

I felt you watching me from across the room
Felt through the crowd the pressure of your gaze
I didn't know what made the air spark between us
All I know is that we both sensed it, we both felt it

You gazed at me while you were talking to him
Your smile over his shoulder said more than words
Without hearing your voice I heard your mind, I heard your heart
I wanted to move, should have moved, but with one last look you turned
    away

I saw you at the door, alone, your keys dangling in your hand
I would have called your name had I known it
You would not look back, just walked away into empty night
By the time I reached the door, I found that you had slipped away

I saw your face for many hours after
All the promise in your eyes and all the promise in your smile
Heading home, I wondered if I'd gone to you and spoken
Was this our chance, our moment? Did I let it slip away?
Just slip away . . .

He strummed a final minor chord, then leaned the Gibson against the mattress. He smiled at her. "Now you see why I stick mostly to singing other people's stuff."

"I liked it," she said. "A sad melody, and a sad thought. Was that us, yeh and me? After the first time we met?"

"Partially, yeah, though it's mixed in with a few other times when I regretted not speaking to someone, all conflated. After what I was told about the Oileánach following that gig, well, I didn't figure we'd be talking again, and the song just kinda came to me while I was noodling on the guitar, thinking about things." His hand rested on her calf, stroking her leg. "I'm glad all of it turned out to be wrong, that you didn't slip away from me."

"Even now? With all this? Even though I dragged yeh arseways into this hash?"

He laughed, once, and his amusement sounded clear and certain. "Yeah. Ultimately, the song's about choices we wish later that we would have made, and how we need to seize those moments when they come or we live with the regret. Regret's a lousy companion." She saw his hand brush over the cloch in his jean pocket, protectively, before he lay back, his head on her belly. The motion made her yearn to hold it once again, to keep it. "What's going to happen now, Maeve?"

She stroked his hair for a long time without answering, closing her eyes again. Inside, the old Morrígan howled, churning her stomach. "I have to find another way," she said finally. "There is one. I know."

They both lapsed into silence after that, as she continued to stroke his hair. His breath was calm and slow, and she wondered whether he'd fallen asleep when he stirred again. She opened her eyes to see him staring at her.

"So . . . this blood magic and sacrifice you talked about—does the person providing the blood have to die?"

"Aye," she whispered, "but then maybe nah. When I had the cloch, before Rory—" she stopped, changing the word she would have used. "—took it, they told me what must be done to open the gateway, the spells and rituals I have'ta use. Yeh've heard the voices yerself now. They're confusing, so many of 'em talking all at once . . . Some of them, at least, said that if someone offered himself freely, I might be able to bring him back afterward, in Talamh an Ghlas. There's a chance. The cloch may have that power left in it."

"You *might* be able to," Colin repeated. "Do these voices of yours believe that's likely?"

"No," she answered simply and honestly. "They don't." She felt her tears welling, a drop spilling out to track down her right cheek. She saw his eyes follow its path.

"Do you believe you can find your 'other way' in time, Maeve?"

She paused. *The lie*, the old Morrígan and the voices of the cloch chorused. *Give him the lie.* "No," she said. "I don't."

She felt his head move under her hand: a nod. "That's what I thought." "Colin . . ."

"No," he interrupted. "Just listen to me. Back home, everyone told me how Dad died doing something he loved, something that meant everything to him, and how he wouldn't have wanted to go any other way. And my mother . . . Mom kept saying how I was wasting my own life, that I wasn't doing anything important or vital, just drifting, and that I should be looking at my father or Tommy or Jen and being like them." He took her hand, strong fingers pressing hers. "That made me angry, but part of me, buried way down deep, agreed with them. I *have* been drifting. I was always looking for something that I was *supposed* to do. I thought it was just music, but now . . ."

He lifted his head, stirring Keara's fog, and his gaze found her own. "Colin," she said, placing a finger on his lips. "Some of the voices back then . . . well, I remember now that they told me blood is required, but not so much. That's the other way. I need to cut yeh, aye—that's the ritual—but it would be just a slash on yer arm to give me what's needed and no more. 'T would have to be deep and long, but it wouldn't be yer death." *The lie . . .* The Morrígan cackled inside her, a sound like a crow's dry cough.

"That would work?" She heard Colin laugh, felt him shrug.

"'T would," she said. "I'm certain. It has to."

"Then there's no problem. I'll do that, Maeve. I'll be your key. I'll take the chance."

The Morrígan shouted inside her, triumphant. *The willing victim . . .* Maeve put her other hand over Colin's, clasping it. She pulled him up to her, kissing him, not caring that he saw that she was crying.

She held him, wondering why the triumph felt empty and hollow.

The Oileánach filled the pub; Colin could hear them inside as they approached with the white noise of a dozen conversations going all at once, though this time there was no music to enliven the gathering. All those conversations went quickly silent as Colin opened the door—creaking on its rusting hinges—and stepped back to let Maeve enter first. The unnatural fog blew in around her and Colin. Colin let the door shut against the fog, standing behind Maeve as everyone's face turned to them. He saw expressions that ranged everywhere from hopeful to solemn to terrified. The room smelled of ale and desperation, of whiskey, hope, and fear.

Those same emotions crowded Colin's mind, along with his own self-doubt about the decision he'd made. The world seemed to be rushing loudly around him, and he could only watch it. *We Doyles have this sense of destiny, or a calling, of something that we're supposed to do.* Tommy's words, which had been echoing in his head since his return to the island.

"Well, Morrígan?" Niall was sitting at the end of bar next to Liam, half-empty pints in front of both and the leather bags holding their sealskins draped over their shoulders. Liam acknowledged Colin with a nod; Niall seemed to be ignoring his presence. "'Tis decided?"

"'Tis," Maeve answered. "Liam, g'wan and run up to Keara's an' tell her she can stop now. Her task is finished, and we're all forever in her debt. With her spell ended, I can finally do me own."

Liam nodded, drained his pint, and slid his way past Maeve and Colin. The cold fog wisped around them again as he vanished.

"An' without the fog, the leamh will be coming ashore in short order," Niall commented. Thick fingers prowled the lip of his pint, smearing the remnants of tan foam there.

"Aye," Maeve responded. "But the wind must clear the fog by itself, and 'twill take time for the murk to be dispersed enough that the leamh will move in. We can hope that the winds are calm today. But yer right: they'll come, and we'll need yeh all to hold them off as long as yeh can when that happens, to give me the time Colin and I need to open the gateway. Niall, if yeh can take your people out into the sea now and make certain the chain nets are up across the harbor to foul their propellers or at least slow them down . . . I want the bean-sí all awake and howling from the shore; that should give pause to any of the leamh who still have any belief in the Old Ways. Get the harpists out playing as they come ashore, again there may be a few who might think it to be Aoibhell's harp and that they're doomed to death, even though Fionnbharr believes she's in too deep a slumber to be roused. In the meantime, I'll gather what I need, and Colin and I will go to the mound; we'll tell Fionnbharr that it's come time for the aos sí to do their part. Lugh, at least, will come out with the aos sí. Then I'll start the spell to open the gateway, an' we go through."

"*He* agrees to all that, does he?" Niall asked, with a glare toward Colin. "He's not going to make a balls of it?"

Colin startled. He'd listened to Maeve's commentary without really hearing it, and now Niall's mockery tugged at Colin's own temper, and he answered before Maeve could respond. "Yeah, Colin agrees. So shut yer feckin' gob, Niall." He said the last sentence with a broad imitation of Niall's own thick brogue. Nervous laughter followed from the others, and Colin half-expected that Niall would lunge for him at the taunt. He fisted his hands at his sides, bracing himself for the assault, but Niall only shrugged.

"We'll see if yeh really understand, then," he said. "If yeh do yer job and we go through, I'll pray yer soul finds *Tír na mBeo*." He lifted his glass toward Colin and drank, then threw his glass against the wall behind the bar, narrowly missing the mirror and bottles there. Glass shattered as those closest to the wall ducked the shards and shouted. Niall laughed at the protests from the others in the pub. "We'll nah be needing the glasses here after today, one way or t'other, and if a little cut bothers yeh, there's likely worse to come this morning. Selkies, let's go; the Morrígan's given us her orders."

A half dozen of the Oileánach rose as Niall pushed away from the bar, all with similar leather bags across their shoulders. Niall nodded to Maeve as he passed. "I hope everything goes jammy for yeh, Maeve," Colin heard him mutter. "We'll need the luck, eh?" To Colin he said nothing at all. The others followed him out with glances toward Maeve and Colin.

"What about the rest of us?" someone asked.

"Yer job is to do whatever yeh can to delay the leamh and avoid them interrupting the spell, but don't get yerselves killed in the process. The leamh won't use deadly force if yeh don't give 'em the excuse, so leave the real fighting to them that leamh weapons won't easily touch."

Colin looked at the uncertain faces in front of them as, one by one, they left the tavern. He wondered if they were all thinking as he was, but he said nothing, nodding to each of them as they passed until only Maeve and Colin were left. "They won't be using guns?" he asked her when they were gone. "You're certain?"

Maeve gave him what seemed a lukewarm smile. "We can hope not," she answered. "An' what good would it do if I told those here anything else?"

"Because you don't know if it's the truth or not."

"Truth?" Maeve gave him a smile that faded even as he saw it. "Truth is as slippery as a wet salmon," she told him, "and as hard to hold onto."

✦ 32 ✦

The Dawning of the Day

FROM THE TAVERN, Colin followed Maeve to Keara's cottage, which no longer poured forth the dense fog. Maeve ducked in the open door. "Aiden? Keara?" she called.

Aiden answered from the bedroom: "In here."

Maeve followed the call, with Colin behind her. A wan and pale Keara lay in her bed, her hair matted with sweat and dark circles under her eyes. Aiden was at her side, feeding her a bit of soup and tea. Seeing Keara, a sense of guilt washed momentarily over Maeve. *Look at her, it's me fault that she nearly died in the effort.* "How are yeh, me darlin'?" Maeve asked. She knelt on the other side of the bed, brushing back the damp strands of hair from the young woman's forehead.

"I'll be fine," she answered, though her voice was but a whisper. She coughed, and a bit of fog slid from her mouth. "I don't think I can do much more for yeh, though. I'm sorry."

"Don't be," Maeve told her, smiling. "Yeh've done more than anyone else could'a. Yeh've made it possible for Colin to come back, and for us to do what we planned to do all along. We'll be in the other world soon, I promise."

Keara's eyes moved, and her gaze found Colin. A glimmer of a smile touched her cracked lips. "Colin, we di'nah think yeh'd come back in time." Her eyes shone with tears. "Maeve said yeh would, said she'd make it so, but I was afraid it might all be for naught."

The words cut at Maeve, even as Keara gave her a look that spoke of adoration and affection.

Aiden was staring toward Colin with hard, dark eyes, his hand clasped in Keara's. "She would have died for the Morrígan, gladly. 'Twas a sacrifice she'd make for all of us. She was willing to do whatever was asked, no matter the cost to herself."

"What you've done wasn't wasted," he told Keara and Aiden both, evidently aware of the undercurrent of their words. "I'm here to help Maeve open the gateway."

A nod, from both Aiden and Keara, was his only answer. Keara's eyes closed, then opened again. "Sorry, m'Lady," she whispered. "So tired."

"You rest, then," Maeve told her, stroking her cheek. "Rest and know that without yeh, nothing a'tall would have been possible. Yeh are the true hero of our tale, and I'll make sure yer part is sung afterward. Would that please yeh, to be part of a song?"

The smile flitted over Keara's lips again, but her eyes closed. Her breathing deepened. "Let her sleep as long as yeh can," Maeve told Aiden. "But when yeh hear the leamh begin their attack, yeh must take her directly to the mound. Them that the leamh capture and put on their ships might not be able to reach the gateway when it opens, and I won't have Keara left behind after her sacrifice for us all. Do yeh understand?"

"Aye, Morrígan," Aiden said. "We'll be there."

Maeve nodded and stroked Keara's cheek once more. Then she rose, swiftly, and with a gesture to Colin to follow, left the room and the cottage.

Outside, the fog was still heavy but already noticeably thinning, and they could both feel the wind off the Atlantic. Colin could see the glow of the sun overhead through the clouds. Maeve glanced upward as well and scowled. "Not much time," she said. "The Old Ones don't have the power they once had, or perhaps the land itself is angry that we're leaving." Maeve sighed and tugged her cloak tighter around her.

"Come on, then," she told Colin. "We have our work to do."

Back at in her own house, Maeve bustled about, dragging the various components of the spell from where she'd stashed them in the bedroom— material she'd been collecting since she and Rory had found the cloch back in '47—and checking again that all the necessary ingredients the voices of the cloch had told her she needed were there. She could feel Colin watching her from the bed as she hurried, putting everything in a small chest. She heard the intake of his breath when she added the scabbarded iron dagger with an ornate copper hilt.

"Yeh know that the spell requires blood," she said, drawing the weapon from its scabbard. The leaf-shaped metal blade was dark with oxidation except where the edges had been filed to a bright polish; the oaken hilt was dull from the ravages of time and the hands that had touched it over the centuries, nearly black in the hollows of the knots engraved in the oak. "'Tis a blade I've kept for, well, a long time, and 'tis the one I must use." She softened her voice then. She could nearly taste the fear in Colin, and that made her suddenly uncertain—which she couldn't afford. The spell demanded concentration and certainty. "Yeh haven't changed yer mind?"

He was staring at the weapon, eyes wide. His hand was in his pocket, and she knew it was wrapped around the cloch. She wondered if the voices were whispering to him, wondered if they were warning him of her lie. *No, they wouldn't do that. They know what the cloch was sent to do, and they know the bard's role.* "It's just . . ." he managed, then stopped to swallow. His gaze moved to her face. She placed the blade back in the well-worn leather and put the knife quickly in the box. "No," Colin said, but the word was no more than a husk. "I haven't changed my mind."

"Those were brave words yeh said to Niall back in the tavern, and to Aiden and Keara as well."

"Thanks." His gaze was fixed somewhere just past her face, or perhaps somewhere inside himself. "They all . . ." He stopped again, licking at his lips as if they were dry. "They all love you, Maeve. And more than that. They worship you. You're the one they'd follow anywhere, to any fate."

"I love them, also," Maeve told him. "I love *yeh* as well, Colin," she added. "An' the way I love yeh t'ain't the way I love them. I hope yeh know the difference. 'Tis what makes this so difficult, for all of us." She crouched down in front of him, taking his face in her hands and forcing him to look at her. She saw his regard snap back into focus as the Morrígan rose within her. Even her voice sounded different to her own ears. "I've told yeh; there's another way, and that's what I'll do: I *will* cut yeh, aye, and 'twill be a deep one but not a deadly one. Do yeh believe me? If yeh would die, then part of me would die with the spell, too."

"I believe you," he answered. He seemed to be searching her eyes, as if behind them there might be another answer, as if he knew that what she just told him was a lie. *Slippery truth, indeed . . .*

He must have seen the despair in her face; he attempted to smile. "It's okay, Maeve. I said I'm willing to do this. You just have to promise me it won't be for nothing."

In answer, she leaned forward to kiss him, a long and lingering embrace. When she pulled back again, she took his hands. "Yer a singer of the old songs, Colin, and yeh know what history and truth they hold for people. I promise yeh what I promised Keara: when the songs are made about this day on the other side, in Talamh an Ghlas, yeh will be a great part of them. Yer name will never be forgotten, not by any of us, and the songs about yeh will always be sung. 'Tis what I can promise yeh for certain."

Colin's eyes narrowed. "Maeve, are you saying that I can't go with you through the gateway? Is that what you mean?"

"Aye," she told him. "Yeh can't come with us to where we're going. The spell doesn't allow that." The corner of his mouth lifted, and his thumb brushed away another tear from her cheek. She hurried on before he could speak, before the Morrígan inside could stop her. "But if this isn't what yeh want, Colin, I won't hold yeh to any promise yeh've made. I'll understand and I'll let you go. All yeh need do is stay here and when the leamh come, surrender yerself an' go with them. But let me be blunt . . . yeh also have to know that if yeh do that, it means the death of everyone else here, mine as much as anyone. None of us will surrender, even if the spell fails. It's yer choice, love. Either way, we were never destined to be together except for the brief time we've already had, as much as we both might have wanted more."

She could see the struggle inside him, battling the vow he'd made. Over the centuries, a thousand heroes had worshiped and feared her, had taken oaths in her name over and over again, and she had watched them fight and bleed and die. Lugh, Cúchulainn, Indech, Odras . . . the names flowed on and on; it was no accident that many named the Morrígan the Goddess of Death. *This is what heroes, men and women alike, do and have done forever. They die, and nothing can stop that—it's their destiny. If his name is to be among their roll, Colin will do the same. A part of him knows that as well as I do.* She watched his face, watched the struggle underneath subside slowly.

Colin nodded, though his cheeks were pale. "I gave you my word," he told her. His voice was like the gravel under a rushing brook. "And I'll keep that word."

As if he'd uttered a premonition, a low, mournful wail sounded through the thinning fog from the direction of the harbor: a ship's horn. Maeve's head came up and she stood, looking a final time into the box to make certain that everything was there.

"We need to go now," she told Colin. "The leamh are coming."

33

America Lies Far Away

*W*HAT THE HELL *am I doing?*

The phrase kept echoing through Colin's head as he walked behind Maeve toward Fionnbharr's mound. The world seemed to have acquired a distance from him. He walked, somehow, just outside reality. Everything around him was strangely sharp and distinct: the sound of his shoes on the gravel of the path, the chill of the Atlantic wind on his face, the masked, failing glow of the sun through the lingering fog at the horizon, the scratch of the wool in his sweater, the movement of clouds against the sky, the sweet scent of grass against the brine of the sea, the lingering taste of this morning's tea and scones on his tongue, the hypnotic swaying of Maeve's skirt as she walked . . .

Every sense was hyper-alert, and he found himself trying to commit each moment, each sensation, to memory as if they were currency with which to barter in the afterworld that was awaiting him. His hand was in his pocket, his fingers clutching his grandfather's stone as he pulled it out to place it around his neck again, and he could hear the whispering of voices within it, but they were faint and contradictory.

She's betraying yeh.

No, this is indeed the moment. Yer doing the right thing.

Yeh can't trust her.

Yeh must trust her.

The interior conversation was difficult to process. No, it was impossible. The words seemed to mean nothing, shattering against his skull. He felt light, almost airy. He wondered if this was a feeling he shared with everyone who faced this kind of crisis, who had chosen (or had chosen for them) a moment where decisions had to be made, where their life would be forever changed afterward.

The voices from the cloch continued to yammer at him, incessantly.

She hasn't told yeh everything or enough.

This might actually be the end for yeh.

What will Jennifer and Tom think? How will Mom react when she gets the news? What will Aunt Patty say? And with that, another thought: *Will they ever really know?* Maeve hadn't told him what would happen with this spell; would the island itself go through the gateway into this other place? If he couldn't go with them, what would happen to him afterward?

Spells and magic and hidden worlds—how can you believe anything will happen at all? This could be a madwoman's delusion. He shook his head, as if the thought could be discarded like a dog shedding water. He reminded himself of everything he'd seen here with Maeve: the selkies, the aos sí, Keara's fog, the underworld beneath the mound to which Maeve had taken them.

No, no, the magic was real. He'd seen it. It *had* to be real.

He had to believe it because otherwise his decision would have no meaning. Otherwise there would be no songs for him.

From the distance, in the direction of the harbor village, there came the bark of two quick but very distinct gunshots. They both paused at the sound, Maeve casting a quick glance over her shoulder. The look on her face was strange, an expression he'd never glimpsed on her before. There was almost an eagerness in the set of her mouth, in the widening of her eyes—as sharp and hard as crow's eyes—as if the disturbing sound was pleasant to her. Her body leaned toward the faint echo of the gunfire, as if she wanted to move toward the struggle rather than away from it.

The Morrigan . . . the voices whispered as one. *The Morrigan . . .*

Colin realized that was who he was seeing: not the Maeve he'd fallen in love with, but the old goddess that was also part of her. That aspect of her was drawn to battle and death, and she wanted to revel in the blood. Then the moment passed, and the Maeve he knew returned, her gaze softening and lines of worry creasing her face. "We have to hurry," she said, though her words sounded like brittle ice to his ears. "They can't hold off the leamh forever, and the spell is long to cast."

She turned back and her pace quickened. Colin remained where he was, glancing over his shoulder toward the harbor. There, he knew, was his rescue, if he wished it. All that was required was for him to run toward the naval personnel who were undoubtedly just now coming off their ships, and surrender himself to them. Why, Superintendent Dunn might be with them. The worst that would happen is that he'd be held for a time before being deported and sent back to the States, back to Chicago and his family; at best, he could plead that he'd come back to the island to recover his guitars, especially his precious Gibson, only to be inadvertently caught up in this turmoil. Eventually—if reluctantly—they'd let him go. He might even be able to travel elsewhere in Ireland, to find more songs and more old tunes, to continue his study.

In time, he might forget the Oileánach, Inishcorr, and Maeve.

In time.

The voices howled in protest. *Yeh ca'nah do that. Yeh gave yer word. The bard is a necessary part of the spell. Yer voice . . . 'twill open the gate.*

"Your grandfather never did go back. I think that always bothered him. At least you won't have that regret." The memory of his Aunt Patty's comments came to him as well. They seemed prophetic now.

"Colin?"

Maeve had stopped, looking back at him. He could tell from her face that she knew what he was thinking, could tell that if he ran, she wouldn't try to stop him, that she almost expected him to do exactly that.

So run! This is the moment when you can save yourself.

But he couldn't will his legs to move. Looking at Maeve, looking at the despair and desperation that wrapped around her as tightly as her red cloak, he found himself unable to act.

He glanced back one last time, then hurried toward her as she turned and continued along the path to the mound.

At the base of the mound, just inside the ring of stones, she set down the box on the grass. Colin, silent, stood alongside her. "Fionnbharr!" she called. "It's time to keep yer promise."

Cold air, as if from a tomb, stirred the folds of her cloak and rushed over both of them. Fionnbharr appeared, standing at the top of the mound under the hawthorn tree, dressed in armor and helm with a sword at his side. A shadowy Lugh stood beside him, holding his spear. "I see yeh still have the fool," he said.

"Shut it," she snapped at him. "Get yer people and go hold back the leamh. Either that or be cursed as coward and traitors for the rest of what little life yeh'll have remaining."

Fionnbharr sniffed audibly. "An' who will do the cursing if none of yeh are left, or if this gateway doesn't work?"

"It will work if yeh give me the time," Maeve answered. "And yer chin-wagging here won't do that. Do it or do'nah, but leave me to my task."

Fionnbharr laughed, mockingly, and she thought for a moment that he might simply fall back into the mound, but instead he waved his hand in summons, and the cold host appeared, ghostly, behind him. Skeletal horses were brought to Fionnbharr and Lugh, and they mounted the spectral steeds. "Get to yer spell, Battlecrow, or be cursed yerself for failing us."

With that, he beckoned again, kicked his mount with his boot heels, and the host of the aos sí flowed past them, frigid and riotous, their voices shouting in the rush of wind that followed. Maeve's cloak billowed out as they went, and she saw their hands grasping at Colin as they passed. She took his arm, afraid that one of them might snatch him away.

Then they were past, a glowing presence winding into the distance down the path and over the small ridge between the mound and the harbor. "Right, then," she said to Colin. "We have to hurry . . ."

She began plucking items from the box. The knife she thrust quickly into the belt of her skirt, not daring to look at Colin as she did so, though she could feel him staring at her. She brought out the herbs and the spices. *"Turn widdershins and scatter them to the winds. Feed the sky . . ."* the voices in the cloch had told her decades ago. She obeyed, taking the powders and dried, crumbled leaves in her right hand and lifting up her hand as she turned counterclockwise. A harsh, cold Atlantic gale touched her as she did so, and she opened her hand. The air took the offering from her with the sound of laughter.

She stooped down to take up the parchment containing the incantation, which she had written down in the cavern of Rathcroghan while Rory slumbered near her. "It's time for your part, m'love," she told Colin. "Put the cloch around yer neck and hold it."

Looking apprehensive, Colin followed her instructions; as he lifted the jewel, the cold, billowing sky-flames appeared again above them, so like the aurora that sometimes appeared in Irish skies, only far more brilliant and imbued with a power that she could feel—a throbbing power swirled down around them and filled the stone as if it were a receptacle. She saw the curling filigrees of the scars appear on Colin's forearm where the sleeve of his sweater had fallen down. His face was lined with a grimace, and she knew he could feel the frigid energy within the stone, burning his hand all the way down to the shoulder.

"Begin . . ." The voices of the cloch clamored, audible even to her, as if ghosts whispered around them. *"Now. Sing, Bard . . ."*

"I don't know what to sing," Colin said into the crackling whirl of the aurora. In the failing sunlight, in the shifting sky-glow of the cloch's spell, Colin was watching Maeve, and in his eyes she could see the echo of the stone's power and the elaborate tracery of it in his arm. Colin's face: trusting and resigned. There was pain in seeing that, as well, and that was troubling to her for more than one reason.

Listen. It will come to yeh, the voices insisted.

Colin closed his eyes. Through the crackling of the energy that was filling the cloch, Maeve could hear the sounds of struggle from the direction of the harbor, and again the chatter of gunfire. Distantly, someone screamed.

Ráisit d'inis nárbo dermar . . . The island protected by a bridge of glass . . .

Then Colin began to sing, and his voice swept everything away: the electric snarl of the sky's power, the rushing of the wind, the sounds of the chaos near the harbor.

> *Ráisit d' inis nárbo dermar,*
> *co n-dún daingen;*
> *sonnach umai*
> *fair co n-druini (clothach caingen).*

> *Linn aíbinn ard immon sonnach*
> *(sorchu scélaib),*
> *ós moing mara;*
> *drochat glana ara bélaib.*

> *No cingtis súas ind óchad dían*
> *chennmas chalma;*
> *tuititis sís*
> *(ba búan a cís) dochum talman.*

As Colin sang, Maeve saw the portal to Talamh an Ghlas open again, the land shimmering as if glimpsed through a foggy window. This time, however, the aurora light of the cloch wrapped emerald tendrils around the edges of the portal, gleaming and writhing, and as the song continued, the tendrils deepened in color and the fog began to vanish, until it seemed that the entrance to the Otherworld stood open and they could simply step through.

"*The spell-words. Yeh must speak them while the bard still sings . . .*" The words rang in Maeve's head, insistent.

She took a roll of parchment from the box on the ground and unrolled it. Maeve began to read aloud the words set there, the words given to her through the cloch while it had been hers to hold. Then, the stone had shouted in her mind as the sky had gone bright with the mage-lights of the land she'd glimpsed beyond this world. The words the voices inside had spoken that evening burned and screamed at her, not letting her rest or sleep until she set them down on paper that night.

Now, as she spoke each word, the inscription flared with a searing, bright flame on the paper and vanished. Her voice seemed to take on power and depth with each syllable as Colin's had, until it seemed that her voice roared so loudly in concert with him that they must hear the spell-song all the way in Ballemór. Above them, in the growing dusk, the mage-lights were ever brighter and more saturated in color, sheets and curtains of shifting hues with the flowing hems of their skirts so close that Maeve felt she could raise her hand to touch them, streaming down to the cloch in Colin's hand and around the portal.

She dared to give a quick glance toward Colin. He was no longer looking at her, but at the mage-lights curling and crawling in above them, and she could see their colors reflected on his face and in his eyes as he continued to sing.

She was coming to the end of the incantation. All that was left now were the final words, the words that required blood and sacrifice to even speak. She took Colin's free arm in her left hand, as with the right she slid the knife from its sheath, the dagger's point gleaming in the colors of the mage-lights. The light descended with her motion, now sliding around her right hand and arm with the dagger, coiling there as they did about Colin's arm and around the portal. Her flesh seemed to be alight. She held the final phrase in her mind; it pounded against her skull, aching to be released.

She glanced again at Colin. He stared at the knife tip wrapped in light and power, and nodded to her.

His eyes closed in anticipation of her strike.

The power snarled and crackled in her mind. *The blood must come now, but nah yet the death. The blood of a willing victim, the blood of one with the ability to wield the power himself, even if he do'nah realize it . . .*

With a grimace, she cut down with the dagger's blade from his elbow to wrist, the edge digging deep into muscle and sinew. Colin sucked in a breath, but he didn't cry out. The blood flowed down his arm, dripping in thick red streams from his fingers. In his other hand, he still held the cloch.

He stopped singing. They could both feel the doorway opening, the mage-lights hissing and fuming around it.

Now the death . . . To finish the spell . . .

Maeve started to move the knife as Colin stared at his wounded arm. She could see the shock on his face, the glassiness in his eyes. His eyes shifted away from the bloody mess and found hers.

The death . . . the voices crooned, but Maeve still didn't move. She argued back to them.

He trusted me. He loved me. He still does.

The voices became insistent. *The spell requires a willing death . . . Yeh must do this or lose the chance . . . A willing death . . .*

"Then you can have that," Maeve said aloud.

"Maeve, go on." She heard Colin's voice as if it were from some great distance, a whisper against the roar in her head, the last words of the spell searing themselves on her tongue. He lifted his head, offering his throat as if he finally understood the lie she'd given him and didn't care, accepting what must happen. He closed his eyes.

The willing victim . . .

Now! She could hold it no longer; she could feel the opening to Talamh an Ghlas looming, the membrane between that world and this one ready to rip open.

A willing death . . . Someone agreeing to be the sacrifice that saves others . . .

And I am willing. That was nothing that the old Morrígan could have said, and she knew then the entirety of how she had been altered and changed.

Colin realized now that Maeve had lied to him. He heard it in the voices that surrounded them, but it didn't matter. *This is why you came here, most of all—to give life to the old songs and those within them.* If that meant his death now, then he would accept that. He clasped his grandfather's stone, as if that could hold him grounded in these last few moments.

His eyes closed, weak and dizzy from the loss of blood from his wounded arm, he waited.

Maeve smiled at Colin. "Remember me, and I'll never die," she told him. She reversed the knife against the side of her own throat and spoke the last words of the spell even as she pulled the hilt hard.

Colin heard Maeve's final words, and he wondered at them. But before he could react, he felt a wind rushing past him, as if the world itself wanted to tear him away from where he knelt on the ground. He still waited for the slicing edge of the knife, but there came instead the splash of hot, thick liquid against his face and he opened his eyes to see Maeve falling, a spray of red still gushing from the terrible wound on her neck, her head canted at a wrong angle. As if in slow motion, the dagger she held clattered against one of the stones at the foot of the mound.

The world screamed her name with him: "Maeve!"

Even as he crawled toward Maeve's crumpled form, the universe ripped open around him. The glowing tendrils in the sky had coalesced, tornadoes of wild colors that framed a doorway into which the island was being sucked, a doorway that sat on Fionnbharr's mound in front of him—and beyond that doorway stood not the gray Atlantic but a land of rolling, verdant hills with valleys clad in dark forests of oak and ash. Even as Colin let the cloch fall back on its chain around his neck and reached one-handed for Maeve, he felt her body being pulled inexorably away from him toward that rip between the two worlds, as if by invisible, insistent hands. He tried to stand and run toward her, but the wind abruptly reversed itself and pushed him back. There were hands in the wind, and voices. Something struck him in the face, knocking off his glasses; he grabbed belatedly for them with his good hand: the cloch, smeared with blood, whether his or Maeve's, he couldn't tell.

He brushed the gore away from his face as he knelt and found his glasses on the ground. The wind was throwing saltwater, leaves, and dirt through the air, making it difficult to see. Maeve was gone; he had no idea where.

Hunting horns trilled, and Colin heard the soft pounding of hooves on earth: Fionnbharr's host rushed past him into the doorway, a fog-ridden haze of riders and voices; Lugh, holding his spear, nodded to Colin as he passed. He saw Niall and Liam, Keara and Aiden among them along with the rest of the Oileánach, riding on ghostly steeds with the aos sí. They galloped through the doorway; he could see their hooves tearing at the turf in the soft hills beyond the rift. "Take me with you!" he pleaded. He lifted his hand and the cloch toward them, but none of them reached out to pull him along with them.

The doorway shuddered, the mage-lights above him sputtering and flaring like dying fireworks. The cloch swaying on its chain and thudding against his chest, Colin pushed himself up again, stumbling forward toward the closing gateway, trying to get through it before it closed, but again the hurricane wind reversed itself and pushed him back. *Nah for yeh . . . Nah yet . . .* voices whispered in his head.

The ground trembled underneath Colin's feet, and terrifying rents appeared in the earth around him as he clawed his way up the hill. The doorway was now but a single thin break in the fabric of reality, the sunlight beyond a mockery against Inishcorr's evening. The standing stones about the mound were swaying and falling. Beyond Inishcorr's cliff, a massive rampart of gray-green water with white foam on its summit, loomed against a sky alive with clouds painted red with the last of the day's light. Towering above him, the water seemed to pause, then—as the doorway closed completely, the green land and the sunlight winking out of existence—the wave crashed down, hard and terrible.

The full weight of the water slammed into Colin, and he tasted brine as he was borne away into darkness.

◀ 34 ▶

After the Storm

HIS ENTIRE WORLD was rocking and swaying gently. Colin forced his eyes to open, then as quickly shaded them with a hand against the sunlight that threatened to blind him. He was lying in a shallow pool of water, his glasses were somehow still on his head, and his vision was bounded by ribs of wood wrapped in tar-covered hide. His right arm seemed to be afire, pain radiating from it so harshly that he cried out involuntarily from the sensation. He tried to move the fingers of that hand, but they obeyed only grudgingly. He looked down and nearly lost consciousness again, seeing a ragged line of clotted blood over a gaping, deep wound, and he remembered Maeve's knife. He closed his eyes to stop the nausea; when he opened them again, his stirring caused cold water to slosh over his wooden horizon.

He was in a small, round-bottomed boat: a currach like the ones he'd seen pulled up on the pebbled beach of Inishcorr's harbor or along Beach Road. Holding onto the side of the boat with his good hand, he managed to pull himself up to a sitting position, blinking into the sunlight.

How did I get here?

He was on the ocean; he could see the unbroken line of the Atlantic horizon, with low, calm swells rolling in. It was morning; the sun low in the east. Turning his head, he saw the high, familiar bluffs of Ceomhar Head with its low farmland spread at its feet, green and pastoral in the morning light. He appeared to be two or three miles or so out from the mainland shore—nearly where Inishcorr itself had been. He glanced over his other shoulder again, seaward, to where Inishcorr should have been visible close by, but there was nothing there at all.

Inishcorr was gone. Vanished. He gaped. The effort of sitting nearly

286

defeated him. The world threatened to go away again, the edges of his vision narrowing. With his good hand, he held onto the side of the currach, closing his eyes and just feeling the welcome heat of the sun on his shoulders.

He remembered nothing after the impossible wave washed over Inishcorr as the doorway to Talamh An Ghlas closed: the wave, taking him into darkness. He had no memory of anything past that moment. "Maeve . . ." He called her name, his voice cracked and broken. He tried to move and felt something move on his neck. He put his left hand around the cloch, holding it tightly . . .

. . . and nearly foundered the currach as a deep horn blast startled him. He turned, the boat rocking wildly with his movement, to see a naval patrol vessel approaching him from the direction of the Ballemór Estuary. "You there in the currach," a crew member on the bow called. "Show your hands!"

Slowly, every muscle aching, Colin obeyed, displaying the ugly wound on his arm. "Right, then," the crew member called back, waving to the glassed-in bridge of the vessel. "Stand by to be brought aboard."

"You can take a break, Sergeant, an' go get some tea if yeh like," Colin heard Superintendent Dunn say to the garda stationed outside his hospital room. "I'll be responsible for Mr. Doyle for a few minutes."

Groaning with the pull of the staples in his arm, Colin used his left hand to push the button on the side of his bed, raising him up to a sitting position as Dunn entered the room, closing the door behind him. The Superintendent glanced at Colin once, nodded silently, then went to the chair alongside the bed and sat. He leaned back, hands laced behind his head, staring at the humming fluorescent lights.

"Water?" Dunn asked.

"No, thanks."

For several seconds more, there was silence. Then Dunn shuffled his feet and brought his hands down to his lap. "'Twas a strange, strange day, that. I still don't half-believe it."

"You were there? On Inishcorr?"

"Aye," he replied, "I was there." His eyes were trapped in tired lines, and the bags underneath were gray and pouched. "An' I still don't know what it was I saw." He was staring at Colin as if waiting for him to answer the riddle, but Colin only pressed his lips together, returning the stare. Finally, Dunn looked away again toward the ceiling. "One of the naval CPOs,

I heard him telling his captain that the Oileánach must have had hallucinogens in that fog they put around the island, because there wasn't any
other explanation for what we saw."

"And what did you see, Superintendent?"

Dunn almost seemed to laugh. He ran a hand over his short-cut gray
hair. "The impossible. Things that were just stories and tales, only they
were there all around us, an' all too real."

"You think the Oileánach could do that with hallucinogens, and that all
of you would see the same things? You think Maeve and the others had the
resources and the science to do that?"

"Nah, I do'nah," Dunn answered. His gaze returned to Colin. "Would
yeh be having a better explanation, Mr. Doyle?" When Colin remained silent, Dunn sighed. "I di'nah think so. Not after the other night when yeh
vanished from Regan's. But that would'nah been anything supernatural,
would it? At least I wouldn't be admitting it if I were you."

"What happens now?" Colin asked. "Am I being charged with something? Am I going to be deported? What about my things?"

"Yer guitars? I'm afraid they're gone with the island and the Oileánach.
I suppose they might wash up somewhere, but they will'nah be worth
anything if that happens."

What about the cloch? Colin wanted to ask, but didn't want Dunn to
know that was the only thing he wanted. When he'd been brought onto
the boat, they'd taken everything he'd had, the cloch among them. He
could *feel* that loss, and the pain of its loss overshadowed the dull throbbing of the healing wound on his arm. He wanted it; he yearned to hold it
again in his hand.

"As to what else happens to yeh, I do'nah know yet," Dunn answered.
"There will be questions, lots of them, and from lots of people who are
angry and confused about all this. But no one from the gardai or the Naval
Services saw yeh there on Inishcorr this time, and there's none of the
Oileánach left to ask." He inclined his head toward the door. "As far as any
of them out there know, as far as *I* know, yeh were just trying to find the
island again when yeh got caught up in the terrible storm, if yeh take me
drift."

"I think I do. Superintendent, I had a pendant," Colin said. "You probably remember it: an emerald-like stone in a silver setting. It was my
grandfather's."

Dunn nodded. "Aye, I remember it. Yeh had it around yer neck when
yeh were found. It's back at the station, along with the rest of what yeh
had in yer pockets. It's safe, and I'll make sure yeh get it back."

"Thank you, Superintendent. Could I have it now? Today?"

"We'll see about that," Dunn grunted and lumbered to his feet. Standing next to the bed, he looked down at Colin. "The woman yeh were seeing out there . . ."

With the mention, Colin felt tears burn in his eyes. "She's gone," he said.

Dunn nodded. "Aye, all of 'em are. Which seems odd, if yeh ask me. Not a single body washed up on the shore anywhere. Do'nah seem possible, that, does it? But I'm sorry for yer loss, Mr. Doyle. I truly am."

The tears seared his skin, tracking down his cheek. He said nothing, and after a moment, the Superintendent heaved another heavy breath. "If yer still around after this all dies down, Mr. Doyle, I'd love a talk with yeh. Unofficial-like, and over a pint."

"You'll have that, Superintendent. If I'm still around."

Dunn's thick fingers patted the sheet near Colin's hand. "Yeh should get some rest," he said. "I suspect yeh'll be needing it. And as to the pendant, I'll do what I can, seeing as it means so much to yeh."

With that, he left the room, calling for the garda to return as he closed the door behind him.

"Breakfast is ready, Mr. Doyle."

"I'll be right down, Mrs. Egan."

Colin pulled a sweater over his T-shirt, being careful as he put his heavily bandaged right arm through the sleeve. He put on the necklace with the cloch over his head, tucking it carefully under the sweater, and went downstairs. The bed and breakfast was full—as were most of the rooms in Ballemór at the moment. The other residents—an older couple from Hamburg, Germany; a single woman from Galway who always seemed to be around whenever he walked into a room; a mid-thirties married couple with two young children from Kansas City—watched him as he entered the dining room and took his seat, though no one addressed him directly. He was a curiosity, a carnival freak to be stared at, but one that was perhaps too dangerous to approach closely. Mrs. Egan seemed to take pride in his presence, as if he were her prized and private possession.

After Superintendent Dunn's visit in the hospital, Colin had endured the inquiries of the various authorities—from the Naval Services to the NPWS to Dunn's local gardai for a week, asking him a thousand questions—some that he couldn't answer, some that he wouldn't. From them, he learned the official tale was that a massive and fast-moving storm front had blown over the island just as the sun was setting, driving the patrol vessels, half-wrecked, away from Inishcorr even as a small battle was being waged in and around the harbor. If those he talked to were coy about the details of the battle and who they found themselves fighting, Colin let that be.

The monstrous swell had been pushed along by the storm, washing over the island, rolling up the Ballemór Estuary, and swamping much of the local coast. When the wave and the storm passed, Inishcorr was gone, not a trace of it left: no flotsam, no wreckage, no hint that it or its inhabitants had ever been there. There wasn't—according to one crewman who took pity on Colin—even a sonar rise on the ocean floor. "'Twas gone like it had never existed," the man said, almost wonderingly.

Somehow, none of the naval personnel or gardai had been killed in the incident and the tidal wave, though there had certainly been injuries and broken bones in plenty. Several of those who had been involved in the attack on Inishcorr and caught up in the great wave found themselves somehow washed onto or close to the *Grainne Ni Mhaille*, the Oileánach's hooker, which had somehow stayed afloat despite its broken mast and torn sails. Superintendent Dunn had been among them.

Colin hadn't been found until the next morning.

To his interrogators, Colin repeated the story that Superintendent Dunn had suggested: that he had once been an innocent visitor to the island, that he'd gone out in the currach to try to reach the island in order to recover his belongings from his former lover and been caught in the freakish storm. He'd had nothing to do with the troubles there—frankly, he wasn't entirely certain *what* had happened that day, and didn't know how his injury had occurred. He hadn't been on the island when the fog cleared and the naval ships moved in; he hadn't been involved in the fighting. Certainly no one had seen him there during the confrontation—wasn't that proof enough he hadn't been there?

It was obvious that the authorities weren't quite certain how to explain the events of that day either, and that they didn't quite agree as to what charges they could bring against Colin or what they could actually prove in court, though they threatened him with everything from terrorism to simple trespassing. Reluctantly, with some prodding by the American embassy and with Superintendent Dunn's influence, he'd been released and his passport and visa, as well as his belongings, including his grandfather's pendant, were returned to him.

Colin had stayed in Ballemór: because that was where his clothes and his room were; because it was familiar; because there he could stare out over Ceomhar Head and wonder.

"More bacon?" Mrs. Egan interrupted Colin's thoughts, proffering a plate with the fatty ham slices that the Irish called bacon. He shook his head, and poked his fork at the eggs on his plate so that the yolks ran like liquid sun to the edges of the toast.

"No, thank you," he told her. "I have plenty here. It's a very good breakfast, Mrs. Egan."

Mrs. Egan smiled as if sharing a secret with him. "The poor lad's been through so much," she said to the table, to nods all around. "We all have. Why, that awful storm just utterly wrecked the marina on Beach Road, and some of the water even poured into the town square down the hill, and there the poor boy was, caught out in the worst of it. I tell yeh, strange t'ings happened hereabout after the Oileánach came. Why, did I ever tell you about poor Mrs. Brennan. . . ?"

Colin stopped listening, eating quickly and escaping the table as Mrs. Egan segued from the curse on Mrs. Brennan to the tale of Darcy's picture. "'Tis the Lord's truth, 'tis, and Father Quinlan would tell yeh the same. Poor Darcy's photograph flew all the way across the room to land right there, in the middle of this very table, sitting there exactly as if I'd put it there meself . . ."

Mrs. Egan paused in mid-tale as Colin rose. They watched, silent, as he picked up his plate and carried it to the sideboard where Darcy's picture now resided. "I'm going out for a walk," he told them. "Have a good day, all."

Colin went into the hallway, taking his jacket from its hanger and plucking a walking stick from the umbrella stand near the door. He heard Mrs. Egan talking to the residents in not-hushed-enough tones. "Poor dear. He goes out walking along the Head every day since he was rescued, no matter the weather. I don't wonder that he's searching for that lost island and the strange girl he loved, who was lost there. Why, 'tis almost like one of those old songs he likes so well . . ."

The closing of the door cut off the rest.

His pants were damp beyond the knees from walking through the dew-wet gorse and the high grass along the ridge of Ceomhar Head. Ahead, he could see his destination: the standing stone overlooking the high sea cliff as if a sentinel. The stone, as always, leaned like a stoop-backed old man, as if one day it might fall over from its own weight to tumble down to the low-land and tidal flats below. Colin placed his right hand on the stone, forcing the stiff fingers there to open and flex. The doctor who had cleaned and stitched up his wound had said that with time and therapy he'd regain use of the hand and be able to play music, but it would probably always be a little stiff, and probably become arthritic in later life. The stone was surpris-ingly warm under his touch in the sunlight as he steadied himself against the fierce wind that blew back his hair and found every gap in his jacket. *There is a power in these stones. Yeh can still feel it, if yeh know how.* Maeve's words. He looked at his left hand, which held the cloch dangling from its chain, and imagined he could feel a faint tingling there. He thought he saw a vision of the stone, standing firm and upright, as it once had.

Maybe. Or maybe that was merely what he wished to feel.

The wind from offshore carried the scent of fish and brine as Colin sat in the grass next to the stone, not paying attention to the insistent damp that immediately invaded the seat of his jeans. The walking stick's brass ferrule prodded the lumpy heather at the cliff edge as he put his chin on the stick's oaken head and stared out over the panorama before him.

The tide was well out, and the lowlands at the foot of the Head were exposed. Instead of a series of low, isolated islands close to the shore, one could have walked over sandy mud from one to another, each with the occasional white farmhouse. To his right, the inlet of the Ballemór Estuary yawned, brown water outflowing to mix with the blue of the ocean. A few boats were out, one of them a Naval Services patrol boat, perhaps even the very one that had picked him up.

To his left, where once the hazy rise of Inishcorr would have inter-rupted the horizon, there were only empty waves and a single fishing trawler, nets still furled on its mast.

Colin wondered if, on some foggy night, one of those boats might glimpse Inishcorr in the moonlit distance: a haunted ghost island. He wondered if he went out there himself, perhaps he might be the one to see the fog-clad outline of the island and the high mound on the seaward side with its hawthorn tree.

He wondered, but he had no answer. There was no sign in the world that lay spread out at his feet, and his companion the standing stone was silent. He let his fingertips prowl the cloch, touching the stone as he stared out, but there were no voices inside it now; when he held it up to the open sky, no mage-lights swept down in answer.

From the branches of a wind-stunted tree nearby, a crow watched the young man seated at the cliff edge. After several minutes, the bird uttered a soft *caw* and spread its dark wings, letting the ocean wind lift it and carry it away, banking so that it rode the wind out toward the sea.

Below, Colin looked up and watched its flight.

Acknowledgments & Notes

I have several people to thank for their help in producing the book you're holding.

First, a special thanks to Dr. Michael Simonton of Northern Kentucky University, who gifted me with some of the handouts he uses in his Celtic Studies courses as well as pointing me toward some excellent sources for Irish Gaelic. Any mistakes in Irish Gaelic are not his, but my own.

Thanks to Michelle and John Donat, for feedback regarding Chicago, their home city. And yes, any mistakes regarding the Windy City are mine, not theirs . . .

And thanks to my first readers: Anne Evans, Denise Parsley Leigh, Megen Leigh, Devon Leigh, P. Andrew Miller, David Perry, Shannon Kelly, Leslie Perry, Bruce Schneier, and Don Wenzel, for looking over various versions of the draft manuscript and giving me their comments—your time and effort are much appreciated! I especially want to single out David Perry, for one of the most insightful critiques I received, one that helped me re-envision the entire flow of the book. Thanks, David! This would be a lesser book without your input.

And, as always, I have to mention Sheila Gilbert, my now longtime editor, whose advice and editorial input I always treasure. Sheila drives me to make each book the best it can be, and I can't possibly thank her enough for her support of my work.

The town of Ballemór doesn't exist (or if it does, I'm not aware of its existence and I've certainly misplaced it on the map) nor does the island of

Inishcorr, but the gorgeous Connemara region certainly does as well as the lovely town of Clifden, on which Ballemór is (very) loosely based. Should you have the opportunity to visit Ireland, I strongly recommend a long visit to the area. You absolutely won't be disappointed.

When I was there, I found myself wanting to stay in Clifden for much longer than I had time. Heck, I even halfheartedly looked at the realtor listings.

Books read in the course of writing this novel whose influence you may or may not see in the text, but which certainly gave me inspiration:

The Táin translated by Thomas Kinsella. Oxford University Press, 1969. A very accessible translation of the Irish epic, Tain Bo Cuailnge. However, the ink drawings that accompany the text I found irritating as often as I found them interesting.

Lost Crafts: Rediscovering Traditional Skills by Una McGovern. Chambers Harrap Publishers, Edinburgh, 2008. This is an essential research book for anyone who wants to know how things were once done.

The Celtic Twilight by W.B. Yeats. Dover Publications, 2004. This is Yeats' relatively short compilation of Irish folktales as related to him by people he met and interviewed. The original publications of the book were 1893 and 1902—the Dover version I read is the 1902 version.

A Treasury of Irish Myth, Legend & Folklore: Fairy and Folk Tales of the Irish Peasantry, by Lady Gregory and W.B. Yeats. Avenel Books, 1988. This volume is actually a compilation of two separate and much older books: *Fairy and Folk Tales of the Irish Peasantry*, a collection of stories edited by W.B. Yeats, and *Cuchulain of Muirthemne*, a retelling of the Cuchulain epic by Lady Augusta Gregory.

The Course of Irish History by T.W. Moody and F.X. Martin. Roberts Rinehart Publishers, 1995. The book is essential reading for anyone interested in a well-researched overview of Ireland's history.

Celtic Myths and Legends by Peter Berresford Ellis. Running Press Book Publishers, 2008. Just what it says it is, a noncomprehensive and nonacademic book of the myths from all around the British Isles, not just Ireland. A decent introduction (and reminder) of the variety of tales and legends that abound in the region.

Over Nine Waves: A Book of Irish Legends by Marie Heany. Faber & Faber Unlimited, 1994. This is just what it says it is, a prose retelling of the various Irish mythologies, broken into four sections. The "Mythological Cycle" retells the story of the Tuatha De Danaan, the Children of Lir, and the Milesians; the "Ulster Cycle" gives us Cuchulainn; the "Finn

Cycle" relates the story of Finn and Oisin; lastly, the "Patron Saints of Ireland" delves into Patrick, Brigid, and Columcille. A decent condensed version of the primary mythologies of Ireland.

Ireland's Pirate Queen: The True Story of Grace O'Malley **by Anne Chambers.** MJF Books, 2003. This is a reprint of a 1998 book published by Wolfhound Press in Ireland. Grace O'Malley is referenced in my novel peripherally, as the Galway Hooker used by the Inishcorr people: the *Grainne Ni Mhaille,* is an Irish term for her. I found the book interesting (if poorly proofed), and well researched. Not much of this appears in my book, but I might use this again somewhere along the line . . .

Irish Journal, **by Heinrich Böll, translated by Leila Vannewitz.** Melville House Publishing, Brooklyn, NY, 2011. Originally written in German, this is the account of Heinrich Böll's travel in Ireland in the early 1950s. Böll was the first German to win the Nobel Prize for literature since Thomas Mann in 1929; the *Irish Journal* is a fascinating memoir of Ireland just after WWII—which is close to the period in which I have Colin's grandfather, Rory O'Callaghan, appear. I used the journal not so much for the description as for the tone and sound of the "voice" of Rory's journal.

Old Irish Folk Music and Songs: A collection of 842 Irish airs and songs, hitherto unpublished, **by the Royal Society of Antiquaries of Ireland and P.W. Joyce.** The book I have is a copy (and not a great one) from the University of Toronto Library of images from the original manuscript of 1909. Still, a fascinating collection of old Irish music, culled from several different collections of old music which became available to the Royal Society and Joyce.

And, of course, there's **O'Neill's Music of Ireland,** which, unlike Colin, I don't have in the original publication, but in Mel Bay Publications' reproduction edition. O'Neill, who emigrated from Ireland to the States himself and became a Chicago policeman, collected from any Irish emigrant or traveler all the old Irish tunes they could remember and transcribed them here in one place: 1,850 airs, jigs, reels, and songs (though, sadly, only the melodies, not lyrics).

Several (but not all) of the chapter titles in this book are titles of tunes in either the O'Neill or the Joyce collections.

Versions of the song "The Ghost Lover" (aka "The Gray Cock" or "The Lover's Ghost") in Chapter 13 can be found in several places with a great variety of verses, going back to *Child's Collected Ballads* by Francis James Child during the latter part of the 1800s, Sam Henry's (b.1870–d.1952) *Songs of the People,* and also in the Roud Broadside Index.

In Chapter 19, we have the traditional song "Mháire Bhruinneall," which has been covered by dozens of artists over the years, the best known of which are probably Susan Mckeown's version or Clannad's. You should give a listen!

In Chapter 24, Colin sings "Cliffs of Dooneen," another of those Irish songs which doesn't have a clear author, point of origin, or age. One suggestion is that the lyrics were written by the late Jack McAuliffe in the 1930s and set to music sometime later by an unknown musician. The cliffs are probably those at Dooneen Point in County Kerry. The song has been performed by several musicians and bands. Look up Planxty, Christy Moore, or Paddy Reilly for nice renditions of the tune, though other versions abound.

The poem that Colin sings to awaken Lugh in Chapter 30 is taken from "Mór ar bhfearg riot, ri Saxan," by Gofraidh Fionn Ó Dálaigh, an Irish poet who died in 1387. This poem is written in Middle Irish, and is part of the story of the Tuatha Dé Danann's struggles with the Fomor. The excerpt of the poem from which the quoted verses were borrowed (along with a translation) can be found at: http://www.karott.com/gaelic%5Creference%5CIrish_Poetry%5CLugh_Comes_to_Tara.htm.

In Chapter 31, we have the lyrics to a song entitled "Slip Away," which despite Colin claiming as his, is an original composition of my own.

And finally, in Chapter 33, Colin sings the poem *Ráisit d'inis nárbo dermar* (*The island protected by a bridge of glass*). One source for this poem is the "Yellow Book of Lecan" (c. 1391–1401 C.E); Gerard Murphy has it under "Otherworld poems" in *Early Irish Lyrics: 8th to 12th Century* (Ed. Gerard Murphy, Oxford, Clarendon Press, 1956). Murphy attributes it to an Âed Finn and dates it to around 920 since the text is primarily in Old Irish with a few smatterings of Middle Irish. The verse comes from the "Voyage of Maél Dúin's Currach" and tells the story of two sailors who rowed out to a mysterious island where they met an equally mysterious woman who enchants them. After a few days on the island, they wake up to find themselves back in their boat, and the island has vanished—that should be enough to tell you why I chose to have Colin sing these verses. The poem may be found on the Corpus of Electronic Texts (CELT) site at http://celt.ucc.ie/published/G400040/index.html. The CELT site is hosted by University College Cork in Ireland, and the brief excerpt from the poem is reproduced here with the kind permission of CELT and UCC.

As always, feel free to visit my own website, which can be found at either www.farrellworlds.com or www.stephenleigh.com.

Appendices

Maeve (Mayv) Gallagher	An Islander woman Colin meets and becomes involved with
Keara (KEY-ruh) Shea	A companion of Maeve's
Niall (Kneel) Tierney	A companion of Maeve's
Aiden (AY-dehn) Nolan	A companion of Maeve's, and Keara's lover
Rory O'Callaghan	Colin's maternal grandfather
Dr. Elizabeth Pearse	Doctor in the IC unit at the hospital in Chicago
Beth Banaszewski	The Doyle family's part-time housekeeper
Bridgett Doyle	(née O'Bannon) Colin's grandmother
Father Frank	The Doyle family's parish priest
Cedric Dunn	Superintendent of the Ballemór Gardai
Máire (MOY-yah)	Maeve's name in Rory O'Callaghan's time
Lucas Flaherty	An Irish fiddler and friend of Colin, band leader
Paidrig (PAW-rig)	An Irish musician, plays concertina
Bridget	An Irish musician, sings and plays mandolin
John	An Irish musician, plays bodhran
Dolan (DOH-lan) Connor	A friend of Maeve's
Liam (LEE-ahm) Doherty	A friend of Maeve's
Joseph Mullins	The proprietor of Mullins' Used Books
Mrs. Brennan	A woman "cursed" by Maeve
John Coffey	First settler of Inishcorr
Fionnbharr (FINN-var)	Leader of the aos sí on Inishcorr
Padraig (PAW-rig) Coffey	Grandson of John Coffey
Patrick Davies	A farmer near Ballemór
Mrs. Naughton	A resident of the Sky Road outside Ballemór

Kieran Martin	A leading seaman on the offshore patrol vessel *LÉ Aisling*
Sean	Radarman on the offshore patrol vessel *LÉ Aisling*
Eithne (EH-nah)	A mythical mortal woman, captured by Fionnbharr and rescued by her husband, a mortal lord

TERMS AND PLACE NAMES (in alphabetical order)

Aoibhell (Ah-VEEL)	A goddess of the sidhe. Hearing her play her harp was a portent that one was destined to die soon
Aos sí (Aess Shee)	"The people of the mounds"—the fairy folk of Irish legend
Babd (Buyb)	One of the three aspects of the Morrígan
Ballemór (BAHL-lee-moer)	A village in the Connemara region of Ireland—pronounced with a slight roll of the final "r"
Beach Road	A road out of Ballemór that follows the coastline of Ceomhar Head, below the Sky Road
Benbrack	One of the Twelve Bens
Bodhran (BOW-rahn)	A round hand drum used in Irish music. The first syllable is pronounced as in "Take a bow"
Brigid	One of the gods of the Tuatha de Danann
Cailleach (coll-yuk)	"Witch"
Cen chaoi bhfuil tú? (Ken fey well too)	"How are you?"—to which "Tá mé togha" (Tah may TAH-chuh—"I'm grand" or "I'm fine") might be a reply
Ceomhar Head (KOH-mar)	A tongue of steep land at the end of the mainland outside Ballemór
Cloch (Clahk)	"Stone" or "Pebble" in Irish Gaelic
Cloch na Thintri (Clahk nah Hintrah)	"Stone of Lightning"
Cnoc Deireadh (Crock Jerrah)	Fionnbharr's mound on Inishcorr
Cnoc na Teamhrach (Crock nah Towl-Rah)	The Hill of Tara near the River Boyle. A complex of mounds and earthworks where the ancient kings of Ireland were reputedly both crowned and buried

Cnoc Meadha (Crock Mah)	The sacred mound of Fionnbharr, located in County Galway, west of the town of Tuam. It was the home of the King of the Connacht fairies, who ruled there. Also reputed to be the burial site of Queen Maeve of Connacht
Connacht (Kawn-AHKT)	The western province of Ireland consisting of the counties Galway, Leitrim, Mayo, Roscommon, and Sligo
Connemara (Kahn-eh-MAHR-ah)	A mountainous region in the west of Ireland. Contains the Twelve Bens (or mountains)
Craic (crack)	As in "That's the craic," which translates roughly as "That's what's going on"
Currach (COR-uch)	A plank-built rowing boat of the Connacht coast of Ireland
Cúchulainn (Koo-HOOL-in)	The hero of the *Tain*, who opposed Queen Medb
Daiddeó (DAD-oh)	"Grandfather"
Éire (AY-rah)	The Gaelic name for Ireland
Filleadh (Fill-eh)	Means both "going out" and "coming back"—also to fold or to bend
Galway Hooker	A single-masted small sailing boat traditional to the Galway region. Usually has a black hull (covered in pitch) and dark-red sails
Grainne Ni Mhaille (GRAN-ya Nee WAN-ya)	The *Grainne Ni Mhaille* is the Galway Hooker used by the Oileánach to travel back and forth from Inishcorr. Grainne Ni Mhaille is a historical figure in Ireland, also known as "Grace O'Malley," who was chieftain of the Ó Máille clan and a pirate in sixteenth century Ireland. She was sometimes referred to as "The Sea Queen of Connaught"
Inishcorr (IN-ish-corr)	An island off Ceomhar Head
Lazybed	A method for cultivating potatoes used in the west of Ireland and also in Scotland, where the tubers are placed on the ground and a mounded layer of turf is placed over them (sometimes with seaweed added for nutrition). The beds are laid out in long rows, with the "channels" between them used for drainage of excess water

LÉ Aisling (ASH-ling)	Irish naval patrol vessel
Lia Fáil (LEE-ah Fall)	The "Stone of Destiny" that sits atop the Hill of Tara. Supposedly where the Irish kings were crowned until the year 500
Leamh (Lee-OW)	A derisive term for normal people used by the Oileánach, meaning "mundane" or "bland"
Letterfrack	A town in the Connemara Region
Lugh (Loogk)	One of the gods of the Tuatha de Danann
Máthair (MAW-hirzh)	"Mother"
Mháire Bhruinneall (MAH-ear WUH-een-ee-al)	Traditional Irish song in Gaelic
Macha (Mah-KAH)	One of the three aspects of the Morrígan
Maimeó (MAM-oh)	"Grandmother"
Morrígan	One of the ancient deities of Irish mythology
Navy Service	Ireland's navy, one of the three standing branches of the Irish Defense Forces
Nemain (Nee-MOHN)	One of the three aspects of the Morrígan
NPWS	"National Parks & Wildlife Services"—a branch of the Irish government
Oileánach (OWE-lee-nok)	"The Islanders"—those living on Inishcorr
Ogham (Owe-um)	An ancient Celtic alphabet, usually carved into wood or stone
Oscail (OSS-kull)	"Open"
Oweynagat (Owen-nee-gaht)	The "Cave of the Cats," one of the sites that make up the Rathcroghan complex. This is reputed to be the entrance to the underworld, from which monsters have several times emerged, and it's also said that on Samhain, the Morrígan herself comes out from the cave. The actual Gaelic is "Uaimh na gCait"
Pléasc (PLAY-usk)	"Shatter"

Rathcroghan (Rah-CROV-un)	Rathcroghan is a complex of mounds and earthworks near Tulsk in County Roscommon. Important in Irish mythology and also the setting for the opening section of the *Táin Bó Cúailnge* and the *Táin Bó Flidhais*
Regan's Pub	A tavern in Ballemór
Roscommon	A county in the center of Ireland
Samhain (SOW-en)	The Celtic festival marking the end of the harvest season and the beginning of the darkness of winter. Commonly held around October 31. The customs of Samhain have somewhat influenced the American Halloween
Sidhe ("Shee")	A common name for the fey folk—though incorrect, since "sidhe" is simply the gaelic word for "mound"
Sky Road	A road with scenic views along Ceomhar Head
Sligo (SLY-goh)	A county in the northwest of Ireland
Sluagh Sídhe (SLEW-uch shee)	The host of the aos sí, sometimes thought to be the spirits of the dead, who pour out from the fairy mounds and sometimes carry off mortals
Táin Bó Cúailnge (Toyn Boe KOOL-na)	The "Cattle Raid of Cooley"—one of the seminal mythological works of Ireland, in which the hero Cúchulainn appears
Talamh an Ghlas (TOWL-uv ahn Gloss)	"The Green Land"—the world to which Maeve and her people are trying to escape
Tuigim (Tigg-im)	"I understand"
Tír na mBeo (Teer Nah Moe)	"The Land of the Living"—in Celtic mythology, one of the "Otherworlds" where the dead hope to find peace
Tuatha de Danann (TWO-ah dah Don-on)	The "people of Danu." In Irish mythology, after the Tuatha de Danann were defeated by the Milesians, they went underground into the sidhe mounds
Twelve Bens	Twelve mountain peaks in the Connemara region